EDIT
AC ADAMS ADAM GAFFEN
NAT PAGA

# Roots of Love

## A COLLECTION OF ROMANTIC ORIGINS

# Table of Contents

# Meet Me at the End

## By Lila Gwynn

At the end of the world, Sera shoots the last spaceship out of the sky.

She doesn't mean to. That's what she tells herself at first. The ship is a two-seater scouting craft, and she's been waving at it with no response as the world around her crackles with fire. There's nothing here but razed earth, metal so hot it simmers orange, the smell of ash. Not even the old Glee Ships factory has survived. Once, it towered over everything else, spitting dark plumes into New Farrum's already-gray sky. When she looks up, the MegQuest Space Station doesn't blink, either, because it's been obliterated. All of her comforts, gone.

She has no way out, and whoever pilots the two-seater ignored Sera even though she's the only living thing left. Even though it would take just a second to save her, and they're supposed to be on the same side in this war.

As the two-seater tumbles down, Sera can only think that if its pilot dies, they will be a tally in her notebook. Another death she's responsible for. But her notebook is destroyed with the mattress she stashed it in, destroyed with her bunk bed in the barracks and everything that made up Sera's life. She has nothing but the skin-tight armor clinging to her and the electromagnetic pulse blaster she's been trained to use solely on MQ ships.

Blaster misuse is not the first rule she's broken today.

The arc of the two-seater hovers gracefully as it nears the scorched ground. At the last minute, it stops its descent, floating. A manual shield comes up, protecting the hull from smashing like Sera so wants it to. She waits, finger on the trigger. There's no way to tell what kind of reaction she'll get.

Nobody comes out. For a second, Sera is tempted to check inside the ship for its pilot. Dead, she's sure. And Sera doesn't have knowledge or access to fly anything. She admits to herself she felt hopeful when the shields came up, but the feeling crashes now. She didn't have much before, but at least it was something. Now what's left?

As Sera turns away, metal creaks. Her hopes soar; the pilot is still alive. The hatch to the two-seater bangs open and a woman thrusts herself out of it, hair wild, a shock of dyed magenta curls fluttering around her face. *Not in regulation.* She wears the same armor-skin as Sera, but she's supplemented it with a jacket—a black one with pockets, many of them full. From a cursory look, Sera determines the jacket lacks the Glee Ships or MegQuest logos that should be prominently displayed on anything manufactured on New Farrum. *Contraband.*

Instinctively, Sera pulls up her HUD to report it. A cursor blinks in the left field of her vision. She thinks up the report quickly, describing the jacket and the wild woman wearing it, but when she hits send, she gets an error. *No network access.* She dismisses the report as the pilot jumps several feet down from the end of the hatch door.

Sera braces herself for anger. Instead, she gets a blank stare. A confident stance, almost as if for a face-off. Blood splatters the pilot's cheek—maybe someone else's. The HUD headset pilots wear covers one of her eyes. Not an implant like Sera's. The metallic armor-skin glimmers against the pilot's body. On her breast is the Glee Ships logo, identical to the one on Sera's, a spherical smiley face blasting off.

Underneath is the name *Delphine,* with the symbol for a pilot next to a gender marker. She's limned in far-off flamelight; she looks like she emerged from the depths of hell.

She's also radiant, the most stunning person Sera has ever seen.

The pilot reaches for one of her many pockets. Sera runs her thumb over the trigger. Whatever the pilot extracts is too small to be a blaster, and if it's an explosive, Sera's reacted too slowly, anyway. She waits for her HUD to identify the object: *vaporizer pen.* Not the kind that vaporizes people, but the kind that vaporizes tobacco. The artificial smell of bubblegum cuts through all the burning.

"Hi," the pilot says. Then: "You want some?"

Sera can't. Not that she doesn't want to, but her lungs are artificial, modified like the rest of her, so she wouldn't feel anything. She can't get drunk, either. "No."

Casually, the pilot leans against the side of the ship. "What's your name?"

"Sera."

"Cool. Delphine. Why did you shoot my ship with an EMP?"

The accusation is so nonchalant that Sera doesn't know how to react, what response Delphine is looking for. She searches the other woman's expression—open, almost curious, so genuine Sera wants to answer honestly, but her instincts scream at her not to. She had shot the ship simply because of something soldiers weren't supposed to feel, something that could ruin you on the field—pettiness.

"We have to let the Glee Ships base know what happened," Sera says with authority. The military objective gives her confidence; this is something she knows well. "I don't have network access."

Delphine snorts. "Me either. The satellites are gone."

This reaction is not what Sera expects. "Then you have to get reinforcements."

"Reinforcements for what?" Delphine gestures at the wreckage of what's left after the companies demolished each other's armies.

Sera does not know who won. Glee Ships, she supposes, since two Glee Ships employees are left. It does not feel like victory, though, without the other soldiers to celebrate with.

"Backup, then. Salvaging the planet." Sera's voice turns up at the end like a question. Through the embarrassment at her verbal blunder, Sera keeps her face neutral.

"There is no backup. There is nothing to salvage." Delphine tucks her vape back into her pocket. "This planet is done for. Everyone left us here."

That can't be true. Glee Ships has poured hundreds of thousands of dollars into Sera's body. She is an investment, and they don't like to waste money. "They wouldn't—"

"They did. All the remaining supervisors flew off together on a frigate. I saw it."

"You're lying," Sera insists, but she knows how pathetic and desperate she sounds. Patiently, Delphine watches Sera's reaction, the journey from fantasy to reality. By the time Sera settles on reality, she understands Glee Ships has left her behind. They think she's dead already, and they have lots of investments. She has overestimated her worth.

"So," Delphine says, having reached the conclusion first.

"So," Sera echoes.

An uncomfortable silence ensues. It's a stalemate. Neither of them can leave. The ship will take at least half an hour to repair itself from the damage of the electromagnetic pulse.

Delphine breaks the quiet first. "My engine was acting up."

"Was it?" Sera asks flatly.

"Well, you delayed my timely escape. You owe me one."

"You want me to look at your engine?"

"Yes. Can you fix it? Put those big muscles of yours to use."

The question makes Sera indignant. She can fix anything. As a child, Glee Ships had her tinkering with smaller components for them already. "Of course I—" she starts, but Delphine is smiling, trying to get a rise out of her. Almost succeeding. "The ship couldn't repair its engine?"

"Nope."

Sera hesitates. Holsters her blaster. "Let me see."

THE INSIDE OF THE SHIP is smaller than some of the other two-seaters Sera has worked on. Already, the lights have self-repaired. The two seats in the front occupy a third of the space, and the combined sleeper-kitchen-bathroom cabin takes up the middle. Delphine leads Sera over the seats and through the cabin to the engine room. It's the tiniest of the three compartments. The proximity of the engine, still warm from recent use, heats Sera's skin.

"It's old." Sera can tell with a glance. "Where did you get this ship?"

Delphine crowds the space next to the engine, looking thoughtful. "Can't say. I wouldn't want you to report me," she teases.

Sera bends over the engine. If it really isn't working, she can diagnose problems, but the toolbox in the engine room looks old, too, and she doesn't have her own. She runs her fingers over the hot metal. "What was wrong with it?"

"Well, it took forever to start up, and it smelled weird when it did."

Sera gives Delphine an incredulous look. "How can you be a pilot and know so little about ships?"

Delphine waves Sera's question off. "Does it look salvageable?"

"It *looks* like the old, rusted engine of a decommissioned ship."

"That's because it is. Decommissioned, I mean." Delphine says this pleasantly.

Sera stares. Delphine stares back.

Between the residual engine heat and the flames outside, Sera's overheating. She isn't due for a thermal regulator until next year—Glee Ships considers it a luxury modification. She reaches for the zipper pull at her throat and yanks it. Just at the point of indecency, she stops, letting the skin under her armor breathe. It helps a little.

Until she notices Delphine gawking at the exposed skin of her neck and sternum.

She can hardly blame Delphine for looking. Her body is patchwork—metal-flesh-metal-flesh—from all the times she's been broken in battle and Glee Ships made her anew.

Too late, Sera flushes with embarrassment. "Stop that."

"Sorry!" Delphine averts her gaze. "Sorry. I didn't mean it like that."

"How did you mean it?" Sera demands.

Delphine closes her eyes. Opens them. "I was thinking you're tough and you deserve a break from all this."

Sera's hand stills. No one has ever offered her the simple kindness of being understood. She thinks to express her gratitude, but she doesn't see how she can. A gift, perhaps. The gift of a functional engine. Flakes of metal come off of the engine and onto her fingers when she resumes her search. Her HUD pops up but tells her nothing beyond the engine's make and model, from over twenty years ago.

"I'm surprised the engine started at all."

"Good thing you shot me down," Delphine says good-humoredly. "Do you think I'd have burned up in the ozone?"

Sera doesn't know how to tell Delphine she's burning now—burning away all of Sera's layers the way you'd peel the skin off an apple.

"Can you bring me the toolbox?" she manages. Delphine reaches behind her for the toolbox, as rusted as the rest of the engine. The tools inside look okay, though. Some screws on the engine appear to have come loose; all Sera has to do is replace them with new ones, assuming the engine itself is functional. There's a reason Glee Ships took this two-seater model out of commission.

Sera feels Delphine's eyes on her back as she works to replace the screws. The urge to impress, to prove her worth, rises in her. She tightens the screws with sweat trickling down her back and wonders what Delphine thinks of her. Despite herself, she does a wasteful little flourish with her wrist as she twists.

After Sera has replaced the screws, there's nothing left to do. She stands.

"You hungry?" Delphine asks, and Sera nods.

THE MIDDLE CABIN IS big enough that a pilot and a soldier could sleep side by side, but not much bigger than that. The two women stand as far apart as they can in this small space. Delphine rummages through a pantry, though Sera cannot fathom what edible food would be stashed on an old ship like this.

"Protein bar." Delphine holds one out. Sera takes it but hesitates as her HUD lights up with calories, nutrients, a reminder of the last thing she ate, and what she's supposed to put in her body now for optimal energy. She is efficient, nearly as efficient as a machine; it strikes her as ironic, in the end times, that she is not set up for survival situations such as this. Another fact in favor of her dispensability.

"Where did you get this food?" Sera asks as she takes her first bite—flavorless.

Delphine nibbles at her own protein bar. "I stole it before this all went down."

"It was over in five minutes," Sera says, "it" referring to the way the world ended, explosions and fire and who-knows-what weapon made to leave only ash in its wake. "How did you prep so fast?"

Delphine stops chewing. In her face, Sera reads what Delphine doesn't say and feels a twinge of satisfaction at being able to discern Delphine's thoughts. "You were planning to run away before any of this happened." A flare of indignance, again, at the rule-breaking, but it doesn't bother Sera as much as she thought it would.

"I got drafted to New Farrum from... well, it doesn't matter. We weren't born into the military there, like you are here."

Delphine's figured out Sera's past, and Sera knows nothing of her. She clears her throat. "You didn't enjoy piloting for Glee Ships," she says.

"Of course not. I've been trying to weasel my way out of service for years. Did you enjoy fighting for them?"

Sera sucks down her instinctual answer. "I completed my service to the best of my ability," she says instead. It's neutral enough.

Delphine looks her up and down. "I bet you did. How many years were they keeping you for?"

Sera's shoulders tense. She's naïve. She's been taught one thing, even as another was happening to her, and though she knew that was the case, it was easier to lean into what was expected of her than to resist it. When she was a kid, they told her ten years of service was all she'd have to give up, and then she'd be free. When ten years had passed, they told her twenty instead. Because she was needed.

She knows, now, she was never needed. More, she has no reason left to resist the things which have built up a pressure in her chest that never goes away.

"Too many," she answers finally, and Delphine's eyebrows shoot up in surprise.

"I didn't think there were modded soldiers like you," Delphine says. "I like it."

That Sera has defied Delphine's expectations brings her an unexpected rush of pleasure. Delphine has defied hers, too. "You like what?" Sera wants Delphine to say *you*, but Delphine shakes her head.

"Nothing," she says. "So you're a Glee Ships rebel, eh?"

Sera has to resist looking over her shoulder, resist pulling up the HUD report system again. Even the mention of rebellion flushes her skin hot. She thinks of the tally notebook. How she consoled herself when questions that stank of rebellion kept her up at night: the *What is my purpose?* and the *What am I fighting for?* questions that were better pushed down to get the job done.

Truth is, she's never seen what Glee Ships and MegQuest *should* have in conflict. Glee Ships started as a spaceship parts manufacturer and expanded into other tech, particularly weapons; MegQuest is a travel agency. Both rely on services from the other, such as MegQuest's hyperdrive travel for Glee Ships product transport and MegQuest relying on Glee Ships' tech to bring tourists to so-called exotic destinations. Seemingly, they're unrelated. The only thing she knows from night whispers in the barracks is the CEOs hated each other, hated each other enough and cared so little for the lives on New Farrum they'd blow up the planet to hurt the other.

"I was joking," Delphine says in response to the serious look on Sera's face.

"I know," Sera says, even though she didn't.

The wall against Sera's back hums. Both women jump up. The engine whirrs from the other room, loud but not abnormal. Everything is operational again; the ship will fly.

"Well," Delphine says. "I guess I should be going. What are you going to do?"

"Um. I don't know."

Delphine nods. "My mom is on Lucerna. I think I have enough fuel to get there." A pause. "Have you heard of Lucerna?"

Sera has. Another thing whispered in the barracks—how Lucerna outlawed corporate purchases of land and thus took away any power the two companies that divided the galaxy could have there. How the people owned the land. The idea of it was so foreign to Sera that she dismissed the planet itself as a myth. But here Delphine is, talking about it like it's real.

"Are you from Lucerna?"

"Originally," Delpine says, and Sera gets another piece of her. "I moved away when I could. Wish I hadn't." Dryly, she laughs. Sera is unused to anyone talking badly of Glee Ships, even by inference. Everything Delphine says builds on Sera's deep-seated doubts.

Delphine makes as if to go into the front cabin. Gently, Sera reaches out and touches her arm.

If this is the last chance she has to speak to Delphine—maybe the last chance she has to speak to anyone—then she wants to come clean. "I was mad."

"What?"

"I was mad you were trying to leave without me."

"I know," Delphine says.

"You didn't stop for me."

"I know."

"Why didn't you stop for me?" Sera blurts, her voice cracking.

"Every modded soldier I've met has been in too deep," Delphine says instantly. Honestly. "I thought you were going to be like them."

Sera thinks of the barracks, the things that happened there when no one was around to hear them. Her notebook, her nightmares. "We're not brainwashed."

Delphine shrugs. "I was wrong."

It's then that Sera notices her hand is still on Delphine's arm. She takes it back. The two stare at each other.

"So," Delphine says again.

"So," Sera says back.

"You need me to be direct, don't you."

"What?"

"I said I have family on Lucerna. Come with me."

"Really?" But Sera feels like she understands Delphine. She knows Delphine is the type of person who means what she says.

"Really. This planet sucks. Do you want to find another one?"

Sera takes in Delphine's cocky stance. No, not cocky—flirty. Delphine has been flirting with Sera this whole time, and she missed it.

"Are you asking me out?" Sera asks, sputtering. "On a date into the universe?"

"Only if you want to. If you don't want it to be a date, I'll still get you out of here, obviously." Delphine clears her throat; she's nervous. Nervous that Sera will say no. "If you decide you hate my guts, I'll drop you off somewhere."

Already, Sera knows she could never hate Delphine.

"Oh, since you were honest about shooting my ship," Delphine adds, "I was checking you out earlier. When you, ah, unzipped your armor."

Sera's mouth is dry. She's been checking out Delphine from the moment Delphine burst from the ship's hatch like a mermaid from the ocean. Never would she have thought the feeling was mutual, that she has something to offer Delphine, too.

"Do you know the way to Lucerna?"

Delphine's lips curl into a knowing smile. "Yes. Do you think this ship will make it there?"

Sera presses her hand to her chest. Her heart is engineered to pump at thirty beats per minute, and it steadies her. "Yes," she says, breathless.

Delphine holds out her right hand. The tip of her forefinger glints off of the cabin's lights. Every pilot has a metallic fingertip, Sera remembers, to operate ships with a touch—metal-flesh, like her.

"Well. We'll start at Lucerna," Delphine continues, as if Sera needs any more convincing. "Maybe upgrade our ship for longer-distance travel. If you want, we can leave the Megara Galaxy completely. What do you say?"

The future unspools before Sera, the possibility of traveling anywhere in all of space and doing anything with this strange woman by her side. Planets and stars she's never seen. No Glee Ships, no corporations, no notebooks stained with remorse. No fighting. Just being, and she doesn't have to do it alone. This world has ended, but hers is beginning.

Sera takes Delphine's hand.

# A Word from the Author – Lila Gwynn

**P**laylist:
Cornfield Chase (Interstellar: Original Motion Picture Soundtrack)—Hans Zimmer

You're Stronger Than You Think (Arcane League of Legends Soundtrack)—Kelci Hahn

Saber's Edge (Final Fantasy XIII Original Soundtrack)—Masashi Hamauzu

**Bio & why I wrote this story:**

I'm Lila Gwynn, writer (and lover) of sapphic fantasy fiction. I've been gobbling up books of all genres from a young age and I recently rediscovered my love of binge-reading when I found the indie publishing community and all the unique, queer stories they had to offer.

I live in the midwestern US with my girlfriend and our three horrifically nicknamed cats. In my free time, you can find me reading (duh), writing, playing video games, or crying onto my phone screen as I attempt to cook recipes above my skill level.

My inspiration for this story is that the real world feels apocalyptic more and more lately, and I'm having to find the things in my own life that give me hope for the future, much like the characters in my story. Additionally, I am a huge sci-fi fan, but every attempt to write it long form has been really challenging because of all the world building involved. It was a real pleasure to dive into a portal to a sci-fi world in short story format.

Check out the completed Olympia the Bounty Hunter trilogy for sapphic urban fantasy with a fairy/vampire romance, or *The Orc and Her Bride*, the first book in a series of sapphic fantasy romances with (you guessed it) orcs at: lilagwynn.com/books[1]

**Thank you's:**

A huge thank you to my friends Matt and Fel for screening all of my stories for glaring errors and assuring me that my writing is good. Thanks especially to Nat Paga for inviting me to this anthology, for hyping up my books, and for writing some seriously inspirational, kick-ass sapphic characters. I owe my partner for her consistent support of my creative endeavors and my kitties for always being around when I need a fluffy hug. Last but not least, thanks to AC Adams for organizing the anthology and Adam Gaffen for editing. It's an honor to be included!

1.    http://lilagwynn.com/books

# Into the Dark

## By C.R. Clark

With every step I took towards the black door, I could feel the tightness in my chest squeezing harder. *The logical part of my brain screamed at me to turn around, but something was pulling me in, like a moth to a flame. I finally was close enough to touch it; I reached out my trembling hand, my lungs screaming for air that would not come-*

MEOW

I started awake, realizing the crushing weight on my chest was my moron cat. Her real name was Belladonna, but I called her that once in a blue moon. I started shortening it to BD, which turned into Bitty or Dot. All these monikers fit; she was both beautiful and poisonous, particularly when hungry, and adorably tiny. When she woke me up by sitting on my sternum? I could swear she weighed fifty pounds.

"Ughhhh, I'm up. What do you want? Is it seriously time for breakfast and peopling?"

Dot cocked her head to the side, licked her lips, and let out an offended MEOW yet again.

*Yes, you lazy lout. Arise and nourish me, lest I wither away into oblivion.* Her voice in my mind was impatient.

I was stuck with a sassy British familiar who was bossy and rather particular about EVERYTHING. Her demands for breakfast rang in my head. A fun bonus. Thankfully, she couldn't talk out loud, or

I'm sure she'd yell at passers-by, local fauna, the TV, anything she thought might listen.

"Yes, my Lady Belladonna, at once do we descend to break our fast and start the day!" I stood up, curtsied at my cat sarcastically, and threw on my robe.

Dot looked at me, rolled her lavender-blue eyes, and hopped off my bed. In true cat fashion she sashayed in front of me, walking out my bedroom door, down the stairs, and into the kitchen.

My little cottage was a bit of a mess. I'd had too many projects and ideas burst into my head and not quite enough focus to finish any of them lately. My kitchen was by far the worst, partly because I had harvested, bundled, and hung all the herbs from my garden to dry, partly because my side hustle as a baker for a local coffee shop-winery-bookstore was booming, and partly because, helloooo ADHD.

*A witch with ADHD, what a combination.*

I swung the kettle over the fire and stoked the embers, boiling water for tea. I threw a few croissants in the toaster oven, grabbed some jam for myself and lox for Dot, and turned on the radio for any relevant news updates this fine Tuesday morning. The perfect combination of your idyllic cottagecore witchy-poo and the modern woman with all the conveniences.

"Oh, if Grams could see me now, Dot, she'd be both intrigued and mortified," I chuckled out loud while my goofy companion actually acted like a cat, chasing a ladybug around the kitchen.

My mother's side was a gnarled tree of witches and their lines. We had had varying degrees of witch, but all with some capacity for The Light, which was nothing more than the family's fancy way of describing magic. My mom was a bit more low-key; having grown up during the Satanic Panic, she'd tried to fit into society a little more than most. My Grams, though, she had been a wild one. A well-traveled, powerful, knowledgeable, and fiercely independent woman, she absolutely radiated Light. Both capital "L" and lowercase. She taught me most of what I know, and the legacy she left behind continued to teach me. She and mom were gone, but little memories kept me going. The ability to chat with them on the "other side" if I needed to helped. I didn't often call; it was a lot of effort and energy, but knowing I could was a comfort.

We came from a long line of what could most closely be described as celestial creatures. Our powers had been given by an angel, and in honor of that gift, the women of my family had dedicated their lives to its worship.

Except for Grams and, by extension, me. She didn't vibe with the entire foundation of the family's "spirituality," so she openly rebuked it. My mom didn't much care either way and went along with it to fit in, but I was ever my grandmother's granddaughter. She fiercely campaigned against the creed and taught me to do the same. I loved her like a mother figure. To this day I'm still inspired by her.

She'd moved my mom and her six other children to this tiny Ohio city after my Pops had died of a heart attack. No amount of Grams' herbs or doctors' drugs could save him from a family history fraught with heart disease and health issues. There was the pesky curse, too, the perfect icing on the cake of his doom.

*Cake.*

Shit, I had a cake order for the bakery to crank out today. Good thing Her Feline Majesty had woken me up. I gulped down my tea, always the perfect temperature and strength when brewed in Momma's teapot, finished my croissants in a few bites each, and pulled up the message I'd gotten yesterday about the order.

I needed a 2-tier vanilla cake with raspberry filling and whipped lemon icing, topped with the adorable "50th Anniversary" topper that Trish had sent along. And she'd added a small list for this week's bakery stock-up:

✓ My family's magical cheesecake
✓ A dozen croissants
✓ A couple batches of XL death-by-brownies
✓ As many loaves of sourdough bread as I could for the
bakery this week

Nothing crazy, but it would require a modicum of focus.

Dot hopped up on the windowsill and dropped a cutting of hyoscyamus on the counter in front of me. Momma used to make me a tea with it when I was little, to calm my fidgety side. Nowadays, I chewed a leaf or two when I needed to complete a task within a specific deadline. Usually, my wandering mind wasn't so bad, but I'd get on kicks and get really invested in something, forgetting the world around me, so this helped keep me on track.

I turned on some music and got to bustling about the kitchen. I didn't often work my craft into my baked goods unless explicitly asked, but I always baked with good intentions. Somehow, the Light always knew when to manifest. I wished my 50th-anniversary celebrators a long, happy life, for easy sunrises and cozy sunsets together. I wished for continued love, respect, and energy to take on the next fifty years if that's what life had in store for them.

Anyone inside the house would never know, but from the outside, the Earth itself seemed to hum whenever I worked. The birds sang louder, the clouds lazily drifted elsewhere, and blooming flowers perked up.

A few hours of focused energy rendered some beautiful results. I'd finished everything on my list, including a few batches of pepperoni rolls. A special treat that was always in high demand, my pepperoni rolls were some of the best in the area, a fact in which, of course, I reveled. The highest honor for the comfiest of comfort foods, and it felt like a damn good magnum opus if you asked me.

I loaded everything into the back seat of my car. Dot was napping in a sunbeam, so I kissed her head and left to make my delivery. It was a pleasant enough spring-ish day, still chilly but warming with the sun. I blasted my Ukrainian folk band and enjoyed the fresh air during the not-quite-20-minute drive to the bookshop.

It felt like any other Tuesday until I turned onto Main Street. My chest tightened and my breath caught in my throat.

*Something was wrong.*

MY EYES SCANNED THE street for any obvious signs of something out of place, and aside from a dog creeping towards a curious toddler with an outstretched hot dog in her hand, all seemed normal. There was a new mural on one of the historic buildings, and the people painted on the side of the old haberdashery had some creepy featureless faces, but again, nothing outwardly wrong seemed to be happening downtown today.

I reached out with my mind, glossing over the townsfolk I passed, searching for any noticeable blip on the Light radar. While nothing I saw could explain it, a growing sense of urgency climbed my chest.

I parked in the 15- minute pickup/drop-off spot outside Tipsy Tomes and loaded up the less fragile parts of my delivery. I walked inside and set them on the end of the counter. Instead of stopping to chat, Trish got a nod as I headed back outside to get the celebratory pastry. I balanced the box in one hand as I dug in my pocket for my keys.

My typical gracelessness was amplified by the anxiety I couldn't explain, and I almost dropped the all-important anniversary cake. At the last second, a pair of tanned hands swooped in from nowhere and steadied the precarious package before it plummeted to the pavement.

Flustered, I looked up from the ground and into the eyes of the person who had saved my ass. *Those eyes.*

The tan, chiseled face matched the hands that were currently extended, holding my cake out towards me. The eyes, however, were otherworldly, and their vast blue depths spoke volumes.

I sputtered an apology for being such a klutz, adding a dozen thank you's for his help and went to take the cake from him. The voice that spilled out from between his perfect lips sent shivers down my spine, but somehow I simultaneously felt like I'd stepped into fire.

"Oh, don't worry about it. I happened to be in the right place at the right time. So glad I could help." He flashed a dazzling smile, "That is one gorgeous cake. And if it's even half as delicious as it looks, whoever gets to eat it will have a fantastic day." He grinned at me, and the deep laugh lines around his eyes told me that smile was a frequent occurrence.

I straightened up and tried to regain the composure that had abandoned me.

I took in the entire scope of my current hero. He was tall and muscular and looked like he might work on a farm, or some other hard labor. I blushed at the thought.

*Okay, reel it in, you immature little schoolgirl.*

His dark hair was tousled, and the sunlight glinted off a few strands of gray hair that ran from his temples down into the heavenly beard he was sporting. He wore jeans, a t-shirt, work boots, and an impressive ring on his right hand. *Thankfully not on his left*, I couldn't help but think. He held the door for me as I delivered my goods.

*What a gentleman.*

"You know, you really saved the day. Thank you again. Can I buy you a cup of coffee or something? This place has the best in town."

"I'd love that," he almost purred. "I'm always up for the best coffee with a pretty girl."

I felt my eyes narrow instinctively and gritted my teeth a little at the "pretty girl" line, but forced myself to relax and smile. Yikes, red flag number one. I'm a grown-ass woman, not a pretty little girl. It felt polite to have a coffee with this guy, because if I had splattered a cake outside Tipsy Tomes, Trish probably would've murdered me. He was a rough-and-tumble-looking guy, so maybe this Southern charm was different from what I was used to.

I unloaded the baked goods and checked the cake in with Trish, before sitting with my mysterious man at a little two-person table in the corner.

Time to be socially awkward.

Trish strutted over to us, giving me a look, which I ignored.

"What can I get for you guys this morning?"

"Oh, I'll have the usual, and whatever my new friend wants. If you want to put it on my tab, that would be great."

It was a dangerously good thing I could have a tab at this place, balanced by an even better thing: I semi-worked here. Between the coffee, the books, and the whiskey, I frequently paid my tabs with my earnings. I was a sucker for a potent drink and a pleasant book.

Tall, Dark, and Handsome ordered a black coffee, the house blend at my suggestion, and one of my croissants. Time to pry.

"So, mysterious stranger who has already saved my ass today, what's your name? Mine's Lenore. I'm basically a contract baker for this lovely establishment and obviously a regular. And clearly the most graceful person on the planet. Are you new in town?"

I was rambling, occasionally meeting his intense gaze, but mostly playing with my hair or excessively tapping my spoon; anything I could do to excuse myself for being the awkward human I was.

"My name is rather old-man-ish." He chuckled, trying to put me at ease. "Thanks to my mother. Most of my friends call me Eddie. I am pretty new in town." Trish brought our beverages. Conversation stopped as we both took long drinks. "I bought some land a few weeks ago outside of town, and I'm setting up a little farm. I worked on my family's cattle ranch back home, but wanted to start over somewhere new."

"Need to start over, huh? What, did you murder someone in your old hometown?" I laughed harder than I should have until I noticed he did not find it as funny as I did.

"Uh, no, I didn't murder anyone, but I have a bit of an unsavory past I'd like to put behind me. Nothing illegal, I swear, and I don't intend to stir up any trouble here. Pinky promise." He smiled wryly at me, and something about his smile made me squirm in my seat.

Sordid past. Mysterious stranger. Weird vibes. All the red flags.

Why the hell was I blushing?

"Well, I'm glad to hear I don't have any serial killer competition. I'm sort of the resident murderer in town, and I'd like it to stay that way." My exceptional social ineptitude tried to make a joke, but my face didn't immediately reveal it, so he grew noticeably uncomfortable and shifted in his seat.

"Kidding! I'm not a murderer, promise. I'm also clearly not a comedian. I'll to stick to my day job."

He raised an eyebrow at me.

"Baking!" I almost shouted. "I mean, baking. For here. Yeah."

*Shut. Up. Now.*

I'm not sure where my synapses got lost, but the neurons were clearly misfiring between my brain and mouth. I desperately wished I would stop.

Eddie sat back in his chair and stared at me for what felt like an awkward eternity. My eyes flitted around the room, bouncing between floor, ceiling, bird poop on the window, no eye contact, an empty chair, sugar packet, goddess help me, my shoe, his shoe, my coffee cup, his croissant, his-

And he laughed, a rich, booming laugh. It made me feel a way I don't remember ever feeling before, like a familiar sweater settling around my entire existence, and the connection between us felt as if I'd known it my entire life. His guffaws pulled me in. We'd heard the first and last joke in the endless universe, and we both ended up laughing so hard we cried.

We fought to catch our breath When we both finally did, our eyes met. I felt the rosy blush creeping up my neck again.

"Wow, people are going to think we lost our marbles." I took a long sip of my coffee. "For a second, I thought I had."

"Don't you have a reputation to uphold here? I'm still the weird new guy in town." He chuckled again, leaning back in his chair and running his hands through his thick, dark hair.

"Oh no, I'm the crazy, witchy lady who lives in the woods. This is pretty on brand for me." I laughed awkwardly, trying to play off the idiotic almost-confession I'd given. Burning witches at the stake and hanging them hadn't gone out of style *that* long ago, and I wasn't trying to bring the trend back.

"Witch lady, huh? I've always wanted to meet a witch." Eddie grinned at me, and my heart did somersaults.

I wasn't sure who this person really was, but I wanted to get to know him better. A lot better, if I was being frank with myself.

THE NEXT FEW WEEKS passed without consequence: working, gardening, baking, the normal. When I made my deliveries to Tipsy Tomes, I hoped I would run into Eddie again. Occasionally, I would. Sometimes he would be at the coffee shop enjoying one of my baked goods, always ready to offer a compliment. Other times I'd see him around town. I ran into him at the grocery store, and he pushed his shopping cart next to mine. We perused the aisles together and engaged in polite small talk while my legs trembled and my heart fluttered.

Finally, I was at the farmers' market one morning looking for some lavender-scented soap and he came up next to me. Not with a casual hello this time, but with determination in his eyes.

"We keep running into each other, so I figured we might as well give this a try. Would you like to hang out with me on purpose sometime?" I chuckled as I met his smoldering gaze.

"You know, that doesn't sound like a half bad idea. When are you free this week? I've got a great local lunch place we could hit up?" I tried to be cool, really, I did, but failed. The flame crept into my cheeks, despite my best efforts to fight the girlish blush.

"I don't mean to be forward, and I hope this doesn't sound weird, but how would you feel about me making you dinner? That was one thing that I brought with me from my old life I still love to do: cooking. In the least creepy way, I'd love to have you over to my place. Maybe tomorrow night?"

I grinned, thinking this was a little odd, but honestly, I liked it. He didn't give me serial killer vibes, and I was usually pretty good at picking up people's innermost thoughts. Though he wasn't an open book, I could get most of what went on in his head. He had some thoughts he kept hidden relatively well, but I attributed that to him being a gentleman and trying not to think the same obscene thoughts about me I was thinking about him.

"Was that too much?" There was a little nervousness in his voice.

"Oh gosh, no, sorry. Lost in thought." I blushed again, betraying those images I'd fought to keep buried. "I'd love to come over for dinner tomorrow. Promise you won't murder me, and we're golden." I couldn't help but laugh at my joke, but he was not as entertained.

"I'd never hurt you. I hope you know that," he said seriously.

"I was trying to be funny and clearly failed yet again. My bad."

He paused a moment and looked at me, and I felt myself wanting to run my fingers through his hair-

"Ha! I get it now. Sometimes I'm not nearly as clever as I think I am. Sorry, nerves."

I found his small confession endearing and adorable and leaned in to peck him on the cheek.

"Fantastic. Here's my number; text me your address, and I'll be over around, what, five? Five thirty?" I handed him a scrap of paper I'd dug out of my purse and scribbled my number on.

His face lit up.

"Yeah! That sounds great! Er- I mean," he changed his voice to a more suave version of his own. "Yeah, that's cool."

We laughed at the shift and nervously parted ways.

Something about his mind hovered outside the abilities of my Light, which was odd, but I loved the mystery. Being able to pick through people's thoughts like flipping through an aged waiting-room magazine was exhausting. I'd been able to tone it down with some practice, to a dull background thrum. When I tried, I could really get in their heads, though. But with Eddie, it was like swimming through the darkness. A calm blackness after being surrounded by the blinding, strobing lights of the rest of the world.

I'd lived my whole life in a haze of mental noise. I remember around my eleventh birthday, I'd started complaining to my mom and grandmother about the "lights in my head". Any other parent might have been concerned, but my mom knew it was part of the Light.

Almost immediately, they began my training in controlling and using it. They taught me to dim and block the swirling colors and flashes when I needed to, to focus on specific pieces to gain information, and to manipulate those lights and sounds when the need arose. It wasn't precisely mind control, more of a mental influence.

The dull roar had persisted ever since. Not as aggravating as it once was, but ever-present. That's why Eddie's mental silence was so pleasant. As I drove home, I contemplated why. Why he seemed so deliciously closed off from my mind.

The rest of the day was spent in quiet contemplation. Tomorrow night was a full moon, so I prepped for my monthly ritual. I had work to do tomorrow, so gathering things and making my preparations early made me feel like I was saving myself from more chaos tomorrow.

Finally, the sun was setting, and I brewed some tea. I snuggled up with my sketchbook and my furry companion and settled into the cozy night.

*WITH EVERY STEP I TOOK towards the black door, I could feel the tightness in my chest squeezing harder. The logical part of my brain screamed at me to turn around, but something was pulling me in, like a moth to a flame. I finally was close enough to touch it; I reached out my trembling hand, my lungs screaming for air that would not come. I placed my hand on the glowing doorknob, expecting it to burn me, but only felt ice cold shoot up my arm. I turned the knob-*

MEOW

"Dammit, Belladonna!" I shouted, causing my fuzzy black companion to jump straight into the air.

*Oh, for pity's sake, woman, what's your problem? I am positively famished, and here you are shouting at me. What's a poor feline to do in this wretched world?*

"Ugh, I'm sorry, Dot. I was having a weird dream, and you startled me. Forgive me?" I scratched behind her ears as she purred loudly, accepting my apology.

THE MORNING PASSED slowly. Dot and I relaxed with some baking and cleaning. We'd settled on five thirty for my arrival, and I fought my brain for hours about how early I could start getting ready to go.

Finally, around three, I jumped in the shower and scrubbed with my homemade body oil, infused with love and some exciting intentions. I shaved my legs, carefully avoiding nicks, and lathered up with a magically moisturizing scrub, more handmade goodness. Amidst the show I was putting on for no one but myself, I felt stupid for thinking anything would happen and he'd notice the extra effort I put forth.

But what if something happened?

I'd dated casually, but mainly a few dates here and there with a couple of guys I'd met outside of town. There are only so many options when you live in a place this small, and things could get weird fast when you hook up with the grocery guy.

I stood in front of my closet, wrapped in a towel, pondering what I should wear.

From downstairs, I heard glass shatter and Dot screeching.

Really? Did we have to do this tonight?

I ran downstairs, and the scene in the kitchen could only be described as chaotic. A giant creature, maybe an owl, was squaring off with Dot, whose hackles were raised as she snarled loudly.

*It is no ordinary bird of prey!* Dot called to me.

"Yeah, I picked up on that." I ducked as the creature swooped towards me with uncomfortably large wings and dangerously sharp claws.

"What the hell are you, and what do you want?" I yelled and grabbed the cast iron pan hanging from its hook.

The toddler-sized thing landed on my kitchen floor, and I swung.

I'm not sure how I missed it, but I did. The weight of the pan threw me off balance, and I stumbled to the side.

I recovered and flicked my wrist, sending a barrage of household items flying at the creature. Surely one of them had to land and at least distract it.

No such luck.

"Don't you have powers, witch? Why don't you use them?" The creature let out a sneering hiss.

I felt something boil inside me. Not the Light glowing, but something else. Something dark.

I tried to shake the feeling swarming within me, but the darkness welled up in my chest. A lava-like heat spread, engulfing and destroying everything in its path.

The thing rose into the air and swooped again, this time catching my arm and tearing three deep gashes in my shoulder.

I gasped and let out a bellowed shout. An unfamiliar burst of blue-black flames came from my hands.

The mini inferno engulfed the space where the creature stood. It let out a wild cackle and dissolved into nothing. The flames filling my small kitchen also disappeared, fading like an oxygen-starved candle.

What was that all about?

Dot sniffed around the area where the intruder had evaporated.

"Hell if I know, it was definitely something evil, though. Wonder what it wanted?"

I was more concerned with how it had goaded me into using my power. I'd used my Light magic on it, but it somehow knew of the abilities I'd given up and worked so hard to get away from. No one knew about them. No one alive, anyway. So how did the bird thing know?

My phone rang, and Eddie's name lit up the screen.

Shit, was I late? I fumbled to answer.

"Hello?"

"Hey, quick question!" Eddie couldn't hide the enthusiasm in his voice. "Assuming you're still coming, red or white wine? Or should I do both? Is that a thing? Any preferences? I'll put out both. See you soon?"

"Any wine is good wine to me." I chuckled at his enthusiasm. "I'm walking out the door; see you soon."

"Perfect, bye!"

EDDIE LIVED ON THE opposite side of town. It was about a twenty-minute drive, but it felt like an eternity as I contemplated the creature that had invaded my home and tried to provoke magic I'd long since abandoned.

My family was no ordinary line of witches. Our Light wasn't a line of brightness and sparkly goodness. Our Light had once been dark magic, something ancient and evil. Until Grams had sworn off the demons, her ancestors had worshiped and crafted their own line. We'd lived happily, forging our lives into something cheerful and light, avoiding the darkness as best we could.

Grams and mom hadn't been able to avoid it forever, though. It had found us when I was seventeen, taking them from me far too early. I'd lived in a few places, bouncing around when people started asking too many questions, or a random demon would pop up and demand I reignite the darkness within me and bend to their will, blah blah blah.

But I loved the Light.

Right?

I loved the magic that Grams taught me and the no-strings-attached sources of the Light. Sure, dark magic could be more potent, but Light served me well, and I saw no need to change anything.

I was so deep in thought I didn't notice I'd missed a turn, forcing me to pull off on the side of the road to get my bearings and get back on track. The cool fall evening was perfect. The clear skies showed off the stars, and a gentle wind blew in from the east. Even a bird was flying back to the nest.

"Wait a second," I said aloud, "is that-?"

The "bird" was actually the unwelcome guest from this evening's kitchen incident, and it was headed right towards me.

Suddenly, I was filled with a boiling rage I'd never felt before. Without thinking, I yelled at it, and the words that came out were not my own but a lost language. The winged beast burst into a glowing blue flame and disappeared.

I was shaken but resolved not to show it. I calmly straightened my disheveled hair and drove off, finally making the right turn onto Eddie's road. While I drove the last few miles, I thought about how the power felt. The unfamiliar feeling fascinated and intrigued me. I loved it, and I knew I shouldn't. It was dark magic, forces within my family line that had gone dormant needed to stay that way. Inside, I could feel the sense of almost-divine satisfaction in finally releasing the bottled-up potential.

Satisfaction that bordered on pleasure.

The delicate tendrils of darkness crept around my heart and mind, caressing the atrophied forces within me.

I SAW THE LIGHTS TO Eddie's house as I rounded a curve and let out the unexpected lungful of stale breath.

*Thank you for that, anxiety.*

I saw his sculpted silhouette step out of the front door. The light behind him hid his face, but I could feel his enthusiasm as I climbed out of my car. I walked to him and kissed his cheek.

"Hey, I hope I'm not late," I said with a coy smile. The shift inside was spilling out, and I felt bolder, wilder.

"Of course, you're the guest of honor! I don't think you could be late to your own party." Eddie laughed, displaying a little bit of nerves with a side of adorable chagrin. My favorite.

He served up a steak stir fry with tons of veggies I recognized from his trip to the farmers' market. There were homemade mashed potatoes that were beyond fluffy, and freshly baked rolls, straight out of the oven. He even brought out a bottle of local wine from the next town over, two actually, one red and one white. We popped open the red and drank deeply as I savored every bite.

"I am insanely impressed. Not to be sexist, but I've not met many guys who can cook this well. And fresh rolls? Now you're speaking my language." The wine helped my enthusiasm.

"I'm so glad you're enjoying it. I haven't had much opportunity to cook since I moved, so this is nice!" He thrived on the praise I offered, and I felt some weird power trip knowing his happiness was in my hand.

We finished dinner and dove into the apple pie I'd brought, polishing off at least three more bottles of wine. We talked into the small hours of the morning. All the while, the darkness within me was growing and spreading.

THE NEXT MORNING, I woke up in my bed, with Dot judging me from her perch by the window.

Again.

*Have a good night, did you? Leaving me all alone here after that thing attacked. I could have died.*

"Oh stop, you're fine. I needed some time to unwind and last night was perfect."

*Disgusting. Romance. I don't want to hear anything else about your evening. I swear, you are more of an animal than I am.*

"Nothing happened. We stayed up late and talked and drank wine. He offered to drive me home, but didn't try to push the idea of me spending the night. I was a little disappointed, if I'm being honest. I really like him. Also? Just because you're an ancient, jaded spinster doesn't mean you need to rain on my parade."

*SPINSTER? I'm only 137 years old. Give me a break!*

I howled with laughter as my feline companion feigned indignation.

We'd moved around a lot in the past few decades, jumping from mountain town to valley village. There had been a tiny mishap a while ago where I'd been cursed with some sort of rabid succubus, and every time I got close to a mortal man, he ended up in pieces. Physically, not emotionally.

Eddie was different. I hoped. The primal urge to kiss him and touch him was almost more than I could bear, but he felt like home. More than anything else in my life ever had, and I didn't want to hurt him.

I set to another day of baking and bustling around the house. I worked my way through yet another droning to-do list, and before long, the sun was sinking low and the stars were peeking through the clouds in the sky.

A firm but slow knock resonated on my front door. I took off my apron and threw it across the back of the kitchen chair, not noticing the poof of flour that rose from it. I walked towards the front of the house, past a mirror in the foyer where I noticed the white powder freckling my face, and tried to straighten myself up before I opened the door.

In front of me stood a wild-eyed Eddie, covered in dirt and sweat, but seeming to shiver despite the warm evening air.

"Hi, I'm so sorry I didn't call. I just—"

"Don't worry about it! You're welcome anytime. Do you want to come in?" I didn't even try to hide the beaming smile that lit my face.

The creeping warmth from my stomach and up through my neck, though, I did my best to keep hidden.

"Yeah, please. I really wanted to see you." He wrung his hands and slowly stepped across the threshold.

"I always want to see you." I flashed a toothy smile, giddy and dissolving fast into some goofy schoolgirl persona. I needed to keep it together.

He shut the door behind him and stopped, looking at me. His eyes skimmed my body, sending shivers down my spine. I couldn't help myself and stepped towards him, wrapping my arms around his neck and entwining my fingers in his luscious hair.

I leaned in to kiss him, rising onto my tiptoes to reach his full lips. Before they met, he stopped me, grabbing either side of my face with his calloused hands.

"Wait."

"I'm so sorry. That was rude." I blushed for completely different reasons than embarrassment.

"No, no, no, please don't apologize. I cannot tell you how much I want to kiss you and touch you and hold you and-" He blushed.

"So what's wrong?"

"Can I talk to you? There's something I need to tell you."

"Of course, please, come sit. Can I get you a drink or anything?" Was it performance issues? Smaller-than-average? Wait, was he lacking the equipment entirely? I started inventing scenarios in my head and simultaneously coming up with solutions. My heart was pounding and my legs were shaking as I walked back to the living room with a couple of glasses of water.

"Okay. This is going to sound absolutely insane. I know. But there's something about you that makes me want to tell you all my deep, dark secrets, and figure the world's problems out with you. I know we only met recently, but you feel right. Lenore, I dare to say I've fallen in love with you already."

The giddy schoolgirl inside of me fought to burst forth and squeal obnoxiously, but thankfully I kept it together.

"I- I feel the same way." I smiled sweetly. So much for keeping it together. "You can tell me anything, and I promise you it won't be crazy. Trust me, I've got plenty of my own weird shit."

"Okay, here goes." He took a deep breath and exhaled slowly. "My family is odd. Odd probably isn't strong enough. Odd, not like matching-sweaters-for-the-holidays weird, but back generations ago, we were—and this is the crazy sounding part—we were cursed."

He paused, his apprehensive face searching mine for any reaction to what he'd said.

All I could come up with to say to set aside his fears was, "Me too! What's yours?"

He laughed, the deep, booming laugh I loved so much. It sent vibrations through my whole body, and I relished the feeling.

"What? I'm serious! Long story short, I'm a witch, and I was cursed a while back. There, that's my deep, dark secret. So, again, what's your curse?"

His mouth hung open in surprise, and some remnant laughter spilled from his irresistible lips.

"Oh, come on. You can't say you're cursed and not spill the tea, Eddie!"

"Umm, well. This almost seems silly. But, uh, when I get, er-close—" He coughed uncomfortably. "To a partner, uh, woman—" He stopped to collect himself.

"Whenever I get intimate with someone, I *change*." He sighed in defeat.

"Change?"

"It's hard to explain, but think of it like a B-list werewolf change."

"Oh, nice. When you're horny, you turn into a wolf?"

"A wolf would make this easy." He rubbed his temples. "And more like a steamy paranormal romance novel than I'd ever want my life to get. No, it's not a wolf. I've tried to find a name for it, even something to describe it and get rid of it, but so far I haven't been able to. So summing it up, I guess it's like a demon?"

"My mysterious, almost-perfect boyfriend changes into a sex demon when he gets turned on? Huh. I thought this week couldn't surprise me any more."

"I understand completely, and I like you too much to let anything happen to you, so if you want I can leave you alo—" He paused. "Wait, did you say boyfriend?"

"I mean. Uh. For lack of a better title, I guess. Sorry. Is that weird? Oh shit. Yeah, that's weird. I'm sorry, I—" He cut off my ramblings.

"No, stop, please. I like it." He took my face in his hands and I felt like he could see my soul with those deep brown eyes. "You really don't want me to leave?"

"Leave? No, why would I? That's the least of my worries. I'm not sure if your brain has really registered what I said earlier, but I'm a witch. We can figure this out. Together." I nuzzled into his hands, breathing in the smell of his skin.

"Oh wait, yeah, you said that!" He almost yelled. "Can you fix me?"

"If I can't remove the curse completely, I can at least help you contain it. Even better, things like that don't affect me, so you don't have anything to worry about."

"They don't affect you, like, at all?" Eddie's eyes grew wide and I could feel his heartbeat quicken.

"Nope." I climbed into his lap and kissed him slowly. "Not at all." I was suddenly sure that whatever he was and whatever I am would go together perfectly. My fears melted away as he wrapped his fingers in my hair and held my body close to his.

As he kissed me hard, I felt his tongue split in my mouth. His hands shifted, and I felt claws tear through the back of my shirt.

The muscles pressed against my chest coiled and shifted, but instead of fear, all I felt was exhilaration. The warmth that grew within me boiled and rose, but instead of terror at the idea of what was coming, I relished the challenge.

This was the beginning. I didn't know where it would go, but I was eager to find out.

# A Word from the Author – C.R. Clark

For my husband, who inspired some of the best parts of my stories, and distracted me from writing in all the best ways. *wink*

For all the people who have ever read anything I've written and given me feedback, compliments, or encouragement. Every hour I convince myself to sit down and actually write the damn thing, I owe to you and your hype skills. I would've given up long ago without you.

Especially Emma, who has never hesitated to read anything I send, and always provides motivation and observation.

For Cara, who ignited the flame in my heart to start writing again, and does all the spooky stuff with me that keeps me inspired.

For AC Adams, Adam Gaffen, and everyone in the Steamy Anthology group who came up with the chance to try something out of my comfort zone, and made me feel like part of a community of likeminded people who love some spice.

Find more of her work at https://linktr.ee/appalachianpennydreadful

# Never Been Wished

## By AC Adams

I awoke to the sight of my prison walls and screamed.

I pounded on the walls. As always, they rang beneath my fists, but didn't give. They never did.

A thousand years I'd been trapped here, maybe more. Time was meaningless. I was trapped until I wasn't. Then I was released until my purpose was fulfilled.

Not once in the myriad moments of fleeting freedom did my would-be rescuer save me.

It made a girl bitter.

My fury faded, as it always did, after a few pointless curses for my long-dead mother, the archdemon who created the djinn, and the life I was condemned to before I was born.

I'm a djinn. A genie. A wish-granter. A life-destroyer.

It's a job, and I hate it.

I was born a djinn, because my mother was a djinn. My father was the man who rescued her from her servitude.

My life was normal until I became a woman, when my powers began to manifest. I was thrilled, but couldn't understand why my mother was miserable. As I grew in my abilities, so did her unhappiness.

Finally, when I was nearly eighteen, I confronted her.

"Why do you hate me, Mother?"

She couldn't meet my eyes. "Because of what I did to you. The curse I laid on you, because I was selfish and wanted a child."

This didn't make any sense to me. "But I have such powers! See?" I conjured a lily though it was the depth of winter. "This is a blessing, Mother. Why shouldn't I use it?"

She smacked the flower from my hand. It landed on the hard dirt floor, battered out of shape.

"Stop it. You have no idea what forces you toy with."

I rolled my eyes at her non-answer. "Then tell me, Mother."

She did.

Djinn belonged to Below, created by an archdemon to tempt people and destroy their lives. We were given the power to grant any wish, exactly as asked, and that was the trap. We weren't permitted to advise or correct the wish to avoid the unforeseen consequences, allowing the wisher to suffer from their greed and base desires. The djinn were granted immortality, with a catch. We existed only to fulfill our purpose, spending our lives trapped in a vessel, free only when summoned.

"Mother, that's ridiculous. You're not trapped, and you're not immortal." I reached out for her hair, fingering the streaks of silver which had appeared in the black strands.

"There is one way, and one way only, for a djinn to escape. The wisher must use one of their wishes to grant us our release."

My mother wasn't finished. "You cannot lure them, or promise them anything in return for their wish. They can't add your servitude to their wish, or they suffer a punishment."

"What punishment?"

"The wish rebounds upon them, and they are turned into a djinn, condemned to the same fate."

And there was the trap. Altruism.

Freeing a djinn required a truly selfless act.

"Your father was a kind man, gentle and loving. He freed me with his first wish. I never expected to feel the sun on my skin whenever I wanted, or hear birds when waking, and I did a foolish thing. I fell in love. When I learned I was with child, I prayed you would not suffer the same fate as me, that whatever magic I'd had as a djinn was dispelled by the wish. For your entire childhood, it seemed my prayer was answered, even after your father died."

I barely remembered him. He died when I was a toddler, but I could still hear his voice in my dreams.

"Then you came into your powers with your womanhood, and I knew my prayers had been in vain."

I thought of all the inconsequential wishes I'd granted myself and paled. If they all had hidden consequences...

"Mother? I haven't suffered anything from the magic I've done."

She shook her head. "You won't. As a djinn, you're protected. You can't give yourself freedom, or alter your destiny, but you'll never want for material things." Mother managed a wry smile. "My captivity was never uncomfortable, unless I desired it to be."

"When does my captivity begin?"

"I don't know, my daughter. Between now and your betrothal, whenever that might be."

I wasn't interested in any of the boys in the village, though I'd known one of them would be my husband someday. The key was someday. I wasn't in any rush.

"Then it may never happen."

Her head shook again. "No."

"What do you mean? I'm not betrothed; I haven't even promised a boy a meeting."

Mother choked down a sob.

"Mother?"

"When your father died, we were destitute. I didn't know what to do. Everything was so different from before I became a djinn, but some things never change." Her voice broke before she continued in a whisper. "I promised you to the son of the village elder in return for our security."

"You did what? Mother, how could you?"

I knew arrangements like this were common, but I never dreamed I was part of one.

"What else would you have me do? Sell myself? Sell you? I couldn't."

I knew this, too. Slaves were common, working the jobs too brutal for the most lowly serf.

"No, Mother, but—"

"There was no choice. I suppose, in the back of my mind, I knew you would never need to be his." I wrinkled my nose. The elder's son was a brutish thug with no humor and less intelligence. The thought of bedding him turned my stomach, but I forced a grim smile.

"In that case, Mother, I'm glad you were right."

Over the next days, she told me all she knew, all she remembered of her life as a djinn. I stopped performing my minor conjurations.

A month elapsed, and I thought perhaps I would escape notice. Then we were summoned to the elder's home for sabbath, three days hence.

"He wishes to make your betrothal official," my mother explained.

That night, I was awakened by a crash and the sound of her screams.

"You cannot take her!"

"It is my right and my duty." The voice that answered her defiance was cruel and raspy. "Do not interfere further. You escaped, but you are not immune to my wrath."

There was another scream, followed by a thump.

"Mother!"

A beast appeared at the curtain which divided my space from the rest of the house and tore it aside. I glimpsed her body, crumpled and tossed aside.

"MOTHER!"

My fury overwhelmed me. For the first time in weeks, I pulled on the magic, summoning a sword to my hands, and flailed at it.

I missed, and it laughed.

"Your spirit will serve you well." An enormous claw descended on my arm, and we vanished.

"DUDE, WHAT'S THIS?"

Ben's friend Natalie held up... something. He didn't know what it was, and said so.

"Fat lot of help you are." She tucked the shiny sphere in a pocket and promptly forgot about it.

I NEVER LEARNED THE demon's name. It transported us from my home into the space that would be my prison in an eye-blink. The space was bizarre. It showed me the container once and explained that it would transform to blend into its surroundings. I'd appear in a place at random and wait to be found. Then I'd fulfill the wishes, be popped back into my cell, and I'd be sent to my next destination. There was no promise I'd be found quickly, but I had no way of telling the passage of time when inside.

It spent a timeless time instructing me in my duties, my obligations, my limitations. What the people could ask for, what they couldn't. And, grudgingly, the conditions of my release. The punishment I'd face for divulging too much.

My prison was comfortable; I'll give Below that much. Anything I wanted, I could wish into being. Except company. I never saw my mother again. I don't even know if she survived its attack. She's long dead now, in any case.

"NATALIE!"

She sighed at her mother's yell from the basement. "What?"

"Time to clean your fall jackets! Bring them down and I'll wash them, and don't forget to check the pockets! I can't replace another phone."

"Whatever." She knew better than to ignore her mother, though. Not after the last time. She still had to cope with a flip phone for another six months.

Natalie gathered the various light jackets she'd worn as the weather chilled, carefully checking the pockets as asked.

*Nothing, nothing, nothing... what's this?*

She pulled an iridescent blue sphere from her jean jacket.

*Oh, the thing Ben found!*

She turned it around in her fingers. It was alluring, and just the right size, about the same as an avocado pit. The light danced and shimmered on the surface, almost seeming to come from within. She felt herself pulled in, losing herself in the starlike glitter, hypnotized...

"Natalie Anne!"

The spell broke.

"Coming, Mom!" She dropped the sphere on her desk, not watching it roll behind the laptop, all the way to the back.

I HATE WAITING.

In some ways, it was easier then, before modern technology. No clocks, no candles, no connection to the outside world, even though I could conjure in anything I wanted. I grew skilled at woodworking, and knitting, metalsmithy and even glassblowing, mostly through trial and error. When you have all the time and nothing better to spend it on?

I could read. The curse of languages was something which was lifted from me when I was imprisoned. Books, though, were rare and monothematic for many years. Gutenberg's press, and the proliferation of texts, was maybe the only thing which kept me from insanity.

It was a close thing.

Now I took advantage of technology and devoured everything I could find.

It was a mixed blessing.

I knew how long it had been since my last taste of starlight.

Starlight?

Yes.

I always loved the stars, twinkling in the blackness of the night sky. They made me feel safe, like there were uncounted beings looking out for me.

It was a delusion, but I still loved the stars, and rarely got to see them.

My benefactors rarely had me outside when I was free, part of human greed. Nobody wanted to share the wishes, or their knowledge or me, so I was kept confined to a room. And my freedom was always brief. Not only couldn't I venture far from my prison, but as soon as the task I was summoned for was complete, I would be sucked back inside.

The sun is easy to see when it shines. Stars are fleeting.

I know when it is, and how long I've been trapped this time.

I don't know how long I have to wait.

But I know next time I'm going to do everything I can to escape.

*KALILI, WHAT ARE YOU doing?*

*She deserves a chance, Faith.*

The sphere emerged from the cluttered depths of the desk, rolled by unseen fingers toward the front.

*You're a soft-hearted demon.*

*Former demon, please.* The mental giggles lingered as the two immortals took their leave.

NATALIE DROPPED HER books on the floor and flopped onto her unmade bed.

"Christmas break. Finally."

It wouldn't be long enough. It never was. Even the longer breaks that college gave her weren't enough to wash the tedium of classes from her mind. Living at home didn't help, but she couldn't afford not to, despite scholarships and her barista job.

Now, though, maybe she could find enough time to have a social life, if only for a few weeks.

Ha.

She sat up and pivoted to her desk, reaching for her laptop. A sparkle of blue caught her eye.

"What...? Oh, I remember this. I wondered where it went." Natalie picked up the sphere and held it in her palm. It was warm and heavy, far heavier than it should have been. She stood to get a better look.

"Wow." She lifted it to the light, caught in the reflections, glittering from within.

I'VE BEEN FOUND!

I know nothing of the person holding my prison, but I know what to do.

*WHAT DO YOU DESIRE?*

Natalie shook her head. Where did the voice come from?

"I've been watching too much Netflix."

*I can grant your desires.*

She frowned, remembering the circumstances under which she found the sphere. "Ben, are you pranking me?"

Nothing except the voice in her head again.

*Release me and I will be yours.*

"Right, and how do I do that?"

*Will it, and it shall be.*

"Sure, I just say that I want you released? Holy shit!" Natalie stumbled and dropped onto her bed.

A woman appeared in the cramped space of her bedroom. No, not a woman, a girl, maybe a couple of years younger than herself. She wore a simple cotton tunic and skirt which draped her legs to the floor. Her hair was brown and wavy, nearly reaching her waist, and her eyes... Though they were brown, golden flecks sparkled in them.

"I'm a woman, if you measure by years, Natalie Anne."

"Holy shit. You can read my mind?"

The woman laughed. "How else could I grant your wishes?"

Natalie shook her head. "Stop. Are you saying you're some sort of genie? Why aren't you in flowing robes?"

"Like this?" Her clothes transformed into a pink, silken confection, but then immediately returned to her previous garb. "Too cliché. And yes, I'm a genie. I apologize for not being blue, or coming from a bottle, but I'm afraid the movie got some details wrong."

This was too much. "I'm asleep, and this is a dream."

"No, Natalie Anne, it's no dream."

"Stop calling me that!"

The woman looked confused. "Is that not your name?"

"It is, but only my mom calls me that, and only when she's pissed at me." A flash of sadness whispered through the woman's eyes, gone almost before it was noticed. Natalie shook her head. "What am I doing, talking to a delusion?"

"I assure you, I'm quite real." The woman reached out and pinched Natalie's arm.

"Ouch! Knock it off."

"Am I real?"

Natalie rubbed her arm, considering her options. Dream, reality, or delusion brought on by stress. She didn't seem to be going anywhere.

"Fine. You're a genie, and you're going to grant my wishes?"

The sparkle of merriment left the woman. "I am, but there are rules."

"Of course there are. Let me see. Three wishes, no wishing for more wishes, can't bring anyone back from the dead—"

"No, I can do that. I don't advise it." She winced in pain. "I shouldn't have said that."

"Right, because it's not your job to keep me from screwing up. Can't wish for love. What else?"

"You must wait for one wish to be fulfilled in its entirety before making another. And you cannot wish for your own death."

Natalie's eyebrows twitched. "Do you get much of that?"

"You'd be surprised."

"This is a lot to take in. Where did you come from? What do I call you?"

She gestured to the sphere, forgotten in Natalie's hand. "That is the current form of my prison." She winced again. "And my name? You want to know my name?"

"Why not?"

The woman's mouth opened and closed as if the simple question surprised her. "Edan."

"Just Edan?"

"Just... Edan."

Natalie stood and extended her hand. "Nice to meet you."

I KNEW WHAT THIS SOCIETY demanded of me.

But I didn't know what to do. Nobody had ever greeted me in such a manner.

After a frozen moment, I put my hand in hers. She clasped mine, warm and strong, and I matched her.

"So, Edan, tell me more." Natalie sat on the bed and gestured to the lone chair. "Like, can other people see you?"

I sat, my head spinning. "What? Yes, they can see me. I'm real, just like you."

I was on firmer ground now.

"Then we need to come up with a story for you, if you're going to be here a while."

"What makes you think I'll be here for some time?"

Natalie laughed at this. "I know the stories about genies, and the shit that happens from poorly worded wishes. I'm going to take my time. You have to stay out until I make my wishes, right?"

"No, I can return to—" I pointed to the blue sphere without calling my prison again.

"Do you want to?"

Again, I was stunned into paralysis. Did I want to? I always did, but...

"No." My mouth took the lead before my brain caught up.

"Then we need a story for you, otherwise my mom will freak." She thought for a moment before brightening. "You're a friend from college who doesn't want to go home for the break, so you're staying with me." She regarded me critically from head to toe. "We'll have to do something about your clothes."

I'd chosen to appear in the garb I wore when I was human. It made my story more believable, but I could see how they might be problematic if...

"What? I'm staying with you?"

"Duh. We have a guest room." She swept an arm over the tiny, cluttered room. "You won't be staying in here."

The next half-hour was a blur. Between us, with much prompting from Natalie, we created a persona and history for me, which would explain my presence.

"Why are you doing this?" I asked as we settled on some minor details.

"I told you. I know about genies and wishes and shit. I won't get trapped into some monkey's paw nightmare."

I let her continue planning, jotting notes, like the classes we were in together and the professors and our mutual hatred for the food at the cafeteria. I conjured appropriate clothing and documents, a suitcase full of clothes and a backpack full of books, a laptop and a phone, complete with contacts and social media.

It was more fun than I'd had in years. Decades.

FOR SOMEONE WHO HAD a genie appear in her bedroom, Natalie bounced back quickly. When Edan asked how, she said, "I've been watching and reading fantasy stories since I was little. It's weird to know some of it is true, but hey, I liked those worlds better than this one most of the time."

A voice from downstairs interrupts her. "Natalie, I'm home!"

"That's my mom. Ready?"

Edan looked terrified. "No?"

Natalie took her arm and led her from the room.

"It'll be fine."

It was. Eventually.

They endured painfully awkward dinner, where Natalie was pestered whether Edan was her girlfriend (and her denials met with poorly veiled skepticism). Then the interrogation ended, with both sides declaring victory, and Edan's presence for the break was taken as given.

It was thrilling.

IT'S BEEN NEARLY A week since Natalie released me.

A week since we began our charade.

And a week since I saw the inside of my prison.

Playing the part of a college student was less difficult than I thought it would be.

Picking up the language, the slang, and integrating myself into Natalie's circle of friends? Simplicity itself, with a little application of magic. Natalie and I decided not to deny any suggestion we were involved. It was simpler, and explained why we were nearly inseparable.

Christmas is tomorrow, and tonight the stars are glorious as we stare out the living room window.

Natalie notices something in my gaze. "You look sad. Why?"

Can I tell her? Well, why not? It's not against the rules to talk about my past.

I explain about my childhood, and the dreams I had of the stars. How much I missed them during my service. Natalie's eyes glisten as I recount my tale. When I finish, she surreptitiously wipes them.

"My family has a tradition."

"Oh?"

Natalie turns to me. "When I was little, my dad told me that if you make a wish on the brightest star at midnight, Christmas Eve, it would come true by morning."

I laugh. "No such thing. I should know. You could say it's my specialty."

Natalie covers my hand with hers. "What could it hurt?"

What could it hurt? How about an unnatural lifetime's hopes crushed again? The prospect of an eternity being an unwilling servant to Below? But I can't say any of this, so instead agree. "Why not?"

She beams. "We'll have to go outside."

I shiver, but follow her to put on coats. "Why?"

"Sirius is the brightest star, but it's south, and we can't see it from inside."

We go out. The snow crunches underfoot, the starlight reflecting like diamonds. Natalie takes my hand and guides us around to the side.

"Up there." She points, and there it is. A brilliant blue-white dot, putting the rest of the sky to shame. "Another minute."

We stand in silence, hands still clasped. Natalie counts down the last seconds.

*I wish to be free.*

After a few seconds, I giggle. "Nothing happened."

Her laugh echoes in the silent night. "It won't until the morning. Come on, we ought to get to bed."

We separate reluctantly at the door and shed outerwear. "What did you wish for?"

"Oh, no, you can't tell your wish. That's between you and the star."

"I see."

I leave her with a secretive smile on her face.

It takes a long time for sleep to find me, but eventually I do. In the morning I wake and stretch, stagger from the bed, and will myself to look presentable. Much easier than bathing and cosmetics.

Natalie comes down a few minutes after me and heads straight for the coffee. I've set up her mug with the cream and sugar she prefers, and she flashes an appreciative smile.

"Merry Christmas," she says after a sip.

"Merry Christmas. Did your wish come true?"

She looks down, then meets my eyes. "Not yet. I think that's your department."

My heart sinks. Here we go.

It's a pity. I like Natalie. She treats me as a friend instead of a servant.

"I'm listening."

She takes a deep breath. "I wish that the life for you we have created over the past week is your reality, and you are no longer enslaved."

My mouth freezes. Normally, I would say, "Your wish is granted," but this time I cannot.

I feel a wrenching, deep within, as if part of me was being torn from me. I cry out and collapse. In my mind, I hear a voice exult, "Yes!" Natalie is at my side in an instant.

"Edan!" She's got me, and I sink into her arms. "Are you—are you alright? Did I do it right?"

"I don't know." The pain ebbs as quickly as it came.

"I'm sorry. I didn't mean to hurt you."

"It's fine." I don't know it's fine, but the lie falls easily from my lips. "Nobody's done that for me."

She nods. "I figured as much."

"Why did you?"

Her eyes gleam again, as they did last night. "Because you sounded so sad, and so lonely. It's supposed to be a season of giving, right? And I thought, well, I couldn't think of a better wish."

I rise with Natalie's help. "Let's test. Make a simple wish, something that can't go wrong."

"I wish I had another cup of coffee, exactly like this one, sitting on the counter."

I twist the mental muscle I've used for centuries to grant wishes, and... nothing happens.

"Well?" Natalie sounds half fearful, half hopeful. I shake my head.

"Try something else. Change your outfit."

I concentrate on a simple test, turning my blouse from red to yellow.

"Nothing." I'm incredulous. Could I be free?

"Natalie, my prison. Where is it?"

We race upstairs and search her room. Nothing. It's vanished.

"I'm... free? I'm free. Natalie, I'm free!" I wrap my arms around her and lift her from the ground, spinning her. "You did it, Natalie!"

I kiss her, surprising us both, but not so much that she doesn't return the kiss.

And of course, that's when the door opens.

"What's going on?" Her mother's voice is stern but tinged with satisfaction.

"The best Christmas ever, mom," Natalie says. I can't erase the enormous smile on my face.

"Yes. Best Christmas I've ever had." I kiss Natalie again, quickly, and put her down.

"Well, I'm glad you two aren't pretending any longer. Now come downstairs. There are presents."

She walks away, and I whisper to Natalie. "I've already had my present."

# A Word from the Author – AC Adams

Oh, hey there!
    Thanks for picking up my little anthology. It's been—
What?

Oh, this is my *author* note?

Lemme switch hats.

Right. Thank you for reading my story! This is not, strictly speaking, a Kalili & Faith story, though they make a cameo appearance. Did you catch it?

I had fun writing this, since it's unlike most of the stories I write. For one thing, it's dual perspective *and* dual tenses, which was a deliberate choice. I wanted to have the contrast between Edan's present and Natalie's past. I'll leave it to you to figure out why.

See, I wrote it for an anthology, but I went over the word count. I gave it to my wife to read, and she told me not to dare cut anything, so I had to write a different story for that submission, and Never Been Wished ended up here.

I didn't really have a playlist while writing it. It was only a weekend, so the music was whatever was in the background. But if I did, it would be:

- I Dream of Jeannie theme song
- Brave by Sara Bareilles

Now for my thank yous. First, always, my wife, my biggest fan and cheerleader. I only drive her nuts on days ending in Y. Next, my co-publisher, mentor, editor, and friend, Adam Gaffen. He kicks my butt when I need it, and I'm a better author because of it. And I'd be remiss if I didn't mention my friend and co-author Nat Paga, who came on board as an editor for this book when Adam and I realized we'd bitten off more than we can chew. She's also a kickass writer! And finally, you. My readers. Knowing that I bring some happiness to you through my words makes the days teaching much, much shorter!

Find me at https://kaliliandfaith.com

AC

# In Search of a Kiss

## By David Green

"Ah, no. Poor little thing."

Turin shook his head. A robin lay dead at the base of a great tree, a bent wing explaining how it had fallen from its perch when taking flight. Bending to examine it, a soft murmur from behind caught his attention.

He'd entered the woods to gather wood for the evening campfire, but he'd hoped he might catch a glimpse of *her*. Turin smiled as Jenna sang softly to herself, walking through the trees as she stroked her hair. She did it often, since he and his parents found her in the wilderness days before. The young woman spoke little, and shyly when she did, but when she sang...

Heat rose in Turin's cheeks. He'd stood gawping for far too long. What if she noticed? What is she called him a Leering Lorca and would never speak to him again, let alone sing in the woods when prying eyes and bold ears weren't present. What if—

"Turin? Is that you?"

The gathered wood fell from his hands, clattering to the muddy forest ground. Jenna stared right at him, her bright emerald eyes wide as twin moons.

"Er... Yes?" Turin cleared his throat. "Yes. I'm gathering wood. For the fire. I wasn't being a Leering Lorca or anything. Honest."

Looking left and right, Jenna moved toward him, hands clasped at her stomach. She wore travelling clothes, clean and mended now, in far better shape than they had when Turin and his parents found her all bloody, battered, and bruised.

"It's okay," she murmured, coming closer. An arm's reach away now. "I'm glad of the company."

Turin gazed at her, only half aware of the slack grin spreading across his face. He'd seen women his age before, of course. Though he and his parents stuck to the quiet places of the world, they occasionally called into the smaller settlements of Parda for goods and supplies they couldn't hunt for in the wilderness or create themselves. He'd even *kissed* more than a few, and once or twice it had gone a little further. Just shy of his twentieth Blood Day, Turin's twinkling grey-blue eyes, steady smile, and wide shoulders brought him admiring glances wherever he went, truth be told. The attention of women—young and old—had stopped robbing him of his senses years ago.

But he'd never laid his eyes on anyone like Jenna before.

With skin like polished obsidian, and eyes of pure, gleaming jade, her silky raven hair cascaded to her lower back, curling at the ends. Though shy, her full ruby lips wore a secret smile whenever she glanced at him, and her voice tinkled like the promise of summer. Tall and lithe, she'd proved herself more than a capable woodsperson too, joining Turin and his parents on the hunt, falling into the crafting of arrowheads and item repair with ease and a steady hand.

And her *singing*. Whenever Turin would come across a secluded pool, he would wait until the moon stood high in the velvet night sky before going alone. Once his skin became used to the midnight chill, he'd float in the water, gazing at the glittering stars and listening to the nightingales profess their deepest admiration for the secret twilight world he existed in.

They had nothing on Jenna. *Nothing.*

Her singing took the natural beauty of her speaking voice and amplified it. Her every cadence was clear as crystal, each syllable throbbing with deep emotion that sent hooks deep behind Turin's navel. Magic coursed through her songs, of which Turin held no doubt. He'd even mentioned it to one of his fathers, Sendal, who'd laughed and fondly murmured about young love.

But Turin held his suspicions, still. Jenna's wounds had healed quickly, too quickly, and the world seemed brighter whenever she stood in his presence. Young love, perhaps? Perhaps...

"It isn't safe to be out here alone," Turin murmured at last, blinking and breaking his regard. He could lose lifetimes in those eyes of hers.

"So you are glad I found you then?" Jenna's lips curved into a smirk. "Do not worry, I will look after you."

Turin laughed, the noise loud in his ears. So rough compared to the sounds she made.

"I meant... Look, we haven't really talked about it, but the state in which we found you..." He swallowed as she gazed at him intently. "Are you in danger?"

Jenna held his gaze for a moment longer, then tilted her head to the side.

"You seem sad. Whatever is the matter?"

"Sad?" Turin blinked, then turned to the dead robin behind him. "Oh, I'd come across this bird. Silly, really, seeing as we hunt all manners of creatures, but at least we offer prayers to Felu whenever we do, and only take what we need. It's just such a pity to find a..."

He trailed off, aware of his babbling as Jenna's smile grew.

"You have a kind heart," she whispered shyly, but she still met his eyes.

A sudden urge to step closer gripped Turin, and his legs almost jerked forward in response. He managed to take a hold of himself. It proved one of his life's toughest accomplishments.

"As do you, I think," he replied, the forest surrounding them melting away. Only Jenna existed. Only she made a sound, her soft breathing clear in his ears. Her scent of strawberries and morning grass filling his head and making it spin.

"You know," Jenna murmured, stepping closer. Turin's lungs clutched the air inside them and refused to let go. *She* stepped closer to *him*. "I believe you are destined for greatness. I know these things, Turin. In fact, I think that is why Felu placed you in my path when I needed you the most."

Greatest? She needed him?

Turin swallowed. "Me?"

Jenna nodded. "I was in danger, but I feel much safer now, though untold perils lay ahead."

"Perils?"

Turin mentally kicked himself. Why could he only speak in single words?

Jenna bit her lip, and Turin almost melted on the spot, his legs quivering. His body desired nothing but to taste the woman standing close enough to kiss.

"Have you heard of the Usurper?" she asked, her eyes flicking away then back again.

Ice replaced the fire in Turin's blood. "Yes. Everyone has. But he's dead."

Sadness flooded Jenna's viridian gaze. "I wish that were so."

She spoke with such shocking vulnerability. At the moment, Jenna appeared smaller, slighter. Alone in the world.

A voice that sounded very much like the one he thought with bloomed in his mind. *Hold her, damn it! Hug her. Tell her everything is going to be okay. She said she feels safe with you!*

"Are you magic?" he whispered instead.

Her smile returned. A secret one, only for him. Kneeling, she gathered the little robin, gently cradling it in the palms of her hands. Briefly meeting Turin's eyes, she gazed down at the dead creature with the broken wing.

And she sang.

The hairs on Turin's arms and the back of his neck responded to the vibrant energy in her voice, rising and standing on end. The words made no sense to him, but the emotion, the melody... The emerald in her eyes and the red in her lips grew in vividness, and her song poured from her mouth and emanated from his soul. Turin didn't breathe, or at least he wasn't aware of doing so. He didn't blink. Didn't swallow. He stood still, not a single muscle twitching as Jenna crooned sweeter than the Heralds of Felu.

A twitch from the centre of her palms caught Turin's attention, and he gasped. The robin's broken wing trembled, then straightened as he watched, healing. The little bird's chest rose and fell, then it hopped to its feet, its tiny head swaying in time to Jenna's song. Turning to look at Turin, it flapped its wings and took flight, disappearing into the vast azure.

Jenna's song ended, and she laughed, clapping her hands. "That little fellow was tougher than it looked and had a spark of life still inside it. You found him just in time."

"You *are* magic," Turin whispered, tears blurring his vision.

"Please do not tell anyone, not yet." Jenna stepped even closer and took Turin's hands in hers. "Please?"

"Whatever you say," he breathed, her eyes filling his entire world.

"Turin..." Jenna hesitated, then nodded. "I do not know you, but I feel... I do not know. It scares me, but I feel I have known you my entire life."

Turin's head bobbed. "I know exactly what you mean."

"Will you search for me?" she murmured, staring up into his face. "If anything happens to me?"

"What's going to happen to you?" he replied, a small frown forming on his forehead.

"I don't know," Jenna whispered, tears in her eyes. "I don't know, Turin. But will you?"

His heart hammered against his ribcage, sending spurts of rushing blood into his ears. "Yes."

Jenna's lips parted, revealing a hint of her white teeth. Closing his eyes, Turin took the plunge, refusing to resist any longer. Their mouths met, and he kissed her deeply, their fingers entwined. Their hands parted, and Turin's found themselves in Jenna's hair, working their way down to the small of her back as he pulled her body closer to his, their heat combining to create a blazing inferno of passion. And, for a moment, the world ceased turning, and time existed just for them.

Young love.

TURIN GRINNED AT JENNA across the unlit campfire as his two fathers gently bickered and bantered. They'd returned from gathering wood hours before, wiping the twigs from their hair before straightening their clothes.

*What is she?* Turin shook his head as colour rose in her cheeks. *Who is she? You know, I don't care. I'm in love with her. Completely and utterly.*

The truth in his heart, sudden as it was, took root there, as sure as the moon rising at night and the sun chasing it away with the coming dawn.

"You know, husband, maybe if you *tried* your magic, this roaring fire you promised me an hour ago would actually exist." Halter, one of Turin's fathers, nudged Sendal, grinning at him. Sendal possessed a hint of fire magic, though he used it seldom. Creatures of Parda sought fire magic, fed on it. Something had happened in Sendal's past which he didn't speak of, something to do with Turin's birth mother. "It's pretty cold tonight, and we want to make a good impression on our guest, don't we?"

The scrape of rock against stone ground to a halt as Sendal threw his husband the most withering stare he could muster. Turin grinned. He enjoyed his fathers' banter immensely, and Jenna appeared just as engrossed.

"Just a suggestion," Halter laughed, throwing up his hands. "Need some help?"

"If I needed help," Sendal grumbled, striking the rocks together with viscous intent, "I'd have asked for it an hour ago."

"Suit yourself." Halter let out an all too loud sigh and leaned back against the travel-bags propping up his head, a mock-content look on his face. "You know, despite the cold, the Stagle Mountains are quite pleasant this time of year. Beats the Mourningwoods hands down. Pity I'm about to freeze my love bits off before I can use them again."

Turin held his head in his hands. "Father..."

A belly laugh exploded from Jenna. All three men raised their eyebrows at one another as her laughter echoed through the mountains.

Sendal snorted with laughter. Halter's gentle way, his serene smile, quick wit, and sarcastic outlook on life worked as a balm against the darkness lurking in anyone's soul, soothing the nightmares of his past. Nightmares Turin often woke from, hazy, disconnected images and voices assailing him. Halter would always be there when he woke, a joke on his lips or a silent, firm embrace waiting. Still, it didn't mean he got to act like a smug bastard whenever he felt like it. With a flick of his wrist, Sendal sent one of his worn-down rocks arcing through the night, straight into his husband's stones.

"Hey!" Halter shouted. "Why'd you do that for? You're lucky I'm not as fey as Cearan himself and I strike you down!"

Jenna chuckled. "Cearan might do that."

Turin glanced at her. "Cearan isn't real."

"So you say," Jenna replied, smiling. "So you say."

"Thought I'd warm it up for you." Sendal grinned as Halter rubbed away at his crotch, the tears in his eyes shining in the moonlight. "Gods, I give up. Sorry, my mind's elsewhere tonight."

"Fathers, we *do* have a guest, you know." Turin glared at his parents. "Behave."

"Yes, prince half-elf," Halter bowed, still rubbing at himself. "Anything you say, sire."

"Half-elf?" Jenna asked, throwing a speculative look Turin's way. "You never mentioned that."

"His mother, my former wife, was an elf," Sendal murmured. "Turin never got the chance to meet her. She died in childbirth."

"Does he get his magic from her, or from you?" Jenna asked. Halter and Sendal stiffened, their faces stony. "Or was that supposed to be a secret?"

"I'm not magical," Turin whispered. "Am I?"

"No," Sendal replied, but he stared at Jenna, and at Jenna only. "He isn't. And I possess enough for cheap tricks, and nothing more. What do you know about magic, girl?"

Jenna smiled sadly. "I know enough. Too much. It returns to Parda in waves, and I am uncertain that is a good thing."

"Well, what matters," Halter announced, taking one of Sendal's hands and entwining their fingers together, "is we are all here together, safe, happy, and in love." He turned his grin at Turin, and then at Jenna, gaining blushes from them both. "And more importantly, I'm more than content with my pet at my side. Even if he can't build a fire."

"Oh, so that's what I am, is it?" The corners of Sendal's lips curved upwards. "A dog?"

"A pretty one." Halter's lips met his briefly, then pulled away. "Not so hairy. And for that I thank Felu."

Sendal returned the kiss, drinking in his husband's taste, his smell. Turin's eyes met Jenna's, and he shuffled a little closer to her, the memories of their time alone cracking like lightning in his mind. She did the same, and the blood pumping through Turin's veins surged at her proximity.

"Want to try the fire again?" Halter asked with a wink, breaking the spell for a moment. "It really is bloody cold, and you promised roaring flames."

"You sod," Sendal laughed. "Fine. Let me find some better stones for the task."

"Of course." Halter rolled his eyes, grinning at Turin and Jenna. "It's the tools he blames. Not the tradesman."

"You be careful, or the next rock I grab will find a soft, squishy and, dare I say, shrivelled target." Halter placed a hand over his mouth, his eyes wide, and shook his head. Turin couldn't help but laugh at his father's theatrics. Sendal stooped, picking up a pair of round stones. "Anyway, go do something other than watch me, will you? It's distracting. *And* lazy. Those rabbits need preparing."

Halter climbed to his feet and saluted. "Of course, creator of half-elven princes. Your wish is my command!"

He sang as he ambled away, an ancient song of the elves' birthplace, in the realm beyond the stars, or so the legends told. It always made Turin smile when he heard it; though Halter had about as much talent for singing as a cat did, he tried his best.

Jenna nudged into Turin's ribs. He gave her a sidelong smile, welcoming her body heat once more. The thought set a fire in his face.

"I know," she murmured. "I cannot stop thinking about it, either. I have never met anyone like you, prince half-elf."

Turin shook his head. "I was thinking the same about you, and don't go blabbing about the half-elf thing. People don't seem to like it, or elves."

"I like them." Jenna took his hand, her touch sending waves of pleasure through his skin. "And I like you. More than like you."

"Er..." Turin swallowed. "I more than like you, too."

"You know, elves *are* magical, and your birth father has the talent, too." Jenna gazed into his eyes. "Are you *sure* you are not magical?"

"I think I would know," Turin replied, shivering. The cold really held a bite. Jenna trembled too. If only his father would hurry with the—

"Fire!" Sendal yelled, his shock clear. Sparks shot from the rocks and into the kindling, the flames spluttering into life.

"Don't sound so surprised," Halter called, carrying over a pair of skinned coneys. "Never doubted you for a moment."

"Liar." Sendal smiled, but then he glanced at Turin, a look of doubt in his blue eyes. Then he shrugged. "It never gets old, the thrill of making something, does it?"

Turin frowned at his father, and his frown deepened. Jenna peered up at him, a finger tapping against his lip.

"What?" he asked.

"Nothing," she replied, that secret smile tugging at her lip. "Nothing at all."

"The fire?" Halter asked, tying a rabbit to the spit. "If you made one more than once in a diamond moon, the feeling would soon wear off. And you'd be better, and quicker, and doing it."

Halter laughed when Sendal's fist sank into his bicep.

"Don't tell me I need to practise my punching, too." Sendal winked at Turin. They sparred often, though Turin's strength had outgrown his father's now, and had done so since his last Blood Day. "I could still take you in a fight, Halter."

"Maybe. You rely on your sword too much. Though if anyone got close enough for you to hit them with your fist with your swordsmanship, they deserve the chance to laugh, you know?"

Turin nodded at that. Sendal's skill with the sword had seen them through more than one tough spot.

"You really are a smug sod," Sendal shot back. "Have I ever told you that?"

"At least five times a day." Halter smiled, patting Sendal's cheek. "Give or take."

"Not often enough, that's obvious." Sendal took his husband's hand and kissed his fingertips one-by-one, then pulled the arm around his shoulders.

"Your fathers really love each other, don't they?" Jenna murmured, watching the pair with sad eyes.

"Yes." Turin frowned at her. "Is that not okay?"

"Oh, no, no." Jenna smiled, but it seemed forced. "It is lovely to see. I envy them."

Nodding, Turin wrapped a tentative arm around her shoulders. For a moment, he thought he'd erred, and she would pull away. Relief flooded his chest when she leaned into him.

A relaxed quiet lay upon the plains beneath the mountains, a stillness that rose to their perch. The moon hanging high in the night's sky illuminated the rolling hills and dirt roads with a silver that danced off the lakes and streams ambling their way across the landscape. Of all the spots they'd rested of late, this place ranked highest. Up there, in the wilderness, Turin could live in peace with his parents forever. With Jenna too.

He let his muscles soften, allowing his eyelids to droop as the crackling of flames lulled him.

"Sendal, I'm glad you didn't make us move deeper into the thicket, away from the road. Now it's not as cold as the Netherworld, it's quite a beautiful view from up here," Halter murmured, shifting to add more twigs to the fire.

Turin's relaxed muscles tightened again. They'd settled beside a path, a dirt-track really, though the group wouldn't sleep in the open all too often. Parda held its dangers, after all.

He glanced at Jenna, remembering her state when they found her, and the danger she'd spoke of in the woods. *'Would you search for me?'*

Turin cleared his throat. "Do you think we should move? We're so remote, it would surprise me if other travellers happen by. After the mountains, there's nothing but the Wastelands, after all. But I'm not so sure it's wise—"

"Peace," Halter called with a smile. "Stop worrying. It's perfect. I was just talking for the sake of speaking. Now, these coneys are cooked, I dare say. Ready to eat?"

Turin's stomach grumbled so loudly Jenna's eyebrows climbed her forehead as she glanced at him. He grinned. "Sorry, I'm bloody starved."

Jenna laughed. "Me too."

"Well, you two would be after being in the woods so long," Sendal replied airily, grinning as Turin and Jenna looked anywhere except at each other. "Ah, young love. Halter, get a move on."

Halter laughed, leaning over the spit. "Catch the rabbits, cook the rabbits, all the while the creator of elf-lords here plays with a couple of stones. Some people have all the luck, eh?"

Movement on the plains killed the retort on Turin's lips. No, not movement. A shadow, a blanket of darkness seeping across the meadow that the moonlight had no effect on.

*A cloud. That's all.* But the stars and moon twinkled bright, the night sky clear for miles.

The shadow grew, rolling and swelling as it hurtled across the plains. And that wasn't all. It moved towards the mountains and the path leading to their campsite. Turin's flesh goosed as his blood ran ice cold. The fine hair on his arms and neck stood to attention. Jenna sat up, eyes wide with alarm.

"Douse the fire," she whispered, grabbing Turin and staring at his parents. "Now!"

Halter spun, a wide grin on his face dying when his eyes locked with Jenna's. "What is it?"

Sendal got to his feet, glancing at the plain, then at Turin. "You feel something, son?"

Turin nodded. "Below us... a shadow in the night. Heading this way. Jenna feels it too."

"I do. We are not safe." She turned, meeting Turin's eyes. "Are you sure you are not magical? Your father did not create that fire, did he?"

Turin shook his head. "I..."

Jenna reached up and placed a hand against his cheek. "And I should not have caused life to bloom in that little bird. I fear I have doomed us all. I am sorry."

Halter spun from the spit, hands falling to the twin-blades at his hips, staring down at the rolling plains. "Where do you... wait, I see it. Moving fast. You're right, it's heading this way."

"Douse the flames!" Jenna cried.

Halter hesitated. "Perhaps it'll bypass us? What would anyone other than the likes of us want up here?"

"Do as she says!" Turin called, getting to his feet and pulling Jenna behind him. "Now!"

The shadow reached the foothills below them, oozing onto the winding path, its inky tendrils swallowing the silver light before it. Clarity struck Turin, sudden understanding he knew as truth.

*I made this fire with my magic. Jenna's right. I am magical. I know it. It wasn't her who called to this shadow. It was me.*

Sendal rushed to the campfire, grabbing his water skin and emptying it over the flames. They evaporated in a fierce hiss, just as the quickening darkness struck their campsite.

Halter's swords rang out. Sendal reached over his shoulder and pulled his long sword from its sheath and Turin's father's pressed their backs together, moving away from the logs and travel bags in step, experienced fighters both. Turin reached behind his seat and pulled out his own sword, an elven blade passed down by his mother's family, the steel crimson and curved. Jenna stayed close.

Turin and his parents had fought together before, against creatures, bandits, and the strange enigmas of the Parda wilderness, but none had witnessed darkness like they did then.

It ate the light. Turin swung his sword, the blade dull in the gloom as he kept watch for movement from the shadows surrounding them. The perimeter appeared darker, like they stood in the grey centre of a storm. The unnatural mist swallowed sound, even the air tasted heavy. Turin sucked it in, his lungs struggling to fill themselves.

A creaking laugh echoed around them, one devoid of mirth. Instead, cruelty and malice fed it.

"An unexpected treat. Which of you is it? No matter, I'll take all of you. More souls for the blade."

A flicker in the deep shadows. Turin twitched his weapon that way, holding the hilt in two hands, back glued to Jenna hiding behind him.

"It's me they want," she hissed, hand gripping Turin's biceps. "When I charge, you run. Anywhere but here, you understand."

"Foolishness," Turin spat. "We all leave together. Together is the safest place."

"'*Safest place?*'" Jenna hissed. "You and I define the word 'safe' differently, you know that? Safe is not here!"

A guttural snarl, followed by a rush of footsteps, snapped Turin's focus back to the shadows.

A horned monstrosity bore down on his parents, one clothed in grime-stained piecemeal armour with the tendrils of darkness clinging to it. A dirty yellow-clawed hand held an onyx-coloured cleaver. A scream came from its muzzled-mouth, its hate-twisted face patched with matted fur, with three eyes flashing red with hatred. Halter and Sendal's startled screams tore into the night as two more emerged from the darkness.

Muscle memory took over. Turin flowed forward, his elven blade angled low, then sweeping upwards, severing the approaching beast's arm at the wrist. It howled as black ichor spurted from the stump, the gush covering Turin's face. He ignored it and carried the movement through, slicing a diagonal gash deep into the monster's armour and through its animal-like face.

It dropped, dead before hitting the dirt. Turin forgot about it. More took its place, and thinking too much about the creature he'd killed would mean his end.

"Stay behind me!" he screamed at Jenna, staying close to her, his eyes flicking to his fathers.

His parents had fought back-to-back too many times to recall. They'd fallen into their practised rhythm, not stopping to check on the other as they fought, trusting their touch, their grunts and snarls, the shuffling of each other's feet, the clang of steel on steel, the weight at their backs telling them the other lived yet as the monsters poured from the shadows.

The creatures fought without order, without skill, a press of wailing flesh and violence flooding the camp site, turning it into a sphere of death. Corpses littered the ground, dismembered limbs piled on blood-slick mud as they fought. Turins's curved sword grew heavy, his forearms, chest, and face dripping with inky blood, his brain taking control when his body wanted to sag to the ground.

He couldn't stop. Jenna had no weapon. Her feet and fists would do nothing against the beasts.

Pulling his blade from the abdomen of the creature he'd skewered, Turin readied himself for the next assault.

It didn't come.

The pause gave his limbs the opportunity to howl in pain and overuse, his sword point drooping. The monsters stared at him, shifting, writhing on the spot like some presence held them there.

"What are you waiting for?" he screamed, forcing his blood hot again.

The monsters cowered, their many eyes fixed on him. No, not on them. He recognised their fear, but it wasn't for Turin. They all peered beyond him.

"Turin?" Jenna whispered. "I'm sorry."

His parents spun, their faces pale beneath the gore and grime. "What in Felu's name?"

A stench thick with rot assailed Turin's nostrils, and the whimpering of the dying filled his ears. His stomach lurched; empty, or it would have voided its contents. He turned, and fear's fist gripped his heart.

"I come for her. I sense it now. Run. You have all fought well, but you all tire." The creeping voice slithered from a growing form in the deep shadows. "I give you this one chance: flee. None of you are a match for me."

A dark tower of a figure loomed above Turin and Jenna, a blade as black as midnight in its fist. Obsidian armour covered it from helmed head to toe; its creaking, nightmarish voice slithering through the cracks in its helmet. It wore the darkness like a cloak. The places the sun failed to reach adopted the shadows. This terror owned them. Its head cocked, freezing Turin to the spot. Behind the visor, it stared at him. He knew it in his bones.

"I have changed my mind. Not only does the girl call to me, you do too, half-elven. Young Light Bearer. But I am the Shadow Master, and I answer to he who eats the sun. You are mine."

"He who eats the sun," Jenna whispered. Trembling. "The Usurper! This is his general!"

Turin shifted, sagged, like a fighter who knew death called. Footsteps behind him caught his attention.

"We love you, Turin. Always. Fight your way free!" Sendal cried, charging past him, Halter beside him, surging toward the Shadow Master.

"No!" Turin cried, reaching out, but his parents moved too fast, sprinting, then sliding together beneath the tower's defence, their swords a blur aimed at the Shadow Master's legs.

They passed through it.

His parents gaped upwards as they slid to a stop in the blood-thick mud. The Shadow Master raised his black blade in two hands and brought it crashing down, the tip ripping through both Halter and Sendal's chests, pinning them to the ground and killing them in an instant.

Turin didn't have the chance to scream. As Halter's head fell to the side, dirt smearing his pale face, his dead eyes meeting Turin's, the darkness flexed.

Shadows surged forward as Jenna sank to her knees. Turin stumbled forward to protect her, tears wetting his cheeks, his heart beating slow anguish in his sunken breast. The Shadow Master moved to take him, but his world had ended in the filth and corpses surrounding him. What did it matter? He and Jenna couldn't withstand such terror.

But she climbed to her feet, teeth shining in the dark.

"If it's me you want, Shadow Master, come and take me!" she screamed, light blooming from her chest.

"No!" Turin shouted, but too late.

Jenna flowed forward, the brightness battling the dark, forcing it backward. Spinning, the Shadow Master wrenched his obsidian blade free, swinging at her.

A blinding blaze flashed, illuminating the campsite from the Netherworld to Felu's Aether.

Shielding his eyes, Turin blinked as the glare faded. Jenna was gone. Gone. The Shadow Master, sword in his fist, loomed above him, the darkness and shadows swirling.

"Are you ready, Light Bearer?" it asked, tilting its head to the side. "Ready to meet your fate? There is no escape."

*NO.*

The voice came from inside. The will of the magic in his soul and the power of his love for the woman beside him. For his parents. The ferocious energy lurking within him, the Light the Shadow Master named it, wouldn't let him die. Not without a fight.

Eyes closed, curved blade falling to the filth from his slack grip, Turin's arms jerked outwards. A buzz inside him built, a tingle in his fingertips running through his arms and into his chest. He vibrated with it. It made his mouth dry, his teeth sticky, but it filled him with life. Alive and aware, so damned *aware*. Turin's eyes flew open; the Shadow Master's assault had slowed to a crawl, the seconds drawing out. Flecks of mud drifted through the darkness, and beyond the shadows, moonlight threatened to break through.

He focused on it, ignored the slow snarls of the monsters behind him, the squelch of the Shadow Master's heavy boot sinking into the mud.

Turin drew on the silver light, giving life to the world beyond the shadows, and it made his blood sing. It drummed in his ears, the beating of his heart all too fast compared to the slow movement of his enemy. Fire ran through his veins; it warmed him, heated him, almost too much. It seared his soul, cooked his organs. Somehow

Turin knew if he kept hoarding this Light, kept drawing it in, he'd become one with it.

*Would that be so bad?*

His eyes fell on the corpses of his parents, their lifeless bodies unmoving. His senses reached out for the missing Jenna. Her smile. The brightness of her eyes. The scent of strawberries and morning grass. Her absence made the tears building in his eyes slide down his cheeks.

*No. I want vengeance.*

Turin, arms wide, opened himself to the Light inside, and forced it into the world.

With a whip-crack of lightning, the lull smothering his enemy's movement disappeared. The Shadow Master's gauntleted hand reached for him, but before a finger fell on Turin, the shadows exploded with glorious Light.

White fire shot from Turin's hands in a wide circle, flooding outwards. Unprepared, the Shadow Master shrieked and fell away, the darkness covering his flight.

His thralls didn't boast the same luck. Their screams reached Turin's ears, the popping of their flesh rich in the night as the Light burned them alive. The white fire didn't harm Turin. How could it? It lived inside him, he'd created it.

Swooning, he fell on all fours, his vision growing grey, the act of creation, of birthing Light into the world, leaving him weak.

*My parents. I must go to them.*

He crawled across the gore-soaked ground, over corpse and limb, the black blade of the Shadow Master fallen beside Halter and Sendal. Turin reached them and collapsed, his outstretched fingers resting against his birth-father's cheek.

"I'm sorry," he whispered, tears mixing with the dirt and blood, "for what I am. It came for me, and I didn't act in time."

He sat up, glaring at the blade that had taken so much from him. His parents. Had it taken Jenna, too? Turin gazed through the film of tears, choking back the sobs.

"I loved her. Even though I didn't know her that well. I loved her." He wept. "I've lost everything."

A soft melody, distant like a memory, drifted across the battle-site. Like one Jenna would sing to herself. Turin wiped away the tears, frowning at the obsidian blade. It came from there!

*'Turin. Turin, my love. I'm here, inside the blade,'* a voice called. Jenna's voice! *'It trapped me. Please, release me. The souls here, they come for me!'*

Turin's eyes flew open. The black blade shone in the moonlight, its edge glimmering with a white light from inside the blade.

"Jenna?"

*'My love, please. I see the Felu, just beyond the veil of darkness! But I'm trapped by the shadows. It feeds on me. Please!'*

"How..."

Turin staggered to his knees, reaching out to grab the hilt. With all the strength he had left, he pulled, wrenching the blade from the muck, the last of his Light flooding into the blade. It flashed once, then settled back into darkness.

He fell into the mud, dazed, slipping from consciousness, the blade laying across him, his hand on his birth-father's.

***Years Later...***

"You know, it's not so bad, this place."

Turin settled into a darkened corner of *The Raven's Wing*, a tavern by the docks in Murties Mallory with a worse reputation than his own. Hood drawn and crimson mask fixed on his face, the other patrons gave him a wide-berth.

A tankard of ale and a smoking pipe lay on the table before him, a candle lending the nook scant illumination. Turin focused, and drew on the fire, pulling it into his Light and feeding the black blade he'd placed across his legs. He didn't care about creatures hunting for magic now. *They* feared *him*.

People knew him. Called his sword the Onyx Death. They called *him* The Crimson Face.

Folk like fancy names for things they didn't understand, Turin had discovered.

Still, it made people leave him alone, even in places like *The Raven's Wing*, and that suited Turin just fine. In fact, he spread many of the rumours of his deeds himself. Now in darkness, he removed his mask, tugging the hood further to hide his more pronounced half-elven features, the points on his ears growing over the years since he lost his parents, his cheekbones higher, and savoured the taste of his ale. He'd slept rough too much of late. A little slice of comfort wouldn't go amiss.

*'I've never liked this place, and I still don't. You're better than this.'*

"Hush, Jenna." Turin closed his eyes, licking the froth from his top lip. Losing himself in the angry shouts of drunkards losing at dice, and the rowdy yells of others 'singing' along to a harassed-looking bard on stage, who had a look on her face that suggested she wished she'd never heard of *The Raven's Wing*, let alone set foot in it. "You're just mad I haven't fed you all day. I'll drain more Light soon."

*'You try being stuck in a blade, no release in sight, with darkness trying to smother you. We'll see how chipper you are, my love.'*

Turin set his tankard down and laid a calloused palm against the black blade. As always, it felt cool to the touch. Flames never warmed it, ice never chilled it. It felt like the flesh on the corpses' of his parents had: empty. But the blade held his love's soul, and Turin fed it Light to keep the shadows at bay. One day, he'd find the Shadow Master again and make the monster pay. First, he'd make him release Jenna. Somehow. Problem was, no one had seen the Shadow Master in years. At first, Turin thought he'd vanquished it, but Jenna insisted the beast lived still, and he trusted his love's word in all things.

"He'll turn up one day. I know it. We're getting close. The Shadow Master can't hide forever. Stay with me."

Turin smiled as he imagined Jenna sighing and rolling her eyes.

*'Because it ended so well for us last time. I know you're doing all you can, and no, I wouldn't be without you. Just... it doesn't matter.'*

"No, go on. What doesn't matter?"

"Going up against the Shadow Master... I'd imagine he'd tell you this is only going to end one way, Crimson Face. Or can I call you Turin?"

He froze as a wizened, white-haired fellow in crumpled purple robes dropped into the empty seat across from him. Quick as a flash, Turin slipped the mask into place, his other hand dropping to the hilt of one of his old short-swords at his hip.

Turin didn't murder, but he would defend himself. Never with the Onyx Death, though. It had stolen Jenna's soul, and he didn't want that fate for anyone. Oddly, it hadn't done the same with his parents. He often wondered why, but the Shadow Master *had* been searching for Jenna. She'd escaped his forces before crossing Turin's path, and she'd apologised countless times for not moving on before that fateful night.

Turin would soothe her. Even though they'd spent more time together as half-elf and sword, he loved her as much as Sendal had loved Halter.

Such thoughts were for another time. Through the mask's slits, he glared at the wizened newcomer. "I'd forget that name as you make your way to the street, old man. And never cross my path again if you know what's best for you."

The intruder's craggy face split into a lopsided grin, his eyes twinkling. "You think it happenstance I met you here in the worst tavern in all of Murties Mallory?" He paused, glancing around. "The whole of Parda, probably."

Turin's white knuckles squeezed tighter. "Who are you?"

"Long I've watched your sad tale unfold, Light Bearer," the old man answered, ignoring the question, and the fact Turin sat straighter on hearing what he named him. *Light Bearer.* "Ever since the Soul Blade—yes, that's its correct name—trapped your poor love. Another Light Bearer, it's why *he* searched for her. It's why you two were drawn together. And now you seek *him.* The Shadow Master. You could have it, you know? Vengeance."

Turin's breath hissed through the slit in his mask. His fingers traced the blade. *The Soul Blade. Aye, an apt name. Make no mistake.*

"Long have I sought the Shadow Master, old man. I lowered myself into the filth of Parda, searching for word of him, and found *nothing!* Now you appear, whispering of vengeance. Begone, before I strike you down. You know what they call me, why they fear me. Do not test me further."

If Turin's threats bothered the wizened old man, he showed no signs. Instead, he peered down at his fingernails, as if considering which one he liked best. The silence between them stretched. That's when it hit Turin. The voices in his head, the magic in his mind. They remained silent in the old man's presence. Since opening himself to his magic on the Stagle Mountains when he beat back the Shadow Master, they'd whispered to him always, a constant flow of words and memories Turin learned to swim in or discard, like wind in his ear.

Now they lay in wait. Silent as the grave. And so did Turin.

"Who are you?" he repeated, hefting the Onyx Death and slamming it onto the table, frothy beer spilling from his tankard.

"Your Light is tranquil, and it worries you. I wondered how long it would take you to notice. You could achieve great things, you know? Trained, of course. Right now, you're a callow youth, just learning their first words. You use them, say them correctly, but never at the right time or place." He looked up, locking eyes with Turin, who gasped. Aeons of experience lurked behind his clear-blue stare; joy and laughter, evil and sorrow, empires risen and smote into ruin. The beginning and end of time regarded Turin, and laid his soul bare. "I am Cearan. You may have heard of me."

Turin sat back, the grip on Turin's old short-sword slack. The Wanderer. Meddler. Sorcerer. Man of myth, whose deeds children learned in the laps of their mothers. Villain and hero, schemer and saviour. Here. Sitting before him. Promising vengeance. Once, Turin had thought him nothing more than a story. Jenna's words, and his own experiences in the wide-world of Parda, had proved him wrong.

Turin swallowed.

"Yes, I've heard of you. You talk of vengeance. Heard enough that whatever you offer comes at a price."

Cearan laughed and leaned forward, resting his forearms on the table. "Doesn't everything? Take your magic. You use it to keep the shadows inside the blade at bay, to keep Jenna's soul safe. Admirable. But you take Light from the world, and use it for selfish purposes. Your talent is a gift, one for sharing. For making Parda a *better* place, and other grand sayings. Through you Light destroyed all of the Shadow Master's beasts, did it not? Turned them to cinder and ash. And let's consider the blade you carry... you use Light to keep Jenna's soul safe, but doing so means it's untethered. Killing again with the blade, stealing another soul? Well, Jenna must go *somewhere*, and that darkness in there grows hungry. You've been wise not to use it, but that cannot always be so. You must face the Shadow Master, and that blade is the only way to stop the creature for good. A necessary task to destroy the Usurper. Yes, he will return. Soon. And the fight will be yours, Light Bearer."

The dead voices stirred, just a flicker, then fell silent, Cearn's presence cowing them somehow.

Turin removed his mask, burying his face in his tankard as he took a deep pull of ale. He met Cearan's eyes. "How do you know this?"

The man shrugged. "You think I wouldn't take notice of one born with the Light inside them? Now. The Shadow Master. You haven't heard word of him in your journey through the hives of Parda's scum and villainy because he laid low beyond the Wastelands, biding his time, waiting for his master's revival. Now he has returned as the Usurper gathers strength. And I know where the Shadow Master will be."

Turin laid a hand against the black blade. The memories of Jenna in the forest bloomed in his mind. When she sang the robin back to life. When they'd kissed. When they shared their bodies in timeless bliss. Before the Shadow Master stole her. Before the Shadow Master killed his parents.

"Where?" Turin growled.

"The Loch Olan, the capital. The Shadow moves, and the Usurper with it. They converge on Castle Parda in the city itself. Everything does. And you with it. Travel there, and the Shadow Master will meet you. Only you may stop him."

"I'm no fool, Cearan. What's in it for you? Will you come and extract your pound of flesh once I'm done?"

The old man smiled. It didn't reach his calculating eyes. Turin's skin crept at the coldness lurking there.

"Let's say our interests in this matter align. Travel now, and make haste. Make no mistake, the Shadow Master remembers you, and desires your Light. You defeated him once—with sheer luck, I might add—and that intrigues him." Cearan climbed to his feet, his robes crumpled and stained, every inch a beggar, until you met his stare. "One more thing. Defeating the Shadow Master will reunite you with your love. This I have foreseen, and this I promise you, if you needed more reason to do as I say. If you want to see Jenna again, if you want to feel her lips on yours, you will do as I ask." He nodded. "Until we meet again."

Turin gawped as the old wizard disappeared into the pressing crowd. *I'll see Jenna again? Kiss her again?*

Draining his tankard, he fixed the mask back in place and readied himself to leave. The whispers returned, a flurry of voices speaking at once with such speed and urgency he couldn't make out the words. He pushed them aside, long since learning how to ignore them.

*'You shouldn't trust him,'* Jenna murmured, her voice echoing from the sword and into his head. One voice Turin could never ignore.

"Did you hear what Cearan said? We can be together again."

*'Yes, I heard him. I heard him, too, when he said everything comes with a price. Tread with care.'*

The crowd parted as Turin strode through the tavern. It even seemed the pipe-smoke did too. He stepped into the streets of Murties Mallory. The crisp sea air filled his nostrils as mist rose from the cobblestoned streets. Of Cearan, he saw no sign.

"Isn't this what you want?" Turin grated, slamming the Onyx Death into its sheath on his back. "To be free of the souls feeding on you?"

*'He didn't say 'free'. Think on his words, the stories you know of him.'*

"Think of the stories they tell of me, the ones I've spread more than anyone, the face I wear so I can walk these roads in search of the Shadow Master. Are they true?"

Jenna fell silent. The damp fog swallowed the echoes of Turin's footsteps as he rushed away from the docks to the stables, intent on purchasing the fastest steed in Murties Mallory. He had his weapons and his magic. He needed nothing else.

*'Just be careful, my love,'* Jenna whispered.

Turin smiled, reaching over his shoulder to caress the hilt. "I always am, don't worry. Three days to Loch Olan if I don't stop to rest. Then we'll see each other again."

Turin wiped at his eyes.

He pushed the ill feeling in his stomach aside with the whispering of the magic in his mind. Vengeance would be his, and so would a life with Jenna. In his haste, Turin didn't see the wizened old man watching from the shadows, or the sorrowful smile painted on his craggy face.

PARDA'S CAPITAL, THE gleaming jewel of the twelve seas, lay before Turin as he reined in his weary mount. The horse had stood him well, its stamina and drive matching his own on the race to Loch Olan. Now it shone below them, bright against the starlit sky. At its centre, dwarfing the rest of the city, stood Castle Parda, its lofty towers and golden domes dominating the other beautiful buildings of the famed walled city.

Turin didn't give any of it a second glance. From the hilltop, his horse heaving and shuddering beneath him, he scanned the horizon, looking for any sign of the Shadow Master. His enemy had dominated his thoughts on the race across Parda. So had memories of Jenna, and idle fancies of a future to come.

His love had remained quiet, replying to Turin's questions and comments with nothing more than murmurs and one-word answers. The whispers of magic had built to a raging cacophony, one he'd attempted to smother with trained ignorance. But the closer Turin drew to Loch Olan, the harder it became to silence them.

'*They know this is a mistake,*' Jenna murmured, her voice cracked and weak. Turin had fed the blade with as much Light as he could muster on their journey, but he knew his love needed more to keep the shadows at bay. '*The darkness inside the blade. The other souls.*

*They know it, too. They're waiting for me to fail, to claim me as their own. The hunger they feel...'*

"You're just nervous. Trust me, please." But Turin felt it too. The heavy air hung with unnatural malice, like it tried to suffocate anyone who had the cheek to breathe it. Just like the night atop the Stagle Mountains. "Soon, I'll see your face again. Kiss your lips. Make up for lost time."

*'I wish it so, my love. Felu's name, I do.'*

Jenna fell silent, matching the oppressive night. The opulent lights of the city beneath took on a different hue, eerie and foreboding, as Turin caught them in the corner of his eye; the blues and purples muted, the yellows and greens sickly. He shook his head, blinked his vision clear, and he found what he searched for.

Rolling shadow, fast moving, heading to Loch Olan's western gates.

Turin reached behind him, his hand shaking with the strength of his grip on the Onyx Death's hilt.

"Are you with me?"

*'To the end, my love. And after.'*

Jenna's voice came through strong, with no hesitation. Nodding, Turin dug his heels into his horse's ribs and cantered off to meet his destiny, and to achieve his vengeance.

TURIN TETHERED HIS horse a safe distance from where he judged the shadow would pass. In truth, he knew it didn't matter. The Shadow Master sensed his Light before, thirsted for it, and it would come for him again.

He waited within sight of the city, its walls looming above him, the lights behind reaching into the heavens. The Shadow Master, with his darkness clinging to him, would swallow it all if he could.

It didn't concern Turin. Only vengeance did. It consumed any other thought. Any other need, all save his desire to run his fingers across Jenna's skin again. To gaze into her eyes and feel her warmth. Hear her song birthed into the world once more.

With the Onyx Death strapped to his back, Turin unsheathed his father's old twin-blades, though he knew they'd amount to as much as sheltering under a single leaf from the rain. Images of his parents' attack on the Shadow Master replayed in his mind. How their sliding lunge had passed through the towering darkness. Only magic had an effect, the Light inside Turin taking over when he'd all but given up hope. Since then, he drew on it, fed the blade to keep the souls from claiming Jenna's, but he'd no idea how to control it as a weapon. Cearan's words returned to him: *'Right now, you're a callow youth, just learning their first words. You use them, say them correctly, but never at the right time or place.'*

He'd said only the blade could stop the Shadow Master for good, too. Truth?

In the distance, the shadows rolled in, oozing across the lush countryside, strangling life from it. The time and place had arrived. Yet Turin floundered still.

Turin closed his eyes and listened to the whispers of his magic. His Light. What did he miss? The pieces of the puzzle to stop the Shadow Master and save Jenna's soul lay before him, waiting to be put together.

The blade on his back. It housed souls in darkness and torment. Did the Shadow Master draw power from it? Was he the Light's answer? The Shadow Master and Cearan named him Light Bearer, said Jenna was one too, and the Shadow Master hunted her. The darkness wanted to consume her, consume them both. Turin quelled the voices of his magic, but they'd told him to run, all those years ago, atop the Stagle Mountains. They'd guided him when all else failed him. Had the answer lay within him all this time?

*You understand.* The voices spoke as one. Tranquil. Warming. Turin smiled at the glow from within. *But we fear you're too late. This foe is beyond you. Fear stops you from losing what matters most.*

What he feared losing most. Jenna.

"Are you with me?" Turin murmured, the weight of the dread sword on his back.

*'Always, my love.'* Jenna answered, worry lacing her words. *'Turin, the souls gather. They feel its master's call. They come for me.'*

"Stay strong. We can do this. I won't let you down. We have my magic."

The stench of rot filled his nostrils. Opening his eyes, Turin found himself in a grey twilight, the darkness pulsating and gathering around him. Red eyes shone from the shadows, too many to count, peering through his flesh towards the Light inside. Craving it. And before him loomed the black tower, the creature who took his love away. The monster who stole his life, his purpose, his happiness, his parents.

The Shadow Master.

"I will have my vengeance," Turin yelled, raising the twin blades before him, hatred setting his blood aflame.

The Shadow Master flowed forwards, then time slowed to a creep. Just as it had all those years before.

*This is not the way*, the magic inside him whispered in urgency. *Can't you make him see that?*

*You?* Doubt struck Turin. *Who is you?* The voices had mentioned no one else before.

*'He won't understand.'* Jenna's voice replied. Weary. Sorrowful. *'Giving me up... he can't do it.'*

*There is another way.*

Turin frowned. "Wait! You lot can talk to each other?"

*'Turin, listen to me. The souls inside you speak to me. They have since this blade trapped me all those years ago. The Light can defeat*

*the Shadow, but only with years of training you don't have. Right now, there's only one way to defeat this monster. The blade. It can't resist it. Above all else, the souls inside crave their master.'*

"But I'll lose you."

*'Better that than the Shadow Master draining your Light. Please. It's the only way.'*

"No. Felu's name, no!" he gasped, shaking his head. But magic built inside him. Making his limbs shake. "I can't lose you! Cearan said I'd see you again! Please!"

He couldn't hold back the fury of illumination inside any longer as the Shadow Master bore down on him, the darkness and its hidden creatures closing in.

Energy and Light poured from Turin as he screamed in defiance. He'd lost Jenna before, he wouldn't suffer such a fate again. Those barren nights and fallow days, wandering, lost, and lonely, descending into the scum of Parda on a quest for vengeance. Not when it lay before him, so close he could taste it. Felu's name, he could!

White flame circled him, forcing the Shadow Master backward. The blazing light collided with shadow, chipping it away as the monsters lurking within wailed in fury and pain.

Turin laughed, tears mingling with sweat as he screamed himself empty; a lifetime of shame, regret, fury, and longing feeding the Light as it assailed his enemies.

*This is not the way,* his magic and Jenna murmured together as he poured himself empty.

He dropped to his knees, weary and weak. His vision flickered, but he saw no stars above. No moon.

Only darkness and shadow.

A creaking laugh reached his ears. "Such might, such untrained malevolence. Such a waste. You know not what you possess, understand little of what you could have achieved. No matter. Last time, you caught me already weakened, unprepared. Now I am ready for your parlour tricks. Your Light will feed my darkness, and I will take what is mine. How I've longed for my blade, and the souls screaming my name, the delicious Light Bearer inside. They hunger for yours and for the one you have sustained, and I will have you both at last."

Shaking his head, Turin followed the mass of black armour dwarfing him to its summit. The Shadow Master's helmed head gazed down at him, the darkness swirling behind him at his command.

'Turin. My love.' Jenna's voice drifted through the fog and confusion of Turin's mind. 'I can't hold on. The souls are too many. You know what to do. Please. Oblivion or beyond the veil is better than the darkness swallowing us. Please!'

Tears leaked from his eyes. But Turin knew. He'd always known. One day, he and Jenna would part. One way or another. In life, or in death.

He glared up at the Shadow Master, tears blurring his vision. "Rot in the Netherworld, monster."

Turin fell forward, towards the dirt, his strength all but gone.

But not all.

Commanding what little he had left, Turin reached behind him, pulling the Onyx Death free, and swinging it in a wide, wild arc. His arm shuddered on impact the moment his face scrunched against the ground, and the darkness screamed.

The sword shook. Turin twisted onto his back, two hands grasping the mighty hilt as the shadows wailed with the anguished voices of thousands. At its centre stood its master, the Onyx Death buried in his thigh. The blade vibrated as the Shadow Master struggled and writhed, screaming with death and fury.

Hands balled into fists, he beat at the blade, but it refused to let go, as did Turin. He clung on as wind whipped at him. Shadows spun, a tempest with him and the sword at its centre, all trapped within its wake.

And still the Shadow Master wailed.

Desperation entered his voice. Light appeared at the wound, where the blade bit through the armour, and spread up the limb, racing between the cracks in the black metal. It exploded from the eyeholes in the Shadow Master's helmet, lighting up the dispersing shadow, brighter than Loch Olan's itself. Turin squeezed his eyes close, the Light still shining from his lids.

Howling, the Shadow Master crumpled, the Light eating his darkness from the inside, until his empty helmet fell to the ground with a thump, the rest of the armour following. The Onyx Death fell to the ground, Turin's fingers still twisted around the hilt, and silence followed.

Breathing filled Turin's ears. The rush of blood. The beating of his heart. But nothing else. Creaking his eyes open, the twinkling stars and shining moon welcomed him. No clouds, nor a hint of shadow. The world still and quiet.

"Just like our last night together, eh? Fitting. Felu isn't so bad, sometimes."

Turin bolted upright. Jenna's spirit glimmered before him, framed against the moonlight, smiling down at him.

"I..." Turin wiped the tears from his eyes. Climbing to his feet, he let the Onyx Death fall to the ground. "I thought I'd lost you. Oblivion or beyond the veil, you said."

Jenna's head cocked to the side. "Cearan said we'd reunite. Guess I should have trusted him."

"But I'll still lose you, won't I? I freed you, but you're moving on. To whatever's next."

Jenna held out a hand, palm up. Turin matched it with his own; it passed through, but he held it there, as if they touched, and gazed into his love's eyes. His life's-love nodded.

"One last gift, to see you one more time. You saved me from that blade. Now save yourself. Live your life."

Turin sobbed, dull pain throbbed in his chest. Jenna wanted him to move on. What life *did* he have to live?

"I don't know what to do, Jenna. Where will I go? I-I wanted one more kiss. Just one."

"Find Cearan. I have a feeling he'll need you yet, and if anyone can teach you, he can. Remember, the Usurper returns, and it is up to you to stop him."

"I love you," Turin whispered, his love smiling through a thousand days of sorrow. "I always have."

"And I always will."

Turin stepped forward, arms outstretched. Jenna copied him, closing her eyes and as Turin embraced the spirit, their lips passed across each other for just a moment before Jenna became one with the silver light surrounding them.

Warmth flooded Turin's limbs, chasing the bone-weary sadness away. Warmth, love, and life. The Light inside him bloomed, and Turin's laughter drifted through the night.

"You didn't think you'd get rid of me that easily, did you?"

Turin spun. Standing behind him, made of light, was Jenna. She reached out and gripped his shoulder. Turin almost fell back in shock.

"You can touch me? How? Why?" he shouted, scrambling back. She was solid!

Jenna smiled. "A gift from the Light. From Felu." The light faded, and she gazed down at him, exactly as she was all those years ago. "You've gotten old. It suits you."

"Years will do that," Turin spluttered.

She held out her hands. "I thought you wanted to kiss me?"

He surged to his feet, his fingers finding hers, his lips pressing against her mouth. Turin drank Jenna in, countless days of need, desire and love made real through a single kiss. An impossible kiss. Their tears of joy mixing together.

"You trickster!" Turin laughed, pulling away and letting out a whoop that echoed across the empty fields. The stars shone brighter in response. "You planned it all along, didn't you? You just wanted to see me cry?"

"My love, I've seen you cry too many times to count. In our defence, we didn't know it would work. But you're the master of Light and Shadow now, so why not?" Jenna smiled at him. "And I have my tricks, and called in a favour when Felu came to welcome me to the Aether. He needs the Usurper stopped as much as anyone, and agreed you needed all the help you could get."

"Felu?" Turin spluttered. "Hang on, 'We'?"

"Yes, me and the magic inside you. It's in me, too. Not to mention the poor souls still trapped in the blade, Shadow Master excepted. How those souls will enjoy feeding on him. You should learn how to free them. They don't all deserve their fate."

Turin stooped and grabbed the Onyx Death from the ground, the blade still cool to his touch. He strapped it to his back, the weight heavier than before.

"To learn that, I must find Cearan." Turin nodded, turning to Loch Olan. "He said everything converged here. I'm guessing he does, too. Let's go find him. And..." He hesitated, but only for the briefest moment before speaking his desire. "Perhaps we can find a room for the night?"

Jenna laughed and kissed his cheek.

Striding to where his horse waited, the Master of Light and Shadow moved through the night, the souls of thousands weighing heavy on his back, the light of his love bright in his heart, and the hand of his lover in his. Their adventure and love beginning once more, and, as the years to come would attest, the stuff of legends writ across the night's sky in blazing stars of light.

**END**

# A Word from the Author – David Green

David Green is a neurodivergent writer of the epic and the urban, the fantastical and the mysterious.

With his character-driven dark fantasy series Empire Of Ruin, or urban fantasy noir Hell In Haven, David takes readers on emotional, action-packed thrill rides.

Hailing from the north-west of England, David now lives in County Galway on the west coast of Ireland with his wife and train-obsessed son.

When not writing, David can be found wondering why he chooses to live in places where it constantly rains.

Okay, why did I write the story?

While this is all about the origins of love, I wanted to have my MC have strong role models to look up at, and to see a healthy and loving relationship between two people and to show love comes in many different ways. Saying that, I felt it was important to have strong stakes, and to show loss, and its effects, also. It comes hand in hand with love, and makes it all the sweeter.

It got me thinking about my first love, and how I remembered it looking back. I wanted to try and capture that idealism and how absolute it feels at the time.

As for thanks: Thanks to Madi, AC, Adam, and, as always, Ollie.

Find David at https://linktr.ee/davidgreenwriter

# Make Me Sweat

## By Nat Paga

Pain and pleasure dominated Nora. Breath hitched, legs burning with effort, she wanted to stop. Yet she could not. Would not.

Gina's excited cries urged her on.

"*Keep going! Harder! YES!!! That's it, c'mon!*"

Nora pumped, giving everything she had. Sweat sprang from her pores with no sign of stopping. It soaked into the scanty clothes she kept on, making them stick like a second skin.

Normally, being unkempt would make Nora anxious. She was surprised when she looked at herself in the mirror and felt powerful.

Sexy, even.

She never thought she could feel those things, especially thanks to another woman. These days, though, she was all about new experiences. She would push herself however hard Gina asked.

Thankfully, the woman had limits.

"Let's slow it down. Match the music's tempo. Good..."

Gina's rhythm ebbed as well. Her body moved to the background samba music, hips curling and bucking in time with the sensual sway. Each subtle shift highlighted the muscle contours that lay under sheening skin. She was gorgeous, built like an Amazonian princess straight from a Wonder Woman comic.

Nora could not help staring. However, as they locked eyes, she looked away in a blushing rush. Head down, she went even faster than before and tried to play off her interest.

After all, it was rude to ogle your spin instructor.

Three times a week, forty-five minutes each class, Nora attended Blaze-hot Spin Studio.

It was not exactly her idea of a good time. Just a month ago, she would have laughed at the notion of strapping herself to a bike in a 100-degree room and paying someone to yell-motivate her.

However, after the recent upending of her life, Nora found herself doing a lot of things she thought she would never do.

What was the standard advice after a breakup? Hit the gym, then good ol' sin. She was still on the first part, but if her wandering gaze was any sign, she was certainly thinking about the second.

In Nora's distant awareness, she heard the music tempo rise. Gina's peppy voice called over it.

"Okay, Wednesday night! Add some resistance, we're gonna climb that hill!"

Nora held back an eye roll. Apparently, though, she did not hide her disappointment enough.

On the bike beside her, a woman who was arguably even more built than the instructor seemed to catch Nora's difficulty. She smirked, giving the sort of side-eye that asked, *If this is too much for you, what are you even doing here?*

A mental image of Nora's sort-of ex in bed with someone else popped into her head. She picked up speed, pedaling until all she could think of was her complete exhaustion.

Unfortunately for Nora, she pushed too far. The physical strain mixed with the overbearing heat tipped her from exhaustion into sickness.

As she felt her dinner fighting back up, she hit the hard stop on her bike. Jelly legs carried her from the cycle room to the much cooler lobby. There, she collapsed on a bench and did her best not to embarrass herself further.

While Nora recovered, the class went on without her. She had been close; only a few songs later, the music stopped, signaling that the ride was over. The other cyclers filed from the spin room, looking far more put together than Nora even after completing their workouts. She held her head down, waiting for them all to leave.

Nora hated giving up. She hated feeling like her ex was right when she told her she didn't try hard enough. That was how she excused getting with Nora's brother, even though they were practically official themselves.

*Screw you, Monica,* she thought. *I damn well did try. Now, I'm going to keep trying for myself and not for you!*

After taking a swig from her water bottle, Nora thrust to her feet. She *was* getting stronger. All she needed was a little recovery. She could finish her ride and probably come out feeling better than ever.

Going in, though, proved a challenge.

Just as Nora reached for the studio room door, it flew open. She almost fell onto her backside. Instead, a powerful grip locked around her forearm and pulled her upright.

Nora landed against a firm yet soft chest. Her heart skipped a beat at the sudden physical contact. She was less excited when she saw who it was that held her.

Side-eye woman.

Nora untangled herself and did not bother to hide her grimace.

*What's she still doing here?*

A quick survey showed that Side-eye seemed to be cleaning up. Nora went from annoyance to disappointment.

"You're putting the bikes away?"

Short-cropped blonde hair held by a purple sweatband bobbed in time with Side-eye's nod.

"Hot yoga needs a clear room. Jeff would be pissed if he got here at 5 AM and had to clean up after us."

"So, you work at the studio?"

The woman laughed. It was a pleasant sound, even if it was at Nora's expense—deep and smooth like her velvety voice. She pointed to a calendar on the door.

"I'm on rotation to take care of it this week. Well, me and Cara, but she ditched class to have date night with her boyfriend. Her loss. I'll take the membership credits for myself."

Glancing at the calendar, Nora read Cara's name and then the one underneath it.

"You're Valerie?"

"Val, actually. And you're the newbie who has trouble getting through a class."

Again, Side-eye—*Val*—smirked. Nora bristled but did not rise to the bait.

"That's me. I'm going to finish now, if that's okay."

"Don't let me stop you. Use the bike on the end. I'll take it last."

"Thanks."

Nora adjusted the bike to her pint-sized height, well aware that Val was watching her all the while. Her butt had barely touched the seat when the woman interrupted.

"You adjusted it wrong. Did Gina show you how?"

"Not really."

Val sighed and muttered something about lazy people. It sounded as if it were not the first time a newbie had been left to figure the Transformer-looking bikes out on their own.

"No wonder you're having problems. You've gotta work twice as hard with your bike set like that. Mind if I give you a quick run-down?"

Closer now, Val stood with her hands on her hips. It only highlighted her impressive physique more. From the abs peeking out from beneath her sports crop top to the sculpted back side, hugged tight in her yoga pants, very little was left to the imagination.

Intimidating, inspiring, or drop-dead sexy? It was difficult to tell which Val was more. To Nora, the woman was a confusing combination of the three.

She was also hard to turn down. Nora hopped off of the bike and nodded.

With a gleam in her amber eyes, Val flashed a surprisingly warm smile.

"Great! First, you have to know what these knobs do—this one adjusts the handlebars up and down, this one moves it forward. This here adjusts the seat and you should..."

Trailing off, Val hesitated. Her hands hovered close to Nora's hips. Even without touching, it was possible to feel the heat that radiated from her own post-workout cooling. She was covered in the same amount of slick, dripping sweat as Nora. On her, though, it was a shimmering glow.

Nora worried she was too 'gross' to touch. However, it seemed Val was simply conscious of overstepping.

"Can I...? I'm not hitting on you, I swear."

Slung over one shoulder, Val's rainbow towel was impossible to miss. Flirting with Nora, though?

Impossible.

"I know!" Nora burst out. "Go ahead, touch me!"

Val cocked an eyebrow. She went on.

"Um, yeah. You want to make sure your hips are level with the seat. And your arm, from elbow to fingertip, should reach the handlebar. Like this—"

As Nora felt Val's steady fingers move and position her, she was glad she could blame her fast-beating heart on the workout. The pulsing between her legs was less easy to explain, but she did her best to ignore it.

When Val released her, Nora tried to look like she was paying attention.

"That's all there is to it. Keep these settings in mind, and your rides should be a lot easier from now on. Try it out."

Nora settled back onto the bike, a bit awkwardly, as Val watched. She started pedaling and was amazed at how comfortable it felt.

"It's so much better! Thank you!"

"My pleasure," Val told her with a grin. Winking, she added, "You know, if you pick the bike next to me tomorrow, I expect you to keep up. You're here for a reason, so do your best!"

"I will!"

Working hard, improving herself *for* herself... Those were Nora's reasons, and she was determined to see them through.

Although, she thought, it didn't hurt to add an extra reason or two. Her gaze caught on Val as the statuesque woman lifted each bike and wheeled it into storage.

Could Nora keep up with her? She wanted to try.

Nora made a mental note to get to class early so she could take Val up on her challenge.

THE NEXT DAY, NORA outplayed herself. She arrived at class *too* early. She was the first one there and had her pick of the bikes. Without knowing which one Val would take, she chose one at random.

Nora sighed. This wasn't high school, she told herself. They were both adults. It did not matter who sat next to whom, and it definitely did not mean they were flirting.

Even so, when Val arrived and had her choice of any other bike, Nora felt her adrenaline spike. It skyrocketed as the woman settled beside her.

"Sup, newbie!"

"H-hey!"

A chorus of cringing internal voices sang at Nora as she tried to wave and almost slipped from her bike stirrups. Mercifully, Val was too consumed with stretching to notice. Or she pretended not to.

Either way, Nora recovered. She focused intently on her pre-workout warmup and not the gorgeous woman next to her bending every which way.

Yesterday's exchange was not flirting. But the more Nora thought about it, the more she wished it was.

Did that mean that she should take the initiative? How were you supposed to flirt? With Monica, she and Nora had been best friends for over a decade before they 'dated.' She always knew that Nora liked her, and things eventually escalated.

How could she do the same with Val?

Well, not exactly the same. Nora did not want to spend another ten years getting close to Val, only to have her heart broken.

It would help if Nora knew something, anything, about Val. She was blunt but nice enough to help a newbie out. She was almost too hot to look at with her cool and cut vibe. She was definitely into other women.

What else?

Just as Nora was about to stumble her way into a conversation, she was cut off by a blast of 90's pop. Class started, and there was no time—let alone breath—for idle chatter.

Gina sing-song shout of, "Okay, Thursday! Time to build those buns. Let's get pumping!" forced everyone's focus to the front.

The ride was brutal. Climbs with intermittent resistance additions, gear shifts, core isolations, and more. After forty-five minutes of punishment, Nora was ready to collapse.

She didn't, though.

Nora made it to the bittersweet end. She moved through post-workout stretches at a snail's pace, careful not to trip at the figurative finish line. Then it was over.

Nora had never been much of an athlete growing up. She coded for a living, and her hobby was gaming, so she spent most of her time in front of a computer.

This was a whole new world to her, and she loved it.

Lost in a hazy endorphin high, it took Nora a moment to realize that Val was talking to her.

"Good job, newbie! You kept up!"

"T-thanks," Nora managed in a shaky breath. "You too."

Around them, the other cyclers slowly filed from the room. Goosebumps prickled over her skin as they opened the doors to let fresh blasts of AC into the stifling studio. Or, Nora wondered, was her physical reaction from the way Val seemed to check her out from head to toe?

It was hard to say, yet she shivered nonetheless.

"You've been coming here for a month, right?"

"Yeah, almost. Why?"

"It's starting to show. Not that I was looking at you before," Val added in a rush. "But those muscles are looking ho—er, noticeable. Keep it up!"

Was that blush on the woman's cheeks? Or was her tanned skin flushed from the workout?

The self-conscious half of Nora thought it was the latter. The growing confident side of her hoped it was the former.

Unfortunately, Val pivoted and left the room before Nora could find out.

A long beat passed before Nora remembered she could leave. She wandered to the locker room in a daze.

Was she really making progress? Enough that someone like Val would see? She was exhausted, but somehow, she felt like she could run another mile.

Since it was a late-night class (the last the studio had before closing) the other cyclers cooled off and left with little fanfare. Everyone was too wiped to socialize or say much apart from a simple, 'see you next time.'

Soon, she was alone.

Nora was still shy about changing out of her sweat-clogged clothes in the wide, open space. In high school, she always changed in the bathroom stalls or after everyone else was gone. Now, though, with Val's compliment echoing in her head, she stripped slowly without thinking.

The second Nora unzipped her front-clasp sports bra, Val entered the locker room. If she were surprised to be flashed, or felt anything at all, the woman did not show it. Without a word, Val grabbed her gym bag from its cubby hole and started changing as well.

Nora tried not to stare. She really, honestly did. However, with her back turned, shimmying into loose jogger sweats and a clean hot pink crop top, Val was too tantalizing to look away from.

Of course, Nora was caught. She forgot completely about the mirror that ran above the sink countertop in front of them both. In it, their reflections locked eyes.

Val cocked an eyebrow.

"I like your pants," Nora tried to cover.

"... Thanks."

Mortified, Nora changed at lightning speed. She murmured goodnight and tried to flee with what remained of her dignity.

Until Val stopped her.

"Wait! Could you do me a favor?"

"Um, sure."

"Agreeing before you know what I want, hm? How bold."

Val flashed her usual smirk, eyes twinkling with mischief. She gestured at the line of bikes left in the studio.

"Cara ditched class again. Could you give me a hand resetting the studio? It goes a lot quicker with two people."

"Oh! Yeah, of course!"

Val showed Nora how to clean and store the bikes. Then, they set to the task. After such a rigorous workout, it was difficult. However, it went fairly fast with two people. When they were done, they took a moment to sit on one of the lobby benches.

"Thanks for that," Val told her. "Wanna help me out again next week too? I'd take you over Cara's flaky butt any day."

Nora tried to keep her cool as she enthusiastically agreed.

Val smirked. Getting up, she scribbled something under her name on the calendar.

Nora read it, brow scrunched.

"'*Newbie*?'"

"So you can get credit for helping. Then again, I suppose you're not that much of a newbie at this point, are you?"

No, Nora thought. She wasn't new anymore, and she couldn't wait to come back.

FROM THERE, NORA DOVE headfirst into her new fitness hobby.

As a software engineer, she felt the need to explore all the facets of something. Over the next month, she sampled every one of the small studio's other classes. Hot yoga in many styles with unique themes, kettlebell strength training, Tibetan chants, and more.

Still, hot spin classes were the highlights of Nora's week.

The memory of her first class and how insurmountable it seemed then made her laugh. Now, she finished every class with energy to spare, and she promptly spent it with Val.

They seemed to be the only ones who wanted to make use of the studio's credit system, leaving the two of them to close up shop most nights. Wiping the bikes down with a sanitizing solution, storing them, giving the place a quick sweep...

Val called it their 'after party.' It was a strange kind of party, with protein shakes instead of booze and manual labor in place of games, but it was the most fun Nora ever had.

Especially since it gave her the chance to get to know Val.

While they never talked about anything overly personal (Val still called Nora 'Newbie', after all), they touched on just about everything else. The more Nora learned, the more her infatuation grew.

A fellow gamer, bad-horror movie lover, and foodie? Val might look like a star athlete on the outside, but the woman consistently surprised Nora with the things she knew about or loved.

Likewise, it seemed Val was enjoying Nora's company. She kept signing up for cleaning duty, and she didn't even ask before handing Nora a spray bottle after class.

But were they flirting?

Nora couldn't figure it out. Until she knew for sure, she would never have the courage to go further. It left her feeling a bit stuck, just like she had been with Monica for the longest time.

Nora sighed.

"You okay? I thought your days of passing out after class were over." Val's joke fell flat.

"It's not that..."

"What is it, then? We can talk about more than surface-level stuff, ya know."

Could they? Or would that ruin Val's opinion of her? Monica had always checked out mentally when Nora tried to talk about anything serious.

"It's nothing," Nora insisted. "You're right. I'm just tired."

Val gave Nora a look. Lips pursed and sinewy arms crossed, she almost appeared disappointed. Her shrug was forced.

"Alright. If that's the problem, a good night's sleep'll help. Here."

Keys jangling in her hand, Val turned off the studio lights and let Nora through the front door before she locked it.

Cool, early-spring air wrapped around them as they stepped into the night. Somewhere between suburb and city, the studio was in a town center on the ground level under some upscale apartments. There were shops, restaurants, and even a currently bustling brewpub lined up along the quiet, walkable boulevard.

Nora had grabbed a parking spot right outside the studio. They stood in front of her car, each waiting for something from the other person. What the something was, was hard to say. Val's expression was blank, even a little frosty.

The familiar urge to hide—from Val, her feelings, and everything else—called Nora.

She ignored it. She wanted to be seen, to say that she was interested in being more than friends, and ask Val out on a proper date.

Nora's tongue suddenly felt like sandpaper. It stuck to the roof of her mouth as she tried to talk, but she forced the words through.

"Well, this is me. Um, Val... I wanted to say I really enjoy hanging out with you. And I was thinking, if you want, maybe we could hang out some more sometime? Outside of spin, I mean."

A genuine smile, not a smirk or her usual sly look, curved Val's coral pink lips. She said something in response.

Unfortunately, Nora didn't hear a word. Her eyes caught on a couple walking toward them, and her world came to a sudden halt.

*Monica.*

Breath caught in Nora's chest. She started sweating even worse than when she'd been in class. There was no way around it. Even if they ducked into an alleyway between shops and pressed flat against the brick wall? They were going to see her. If she got in her car and made a quick escape, they would recognize it thanks to the decal on her bumper. She loved the Pokeball sticker when Monica gave it to her, and now she hated it more than anything else.

Val noticed Nora had been reduced to a shaking leaf. She glanced back at the catastrophe coming their way.

"Someone you know?"

"My ex," Nora whispered.

"Huh. He's cute for a guy, I guess."

"Not him. That's my brother, Alex. The girl next to him."

The girl walking arm-in-arm, lovey-dovey as could be, with the most hurtful partner she could have picked. Nora felt like throwing up, metaphorically and literally.

Val, however, was shocked for a different reason.

"*Her*? You mean you're—"

"I like who I like," Nora snapped. She immediately felt guilty, since Val had no way of knowing. It wasn't like Nora had said anything about her romantic inclinations. She was not as courageous as Val, who was open about what and who she wanted.

Thankfully, Val didn't hold it against Nora. In fact, her eyes twinkled with a sort of mischievous amusement.

"Wanna mess with them?" Her voice was a conspiratorial whisper, but Nora was having trouble focusing. Her anxiety mounted to a fever pitch, attention torn between the happy couple and the gorgeous woman before her.

"W-what?"

Val shifted. One of her toned arms rested against the wall, almost trapping Nora. Her other reached up to hook a frazzled auburn lock behind Nora's ear and lingered there.

"What would they say," Val murmured, leaning in close, "if they saw *this*?"

A warring dichotomy of senses struck Nora. The unyielding, cold brick behind her versus the springy soft warmth of lips pressed against her own. The hotness of breath that was not hers, and the crisp breeze.

If her mind had been in overdrive before, now it was completely short-circuited.

Who was Monica again?

Nora forgot entirely about her ex as she lost herself in Val's kiss. Sweet and permission-seeking at first, it deepened as she allowed it. Her lips parted, and Val followed suit. Their tongues teased, taking turns tasting each other.

Nora's hands moved on their own. They found their way to Val's bare waist, beneath the hem of the woman's crop top. Her fingers tensed, desperate to creep up and play with the piqued nubs poking through the athletic mesh material.

They melted against one another until there was no space between them. Lips smacking, muffled moans matching in fervor, Nora almost missed the sound of a gasp. The screech of her name was less easy to ignore.

"*Nora?!*"

Heady daze dashed, memory of what was *actually* happening hit Nora like a cold splash of water. The kiss was a performance and, judging by their audience's unhinged jaws, they deserved a standing ovation. Val pulled back barely enough for Nora to turn and face the pair.

"Hiya," Nora replied as naturally as she could, which came out more stilted than if she said nothing at all.

Panic flared inside Nora. Monica's expression was borderline caustic, while Alex's was simply perplexed. Her brother had no idea that Monica and Nora had been anything aside from best friends or even that she was gay. It was a hell of a way for him to find out. Yet part of Nora felt a petty pang of satisfaction.

As Monica surveyed Val, her jealousy was palpable. She dropped Alex's arm and crossed hers over her chest.

"Well? Aren't you going to introduce us?"

As Nora stuttered excuses, Val answered over her.

"Valerie. Valerie Valentine. I'm Nora's partner."

"Her *what*—*!*"

"Spin partner," Val clarified with a grin, well aware of what she'd implied.

With one arm draped over Nora's shoulders, Val's other extended for a handshake. After a delay, Alex took it.

"Nice to meet you," he returned in an admittedly welcoming tone. "I'm her brother, Alex. This is my girlfriend—"

"Nora's best friend," Monica corrected icily. "So you're the reason she's been ghosting me."

"It's not her fault. I've been busy." Nora couldn't help squirming as Monica rolled her eyes.

"If you wanted to spin, we could've gone together. You don't need to get with some rando."

"Oh, don't worry," Val countered. "Nora and I have gotten to know each other *real* well all these late nights. Right?"

"Er, right..."

"See, I needed a partner who could keep up with me," Val went on, laying the innuendo thick. "Nora, she's the best I've ever had. Since you two are close, you must know what a catch she is."

Val's easy but pointed tone seemed to make Monica seethe even harder. Alex smiled beside her, oblivious.

"Well," he said, "we've always known Nora's been waiting for the right person. It's nice she's finally met someone who fits the bill. Our Mom and Dad would love to meet you."

"*Alex!* Don't tell them! It's too soon to talk about anything like that. We're—"

"We're taking things slow," Val interrupted without missing a beat. "But I'd love to meet them sometime."

Monica didn't bother to hide her snort. She tugged on Alex's arm like a pouty child.

"C'mon, babe. Let's go already. I'm tired."

"Oh, um, okay." To Val, Alex offered, "Again, really nice to run into you both. Nora gets wrapped up in things, so we didn't think anything of her keeping to herself the last couple of months. I'm glad she's been having fun."

"Likewise. It's been a blast."

Monica practically dragged Alex away as he waved goodbye.

Alone now, Nora and Val stood on the sidewalk beneath a street lamp's fluorescent glow. It was impossibly awkward. Nora could tell Val was looking at her, but she couldn't bear to face the woman.

How could she, after such a mortifying encounter with her ex? After that *spectacular* kiss?

While Val probably found the whole situation hilarious, Nora wanted to crawl into a hole and hide.

So that was what she did.

"Whelp, I'm gonna head home and crash."

Nora wormed her way out from under Val's arm and beelined for her car. The voice that called after her was hopeful.

"See you next week?"

"Yeah, see you!"

NORA LIED.

She stopped going to classes entirely. Her apartment became her fortress of solitude. She left only for necessities or the occasional pity drink at the bar down the road. Work, game, sleep... her days reverted to their old pattern of self-imposed isolation.

Nora told herself she was fine. She was used to being a homebody. If she really wanted to cycle, she could buy a bike of her own and never pay a membership fee again. However, she knew it wouldn't be the same.

She missed the short drive to the studio and the amp-up music she played along the way.

The studio itself with its calming atmosphere and peppy instructors.

A certain someone with killer abs...

But every time Nora got her gym bag together and started for her car, she couldn't bring herself to go. She stood paralyzed in front of her door until it was too late. Then, the self-loathing set in, and she retreated further inward.

The barrage of texts Nora received did not help.

First was Monica, late that night after their run-in. She sent paragraphs describing how hurt she was Nora was pushing her out, how she felt replaced, and, really, a bunch of narcissistic nonsense. When Nora did not reply, she sent follow-up texts that ranged from apologetic to apocalyptically angry.

It was all Nora needed to realize she was fully and completely over the woman.

Alex's texts were nicer, if not equally painful. He said Monica had been coming onto him for years, and he had no idea there was anything deeper between her and Nora apart from friendship. He hoped they could work through things as a family, since that's what they were.

Nora told him she understood, but needed time.

Her parents also sent several texts. She was fairly sure that Alex and Monica would not out her to them, but they knew something was up. Thankfully, they backed off after she kept up a stalwart grey-rock strategy.

This was for the best, Nora thought. If she didn't let anyone in, if she kept to herself, she wouldn't get hurt again. She repeated the mantra and stuck to it.

Until she got a different text.

Two full weeks after Nora stopped going to spin, her phone lit up with a message from an unknown number.

*Hey Nora. Sorry to text you out of the blue. Got your number from Gina, but don't be mad at her—I lied and said I owed you money. I wanted to apologize for making things weird. I crossed a line, and I can't say enough how sorry I am. Please don't stop going to spin because of me (you've been making so much progress!!!). I'll go to a different gym if that helps, let me know what I can do.*

*—Val*

Nora's phone was like a block of lead in her hands. She felt more awful than before. The drama with Monica was not Val's fault. It might have lit a powder keg, but Monica filled it herself by getting with Alex. Nora was going to move on. She had to. If Monica didn't want to accept that, and her texts very much made it seem that way, it was her problem.

Val offering to go to a different gym? A terrible sinking sensation opened up in Nora's stomach, the feeling of something slipping away she would never get back. She reread the message.

That word, '*progress,*' stared back at Nora. She *had* been making progress. Week by week, class by class, the effort she put in eventually came back.

Weren't most endeavors like that? You have to go and *do* the thing, leave the fortress, to see the results you want. Maybe you won't get exactly what you're looking for, but you'll have tried.

Nora wanted to try.

Before she could stop herself, she typed up a quick response and hit send.

*Don't worry about it. I've been busy lately. See you at class tonight.*

For a full minute, Nora stared at her phone, rereading both messages. Her heart skipped as she watched the three-dot typing indicator pulsate for what seemed like an impossibly long time. Then it was gone.

A simple *'great!'* was all Val texted back, but, somehow, Nora could read a world of relief in the single word.

Maybe because she felt it too.

She clutched her phone to her chest and took a steadying breath through her nose. The giddy elation that washed over her was indescribable, and the panic that followed was familiar.

She checked the time. It was 5PM. Spin was at 8.

Nora had eaten a cold, leftover slice of pizza for breakfast today, and that was it. Her body wasn't going to like this.

Tough luck, Nora told herself. No more cop-outs or giving up. She could put up with some discomfort, emotional or physical, if it meant she could get out of the rut she'd dug. Even if things with Val didn't progress the way Nora was hoping, that was still what it was.

*Progress.*

THERE WAS AN ART TO motivation. Kindness and platitudes could drive a person to greatness. However, sometimes, cruelty was even more effective.

Right now, Gina was being *extremely* cruel.

*"C'mon, slackers! I see those baby turns! Just 'cause you've been skipping doesn't mean the rest of us are gonna slow down. Bump that resistance and keep up!"*

Nora felt called out.

Her fingers fumbled as she reached for the knob. She added a turn and forced her legs to match the music's beat. The bike's wheels churned in slow motion, struggling along with her. But she kept moving, and so did they.

Since Val came into class right as it was starting, she ended up on the last bike available, on the other side of the room. It was impossible to look her way without being obvious. Even so, Nora worked up the courage to glance at her in the form-checking mirror.

It was worth being caught.

Val looked incredible. Wearing a tight white sports bra with black yoga pants, her chiaroscuro aesthetic was like something out of a renaissance painting. Light and shadow rippled over her glistening form, highlighting muscle contours with every dramatic move of her body.

Had she gotten even hotter?

Nora was flabbergasted. A woman who looked like *that* had kissed her? The memory of it, how her lips moved and bounced (the tantalizing proximity Nora's hands had gotten to *other* bouncing parts), was more motivating than Gina by a mile.

When she could tear herself away from gawking at Val, Nora pushed herself to the limit. For every drop of sweat that landed in the growing puddle beneath her bike, she added a resistance turn. And she was sweating enough to make up for the weeks she missed.

Nora went into a sort of exhausted fugue state. Faster and faster, harder and harder. She would not let herself give up again. Unfortunately, her body had other plans.

If cycling was something one did often, investing in the proper equipment was important. Clothes that could take the ridiculous outpouring of sweat, a sizable water bottle, and a towel were all musts. Cycling shoes, ones designed to clip into bike pedals and transfer power more efficiently than regular shoes, were recommended by every class regular.

When Nora's normal sneakers slipped from the stirrups, she knew it was entirely her fault for not listening to the advice. The pedal kept going without her foot and slammed into her calf with such force that she could not hold back her yelp. She hit the brake on her bike, stars streaming over her vision.

Gina slowed her pedaling, but Nora waved her off. The last thing she wanted was more attention. The music was so loud, and everyone was so focused on their own workouts, that only a couple of people noticed. Shame surging, she disentangled herself and limped from the studio.

It was a small mercy that the lobby was empty. The cyclists were the only ones left in the building, so no one witnessed Nora's graceless stumble to the locker room. She made it to one of the toilet stalls and collapsed onto the seat.

Nora cried. All the frustration, embarrassment, and disappointment bubbled to the surface.

As the locker room door creaked open, she tried to muffle herself with her towel, not that it was hard to tell where she was. With only two stalls and a set of showers in the back, the locker room was smaller than most. A set of well-worn black cycling shoes stopped in front of Nora's hiding place. Val's familiar voice came through the door.

"Hey there, you okay?"

" ... "

"You don't need to be embarrassed. You're not the first person to slip their pedal, and you won't be the last. I grabbed a first aid kit."

" ... "

"Newbie?"

Finally, something in Nora burst.

"Stop calling me that! It's Nora! My name is Nora! You know it is, so why do you keep making fun of me?"

A beat passed. When Val replied, her voice was a long way from its usual confident boldness.

"It's not like that. It's just, I've never been good at flirting. Sorry, Nora. I'll leave this here and go."

Go? She couldn't go, not now, not when Nora had made the effort, kept making progress!

Val placed the kit down on the floor outside of the stall. As she drew her hand away, Nora grabbed it on impulse.

"Wait. Could you help me with my leg? And maybe we could... talk?"

It was all Nora could manage to say, but it was all she needed. She unlatched the door. Wordlessly, fingers laced, Val led her to the showers.

"MY RELATIONSHIP WITH Monica was unhealthy."

Sitting on a tiled shelf beneath a periodically dripping shower head, Nora opened up. It was difficult. She felt silly admitting the sordid details of her failed romance to anyone, let alone the person she was interested in.

Val listened patiently as she tended Nora's leg.

"She always knew my feelings for her went past friendship. Even though she teased me for it, there were times she acted like she felt the same. Times it felt like we were a proper couple. But whenever she had a new guy she wanted, she would drop me."

"She liked the attention."

"Yeah, I think that's what it was. For years, I told myself she would stay with me if I kept trying. So I did. I was her backup date for every holiday and wedding. I celebrated every little thing she accomplished, satisfied her in any way she wanted—and I mean *any*. In the end, she told me I didn't try hard enough to be her girlfriend. Right after I caught her in bed with my brother."

Nora hissed as Val pressed an alcohol pad to the pedal-skinned patch on her calf.

"Sorry," she said. "Stings, doesn't it?"

With a sniffle, Nora nodded.

They both went quiet. Nora tried to gauge Val's reaction, to guess how pathetic she sounded. However, Val was intently focused. She finished with the alcohol pad and dabbed a cream over the worst of Nora's wound. It was soothing, but so were the nimble fingers kneading it, making just enough contact.

"It sounds like she put you through a lot," Val commented without meeting Nora's eye. "You're still trying for her, then? Getting in shape, going to spin... You want to win her back?"

"*Fuck no!*"

At Nora's outburst, Val looked up. Nora didn't curse often, but it slipped out now. At least it was appropriate. She swallowed the lump in her throat and tried again.

"I don't want to be a second choice or have someone tell me I'm not trying enough for them. I want to try for myself, if that makes any sense."

Nora was still overheated and sweaty from the workout, but Val's laugh made her cheeks burn even hotter.

"What? Is it that funny?"

"No, not at all. I think it's a good way to live. And when you're trying your hardest, people notice. I know I sure did."

"R-really?"

A sopping lock of blonde hair fell over Val's face as she nodded. She swept it back, and there was a guilty shift in her eyes.

"To be honest, you were right. I've known your name for a while now. I asked Gina after the first few times I saw you around."

"You did? Why?"

"Why do you think? I saw you coming here, week after week—an adorable redhead who keeps pushing herself, smiling even when she's sweating her cute ass off—and I wanted to know more about you."

"Well, now that you do...?"

Val did not reply right away. She finished wrapping Nora's leg with a clean strip of gauze and repacked the kit.

As Val stood, the space between them seemed to shrink even smaller. With the curtain closed, the shower stall seemed barely big enough for the two of them.

Over the heady buzz she felt, Nora struggled to hear what Val said next.

"The other night, before those two showed up. You asked me out."

"I... I did."

"You didn't hear what I said, did you?"

Eyes trained on the shower drain, anywhere that wasn't Val's face, Nora shook her head. Two gentle fingers tilted her chin up and forced her to look.

"Ask me again."

For longer than was probably acceptable, Nora forgot how to speak. Was this happening? Her chance to say how she felt and ask for what she wanted in a way she never dared with Monica?

Val wore her usual sly grin. Still, there was an extra element behind the expression: anticipation perched on the border of nervousness.

At least that made two of them.

In the name of progress, Nora asked.

"Val. Do you wanna go on a date sometime? With me, maybe?"

"Yeah, Newbie. I'd like that."

There was hardly any distance left between them. They closed it in perfect sync, lips meeting in a matched tempo of fervency unleashed.

Salty tang and sweet saliva swarmed Nora's senses. The rush of it all—the intoxicating taste, the electrifying skin contact spurred by slick sweat—made her glad she was sitting. Nora's legs curled around Val's waist, arms around her neck, drawing them close as possible.

It wasn't close enough.

As Nora pulled back, Val cocked an eyebrow. She understood what the problem was once she saw the way Nora looked at her chest. Or, more accurately, the article that hid it.

"Hm. I suppose it is in the way..."

In a dexterous dip, Val unzipped her front-closing sports bra. Still, the fabric clung tight. Smooth, swelling breasts were held in place by a tease of a hook clasp. Her eyes twinkled as she released it, letting them spring free.

Nora had never wanted to touch another person so badly in her life.

At Val's eager nod, Nora took one mauve nipple into her mouth and fondled the other to her heart's content. Her free hand wandered and roved wherever it could reach, lost in the newness of Val. The woman's muscles, her scents, the throaty, pleasured purrs she let loose to punctuate every suckle, made Nora desperate to discover more.

Unfortunately, her expedition would have to wait.

With a crash, the locker room door burst open. Val caught Nora as she leaped. They stood, statue-still, as the other cyclists filed into the room.

Over all the usual post-class chatter, someone called for Val.

"You still here?"

"Yeah, in the back. What's up?"

"Was Newbie alright? Seemed like she took a pretty hard hit."

Gina was right on the other side of the curtain. One casual sweep could move it aside and reveal the illicit activities within. Despite this, she stood there, none the wiser.

Nora couldn't say whether she was more terrified or turned on.

"Oh, she's fine," Val answered, cool as could be. "Just a little banged up. She went home early."

"Ah, okay. Think she'll be back next week?"

Eyes locked with Nora's, Val answered, "I think she'll come."

One tapered finger slid down Nora's chest and hooked the waistband of her shorts. As Val spoke, she tugged, and it sent throbbing shockwaves through Nora. They were so intense she had to cover her mouth to hold back her whimper.

"Cara skipped again," Gina continued, still unaware. "You know you're on cleaning duty, right?"

"Yep. Gonna shower first, then I'll get to it."

Val reached past Nora and turned the knob. Tepid at first, it warmed considerably in seconds. Or perhaps it was the way Val stripped her remaining clothes. Naked, she pulled Nora against her bare body and held her while the water cascaded down on them both.

"I can stay and help if you want," Gina offered. "Otherwise, I'm heading out."

"You go ahead. I'm going to take my time."

Gina's footsteps faded into the background, lost under the rushing water.

Val moved to kiss Nora. Instead, Nora kissed her first. She took initiative and loved it.

Nora felt Val's smirk curve against her own. Class might have ended, but their session had just begun.

# A Word from the Author – Nat Paga

My name is Nat Paga. I'm a part-time writer, full-time Hobbit. When I'm not coming up with stories about strong women who like to kick and touch butts in equal measure, I'm probably cooking something that'll knock your socks off. I live in the part of New Jersey that considers itself a part of Philadelphia. My favorite pastimes are cuddling my human while we watch bad horror movies, just about anything nerdy, and hot yoga.

My ongoing weird-western romantic adventure series, Ashe & Dez: Gals with Grit is my largest project to date. That, along with Make Me Sweat, were born out of a desire to let my Sapphic side shine.

Thank you for reading our anthology! To find me and my stories, follow @natpaga_writes.

I'd like to thank our wonderful editors and organizers, Adam and AC, for making this anthology possible. And Lila, too, for her awesome contributions.

Playlist

Valerie—Amy Winehouse

I'm Still Standing—Elton John

# Gaea

## By Lou Grimes

Today, I must kill.

It's no different from any other day. Often, I kill.

That's the circle of life. Everything has a cycle. If we didn't have it, my Heart Stone would be overrun, and it would find a way to destroy everything.

What I must kill is a human.

No matter how many times I kill, it's never felt right. I must do it to even the balance, but I don't relish in it like my friend does. I feel every single discomfort, pain, and death. Sometimes, it is unbearable.

There's a balance I am bound to keep, so I must kill. If I don't, the Earth will die from excess. I don't remember how I came to be, but one day I simply was.

When I watch the people, I wish I was one. To live in a world where I didn't have to kill. That's not who I am, though.

I sigh.

I transform into something else to see more.

On a bird's wings, I glide across the village. The feathers ruffle from the wind. My talons are tucked at my side as I search.

There are buildings of stone scattered about.

From the sky, I see the golden lights of each living thing. At the end of the village, there's a light not as bright as the other ones. One blow from the wind could snuff it out.

I use another gift, the ability to share space within a being, to transpose from person to person in the village. When I find a cluster of people standing around a human who's covered in wrinkles and slate hair, I stop. The dim light blinks.

Never do I look at their faces. I don't want to remember the ones I take their spark from, nor their family members.

I charm the rest of the spark out.

Now, he will go to Hades' realm to wait to be reunited with his loved ones someday.

I move through the town, hunting for the right one. The spark is still clutched in my hands. I charm some more energy into it as I go.

At last I spot the perfect home. I stop at the wooden door, noticing a gravestone out front. It's too small for an adult. Moving inside, I find a couple who are having dinner with one child at the table.

I press the energy into the mother's stomach, sparking life where there was none.

A soft smile crosses my face, though tears well from sadness.

This is the part I enjoy. This makes my duty to balance worth it.

After it's done, I weep for the loss like I always do. Tears pour down my cheeks, falling to the ground. They will nurture the land around me, replacing death with life.

"Are you okay?"

I still, not answering. From behind, I look human, but once I turn around, all will be revealed.

I can't resist the human experience this person is offering me. Its temptation calls me greater than the aches of the earth that I'm feeling right now.

I want to know everything. I turn around to find out.

A tall and lean human stands before me. He's a farmer I recognize from the fields. His long white tunic is stained from working in the dirt. Thick leather boots protect his feet.

Dark eyes with thick black eyebrows widen at the sight of me. When he shakes his head to clear his vision, his silky black curls bounce. Long black eyelashes flutter as he blinks, hesitant about how to answer. His lashes are accentuated by an angular face and long nose.

"Oh Goddess, I did not mean to disturb you," he stammers. "I thought you to be a crying maiden in the forest."

Though awkward, his admission pleases me for a reason I can't quite explain. A coy smile tugs at my lips. This is my first interaction with a human.

"I was crying, but you've distracted me from my Heart Stone's pains," I say.

"I didn't know gods cried," he murmurs, staring at me with wonderment.

"Some do."

"It's nice to meet you. I'm Galen, son of Ganas." When neither of us speaks for a minute, he adds, "What are you called?"

"The gods call me Gaea."

"Why were you weeping?"

"One of your kin has died. I did not want to do it, but the balance must be righted, or everything will perish." It's simplified, but enough for now.

"You should not weep, for he lived a good life, and enjoys his reprieve from a long life of hard work."

"I did not think of it like that." I hadn't. This was a new concept, that death could be a relief. There's a change in the air, but I know Galen doesn't feel it. I do.

"Return to your people."

"I am blessed to have met you." Galen bows. "I will make a sacrifice in your name."

My head snaps up. "I don't want anything sacrificed for me. If anything, keep doing everything you are already doing."

Galen raises an eyebrow then nods his head. I watch him leave for the sake of knowing I am no longer alone.

"I know you are there." The woods appear empty, but I know better.

"How?" I hear my old friend wonder.

"I just do." I don't tell him that even the air feels his violence.

I glance over at him. The god is cloaked in black, no doubt coming back from igniting some kind of mischief. He's not the type to hide his appearance. I still feel his cold black eyes upon me. If I felt cold as humans do, I would shiver.

Though I don't know why, we are old friends. Indeed, we are an odd pair. I've always felt a certain kinship with him, defying all sense.

The imposing figure takes a step closer to me. He doesn't need to show off, but I don't think he can resist.

"Making friends, are we?"

I ignore his question. I don't play the games the other gods do. "What are you doing?"

"You know what I'm doing," my friend answers.

"I do. I have work to do." I don't want to be here for whatever he is doing.

Though I wish for it, I can't escape the death of things. Even though it's necessary, I still don't wish to see it. It's everywhere. It clings to this world as strongly as life does, a balance as ancient as life itself.

Transposing away from him, I don't even give him time to answer.

Wings beat beside me as I cut through the air. Exhilaration floods me as my ears are laid flat. I twist and turn until the landscape is even before me. I glide through the sky, watching a nearing range of mountains. A golden orange world lies before me as the sun sets.

Razor-sharp talons are curled at my side. A roar breaks out of the Griffin as he dives for a meal, and I transpose to another.

Water surrounds me as I swish through a river. Other fish bump into me, for I am surrounded by my school of friends.

The current flows through me as I follow it around every river bend. Aquatic plant life of bright vibrant colors paves my road as I move through it, weaving about.

Claws snap around my scaled midsection, tearing my scales up. Bubbles erupt out of my mouth out of surprise as I am ripped from the water. I gasp in the air. As the Griffin shrieks above, I squirm for a minute before transposing to another creature, knowing this one's end.

I thunder across the plains, hooves flying and mane whipping. My herd follows behind me.

A scent hits me moments before I round a hill. I dig my hooves into the dirt, but it's too late. My momentum carries me over the hill as I transpose into the next creature.

Onyx leather wings unfurl out behind me as I wait for my dinner to come to me. I am the father of monsters; I should not have to wait. The humans call me Typhon.

Snake headed tentacles twist at my beard. My tails swish behind me with even larger snake heads than the ones in my beard. All three of them are as hungry as I am.

My tails open their slitted mouths, and one swallows a creature whole.

Before it's swallowed, I transpose, returning to the land once more.

I breathe with the trees, breaking through rocks with my roots. I move mountains. I devour decay. Pebbles are broken down to make way for streams of nourishment. My will heats and cools the very air. I make creatures from the tiniest of flies to the largest gargantuan I can forge. I create the monsters that roam my Heart Stone.

Though I am everywhere, I am nowhere.

That's a problem sometimes. When I am everyone, I feel everything.

Hot agony sears across my Heart Stone. Jagged lines flow from the burn spot as the burning advances through the root system nearby.

Following the ache, I stream through the land, cut through the mountains, roll with the leaves in the wind. I transpose through every pebble, sand seed, and rock that scatter about on my Heart Stone.

On little feet with claws, I scramble through the woods as hard as I can make myself go. A long tail shifts about behind me, giving me the perfect balance as I jump. My large ears flick as I move onward to escape the fire's wrath.

I know each crevice of my Heart Stone.

Before I break into the clearing, I recall the valley. It was covered with flowers, grasses, and was home to many woodland creatures. Now it is black as the fire persists, and the flame licks everything around it, burning more.

The humans have their masks down low, protecting the air they needed to breathe in. Animals of all kinds scamper away from the fire.

I pause with rapt attention.

Burning is a normal cleansing of the land, because that's how a balance can be achieved. You remove the old to make way for the rebirth of all things. It's a natural occurrence, like a lightning strike causing a fire. It will burn fast, and just enough.

However, this burning is uncontrollable. It lights things faster than any fire I have ever seen.

The smoke smells unnatural. The entire burn feels different. It feels intentional, more agonizing than any natural fire I could create to maintain balance. It's not natural, or forged by any natural occurrences.

The humans watch too, from the hill. The animals fleeing feel the poison as it chokes everything in its wake.

No more. The fire has been burning too long. I swirl the clouds up. They darken, and fat raindrops fall. At first the smoke hisses, but then it flares up worse than before.

I blanch.

The fires swell taller and more powerful. This blaze would burn my entire Heart Stone to nothing more than cinders.

I've made things worse. Just as soon as the rain came, I take it away. I don't know how to stop this.

After some time, it stops burning. For miles, the scent of smoke and ash fills the air. Smoke rolls into the sky.

I take a moment to realize I am no longer alone. I glance out of the corner of my eyes at my old friend, refusing to hide my emotions. This time, his hood is gone. His brunette hair is cut short, causing it to stand straight up some. He still wears the cloak. I realize it's covered in ash.

"What is this?" My fury mounts. Deep in my heart, I know this was his doing. Though maybe he never lifted a finger, he caused this.

"They call it Sea Fire," he says. "The humans that you love have created a fire stronger than your own, using all that you have given them. A fire even you can't put out," he adds, goading me. His dark eyes pierce into me. My old friend wants me to react, but I won't give him the satisfaction of such things.

Needing to be alone, I leave him to boil in his own hate.

Sobs echo through the forest all night. Eventually, I will try to fix it. I am not even sure it can be fixed. I have to try, but I am not ready to do so.

The spot has been aching since the fire. The day after the burning, an irritating itch has increased from the patch.

I have felt nothing like it, so I move across the earth, unbidden. I find Galen scraping the spot. Sweat makes his black whorls shine. His white tunic is already drenched.

Before I break the silence, I watch him for a while.

"What are you doing?" I ask.

Galen jumps, but then bows.

"You scared me. I am cleaning this land so that I may plow it."

"Why? You have more than enough food plots to have a bountiful crop next year." I watched him do each one.

"I'm doing it so that you won't weep anymore. We didn't realize it would burn this much. I'm so sorry." Galen appears sorrowful at how much anguish this has caused me.

Heat warms my heart. A gentle smile spreads across my lips. Galen's eyes follow them.

"Thank you, Galen," I say.

Galen grins, making his entire face light up. He continues his scraping. There's a new speed in his manner as he does.

Every day after that, we meet in the same spot. I watch him fix what my friend has done, and then we talk until well past sunset. Galen tells me about his world, and I do the same.

After a time, it isn't long before the burn is sprouting new life.

The next time I sense Galen, he is not covered in the earth. He no longer smells of salt and dirt. His clothes are absent of sweat and stains. In fact, the clothes he wears are the most complex set I have seen on him.

I almost frown at the sight of him without the earth lingering on him. He has scrubbed himself clean. His secretive smile stops whatever inappropriate question I was about to ask.

"What?" I want to know what he is hiding.

"I have something for you." Galen holds his hands behind his back. "A gift."

"What is a gift?" Curiosity gets the best of me.

Galen pauses before answering. "Giving with no expectations."

I contemplate his words, but they hold no meaning for me.

"I don't understand."

"Perhaps not now, but you will. Close your eyes, and hold out your hands."

"Okay." My voice is breathy as I close my eyes and hold out my hands.

With all the gingerness in the world, Galen places something in my upraised palms. It's harder than any regular cloth I've touched, almost the stiffness of animal hide.

His touch lingers longer against my skin than necessary, but I don't protest.

"Now, open." There is a thickness in his voice that wasn't there before, as if he is struggling with his own emotions.

I do.

Confused by what I see at first, I frown. My head tilts, uncertain at what this gift is.

From all my watching, I've witnessed some human customs in my life, but I'm also maintaining balance over an entire world as we speak, so I don't understand them.

Galen smiles again.

"It's your disguise. There's a festival tonight, and I want you to come with me, if you want to?"

Still hesitant, I process what he says.

An edge of worry sharpens Galen's eyes after a moment. "You don't have to, but I would like you to see more about humans."

"I would love to." I'm not sure what I am getting myself into, but I can't wait and the excitement surges through me. "How do I wear it?"

"Here, if you don't mind, I'll tie it for you."

In agreement, I extend my palms.

Galen steps forward, taking the piece of hardened material, and steps behind me. Goosebumps prickle up. I've never let a human come this close to me. Galen moves another step closer, and I find it hard to breathe. My Heart Stone quickens.

I focus on keeping my Heart Stone steady. The speed it spins picks up by a fraction, but it's enough. The air surrounding us tries to heat, but I stop it from rising more than one degree.

When I get it under control, my focus returns to him.

One of his hands comes up one side of my face, and the other comes up with gentleness on the other side. There's such slowness in his movements, as if I'm a skittish creature a single second from bolting into the forest.

Fingers hold the mask to my face while his expert hand ties the cloth together. It goes tight against my cheeks. He stills for a second before he releases it enough to keep it on my face.

"Is it too tight?" Galen asks before he finishes the knot.

"No, I don't think so."

When he finishes, he steps in front of me with a soft grin. "You look so beautiful. Here's the cloak."

Galen takes a long piece of cloth from the sack he brought, with the same stitching as his own. I'd be a fool not to see it matches. He hands it to me and helps me put it over my shoulders. He ties it around my waist.

"With the light fading, you can pass for human, since everyone has been in the ale for a while now." There's a note of humor to Galen's voice. "Not to mention, everyone will be in costume."

The corners of my mouth tilt up, echoing his.

That's how I end up staring at a set of gates. They are closed, but they appear welcoming from the warm lights behind them. Music flows through the air.

The guards open the doors to reveal a town of modest size. The streets are packed with people. Many converse in groups, holding drinks in their hands. Children run around the streets, playing games, and other people are doing things I don't even know the names to.

I've seen every inch of this world, and yet I've never seen anything like this. I grin, taking it all in.

Galen loops his arm around mine as we stroll through the town together. The air is loaded with scents I've never smelled. The smells float in the smoke of the fire pits. There is a hint of people mixed in there somewhere.

Galen stops up short and pales.

"Do you eat?"

"I can, but I don't need to," I answer. "I have tried food before and found it distasteful, but that was a long time ago. Perhaps human food has progressed since then?"

"We've moved beyond mere sustenance. Here, let me show you what we've made from the things you grow for us." Galen pulls me to the table overflowing with meats, cheeses, breads, and fruits.

He hands me a couple items, then pairs a few things together. One is salty, but then he matches it with a fruit that bursts.

"It's amazing."

He smiles and moves to gather a few more things. While he picks the next ones, I notice a group of people off to the side. They move together in a similar pattern. It's captivating, like the way the trees in the forest move together.

Galen sees my shift of attention.

"Come on. I love to dance." Galen leads me toward the throng of people.

This time, it is my turn to stop short. "Dance?"

"Dancing. It's not as hard as it looks." I'm dubious, but Galen bows to me before we step closer. I mimic him, step after step. In the end, I am giggling like the girls in the mob. We spin around and step this way, and then that way.

After a while, we stop. We both need a break, and Galen's salted earth scent has returned. I can't get enough of it.

Galen looks about, pondering the next thing we should do. He brightens at whatever he has come up with.

"I believe we can catch the end of the last act." Galen nods into town.

"Act?" Humans are so odd.

"We dress up like the great heroes, warriors, or even the gods. We act out the great deeds or tragedies they are known for on a stage."

I'm frozen. I don't know how I feel about his explanation, but I don't want to disappoint Galen. I need to understand.

"Show me."

Galen extends his hand for me to take. We head deeper into the town.

We don't make it far when we come upon a mass of people surrounding a large wooden structure. Cloths hang down each side. There are people standing on the platform, dressed in grander robes than I have seen tonight. This must be the stage Galen mentioned.

Stepping forward, Galen gets us a better view.

"Help me, help me Apollo, Goddess Athena!" a young man calls, running across the stage.

Screeching, three women in long white robes chase after him.

A chill run through my body at the sight of them. I can't look away from the three women. It's not their screeching that draws me. It's the wildness they portray, the rage they try to convey.

"They are the Furies." Galen murmurs in my ear.

"Are they?" I recall the real Furies, pale compared to these women. The ones I know are calm and collected. They rule emotions from afar. Not these monsters who search for criminals in the dark. I watch more, trying to reconcile the perception and the reality.

They think the Furies are everywhere, but they are not. The Furies I know control the dark parts of the mind that call for vengeance, retribution, and justice. They make people remove the bad from this society. They are there when a father kills his son's murderer, when a mob takes justice into their own hands, when a victim kills their offender.

Always, they are there.

The Furies even can reach the gods. My friend is proof of that. There is little doubt he's never not been hounded by the Furies.

A soft laugh escapes me.

"What?" Galen asks.

"Thank you. I'm having a good time. It's very eye opening."

We watch the last few minutes, and when it ends, we make our way out of town. It's a gradual progression as we enjoy each other's nearness.

When we stop at our usual meeting spot, I turn to face him. He moves to take my mask.

Closing my eyes, I savor his touch. For a minute, I feel almost human.

As he does, he comes around, holding my chin in his hand. Galen lifts it up, and our lips press together. Once he draws away, I miss it.

"Goodnight, Galen."

"Goodnight, Goddess." Galen teases me and I smile. He turns and I watch him return to his town.

"This is going to end badly." The presence beside me finally speaks.

I sigh, irritated. I'm tired of being watched.

"You don't know that."

"I do. The closer you get to him, the closer you get to humans. They won't stop. They'll create more things like the Sea Fire so they can hurt you. War is as embedded in them as it is in me."

I shake my head. "It's you that's doing this. Not them."

"I will show you." His voice is resolute, full of promise and horror.

I know he will, and there's no hope of convincing him otherwise. All I can do is wait for it to come.

The next day, my old friend proves it. A familiar scorching hurt hits, making me cry out as my knees hit the floor. This time, it escalates so fast. It burns so much that I have trouble keeping the consciousness that is me. By the time I get there, the whole forest is gone, yet this is not the worst. At the center of this forest once stood a town

"What have you done?" I ask, knowing this work belonged to my long-time friend.

This time, his cloak opens, revealing some glinting metal underneath.

"You don't understand. You need to comprehend what they are capable of." His eyes bore into mine. "This is the beginning. It will only get worse."

"Not all of them are like this." Images of Galen flash before me.

"It didn't take much convincing for them to use the Sea Fire for war."

"What about the ones who take care of the land and other people?"

He shakes his head. "All I want is for you to see what you have fallen for, what they truly are: animals."

"Why?" I need to know. I think deep down, I've always known, but refused to see it.

"I love you. More than they ever could."

The words tumble from my mouth before I can stop them.

"I love Galen."

"I know you think you do, but I'm going to save you from them, and him.".

"This isn't love. You have hurt me beyond repair." I know this will never heal.

"No, this will grow back in time. As you will heal from what I do next, too, yet you might think you are hurt beyond repair."

This time, he disappears.

I know where he's going. I transpose to where he will be.

My old friend stands in the field, facing Galen. His cloak is gone.

Galen's face is pale white at what he sees. I can't fault him. What he faces is a god in a full body of armor.

"Ares!" I scream, wanting him to focus his attention on me. "I thought this was all about me."

Ares turns to me. There's a long scar down his face. It goes from his forehead to his jawline. "It's always been you."

Galen pales and meets my gaze.

I dig into the surrounding ground, drawing metal, and then twist the hoe he was using into a spear. "I'm not so sure anymore," I say.

Galen nods and raises his spear.

Ares takes one step toward Galen, and I move in unison, knowing Galen is no match for Ares.

Ares raises his sword in challenge. Galen answers the call with his spear, but I know I can't let him fight alone. He won't win. I might not either, but it is better than the alternative.

Ares dodges forward, clanging his sword across Galen's spear. Sparks erupt because Ares is stronger than any mortal man, but there's nothing stronger than love.

Galen holds his own.

When I see an opening, I scramble the soil beneath Ares's feet. He staggers as Galen deals a few thunderous blows to him and his shield. The impact sends Ares a few steps back, so Galen gives him a couple more.

Ares stands taller, not deterred by the few hits he's taken, but he's the god of war, so I'm not surprised.

I throw boulder after boulder at Ares, but his shield protects him.

Galen goes in for a few stabs and slashes. Ares keeps coming back, stronger each time. Sweat is rolling down Galen's cheeks.

I blink. I need to get rid of Ares's shield or we will never stand a chance against him.

Focusing on his shield, I shift the very metals that forged it.

It decays at the touch of my will.

Ares narrows his eyes as his shield crumbles. He casts it aside, taking his sword into both hands. He twirls it around, testing the weight.

Ares thrusts it at Galen again, striking him on the shoulder. Galen hisses, taking a few steps back.

Water explodes out of the holes in the ground. I collect it into something more potent. It knocks Ares back before it he can finish the blow on Galen. Galen scrambles out of the way as the wild water whips about.

Something barks to the side. Two sets of glowing ruby eyes bounce through the trees. I watch as two monstrous dogs come bounding out of the forest. I know them of old. Their hair is shaggy and uneven. Scars cover their bodies, trophies earned from following Ares into battle time after time, too many to count.

They might as well be Cerberus's cousins. These curs' claws rip the earth with each step.

Ares's dogs would kill Galen in seconds, but he doesn't flinch as he raises his spear in the air.

One dog locks onto my forearm, and I topple to the ground from the weight of it. Bite after bite, so many I lose count. First, they latch onto my arm, my side, and then my head. It all blurs together. I can't discern one bite from another.

"Gaea!" Galen shouts for me, but the dogs are too swift. They do more damage to my flesh.

The more I endure, the more the world rumbles in sympathy. All I want to do is release this agony. If I do, I will destroy everything I have built from the ground up. And yet I can't stop myself from ripping my heart out. If Ares wants my heart so badly, I'll give it to him. I'll give it to him in pieces. Every single pebble, rocks, and thing that makes up my Heart Stone, I will bring the whole thing down on him.

The hate and vengeance twist inside of me, making me rage harder and harder, but I force myself to remember the reason this fight began.

Love.

My love for Galen is the reason I started, and I will let it be the end of this for his sake. I bottle it all up, and then focus my power on keeping my hurt contained. The world can't handle this level like I can.

I come out of it in time. By "in time," I mean I see Galen putting a spear through one of the dogs' lungs.

"No!" Ares shouts, but it's too late. His dog lets go of my flesh and falls to the ground. It wheezes a few seconds before it goes silent.

Ares charges Galen, sword swinging as he runs. Galen tries to remove his spear from the dog's side, but he can't. He leaves it and tries to dodge Ares's attack.

Ares is too agile, and his blade slides through to Galen's lungs.

"Now you see him for what he is, no better than any other human. Now we can be together," Ares says, triumphant.

"Get away from me!" I scream. I shake the earth and send Ares hurtling back.

I run to Galen's side. I fall to my knees, clutching the man I love to my breast. A sob escapes me.

"I wouldn't have changed anything, my goddess." Galen whispers in my ear as his heart takes its last beat.

My Heart Stone trembles as I do. The very plates shift, pushing and pulling apart, causing quakes across my heart.

For once, the tides have turned. The Earth feels my suffering.

It threatens to break my Heart Stone in pieces, but before it does, I dig into the roots, flowing through them and every stem to a place where no one knows my name.

Galen's head falls back as his soul leaves his body to join Hades, like all the other humans.

For a moment, I don't recall the cause of my anguish. It's not my Heart Stone that did this. It's the God of War.

Before I can stop myself, I stagger up and charge at Ares.

The God of War throws his sword up to defend himself.

When I knock it aside with the wind, Ares stands frozen for a moment. I take up the discarded spear. I want to do this the old-fashioned way and stab at him, picking up speed with each thrust. Ares has trouble blocking me.

I duck, and then jab up at his heart. Ares blocks it at the last minute, and then continues his swing.

Right before he chops my head off, he diverts his swing. A lock on my hair falls to the ground. Ares pales.

I bark a laugh.

"Is this your love?" Sarcasm drips from my words.

"I didn't mean to. I don't know any other way." The admission pains Ares.

"I feel sorry for you because you'll never know true love. War is your true love." I snort and add, "Galen loved me so much he died for me. You love me so much you'd kill me."

Ares clenches his jaw. I might as well have sent an arrow to his heart, laced with the most powerful of poisons. Truth. At first, he had no intention of killing me. Now, he has to defend himself. I am out for his blood as sure as the Hades hounds themselves. He knows it.

There's one way to fight the god of war: fight dirty. Before he can react, I throw the sand I have all around me. It glitters as the sun shines on it.

He summons a shield and throws it up between us, holding it more perfectly than anyone else can.

I snarl, relenting with the sand.

Ares tips his shield back. His sword cuts through the air, flashing.

I crash the mountain on top of him. Rocks slide from the mountains, falling. They land beside us, almost taking out the angered god as they do.

He stabs at me. I explode into dragonflies. He stumbles as he loses his balance, and I go in for the kill.

Roots burst forth from the earth, curling and twisting to protect me from Ares's attack. Ares staggers, which I use to my advantage. I dig into the caves around me, dragging the gems from my Heart Stone. Once they are collected, I send a volley of crystals of all colors at him.

He dodges each one.

Birds of all types swarm the air above him. They dive bomb him, pecking and slashing with all their might.

Ares cuts down a few. He extends his arm, and blood magic pours from it.

Vultures came out of every fissure. They attack the swarm of birds I called to me.

Feeling their ache, I release my hold, knowing Ares will do the same. He feels for his vultures like I do all the other birds. This similarity disgusts me but is familiar, and a thought forms.

Blood rolls down his cheek. He touches his fingers to the droplets. I grin at the sight of it.

I turn up the heat, scorching the air around him, like he scorched my Heart Stone time after time with his wars.

Ares falls to his knees, sucking air. From his shocked look, he didn't think I would give him such a fight.

While he's on his knees, I drive the blade as deep as I can. The flesh rips. Blood oozes from the wounds as I bare my teeth, cheering for his death.

Since he took my heart from me, I will carve his out of his chest. "I think I know now why I've always felt a kinship with you." I press the blade deeper. "I see the same rage in you that lives in me. It's the rage that connects us. No one else knows the levels of rage we face. I convert mine into the earth, but you feed yours."

Ares's eyes widen in shock. The thud of his body landing reverberates through the ground.

"I will save you from yourself. I will follow you for the rest of time." Blood beads his lips as he whispers. "War restores me. The humans you love so much will resurrect me. I will find you, and we will kill them all together. I will save you."

Ares draws his last breath as I watch. This one death I shall watch. I must watch. Though I've always hated death, I don't look away from this one. I need to see him die.

I stare at the bodies, realizing two things.

First, in this moment, the humans are safe from Ares. And second, Ares will return, but he will have a hard time finding me. I shift my body to a human form, and head to the furthest village I can find from Greece. I hope to find peace and savor it. As I transpose, I can't help but wonder if I will find the peace I'm looking for when the man I love is gone.

My heart aches as I wipe my mind of all memories, for I will find no peace with a broken heart. I think I've earned it.

The gods can keep their madness.

Goodbye my love, for I am Gaea no longer.

# A Word from the Author – Lou Grimes

L ou Grimes was born and raised in Texas. She writes in the comfort of her own home. When she is not writing or working part time, she is outside gardening, swimming, and hiking. Another favorite pass time of hers is anything that involves creating art and traveling as much as possible.

When she was growing up, her nose was either stuck in a book or stuck in her own daydreams. Her main objective as an author is to create a world that people want to get lost in.

Playlist:

- Everybody wants to rule the world By Lorde
- Arcade by Duncan Laurence
- Rise by Katy Perry

I wrote this story because I think Gaia's story hasn't really been told like this. Mother Nature loves us and helps us in so many ways. I think we forget or don't appreciate everything we have because of Mother Nature.

I also wrote to raise awareness about our terrible environmental impact on this world.

Though this Earth loves us, a majority of men are like Ares and don't care for this Earth like they should. I am working on doing at least a standalone with Gaia as the main character which will tie into this.

# Forces of Attraction in a Two-Body System

## A Cassidyverse Story

## By Adam Gaffen

The hallway was crowded, and fifth form cadet Katy Montgomerie shouldered her way through the mass of her fellow students. She paused at a window and shivered.

January in the Northern Imperium was horrible.

January in Marquette, the home of the Northern Imperium Naval Academy, was undeniably worse. Marquette was firmly in the snowbelt, where the first flakes could appear as early as September, and the last flakes might not land until June. In between, they piled up.

And up.

If Katy's memory served, it looked like 2094 would be worse than '93. The window she gazed out was a full four feet above the ground, but the snow reached halfway up the pane.

"This sucks."

Katy didn't flinch at the sound of her best friend's voice. It was a game she and Keely Shae played, seeing who could successfully sneak up on the other. Despite Keely's height advantage—she was barely five foot two, while Katy topped out near five foot seven in the antiquated system only the Imperium still used—she rarely got the jump on Katy.

"You just hate it because you can't see out."

"You giraffes have an advantage over us normal people."

Katy laughed and ruffled Keely's short-cut red hair. "Normal people wouldn't be here in January."

Keely swatted the hand away. "Point."

Together they continued through the hall, which emptied quickly as they progressed from the 100- and 200-level lecture halls into the more rarified air of the 500-level seminar rooms.

Fifth form students had fair flexibility in their schedules, a quirk of the system NINA employed in its academic programs. All general requirements were completed by the end of the second form, while the courses the various occupational specialties demanded took most of third and fourth form. Fifth form, which was optional, allowed cadets to take courses that interested them.

"Where is everyone?" Keely asked. The hall was empty except for them.

"You expect a crowd? It's a pretty esoteric subject."

"Maybe."

"Oh, come on. It's "The Application of High-Energy Lasers for Space Exploration." I mean, I'm a physics and mathematics geek, I know why I'm taking it. You're hoping to get into space after your term of service is up. How many others would you expect?"

"Me."

They turned at the voice ahead of them.

"Hey, Dawan, what's up? I didn't know this was your thing."

Another fifth form cadet, Ryan Dawan emerged from the alcove that had hidden him. "Naah, but I heard the prof is hot, so I figured I'd check it out."

"Ryan, you're a swine." Keely slapped his arm, and Katy chuckled. He was a nice enough guy, and her friends thought he was cute, but she didn't feel anything particularly for him. Or against him. She wasn't into girls, either. It was a product of her non-traditional childhood, and not something she paid much attention to.

She was amused when her friends were ogling someone they found attractive, though. It wasn't all bad. She could at least appreciate their aesthetics. She simply didn't understand the life-or-death urgency they put into it.

"What? A guy can't look?" He turned to Katy. "So what's the deets, Katy?"

"Why do you think I know anything about her?"

"Because you know all the shit going down on campus."

It was true. Between her childhood shyness, which she'd battled to overcome with brilliant success, her cadet-cut brown hair, and her willowy beauty, Katy had found herself at the center of a great web of information. Need the name of the cute second form in Modern Tactics? Ask Katy. Which courses were easy A's? Ask Katy. Something new coming from the administration? Ask Katy.

She sighed.

"Dr. Lorelei Stewart. Double doctorate in both Plasma Physics and Atomic and Laser Physics. I heard she was let go from her last position and this is a temporary gig until she can get back into research."

"What was her last job?" Keely, fascinated despite herself, asked.

"Professor at one of the public tech universities in the People's Republic."

Dawan whistled. "And she was fired? Damn, I thought you had to be in the grave to get fired by the Republic, as long as you spout their bullshit."

"That was her problem. "Physics doesn't care about opinions, viewpoints, or political correctness. It's a fact, or it isn't. Period." That's what she's supposed to have said to the board when they were questioning her about something she taught."

"My kinda prof," Keely said, and Katy nodded. Keeping her opinions to herself had never been her strong suit. She blamed her parents.

"Hey Katy, I didn't get to tell you before the term ended. Nice play in the fourth quarter."

She blushed but bit back the automatic denial. It *had* been a nice play, dammit.

Thanks to the unusual circumstances of her childhood, her willowy appearance was deceptive. That seemingly fragile beauty concealed a wiry, muscular frame, which meant she was much stronger, and faster, than most other women her size. So much so that she'd been persuaded in her first form to try out for the Academy football team, making it as a cornerback. Her speed and quickness—and don't ever let anyone tell you they're the same thing, because they totally weren't—made her a natural defender.

She might have been the lightest player on the team, but no wideout overlooked her abilities to get between them and the ball. During the playoffs last month, she'd been key to their semi-final victory, picking off a pass and returning it for a pick-six. Only a dirty play in the second quarter of the championship game, giving her a concussion and forcing her out kept her from repeating her heroics.

"Thanks."

Now three strong, they walked abreast the last yards to the seminar room.

Dawan held the door open. Keely batted her eyes at him, adding a Don't Screw With Me smile for good measure, while Katy didn't give him that much. They passed into the dimly lit room.

"Glad to see I have a class to teach."

The voice was deep and throaty, and Katy's breath hitched as it resonated through her mind and then lower.

*Whoa.*

Katy couldn't see the speaker as her eyes adjusted, but it seemed to come from... She squinted.

"Come on, sit down. Lots of space, so I'm not letting you get away with hiding in the back."

A figure was seated at a desk to the right of the podium, but that couldn't be the professor. Keely reached the same conclusion.

"Is that Dr. Stewart's kid? What's she doing here? Where's the professor?"

Katy shrugged, but before she could answer, the figure said, "I am Dr. Stewart, and I can't help my height."

"Oh, shit." Keely's words echoed Katy's thoughts.

*She's your professor, dummy! Not another cadet!*

"Nice move, Keels," Dawan muttered. Louder, he said, "I think I have the wrong class. I'll go to the registrar and straighten it out." Without waiting for an answer, he turned and marched out of the class.

"Now then, if we're done?" The figure did something, and the lights came up. Katy didn't quite gasp.

Dr. Stewart was short, yes, but muscular and perfectly proportioned, with olive-tinted espresso skin. Her dark, curly hair barely came to her shoulders, but it was her eyes that Katy was drawn to. They sparkled with intelligence and humor, as if in recognition of the unusual circumstances and relishing every second. Katy dropped into a chair without realizing she'd done so, and Dr. Stewart suppressed a smile.

"Two students. Well, better than my last class." She stood and walked behind the podium. "Attendance won't take long, and I'll certainly know if either of you skip class." She glanced at the lectern. "Shae, Keely?"

"Here." Dr. Stewart nodded in Keely's direction, as if noting her appearance.

"That makes you Montgomerie, KR. No initials, just KR?"

Katy flushed, her momentary trance broken. The story behind her name wasn't one she was comfortable sharing, even in such limited circumstances. "I go by Katy, professor."

"You can explain it to me after class." She made a note, and Keely reached over to squeeze Katy's hand in sympathy. "Now. I'd like to think I'm not an ogre, so I prefer to be called Lorelei. If you're feeling formal, you can call me professor. I've earned that, despite what the boobs in the Republic think."

Keely shot Katy a glance, as if saying, *How did you know?*

Dr. Stewart, Lorelei, ignored the exchange. "I'd like to get to know you two better and get a feel for your background. This is a 500 level course, so I'm hoping you haven't drifted in here accidentally, but if there are aspects of your education which might give you issues, it's best to identify them now. Keely, we'll start with you."

"... TODAY'S LECTURE. YOUR assignments are available on the Academy server, and I expect you to complete them on time. I don't accept assignments after the deadline without explanation." Lorelei looked at the clock. "Fifteen minutes early. That won't happen often. Keely, you're free to go. Ms. Montgomerie, come with me."

She'd used Katy's surname the entire class, hammering home her point about her initials. She wasn't trying to be evasive, but her initials were part of her tangled history, and she barely spoke of it to her closest friends. How much less interested was she in telling a professor she'd known for two hours?

Then again, there was something about Lorelei...

The first lecture had been amazing. Katy signed up because, as she said, she was a math and physics geek. But Lorelei brought a passion to the subjects which floored her. If she wasn't in the command track at the Academy, she would have jumped at the chance to follow Lorelei wherever she went, as long as she kept weaving her magic.

With a sympathetic glance, Keely made her escape. Katy fell in behind Lorelei as they left the room.

"You can walk next to me, Ms. Montgomerie." Lorelei's tone was amused, with a hint of Don't Make Me Repeat Myself, and Katy lengthened her stride to catch up.

"Your background is quite impressive. I hadn't realized the Academy had such a robust physics department."

"The Imperium Navy is serious about their officers gaining a solid understanding of their fields, ma'am."

Lorelei laughed, a robust thing. "Don't call me ma'am, either. I can't be over fifteen years older than you. Tops. You're a fifth form, so you're twenty-two?"

"Twenty-six, ma—Lorelei."

That earned her a look which promised questions, but all Lorelei said was, "Hmm."

The rest of the walk was done in silence. Lorelei's office wasn't particularly well-placed, as could be expected for an instructor who would likely only hold a temporary position. But it was quiet, and comfortable, bearing the evidence of her touch in the furnishings. Multiple workstations dominated one side of the room, while reference texts filled a bookcase on the opposite wall. They were genuine books, not electronic versions, and Katy blinked.

"I prefer them to e-texts. Sit, please." Lorelei gestured to the armchair before her desk, settling into her seat behind it. "Now, please. An explanation?"

Katy sighed. It shouldn't be difficult. She'd been telling people for years, and this was one professor. At least it wasn't public.

"I was born intersex." Katy peered at Lorelei, watching for any of the usual reactions, but didn't see any. "My parents were really old-fashioned and refused to be told my sex before I was born. All they cared about was whether I was healthy."

Lorelei nodded, still not saying anything.

"Since they didn't know, they had two names ready for me. If I was a boy, I would be Richard, and if I was a girl, Katherine. When they found out from the doctor, they had a dilemma. Instead of giving me either of the names, they gave me the initials KR, and called me Kiri."

"Very forward-thinking of them."

Katy's laugh was bitter. "It was a pain in the ass. Do you know what it's like to learn you're different from the other kids in a way you can't understand, much less explain?"

Lorelei gestured at her diminutive self. "I was this tall in fifth grade."

Katy waggled her hand in a so-so gesture. "But there were always short kids, and being short was pretty normal, right? Intersex wasn't. I had so much trouble the first couple years of school. The girls didn't accept me, and the boys picked on me."

"That must have been painful. How did it stop?"

"My dad moved for a job, and I transferred schools. I was seven. Over the summer, as they planned the move, we talked about who I wanted to present as."

Lorelei winced. "It doesn't seem fair."

"No, but my parents were doing their best. They included me, and listened to what I wanted. By the time we moved, I'd decided I felt more feminine, more connection to the girls I'd known. They hadn't accepted me for who I was, but at least they weren't mean about it. When we got to the new town, I was introduced as Katy, and KR was just a blip on the birth certificate."

"I see why you didn't want to discuss this in class. Is Keely...?"

"She's one of my best friends and knows the story. I'm just—it's sensitive." Katy steeled herself. She didn't need to say anything else, but her tale wasn't finished, and she hated leaving anything for later. "I took testosterone suppressors and estrogen and progesterone enhancers through my teenage years. After graduation and my eighteenth birthday, I had gender affirmation surgery."

"Is that why you're older than the other cadets?"

Katy nodded. "I was accepted to NINA in high school, but deferred it until after all the surgeries were complete and my body fully adjusted to its new reality. It took four years, which was a little surprising, but it gave me a chance to grow up and get some real-world experiences. I also took some extension courses, nothing for credit, just fun."

"Ah, that explains your advanced standing in the physics classes."

"Yes, prof—Lorelei." Katy dropped her eyes, then raised them again. "Are we good?"

"Yes. Thank you, Katy, for taking the time to explain. I appreciate it."

Katy stood to go but stopped when Lorelei cleared her throat.

"One last question?"

"Yes?"

"Does anyone still call you Kiri? It's a pretty name."

Pretty? Did she just say her childhood name was pretty?

"Just my little brother. And one person I dated."

"Was it serious?"

"I thought so, and it was, for a time, but I'm sure you know how those things go."

Lorelei made another note, which Katy hardly noticed. Pretty?

"Thank you for your time. See you next week."

Pretty?

"REALLY? SHE SAID YOUR name was pretty?"

Katy nodded, chewing on a mouthful of salad.

"How do you feel about it?" Katy's dinner companion was her other best friend, a fellow fifth form, Jennifer Martinez.

"Weird, Alley. Definitely weird. I mean, she's my instructor." Everyone called her Alley, from her middle name, Allison.

"It's not like she called *you* pretty." Alley and Katy turned their attention to Keely. "What? I'm just saying it's an innocent comment. Like saying a flower is pretty, or a sunset. Your name isn't you, after all."

Alley waved a fork at Katy. "Definitely something to consider. She might be nervous about having such a limited class and wanted to make small talk to put herself at ease, especially after you nuked her from orbit with your childhood story."

Katy winced. "You think it was too much?"

"Maybe. I mean, you're very open and relaxed about your history, and the Goddess knows Keels and I don't care, but yeah. It might be a little much if you're a new instructor asking about a name."

"Shit."

Keely rubbed her forearm sympathetically. "Don't worry, Katy. It's not so bad. I mean, she didn't run away screaming, right?"

"It was her office, Keels. Besides, I don't want to date her." She didn't. Just because she saw Lorelei's smile in her daydreams didn't mean she wanted to go out with her. Right?

Alley and Keely shared a glance, then Alley whispered, "Nobody said anything about dating her."

"Neither did I!"

Dinner fell into an awkward silence, but they'd been friends for nearly five years. No silence could last terribly long.

But it gave Katy something *else* to think about.

""CAN YOU DESCRIBE THE relationship between thrust and payload, as it relates to using photonic rather than chemical propellant?"" mocked Keely as they returned to the busier area of the building. "No, I can't. That's why I'm taking this class!"

Katy chuckled. "I know you didn't expect it to be easy."

"No, but it's only the second week!"

"And it was in the assignment she gave us for this week."

"… It was?"

"The one I asked you about yesterday, and you said you'd finished?"

"No, no, I told you I was done with it." To Katy's quizzical expression, Keely explained. "I might have gotten so frustrated that I threw my terminal against the wall and spent the rest of the night putting it back in working order. Not saying I did, just I *might* have."

"Keels, you know you can come to me for help, or send Lorelei a message."

"Oh, she's "Lorelei" now?"

"Knock it off, Keels. She told us to call her that the first day."

"Which you refused to do. I remember, all class long, you called her professor. Now she's Lorelei?"

"You're making too big a deal out of nothing."

"Am I?"

"Yes." Katy's voice made it clear she didn't want to discuss it further, so Keely let it drop. At least, for now. There'd be enough time to tease Katy later.

"Fine. I need your help."

Katy nodded. "After dinner?"

"Sure."

KATY SQUIRMED IN THE comfortable chair. Instead of announcing grades and moving on, Lorelei forced her students to make appointments to review their work during office hours. It made her nervous, considering none of her other professors did this.

And not simply because she was unsure of the conclusions she drew. Had she been obvious about her attention being more than just the subject matter? Did–

"Katy, can you explain the answer you gave for equation twelve point three?" Lorelei looked up from the screen. Katy, caught examining Lorelei's expressive face, quickly ducked her head to her tablet.

"Twelve point three?" She called it up, trying to remember her thinking from when she was doing the work six days earlier. "Oh. It seemed like there were some unfounded assumptions in the establishing equations. I dug into it, researched it based on what I could discover, and calculated from there."

"And what made you think there were unfounded assumptions?" Lorelei's voice wasn't harsh, quite, but it wasn't the understanding professor she presented in class.

Katy shot back. "They gave unrealistic results when you left them in place. The thrust that these imaginary photonic boosters produce? It was exaggerated by two orders of magnitude!"

"Because it's a design I'm working on that hasn't gone public!" Lorelei exclaimed, then clapped a hand over her mouth. "Forget I said that."

"You're using us to check your theories?" Katy was incredulous. Using students for research assistance was common, especially in post-graduate studies, but doing so without their knowledge was an ethical violation.

"No." Was there a hint of something unsaid? Katy didn't wait for more.

"It seems like it." Katy was always decisive. It was a trait which served her well on the field, never hesitating to break on the ball or cut the angle to intercept a player. Now she made another decision. "I'm going to the Dean."

"Wait. Let me explain, and you'll see it's not how it looks."

"You can explain it to her." Katy strode from the room, ignoring Lorelei's sigh of distress.

"YOU'RE KIDDING!"

Katy shook her head in dismay.

"I wish."

"Jesus! Katy-bird, what are you gonna do?"

"I don't know. Really," she said in reaction to Keely's stare.

"It's a slam-dunk! She's using us for research without our consent. That's totally bogus!"

Keely's old-fashioned phrase pulled an unwilling smile from Katy, but it faded instantly.

"If I go to the Dean, she'll get fired."

"That is so not your problem!" Keely examined Katy's face. "You think it is? You don't want to get her fired?"

"I—well, no."

"Why not? Just because you opened up to her about your name?"

"No, of course not!"

"Then what?"

It was time for evasive maneuvers. "If she gets fired from here, her career will be over. I don't want that on my head, especially if it was an honest mistake."

Keely sighed and shrugged. "You're too soft, Katy. But if you won't say anything, I won't either."

"Thank you."

Katy couldn't pinpoint why she was reluctant to follow up on the violation. Was it her sense of fair play? What she said to Keely was true. The accusation of ethics violations in research would probably be enough to end any hope she had of remaining in academia. If she planned on moving to private research, it wouldn't be as devastating with the right employer. It would limit her choices, though.

So what?

*Katherine Elizabeth. Keely's right. You're soft.*

Telling herself didn't change her mind.

EVEN IN THE TUNNELS which connected the buildings of NINA together, it was possible to hear the howling winds of the late February storm.

Howling winds couldn't drown out their conversation.

"I'm thinking of dropping Lorelei's class."

That did it. Keely halted, forcing Katy to a standstill as well.

"What are you talking about? You love this stuff, and you're so good at it! Is it the research question?"

"No! No," she repeated, with less emphasis. "I think you're right. It was an honest mistake. I just—" She didn't know how to express her feelings, but she knew Keely wouldn't let her off the hook. "It feels silly. I don't need the credits, and what am I gonna do with it?"

"Tell me another one, Katy! What's the real reason?"

"Really, Keely." She'd be damned if she told Keely before she admitted anything to herself.

"Fine, whatever, but if you drop, I drop. I won't be her sole target when she asks one of her impossible questions." She smiled malevolently. "If you're really my friend, you won't do that to me."

"That's not fair! I've had your back for five years now!"

"Never said it was." Keely resumed walking. With a frustrated growl, Katy followed.

"Keels...!"

"Not listening to anything except you saying you're sorry and not dropping the class."

"You play dirty, Keels."

Keely pivoted on a heel and took two fast steps back to Katy.

"I'm not going to let you do something stupid because you're all conflicted about whatever you won't talk to me about!"

"Jesus, Keels."

"Don't pull your mystery sky father crap on me, Katy." Keely's tone softened to something just barely audible. "Talk to me, Katy-bird. It's me, Keely, remember? The one you went to for advice before your first date with Drew?"

"It's not like that!"

"Feels like it to me. Look me in the eye and tell me you aren't attracted to her. Go ahead. I'm waiting." The seconds ticked by, wind whining through the permacrete walls.

At length, Katy mumbled something which might have been *"maybe a little."*

Keely resisted the impulse to tease her friend. "What are you going to do about it?"

An incoherent mutter and a shrug were all Katy could manage.

"You want to try again?"

"She's a professor!"

Keely shrugged, and Katy was momentarily annoyed with her friend. After all, it wasn't her love life on the line.

"And I don't even know if she's into women. God, how do I ask that? Excuse me, professor, but who do you prefer, men, women, both? I can't even think of a subtle way to ask!" Katy covered her face in her hands.

"Screw that. If she's not, you're no worse off."

"Dating a professor?"

"A temporary professor. She's only here this semester. I'm sure that makes a difference."

Katy's glare showed her skepticism, but Keely was undeterred.

"Knock it off. Your tough-girl act doesn't fly with me. Come on, Katy. Let's head to the caf, get some scones and coffee, and figure it out."

"You sure, Keels?" There was an undeniable note of hope in Katy's voice.

Keely linked her arm with Katy's. "Have I ever steered you wrong?"

"Lots."

"Not this time. I promise."

*HOW AM I SUPPOSED TO do this?* Katy thought. *Sure, talking about it with Keely was so easy. Ask her out, nothing romantic, just coffee to discuss her secret project. Of course, we talked about it six weeks ago, and I haven't done shit with it since, but the principle's sound.*

She sighed.

The way Keely laid it out that afternoon? It all made sense.

"If you're attracted to her, you have to know if it's her personality or just her body. Even I can admit she has a great ass," Keely had said. "That means one-on-one time where you can talk about things other than physics, which means out of the classroom and her office."

*Even if Keely was full of it about the asking out, she was right about her ass.*

"..."

"Excuse me, Katy? I didn't hear you."

Oh, shit. Did she actually say that? *Play dumb!*

"I'm sorry?"

Lorelei shook her head and turned back to the old-fashioned whiteboard she used instead of a portable screen.

Keely scribbled on her personal padd and turned it so Katy could see it.

*You have it bad.*

Katy rolled her eyes and returned to the lecture. Keely pulled the padd back, took a few notes, and then pushed it back for her to see.

*Today. You've stalled for weeks!*

It was less an ultimatum than a statement of fact. The fifth forms were scheduled for a final pre-graduation training cruise the first week of April, extending into May. Their graduation and swearing-in ceremony would take place a week later.

Damn. Katy risked a glare at Keely, but she was ostensibly focused on the equation Lorelei was writing on the board.

The rest of the period passed in a blur. All too soon, Keely was stuffing her padd into the ratty backpack she'd come to NINA with five years ago and bundling into her parka. It might be the end of March, but spring in Marquette always ran late.

"See you at dinner." She dropped the breezy farewell before heading out.

"Traitor." Her hiss didn't stop Keely, but it caught Lorelei's ear.

"Katy, did you need something?"

*Now or never.*

"I. Um. That is. I want to ask you if you wanted to, uh, have a coffee with me. To talk. About your project."

*You sound like a blithering teenager!*

Much to Katy's surprise, Lorelei didn't immediately refuse her.

"My project?" She projected innocence, but Katy knew it was an act.

"The one behind your equations that threw us off? I want to know more."

"Why?" Innocence was gone, replaced by suspicion. "To turn me in for ethics violations?"

Despite herself, Katy flushed. "No!"

"No, Ms. Montgomerie. I won't be taking coffee with you *or* discussing projects that don't officially exist. Now, I believe you have another class shortly?" She swept her belongings into a bag and stalked out the faculty exit.

"That went well. Damn." Katy froze momentarily, then jumped from her chair and followed, pushing through the door.

"Which way?" She recalled the location of Lorelei's office and turned right, hurrying. After several yards, she thought she heard footsteps ahead and risked calling, "Lorelei! Wait!"

The footfalls stopped, then redoubled.

*At least I know it's her.*

"Lorelei, please!"

This time there was no stop, just hesitation before that beautiful, husky voice called back to her. "Katy, you shouldn't be back here. Go to your class."

Katy didn't slow. "Two minutes. That's all I want."

The footsteps stopped again. Katy took that as a good sign and hurried. Coming around a corner, she noticed Lorelei barely in time to stop, but not soon enough to prevent running into her. She threw out her arms and caught the smaller woman as she tumbled, pulling her in.

"Shit, I'm sorry!" Katy blurted.

Lorelei didn't respond for a moment, recovering some measure of equilibrium. Only when an electric tingle started running from Katy's fingertips to her elbows did she release her hold.

"You have my attention." Lorelei didn't sound pissed. Instead, she almost sounded amused.

"Lorelei. I'm not good at this."

"Running people over isn't what you usually do? I caught your last game." One dark eyebrow arched, and Katy flushed.

*Settle down.*

"Not in corridors." Then what Lorelei said hit her. "You were at the championship?"

Lorelie nodded. "I was, and most of your home games, too. NINA was recruiting me, so invited me to several games during the year. You're a hell of a player."

*She watched me play?* Katy knew she was good, but she wasn't a headliner. Lorelei wasn't done yet.

"I was really impressed by your performance in the last game of the regular season. What was that, three passes defended and a pick, plus four solo tackles?" She whistled. "Damn impressive for someone who can't top one-forty."

"Th-thanks. You saw my games?"

"I did. Have you thought about going pro? After your service to NINA?"

"P-pro?" Katy couldn't believe where this discussion had gone.

"Sure. You've got the talent. In the championship, the pick you made in the first quarter was a thing of beauty. No wonder they cheap-shotted you out of the game."

This had to be a dream. Or a joke. Or maybe she slipped and fell and knocked herself out and was hallucinating.

*Stop it, Katy! Look at her. She's sincere, she cares, she's interested in you, so ask already.*

She pressed her lips together and drew in a cleansing breath. "Lorelei. I like you. I enjoy spending time with you in class, and I want to find out if maybe you do too. Outside of class, I mean. Not in class. Enjoy spending time with me, that is."

*Oh, Jesus. Babble much?*

Lorelei chuckled. "Are you asking me on a date, Katy?"

Cornered, Katy retreated to monosyllables. "Yes."

"You know I'm a professor. Not only a professor, but *your* professor. Dating you would cross all sorts of professional and ethical boundaries."

"Yes."

"And I'm only here for a few more weeks until the semester ends."

Katy didn't know this. "You're leaving?"

Lorelei nodded. "This was only ever temporary."

One word. That's all it took for Katy's half-imagined visions of the future crumbled, dissolving into so much technicolor rubble, and she gave a sad nod. "I'm sorry to have troubled you."

She turned to go. A warm hand reached out and pressed against her arm.

"I can't date a student, and certainly not one of my students."

Katy nodded again without turning.

"But in May, I won't be your professor, and you won't be a student."

*What?* This was an angle she hadn't considered.

Lorelei, as if unaware of the wash of hope that swept through Katy, continued. "If you can wait until then? I'd love to go out with you."

Katy slowly spun, hardly believing her ears.

"R-really?"

"Really." Lorelei shook her head. "I know it's terrible of me, but something about you has pulled at me all semester. No, earlier. Seeing you move during the games, your grace and fierceness combined into one alluring package. I'm glad it wasn't one-sided."

Katy beamed. "Not at all one-sided."

They both fell silent. It was at least a minute before Lorelei remembered her hand on Katy's arm and pulled it away. Katy felt the loss immediately.

"So."

"So." Lorelei looked down at her feet, then back into Katy's eyes. "Can you wait that long?"

"I've been fighting this since January. A few more weeks? I can be patient."

Lorelei chuckled, a sound Katy instantly fell in love with. "You youngsters don't know anything about patience."

"Hey, I'm not that young, remember? I'm twenty-seven now."

"Less than ten years younger." Katy wasn't sure she was supposed to hear that. "Huh. At least I'm not robbing the cradle."

"Not at all."

Lorelei nodded sharply, breaking the spell. "Very good. I'll see you in the next class." She started away.

"Lorelei?"

She looked over her shoulder at Katy. "Hmm?"

"I'd like it if you called me Kiri."

Lorelei's smile was brilliant. "I will... Kiri."

# A Word from the Author – Adam Gaffen

Here we are again! Another anthology call from AC, and I trot out another story from my Cassidyverse.

This time, I got to dive into the backstory of a pair of secondary characters who, honestly, don't get much page time, which I probably ought to correct one of these years. Okay, I have to give you some backstory here so you have context.

My main character through most of the books is Kendra Cassidy, and she's determined to pull humanity into space; specifically, to the stars. In the process, she ends up irritating the Solarian Union and has to fight them off, leading her to create a navy. But she's a retired actress and assassin (don't ask), and doesn't know the first thing about military protocol. When the best commander for a new starship is Kiri, and the best available engineer is her wife, Lorelei, Kendra doesn't blink. She makes it happen, protocol be damned.

For this anthology, I thought it would be fun to go back and find out how they started. It's mentioned, briefly, when I introduced Kiri, but there's nothing like the detail you get here.

My playlist is pretty short.

Hot for Teacher by Van Halen

The Art Teacher by Rufus Wainwright

Thank you for reading my story. It's a privilege to spend my days creating for you, and something I hope never to stop appreciating. My wife, Michaela, is the most encouraging and supportive person

I've ever had in my life, and that's only the beginning of the marvel which is her. AC and Nat, my co-editors, who have taken on more and more with this anthology. And once again—thank *you*.

To learn more about the Cassidyverse, go to my website, https://cassidychronicles.com, and check it out!

# Kissing the Boss

## By Madilynn Dale

I rest my chin on my hand as I watch Professor Montgomery prattle on. He stands before a giant white board with a pointer, and the red letters blur into nothingness. Physics is not my cup of tea, but I try my best to take it all in. I don't know if it's the dark classroom and its wooden tables, or that the classroom is in the basement, but I'm always tired during this class.

My reader calls to me, daring me to pull it from the bag and dive into one of my romances. It's not like anything the Professor says won't be in the powerpoint he emails after each class, so why shouldn't I have some fun? A little escapist fantasy can't hurt, right? I can almost see the cover of the latest book. "The Boss's Lips." Yummy.

A soft buzz reaches my ears from the black bag resting at my feet. It's my cell phone, but is it a call or a text? It doesn't buzz again. It's not a call, but who texted me?

I discreetly lean down and dig it out. Glancing at the screen, I see the message is from my newest coworker. Greta already has a bad habit of getting on my nerves. It's never good when she reaches out.

**Greta: Hey Cindy I can't work tonight and need someone to cover my shift. Can you do it? It's the 5 p.m.-close shift.**

I frown, trying to recall which assignments I have due tomorrow. I was hired to work part time, but she's called in a lot lately and I've been pushed into full time. It's getting annoying, but having the extra cash has been nice. Broke college kid, after all.

**Me: I'll cover tonight but this needs to stop. You're making this a habit. I can't always cover for you.**

**Greta: I know, I'm sorry, I promise I'll make it up to you.**

I roll my eyes. She always says that but I've yet to see anything other than her usual, which is doing as little as she can while on the clock and still make bank in tips.

**Me: You better. I'm tired of covering for you.**

I slide my phone into my bag and resume watching my professor. It seems I didn't miss much while messaging. I believe this class is going to be my death.

As time goes on, I let my gaze wander around the room and tap my pen. I try not to look around too much since this class is with an ex-boyfriend, but I can't help it. Thoughts of what I need to do before work and who is working tonight drift through my head. I hope my favorite people are there. It makes things so much easier when they are, especially if *he* is there.

I blink as Professor Montgomery passes out small booklets for us to work on for the next week. Yay for Physics problems! He dismisses us as the papers reach my row. I grab mine and pass it on before standing. The papers slide into my bag and I tense as someone stops at the edge of my table. I glance up and frown.

"Can I help you, Andrew?" I sling my bag over my shoulder.

"Can I buy you a coffee? I'd really like to sit down and talk about what happened between us. I think we can make things work." He picks at the strap on his bag and follows me as I head toward the door.

"No, I don't have time. I've got work later and I need to get some homework done before then."

"You could do that while we talk. I don't want you to give up on us yet. I love you." He stays at my side.

I sigh in frustration. "No. You know I can't focus on my work if someone's chatting with me."

"Just give me a chance to do things right this time, Cindy." He grabs my arm, forcing me to face him at the base of the stairs. "I was going to propose to you before we broke things off. I want to spend the rest of my life with you."

I grit my teeth, purse my lips, and glare. "Is that supposed to make me take you back or something? I said no. You know what you did to make me unhappy. Relationships don't work that way."

He gapes for a second before forcing his jaw closed. His hand tightens on me. "It'll be different this time. I promise. You can do whatever you want, within reason. I'll even let you go out with the girls."

I yank out of his grasp and wipe at my shoulder nonchalantly. "Conditions, Andrew? This was about more than letting me hang out with my friends. You controlled everything I did. Do you know the worst part? I let you. I was blind, but not anymore."

"Please Cindy. Don't do this to us."

I roll my eyes as I turn away from him and move up the stairs. I don't wait to hear if he has anything else to add. This conversation is over, and I've got shit to do. I refuse to go back to the past. I deserve to be happy and I'll be damned if I let another man, no. He wasn't a man, just a boy in a man's skin. But nobody will control me like he did.

HOURS LATER, AFTER stopping by my apartment to change and switch gears for work, I park in the small lot behind the old diner. My car door creaks as I get out and I glance around. The diner here caught my eye as I was exploring the area near the school with its retro 60's style décor and easy-going environment. It reminded me of listening to my grandparents' cassette tapes as kid when they raved how amazing *Elvis Presley* was. Although he's not plastered all over the walls, the comfortable atmosphere takes me back to a less stressful time in my life.

Slipping through the back door, I clock in. I'm a bit early, but I've always said, "If you're early, you're on time and if you're on time, you're late." Tucking my purse in the bottom cubby of the shelf system, I slip into my apron and head through the back of the kitchen. I stop in my tracks and fumble with my apron as the door closes behind me.

He's here. The boss. Not Adam, the manager, but the big boss. Holy fuck.

He's leaned over, focusing on a ticket hanging above the grill. He's calm yet intense, and something about his face makes me blush. Oh, to have him look at me with that intensity. A woman can dream, right?

I try to spin on my heel to give myself a minute and check my makeup, but his words jerk me to a halt. "Hey Pancake, I didn't know you were working tonight."

I slowly turn to face him and take in his gorgeous smile. His blue eyes dance with mirth behind the glasses that sit slightly crooked on his face. His dirty blonde hair is styled perfectly as usual, and his slim build shows off his toned muscles.

"Hey Ethan. Yeah, Greta messaged me." I shrug and return to fighting with my apron.

"Huh. She didn't let any of us know. Maybe she messaged Adam. He had a family emergency to take care of. Do you need help with that?" He moves toward me, but stops as I hold my hands up.

"Nope, got it. So, has it been busy tonight?"

He shrugs as he moves back to the black flat top grill where a couple of burger patties sizzle. "No, steady. I'm hoping it'll pick up more later. You know how it gets toward the holidays."

He flips the patties and his face drops into a slight frown. Business is much slower during the holidays and it affects us all. I lean against the doorjamb and glance at the small dining room. The walls are covered in old photos of celebrities above the booths, and a couple of red topped tables cover the middle of the black-and-white checkered floor. The counter where our waitress items are is red.

Lucy, another server and a few years older than me, stands chatting with one of the few occupied tables. It's our regular Wednesday night couple who come in for burger combos and dessert. They're such a lovely pair.

I wash my hands and gather my thoughts as I enter work mode, turning my attention back to Ethan as he's plating the food. "Yeah, the holidays are no good for business. Does that mean we'll get out of here quickly tonight? Since it's been slower?"

"It's me, so you know that answer. Hot food!"

I laugh and grab the food from him. He's cleaning the prep area as I move off. Any time he closes our diner, we finish quick. It's like he brings in a new energy when he's here. It's refreshing.

"Hey, Anita and Carl, here's your food." I smile as I place the baskets in front of the older couple. They've been eating here since the restaurant opened.

"Oh, thank you dear, we were just catching up with Lucy here. How's school?" Anita picks up a knife and slices her burger in half.

"Busy, thanks for asking. Are you guys ready for the holidays?"

Carl clears his throat. "I think we are. Anita had all the shopping for the grandkids finished last month."

Anita sets her burger down and looks at Carl affectionately. "That's right. Not that you know what any of it is, but we're ready to see them all."

"That's great. Well, you guys enjoy. Let us know if you need anything."

"Thank you dear, you know we will." Anita chuckles as she returns to her burger.

I smile and turn to Lucy as we walk away from the table. "Anything we need to do at the moment?"

Lucy shakes her head. "Everything is filled and ready to go. Let's hope we get a bigger rush than last week. I'll grab what's in the tip bucket so we can split from here on out. Greta messaged you?"

"Yeah. She's going to lose her job if she keeps this up, like the last waitress who called in all the time."

Lucy sighs. "I knew she wasn't ready for a job from the day she started. Not many sixteen-year-olds are. Did Ethan know she wasn't coming in?"

"Nope. He didn't say much about it. I'm glad we're working with him tonight. We won't be here until midnight scrubbing up."

"Same. I overheard him on the phone. He mentioned he would be here more often." Lucy grabs the container of silverware, and we start rolling.

"Oh? That would be interesting."

She shrugs. "It pays to ear hustle."

I laugh, knowing I'm as bad. In fact, Ethan now walks outside if he can when I'm working with him. It's not like I purposely hover to hear what he's saying, but something about him seems to pull me in.

We spend the rest of the evening taking care of customers and cleaning. A small rush comes around seven, but it doesn't last long. It leaves me feeling energized, or maybe it was the couple of cups of coffee I had during the evening?

When the last customer walks out—after closing, because we aren't the kind of place to kick people out before they finish eating—Ethan locks the door. One thing I love the most when he closes is that he hooks his Bluetooth to the fancy jukebox and cranks the music.

I smile as one of my favorite pop songs blares through the speakers. He meets my eyes briefly before moving to the counter. It's paperwork time for him while the rest of us clean the diner from top to bottom.

I grab a broom and sweep under tables as Lucy follows behind with a mop. Lucy clears her throat and I glance at her. "How long have you had a crush on the boss man?"

I blush. "Who said I had a crush on him?"

She lifts a brow and cocks a hip to the side. "It's pretty obvious, dear."

I purse my lips. "You think he knows?"

"He looks at you the same way you look at him."

"No, he doesn't." I glance across the room at Ethan. "There's no way."

"Girl, everyone who works with us sees it. How do you not?"

"Well, he hasn't said anything." I turn back to my broom and try to drop the subject.

"Well, maybe you should? I mean, maybe it has something to do with the fact that he's our boss? I don't know what the rules are with that type of thing, but there's probably a way around it." Lucy shrugs and begins scrubbing again.

"I guess you're right, but I don't want to just say, hey I like you. How dumb does that sound? Plus, what if he doesn't like me like that?" I know we flirt often, but butterflies dance in my stomach as I think about talking with Ethan about this thing.

"I think you should give it a shot. The worst thing he could say is he's not interested, and you can keep on keeping on like you've been doing." She smiles and finishes scrubbing the floor.

We do a final run-through and double-check everything a couple of minutes later.

"Alright everyone, I'm done. Where are you on your tasks?" Ethan closes the drawer to the cash register.

"We're done up here." Lucy responds cheerily and elbows me playfully. I nod in agreement.

"What about the back?" Ethan turns and peers through the door to the kitchen.

I admire his physique as he leans through the door. I love how his jeans hug his hips and I even notice the tattoo peeking out from his shirt as it rides up in the back.

"Okay, everyone is finished. Let's grab our things and get out of here." He spins around and meets my gaze.

I flush as he grins. I've been caught.

"Everyone out the front. Once we're all out, close the door so I can set the alarm." His voice is more energetic than it was at the start of my shift.

We file out the door and wait for Ethan to finish up. We stay close together, because the lighting behind the diner is terrible and if you don't park close to the buildings, it's pitch black. The city has yet to change it.

Finally, he slips out the door and double checks the lock. "Alright, everyone's free to go!"

The cooks cheer and rush around the side of the building. I laugh loudly as they do, and Lucy twirls away. She'll always be young at heart.

"What are you doing the rest of the evening, Ethan?" It took all my courage, but I ask and lock eyes with him.

He shrugs. "I don't know really, hadn't thought about it. I guess go home, make a drink, and chill. What about you? Any homework to catch up on?"

"Probably. Not that I want to do it. Physics is going to be the death of me this semester."

He laughs. "I bet you can handle it. What's so difficult about it?"

I roll my eyes. "All of it. I'm not a math kind of girl. Give me books and I'm good to go, but math problems? Nope."

"That's funny. I'm the opposite. I like books. I just don't have a lot of time to read with how much I work." He smiles and we stop next to his car.

I glance around and realize that I parked close to him. "What's the last book you read?"

He pauses and leans against the front of his Camaro. "I think it was horror? It's been so long, it's hard to recall."

"I have to be in the mood to read horror. I've got a vivid imagination, so those become too realistic for me. Then I have nightmares that don't go away for weeks."

"Wow, that's crazy."

I shake my head. "Sometimes they aren't fun."

"What do you do to make them go away?" He frowns. I move closer to lean against his car.

"Well, I try to get lost in another book to put my brain in a different space, but it doesn't always work." I shrug and he offers me a smile.

"You can text me next time. Maybe we can talk, and you can move past whatever freaked you out?" He leans further into his car and stretches his arms.

"Do you really want me to do something like that? It could be like 4 a.m. when I text you. Wouldn't that mess you up for the following workday?" I tilt my head sideways, thinking of the last time I stayed up so late reading.

"Nah, it would be okay. You're fun to chat with." He pushes off his car. "Shouldn't you be heading out to do some homework soon, though?"

I shrug. "Why? Am I bothering you?"

He shakes his head. "No, just checking to see if you're comfortable hanging out with me in the middle of a parking lot at night. Not that I would ever do anything to you."

I blush at his words and glance around us. Sure enough, only my compact car and his remain in the lot. The surrounding air is cool and I glance up at the few stars I can see past all the lights. It gives me a moment to gather myself.

"The stars are pretty, from what I can see of them." His words are soft, and I glance from the sky to his face.

"They are. What have you got going on this week? Any plans for the weekend, maybe with a girlfriend?" I smile, pretending to be chill as I fish for information. Should I tell him how I feel? Would that be weird? Lucy said I should go for it.

He leans back into his car, getting comfortable again. A smirk rests on his face. "Not a lot, really. I moved into a new house in Lotta, and I'm still working on getting things unpacked."

"You drive here from Lotta? That's almost an hour's drive! How do you manage it?"

He shrugs, and his smirk stays. "It is what it is. With the way I drive, it's honestly not that long. I've had to drive longer to work before. It's part of what I do."

I reach up and twirl my hair around a finger. "Doesn't that ever get tiring? What does your girlfriend think?"

"You're pretty curious about this mysterious girlfriend, aren't you?" His question startles me, and I blush as I continue playing with my hair.

"Do you blame me? I don't want someone threatening me for talking to you alone. She could think you're being unfaithful."

He laughs and shakes his head. "I don't have a girlfriend to be concerned about. I haven't quite found someone I connect with. I mean, there are a few maybes, but I don't know if they feel the same way, and there are other complications."

I drop my hand from my hair and arch my brow. "What do you mean by complications?"

He lets out a deep sigh. "It's difficult when you're in my position. If you find someone you like, but they work under you? You have to go about it a certain way. For one, the company typically doesn't like those individuals to work with each other. Also, people think I have a ton of money with my position, so I have to weed out gold diggers as well. I blame my car."

I chuckle, cross my arms, and rest a fist under my chin, stealing a moment to think over his words. "So, if someone, like, I dunno. Let's say like me, right? So if I liked you and wanted to date you, we wouldn't be able to work together?"

He tilts his head and looks at me curiously. "That's correct."

"Would it be hard to see you if, say, that situation happened?"

He purses his lips and eyes me for a moment. "I doubt it. Why do you ask?"

I glance down at my feet and make circles with my foot in the dirt on the pavement. I remain quiet for a moment as I search for the confidence to confess my feelings. If I do this? There's no turning back. If he doesn't feel the same, well, I'll figure it out from there.

"Cindy, why do you ask?" Ethan rests a hand on my shoulder, pulling my attention away from my foot. I look from the ground to his hand, then follow his arm with my eyes until I meet his gaze. I gulp and ignore the buzzing in my stomach.

"Well, um." I take a deep breath and let it out slowly. "I like you."

His eyes widen at my words, but his hand stays on my shoulder. He stares at me and neither of us moves. It's as if time has frozen.

"You do?" His words are raspy.

I nod and his face breaks into a huge smile. He drops his hand and pulls me into a hug. He rests his chin on top of my head as he says, "I like you, too."

"You do?" I'm astonished he feels that way. I feared this would be one-sided.

"Yes. How could I not? You're beautiful and kind, smart and hardworking. We connect in a way I've only found a couple of times before. Of course, I like you."

I step out of his arms and meet his gaze again, struggling to process what he said. I know we've worked together for some time, but wow. How does he already know that much about me? "You like me, like me?"

"I do. I know that'll make the work stuff complicated, but we'll figure it out as we go. I'm only at this store temporarily, so that'll make it easier. If we date, I have to let the upper bosses know. I hope you're comfortable with it, but there's no getting around that if we pursue a relationship."

I gulp, thinking of all the things he mentioned earlier. "You'll have to go to a different store and not work here again?"

He nods. "Yes, but if we're dating, you'll see me plenty. Speaking of which, do you want to go on one this weekend?"

I smile and excitement courses through me. "I would love to. What are we going to do?"

He scratches his head as he ponders for a few minutes. "How about we grab some coffee and walk around the mall? Or we could grab dinner or something? What do you want to do?"

I laugh. "You're asking me on the date here. All those ideas sound good. I can always go for a coffee, so let's do the mall and coffee thing."

He pulls me back into a hug and chuckles. "In that case, it's a date. We better get out of here before it gets too much later. After all, you still have class tomorrow."

I roll my eyes. "I'll text you later. Have a good night, Ethan."

He releases me from the hug and meets my gaze. "You too, Cindy."

I SPENT EXTRA TIME fixing my hair and makeup this morning. I know he's seen me with little makeup at work this summer, but going on a date is different. I want to look good, and it helped distract me from the cartwheels happening in my stomach.

The mall is busy when I arrive to meet Ethan. I smile as if I won a trophy as I make my way to the small coffee shop we agreed on, fidgeting with a strand of hair. People move in and out of stores with shopping bags and I pass a few groups of teenagers chatting and giggling. It's such a weird thing to me, since I grew up in the country and the closest mall was two hours away. It adds another bit of nerves on top of what I already feel, and I focus on my breathing to calm them as I near the coffee shop.

The café and coffee bar stands out from the other shops with its brown tones and heavy scent of fresh-brewed coffee. Small tables are scattered away from the bar, and a few comfy chairs are positioned around coffee tables. Calm music reaches my ears and seems to help.

I spot him before he sees me and can't help but scan him up and down. This is the first time I've seen him out of work clothes. While he still wears jeans, these appear nicer, and he has on a clean shirt. His hair is styled as it usually is, but his posture appears more relaxed. Will he be as chatty as he was after work the other night? I know he's easy to text with, but face to face is always different and this is not a platonic thing anymore. We're actually going for it.

I hope.

I make my way toward the table he's at, and his face breaks into a glorious smile as his eyes meet mine. "You made it! Did you have trouble parking?"

I nod lightly and he offers me the chair opposite of him. A cup of coffee rests on the table in front of it.

"Yeah, it was crazy. I guess you can tell it's close to the holidays when it's like this? Thanks for grabbing me a drink."

"I got a white mocha. That's what you like, right?"

"It's my favorite. I'm glad you remembered." I smile and grab my cup, inwardly doing a happy dance as I take that first sip. The perfect coffee drink, and he remembered our conversation.

Ethan grabs his own.

"Are you drinking a mocha?"

He smiles after taking a sip. "Of course. I told you it's the only flavor I'll drink."

I laugh merrily before something catches my eye at the coffee bar behind him. My heart rate increases, and I feel like hiding.

"Oh, no." I try to duck, but I know I've been spotted.

"What is it?" Ethan swings around and sees the barista making his way around the counter.

Before I can answer, Andrew's at the table, hands on his hips, and looking at me accusingly.

"Really, Cindy? Dating your boss? Seriously? That's why you left me?" His nostrils flare and face flushes. A dirty towel hangs on his shoulder and there are coffee stains on his apron.

I roll my eyes, take a deep breath, and square my shoulders as Ethan looks between us, confused. "No, Andrew, I left you because you were a controlling asshole, and you can't change that despite what you believe."

Andrew glares at me and turns to Ethan. "I hope you enjoy my leftovers. She can be a clingy pain in the ass. If I were you, I'd walk away now. You'll regret staying with her if you don't."

My mouth drops at his words, and Ethan stands. The two stand eye to eye. Ethan's face turns from joyful to stern. His jaw is set and there is a small tic in the muscles below his ear. He crosses his arms across his chest and glares. "Sounds more like you're the leftovers, Andrew. Do you understand me?" He doesn't wait for an answer. "How about you get back to your job before I call your manager? I know him well, considering I went to high school with him."

Andrew sneers. "You're going to pull that card on me?"

Ethan smirks. "If you'll mind your business and leave us the hell alone, maybe I won't have to."

I glance toward the counter. Another man in a polo stands with his arms crossed watching us. His jaw is also clenched, and I can't help but wonder if he senses the tension around our table. Will he kick us out? Or fire Andrew on the spot? Not that I would be upset seeing him humiliated after this stunt.

I glance at Ethan, trying to figure out what happens next.

"On second thought, Andrew, looks like your boss has already seen you. Better hop to it." Ethan waves at the man at the counter, who returns it.

Andrew looks over his shoulder and pales. He looks at me and wipes his hands on his apron. I notice his shakiness as he moves his hands away. "This isn't over. Mark my words. We will talk about this, Cindy."

"'Mark my words', Andrew? Who are you, Dr. Evil? Whatever." I pick up my coffee and take a sip. "I have nothing more to say to you, and there's nothing you can say I want to hear. We will never get back together, even if hell freezes over and Satan takes up ice skating."

Andrew glares at me, then glances at Ethan. He grinds his teeth and purses his lips, fighting to keep his mouth shut.

"Get lost." Ethan shoos him like one would send kids to play.

Andrew does it again. He looks at Ethan, glares at me, and turns his gaze to his boss across the room. Finally, he moves away, and my shoulders lose some of the tension I didn't realize was there.

Ethan returns to his chair as Andrew reaches the counter. "He seems pleasant. I bet he's a hit at parties."

I shake my head, chuckling. A glance shows Andrew standing behind the counter, talking with the man in the polo, and my chuckle dies. "I thought he was better than that once upon a time. When I was with him, I lost who I was. It took me a long time to find myself again. I didn't realize he worked here, and I'm sorry he was being a pain."

Ethan looks at me with concern. "It's fine and not your fault. How long ago did you split up?"

"Two months ago? I know it doesn't seem long enough for me to find myself, and I'm still working on it. Being away from his influence has made a tremendous difference. I didn't realize how much he affected me."

Ethan sighs, "I get that. I was in a relationship like that years ago."

I nod. "So, do you want to stay and finish our coffees or walk around?"

Ethan looks over his shoulder toward the counter where Andrew and his boss appear to be in a heated discussion. "Let's walk around and talk. I'm sure my buddy will text me about this later. He's a good man."

I smile, relieved we don't have to sit here and deal with my ex staring us down. Not exactly a comfortable first date.

Ethan takes my hand as I slide from my chair and gives it a squeeze. "Tell me more about your family. What are they like?"

TIME LOSES MEANING as Ethan and I get lost in conversation. We wonder through a few shops as we talk about life and some of our hobbies. I'm elated we have so much in common and curious about our differences. He shares more about his love of paint ball and video games as we snack on pretzels from a store close to the coffee shop.

We move on, walking until we realize we could go somewhere else and chat for a while, maybe even grab something later for food. This spurs our decision to move our date elsewhere.

Specifically, my apartment.

As we navigate traffic, I can't fight the dreamy smile glued to my face as Ethan follows in his car. I can't believe I suggested it, even though I tell myself it was purely practical. His place is further off, and he didn't want me driving back late at night from there. Still, it's hardly your usual first date location, and I'm thankful my roommate is gone for the weekend. It'll be quiet and just us.

"I know this isn't the best apartment complex, but it's affordable." Ethan follows me up the stairs to the third floor.

"It could be worse. Are the rooms drafty?"

I laugh, remembering some of the horror stories I've heard regarding drafty apartments. "No, thankfully, and we have our own washer and dryer. No laundromats or hauling laundry to a laundry facility like some complexes force tenants to do."

"Nice. I had to do that with my first apartment. I decided I would aim to rent houses after that until I could save up enough to buy one. Then again, the company has me moving to so many places it's not worth it yet. In the future, I'd like to. Settle somewhere, I mean."

I nod as I slide my key into the lock, and cringe as I notice the white paint flaking at the bottom. Ugh. Great first impression.

"I haven't even considered buying a home yet." I push the door open, and he follows me. "Welcome to my humble abode."

I watch him look around the small apartment with its dark brown couches, a gently used rug, small tv, and attached kitchenette. It's not huge, but it works. My roommate and I each have our own room, which gives us the privacy we need.

"It's not bad." He smiles.

I laugh. "It could be better, right?"

He laughs in response and grabs my hand. I squeeze his in return and lead him to the couch.

"Movie? We could order some pizza later if we get hungry."

"You've found my love language." He chuckles.

"Oh, food?" I ask curiously.

"Nope, pizza."

"Really? What's your favorite?" I smile as I pull out my phone.

"I prefer a New York style cheese pizza over anything, but I'll eat whatever. Do you have one you prefer?" He scoots closer to me on the couch until our shoulders are resting against each other.

I pull up the pizza app on my phone and begin looking for the pizza he mentioned. "Cheese is my go-to. Occasionally, I'll crave pepperoni or something, but I'm happy with cheese nine times out of ten."

"I guess changing it up now and then isn't too bad. Do you want me to pick a movie to watch while you order the food?" He grabs the remote from the coffee table in front of us.

"That would be awesome. It won't take me long." I glance at him, then back at the app as I finish placing the food order.

"Do you like rom-coms? This one looks fun." He points toward the TV with the remote as a scene plays out between a couple standing on a platform doing a talent show.

"I don't really consider it a rom com. I know it's funny, but then it turns sad as the season ends. She goes through so much pain." I frown as I set my phone down.

"It does, but it was the first thing that popped up. We can pick something else if you'd like?" He hits the menu option to look.

I shake my head. "No, this will do. I love how it focuses on the way she processes her grief, even if she gives herself more in the end. It's not like she knew she was creating her own isolated world where she kind of controls everyone."

"How many times have you watched this, exactly?" He smirks and sets the remote down.

I shrug nonchalantly. "Only twice, I think. I've seen some different posts that explored the themes of the show. There are some fascinating conversations and comments about them."

"Interesting. I do that a lot, too." He slides his arm around my shoulders, and we relax into the show, letting the conversation ebb and flow. We play episode after episode around the arrival of the pizza. After binge watching for a few hours, we stretch and check the time.

"Holy cow, when did it get so late?" I jump up to clear away the pizza box.

Ethan stretches, and I catch a glimpse over my shoulder as I head to the kitchen. I smile at how *right* he looks sitting on the giant sofa, warming me from the inside at how comfortable he is around me.

I walk back toward the couch, unsure if he's ready to leave or not. I don't want our night to end, but I'm not ready to spend all night together. He reaches for me, pulling me from my thoughts, and I squeal.

"The time is fine. I've enjoyed spending our evening together. How about you?" He wraps his arms around me and pulls me closer to him on the couch.

I smile as bees buzz in my stomach. Is he going to kiss me? Are we ready? It's a big step, a step into uncharted territory. "I've enjoyed it. Can we do it again?"

"I hope so. How about dinner Tuesday night?"

"I would love that." My heart beats faster as he leans closer to me. I can smell the cologne he's wearing and my heart melts. It reminds me of cool nights and warm spices. I glance at his lips, then back to his eyes, trying to determine which of us will move first.

"Is it okay if I kiss you?" He's breathless, glancing at my lips and pausing a few inches from my lips. His breath is warm as it moves against my skin.

I nod and his eyes light up. He leans in and his lips meet mine with the softest of touches. I feel a jolt of energy course through me and our kiss deepens. It's amazing and I lose myself in it. His arms slide up my torso and under my shirt, but no further. I wrap my arms around him in response and our tongues meet. Soon I'm pulled across his lap and we lose ourselves in the sensations.

All too soon, he pulls away and we smile at each other, both a little breathless. My cheeks feel warm, my lips swollen from the time spent locked with his. We rest our foreheads against each other as I straddle his lap.

"I better go." He leans in and gives me another gentle kiss. "I'll text you when I get home."

I smile, feeling as if I'm floating. I could easily go for another round of kissing with him. It's addictive and a surprise. When was the last time I had fun kissing someone and didn't end up hating it after the fact? This kiss was the best one I've had in years.

I try to keep this out of my voice and fail. "Thanks for a wonderful date, Ethan."

I slide off his lap and he stands, stretching. "It was my pleasure, Cindy. I'll talk to you tomorrow." He leans in and gives me one last kiss. It's sweet and over too soon.

He pulls away with a smile. I follow him with my eyes as he moves to the door to let himself out. Once he's closed the door, I flop my head back. Did that really happen? With my boss? He's amazing. I don't think I'll ever get used to this. I still can't believe he likes me and now we're officially dating! Eek!

I sigh and push up from the couch. It really is late and unfortunately, I have to work on school stuff tomorrow. After stretching, I head toward my room. Even if we don't work out, this night will be a memorable one.

I mean, it's like one of those books. But how often do you get to kiss the boss in real life?

THE END

# A Word from the Author – Madilynn Dale

Madilynn Dale is an author, blogger, freelancer, reader, mother, outdoors enthusiast, wine lover, and over all creative. She's a host for several shows featured under Go Indie Now's wide umbrella, hosts a podcast channel of her own, and loves to travel. Madilynn enjoys chatting with creatives from all areas of the field and letting her viewers see the authentic side of each one of them.

Madilynn is an Oklahoma author and holds several different degrees. She has a bachelor's degree in Kinesiology and an associate degree in Physical Therapy Assistant Sciences. Her creativity stems from something deep within, and through her bond with the creative flow, brings her stories to life. She never envisioned herself as a writer but took a leap of faith while pregnant and began a new journey. She enjoyed writing short stories as a kid and has been an avid reader since grade school.

Madilynn's hobbies, when not writing, include reading, baking, crafting, hiking, playing with her son, caring for her rescue pets, and horseback riding. She loves to travel and explore. One day she hopes to expand her travels and see the world, but in the meantime, you'll find her working on her next novel.

**Playlist**
Fuck You by CeeLo Green
Party Rock Anthem LMAFO
Stone In Love by Journey
Jamie All Over by Mayday Parade

https://open.spotify.com/playlist/
1wUdwCZO3BCfqateKmXmLU?si=f2eb57bdd3244067

**Why**

This story ended up being something more personal to me. The idea hit me like a ton of bricks after seeing the theme for this collection. With that in mind, I let my fingers and mind play across the keyboard to create this sweet story. Inspiration for this short thing cam from how I met my husband. I was a waitress in college, and he was my boss's boss. More drama surrounded us then what is in this sweet story, but I hope the characters were able to share the beginning of what became a lasting love. For ever an always.

# Coming Home

## A story from the Black Devil Omegaverse

## By Dani Hermit

*This story takes place several years before the start of Infernal Affairs, the first book in the Black Devil series.*

### One (Gran)

Being murdered was nothing like he expected.

Gran Martelli had long ago accepted that he would end up murdered. That was the fate one signed up for when they were part of the mafia. Being a highly trusted and much-beloved member of the Martelli family, a pillar of support for the newly appointed leader, put Gran in a position with equal power and danger. Despite how fiercely his cousin Liam had promised to protect him, Gran held no illusions about what he was getting into.

Now that he was finally murdered, Gran had to admit it was rather disappointing.

He'd not gone down in a blaze of glory, gunshots ringing out and his fur splattered with blood. He'd not taken a bullet for Liam. He hadn't been stabbed, poisoned, or strangled in a dark alley.

Gran had been lured into a deep, dark hole and forgotten.

He hadn't died the first day. Nor the second. Gran had no idea how many days it had taken him to die. He'd laid in the darkness and felt his body slowly fading around him. He drifted in and out of consciousness, never sure if he were awake or dreaming. His body ached from hunger and thirst. There was a drip of dirty water he reluctantly lapped at, but even that eventually dried up.

The worst part was when the delirium set in.

Gran had no idea who he was or where he was most of the time. His body felt weird and swollen but also too small. He wondered if being a chubby tom had prolonged his suffering. He never missed a meal, and there were so many delicious treats in the world. But as he lay in filth, uncertain if he were alive or dead, Gran bittersweetly savored the memories of every piece of pie and cake he'd ever eaten.

In and out of fevered dreams, he saw the Demon's face. How had he forgotten it? The Demon had been in this hole when he'd arrived. It licked him, snarling in a low, terrifying voice. And when it finally left him behind, it had been wearing Gran's face.

And the no-fur at the top of the stairs. Was he real or part of the fever? Why was he in a white lab coat? Gran couldn't remember that particular no-fur from the Martelli stable. He wasn't pretty like the other ones. He was... strange, with mismatched eyes. Liam liked to collect unusual no-furs, but this one wasn't just some outlier.

He was scary.

When the world turned bright white and cold, full of winter's sweet, clean smell, Gran assumed he was hallucinating again. But the cold didn't go away. The dampness of melting snow seeped through his fur and into his skin, cooling the discomforts that had overtaken his entire awareness.

For the first time in Gran didn't know how long, he closed his eyes and slept.

A huge shadow fell over the tom as he came back from unconsciousness. His waking eyes were not ready for the sight before him.

"Sweet gods, don't eat me!" Gran screamed, surprised that he could make sounds after what he'd been going through. Pushing at the snow with his paws, he tried to scuttle back from the creature looming over him.

*A Demon.*

It was three times as big as the one that had stolen his face. The teeth and multiple limbs were the stuff of nightmares. And the smell...

Okay, the smell was quite nice, like cinnamon pastry cream. But that was surely just to lure him in to become a meal for the big, toothy creature lumbering towards him.

"Stay away!" Gran managed to get his paws under him, and he fled in the opposite direction of the Demon. Maybe he had enough adrenaline from his panic to get away. At least he could live for a few more minutes.

## TWO (WOUND)

The Demon called out to the sickly-looking tom, but he lost him in a sudden blizzard. Going back to his home, a warm cave carved out of a mountain, he shrunk down to a size where he could work with his medicinal herbs and tools.

"Wound," The Demon spoke to himself. He had a bad habit of that. But living in the coldest, remotest part of the Underworld didn't create a lot of social interactions. He usually had to settle for talking to himself. "What were you thinking? A nine-foot-tall monster isn't exactly inviting."

He had rushed out as soon as he sensed the anomaly in his realm, more worried about the condition of the misplaced soul than his own appearance.

Souls rarely came here. The Black Devil, Lord of the Underworld, used to come more often once he and Wound called a truce. That had taken a few centuries as King, the current Black

Devil, had defeated Wound, the former avatar of the Black Devil, for the Throne with cunning and brutality.

In the battle, Wound was damn near eradicated. The Fates intervened and made him Steward of the Underworld, giving him The Book of Changes to oversee. He was stripped of his avatar powers, turned into a Demon, and exiled to the Winterland - a cold, sparse, lonely place.

He learned Demon medicine and became useful to King, just in case the Black-furred tom got twitchy and sought to take him out completely. It gave him a little leverage.

Having been a doctor in his former life before the Throne chose him for the job, it wasn't a far stretch for Wound. He relished the familiar role that didn't require tormenting souls, which Wound never embraced.

His world had been a different one. Ancient history, really. Unlike the current Black Devil, Wound had been born a Hare. So much had changed, and to avoid facing those changes, Wound lived a very secluded life.

The only tom soul he regularly saw, more or less, was the Orangelo who came to the Winterland to paint landscapes. But he was a special case and a healthy, robust soul that chose to spend time here.

Newly dead souls *never* came here. They weren't strong enough to handle the realm's icy chill or intense energy. You needed years of acclimation to the Underworld before you went to Wound's realm.

This newly dead and newly Demon-murdered soul had no business being here. And every moment he stayed outside, the tom soul risked what amounted to spiritual frostbite and possibly fading out. It was rare, but using the signature Wound could see in the tom's auric field, he could tell his life had been interrupted by supernatural means. Not spun by the Three Toms of Fate. And very traumatizing.

The tom's soul should have gone somewhere much gentler to start to acclimate. Poor creature. Wound couldn't leave him be. Couldn't abandon him.

"But how to find you?" Wound collected up some of the jars he'd need. "How do I coax you out?"

The Demon started mixing up a sweet concoction. "Toms like milk. Warm milk, especially. At least, I think that's right." He was unsure. He hadn't been Topside in a very long time. He was sort of exiled unless the Book of Changes told him otherwise, and the Book hadn't done so since it became his to protect.

Wound poured the mixture into a huge, colorful bowl he usually used for crushing herbs. Then, he glamoured himself into a form he'd not taken in a long time, a Grey-furred tom. He headed outside to find a spot to leave the sweet treat that packed a little extra dose of sleep aid, hoping to entice the newly dead tom.

Once Wound could take care of him, he could get him on his feet and to where he belonged.

Setting the bowl down, he backed away and hid behind some pine trees. All he could do now was wait.

It took about half an hour for the Tawny tom to reappear out of the snow. His pink nose twitched, sniffing at the lingering steam from the warm milk. He had green eyes that matched Wound's memory of spring grass. Those pretty eyes went wide as the tom looked around, probably looking for a threat or the owner of the warm bowl of sweet milk.

Finally, the tom crept forward and stuck his tongue out to taste the milk. He narrowed his eyes, looking at it for so long that Wound started to think that perhaps he had been wrong about toms liking warm milk. The tom made a weird jerking motion with his shoulders and picked up the bowl, dumping it down his throat. The poor thing seemed to be starving. He even licked the final drops out of the bowl.

The tom staggered away less than a minute after he'd put the bowl down. He made it about three steps before he pitched face-first into the snow.

Wound moved quickly, collecting the thin, practically weightless soul in his arms. He would conjure a warm bed when he got them both back. The bowl would return to its place on the pedestal as it always did.

"Don't worry, sleepyhead. I won't let you fade." Wound gave the tom's head an affectionate nuzzle.

### Three (Gran)

Waking up in a warm bed was not what Gran expected to happen. Once he'd drank down that delicious - definitely drugged - warm milk, he'd half expected he would wind up some Demon's snack. At least, he hoped all they wanted to do was eat him. He had heard some pretty scary stories about other demonic hungers.

Shivering, Gran pulled the blankets up over his head. He wanted no part of the world outside this warm little nest he'd found. Maybe some tom had found him in the snow. Maybe he was safe and not dead. That would be nice. Once he was back on his feet, he could find Liam and... and... What exactly?

His mind was a little fuzzy on what he should tell his cousin. But he should know Demons were infiltrating his organization. That felt like important information Liam needed.

Later, though. For now, Gran was going to hide and sleep some more.

A sound and a scent made him sniff his head out from under the blanket. It was a food smell but not quite a food smell. Another, deeper sniff brought the scent of herbs and fire. He was smelling some kind of medicine, probably a strong tea. He didn't want to take any medicine. He was fine. Just tired and hungry.

Gods, but he was so very hungry. So much so that the smell of the medicinal herbs was making his stomach growl and his mouth water. Even a healing broth would be welcome right now. Or more of the sweet, warm milk. He wondered if there was more of that. Was there someone here he could ask for more?

"It's nice to see you awake." A voice that was not likely a tom or Demon addressed him. It was soft and had a bit of a high pitch. It reminded him of Turquoise, Liam's favorite no-fur in the stable. The furless hand on his forehead confirmed it. "But you are very unwell."

"Am I?" Gran asked, peeking at the little no-fur from under the warm blankets. He was adorable but somehow awkward as well. Did he have a tom around here who'd be mad that there was some stranger in his bed? "I thought I was dead."

"Yes. But the dead can be very unwell. You see, your auric magick is sort of a lifeline. No, bad choice of words, let's say soul line. Anyway, you need it to stay, hmm, in existence." The bright-eyed no-fur began to pull the blankets down Gran's body. "The good thing is I know what you need."

"Do you?" Gran watched the no-fur move with curiosity.

He would have preferred to have stayed under the blanket, where it was warm. But the no-fur pulling it away to reveal his naked body made Gran think some very non-healing thoughts. The only thing the once-chubby tom liked more than food was no-furs. They were so pretty and tasted so sweet.

Gran tried to resist licking his lips as he watched the no-fur work. He really shouldn't be thinking about him like that. He didn't even know his name.

"I do, and the good thing is, it's what my body was made for. If, of course, I please you, and we can get..." The violet-eyed no-fur smirked as he removed the blanket all the way. "Wonderful, that doesn't seem to be a problem. You're dead but not *that* dead. Oh, sorry, that was a terrible joke, wasn't it? But nice to see it still works."

"Not as nice for you as it is for me," Gran replied shyly. "The only thing sadder would be if I couldn't eat."

Gran watched the no-fur as he crawled onto the bed. He stopped him from going any further. "Um, not that I don't appreciate the offer, but... I... I don't know your name or if you have a tom or anything about you."

"I'm a healer. My name isn't important. You come from the Topside. You don't have to be polite. But you can give me a name if you'd like, as I understand it is done up there." The no-fur began to stroke Gran's chest with both hands, fingers running through the lighter fur.

"Giving you a name stakes a claim, little one," Gran said softly, moving his paws from the no-fur's shoulders. He skimmed them down his sleek little body. "I am happy to accept the healing, but I don't think you understand the weight of what a name would be. I can't saddle you with it. Not when I have nothing to offer, seeing as how I'm dead and all."

"I only offered for your comfort." The no-fur stretched his body in a slow seductive way before scooting down to rub his seeding pocket against Gran's ready cock. "I know what I am. And I know I am the only thing that stands between you and oblivion. Which seems to give me power over a Tawny-fur tom I shouldn't have. So why don't you act on instinct, my big sexy Tawny, and break me." The last bit was whispered against Gran's neck. "Set both of our powers and bodies ablaze."

"I was thinking of devouring you," Gran murmured against the no-fur's soft skin. He arched his body, surprised to find his cock slid home with no effort. This no-fur was more than ready for him. Unlike many toms, Gran wasn't prone to violence during sex. But he was still a tom and always down for fucking.

He pushed up, rolling the no-fur onto his back and shifting his hips to plunge even deeper. He rode the no-fur for a few strokes before pulling out. Gran moved down his body, slowly savoring every inch with his mouth until he came to the sweet creature's hard cock and eager seeding pocket. He hungrily drove his tongue into the no-fur, lapping the sweet juices.

Purring, Gran wondered if anything was so sweet as the sounds of a no-fur being pleasured. They were rarely given a chance to feel their own desire, but Gran reveled in it.

**Four (Wound)**

Wound had done what was required to provide hope for the tom to make it to his audience with the Black Devil. However, what the Tawny was doing to his body was a distraction he hadn't expected. It was making any kind of diagnosis difficult.

But then Wound had never transformed himself into a no-fur before. It hadn't been easy, but a first pass over the Tawny's aura had shown he needed the healing boost only a deep connection with a no-fur would provide.

However, it wasn't supposed to be bliss. It was supposed to be an unpleasant surgery—in, out, and done.

Instead, Wound was squirming, and his head filled with dizzying sparks. And when the tom paused what he was doing and gave him the most beautiful smile, something so shocking happened that Wound almost lost his hold on his glamour. The Demon felt his heart swell, filling with an impossible word. *Innehavre* - the term used to describe the connection of fated mates - usually was for a tom and a no-fur, but it could happen to any set of souls.

But it was there in the Tawny's entrancing emerald gaze. *Innehavre*. Wound stumbled over his words, but he wanted to know.

*Had* to know.

"Tell me your name, please."

"Gran," the Tawny replied. He flicked his tail nervously. "It's short for Grandeur, but that name never fit me."

"Somehow, I disagree."

Wound was breathless.

He was feeling things he didn't remember from when he was Topside. Certainly things he never dared to hope for while he had been the Black Devil, before he was violently forced to take on a Demon's life and form. Those feelings overwhelmed him now, making him say things he never imagined would come out of his mouth.

"It suits you. You are bringing warmth and color to this whited-out, empty place. Please take me. I must have your cock inside me. Now. Don't make me wait."

"I wouldn't dream of it," Gran replied, taking his time about working his way back up to Wound's mouth with licks and nibbles all over his body. He wrapped one arm around Wound's waist, lifting him a little to meet his hard cock. Gran eased inside Wound's no-fur body, taking time with his sweet torment.

"There's a wickedness to you, tom. Makes me wonder what you did Topside."

Wound had to fight not completely to lose himself. He saw the places where Gran's aura was trying to come apart and where his essence was starting to eat at itself. Closing his eyes, and praying he could make it through this without losing hold of the mix of their auras, he felt the climax of a no-fur for the first and probably last time.

Wound was forming a bond with a tom who could never be his. The Demon was now aware he could only hold the no-fur form for ten, *maybe* fifteen minutes. He tried not to clutter his thoughts with heartache. There would be no Gran to be heartbroken over if he didn't get this right.

Using his healing skills, he grabbed hold of their mingling auric signatures and made Gran burn brighter.

**Five (Gran)**

Everything went soft, fuzzy yellow. It felt like warm sunshine pooling around Gran's body and invading his senses. It stripped away the feeling he was getting from the little no-fur who wasn't a no-fur. He wasn't entirely sure what the healer was, but he'd seen more than the slim little body as his special magickal ability to see the truth came to life. He'd also felt something more.

Gran had no idea what he was feeling, but he knew that he wanted to feel it some more. The golden light was so soothing, so warm... He didn't have a choice but to drift off to sleep. He hoped he hadn't left the no-fur - whose name he still didn't know - wanting. After a nap, he could see repaying the healer's kindness.

Gran had no idea how long it had been since he passed out, but he woke up alone in the pile of blankets. He would be lying if he said he wasn't disappointed. It didn't seem fair that he was the only one using the comfy bed nest while the healer doing all the work was left sleeping... where? He hadn't seen anything outside of the blankets. Even when he'd been coaxed out for the magickal sex, he hadn't looked at anything other than the pretty no-fur.

Poking his head out from under the blanket, he saw a cozy little room. It had to be a guest room because there wasn't much other than the bed and a small table. The white wood on the walls was charming, but there was no decor. The longer he looked at the room, the more he thought maybe it was more like a hospital room than a guest room in a house.

Stretching out his limbs, Gran tested to see how he felt. Nothing was broken, and he didn't feel any bruises. There was some stiffness and soreness here and there, but nothing like the aftereffects of hypothermia. After running around in the snow, he was surprised his body wasn't covered in chunks of ice.

Pushing the blankets away, Gran slowly found his way to his feet. There weren't any clothes or even a robe in the small room. He pulled the lightest blanket off the bed and wrapped it around himself. Although, after what happened between himself and the healer, he wasn't sure that decency was a concern anymore.

Gran wasn't entirely sure what he was looking for as he padded out of the room into a long hallway. Food? Water? He wouldn't turn either one down, but he was peeking into the open doors of other rooms in hopes of finding the healer. Instead, he found a comfy sitting room with a soft chair, a large fireplace that already had a fire going, and a basket of pretty purple and blue yarn.

In the basket, he found a set of knitting needles. Settling in to wait for the healer here, Gran began fiddling with the yarn, wondering if he could remember how to make a sweater. He'd seen the wintry landscape through several windows, and the healer had been naked. He needed a warm sweater if he was going to stay toasty in this place.

Gran must have dozed off because the sound of footsteps passing by the sitting room door made him jump. Wiping a spot of drool from the corner of his mouth, Gran called out to see if that was the healer.

"Hello? Healer?" Gran felt dumb not being able to use a name, but at least 'healer' was less rude than anything else he could think of to call him.

**Six (Wound)**

Wound almost dropped the firewood he was carrying in his large paw. He didn't expect Gran to be awake for another day or two. He switched from his smaller Demon form to an even less intimidating tom form. A harmless, slightly pudgy Grey-fur who wore a fringed vest and tie-dyed jeans. He completed the look with little round glasses with yellow lenses. He had seen this fashion not that long ago in the Book of Changes and thought it would set Gran at ease to see someone dressed like the toms he would have encountered topside.

What he didn't consider was that most Demons had only a vague idea of time for Topsiders, and Wound was no exception. His fashion was a good fifty years out of date.

Wound had decided to introduce himself to Gran in this guise, get him well and on his way as soon as possible. That hadn't stopped him from using his auric magick to turn his mountain cave into a quaint little cottage that had more rooms on the inside than any cottage could. It was a cozy home for Gran to convalesce.

Not stay.

That dream was ludicrous. There was no way Gran felt what he felt. It hadn't passed as Wound was sure it would once he was violently shaken out of the no-fur form.

*Innehavre.* The word, the bond, resounded through his whole body every time he snuck a peek at the sleeping Tawny-fur.

To save them both the pain of what would never be, Wound would explain the no-fur away as a hallucination if it came up. Though he hoped it wouldn't.

"Yes, tom. I am right here. Are you in the sitting room? I was about to build a fire."

"Someone already did," Gran replied, pointing to the fireplace. "Oh, it must have burned down while I was dozing. A fresh one would be nice if it's not too much trouble."

The Tawny-fur gave Wound an odd look. "You're... uh... purple. That's different." That didn't seem to be all the tom was seeing, but if there was anything else, he didn't mention it.

"I'm what?" Wound hid the concern in his voice. Maybe the Tawny wasn't making the progress Wound hoped. At this rate, using hallucination as an excuse would be easy. "Oh, you must mean my eyes. How can you tell through my tinted glasses?"

Gran blinked a few times. "No, I swore your fur was purple." He rubbed his eyes. "Maybe I'm still tired. Or I've been staring at this yarn for too long."

Wound was going to have to find a mirror. There was a chance his glamour had gone wonky because of how much energy work he'd done on Gran. He was supposed to be gray and white striped, but for all he knew, he was purple-striped or worse. "Don't worry about it. If your worst symptom is seeing strange colors, I'll take it. Now that you are up and about, would you like me to make you breakfast?"

Gran's entire face lit up at the mention of food. "Oh, yes, please. I could very much use something to eat. I feel so empty. Is that part of the healing? Or..." The Tawny-fur's face darkened as he trailed off, his mind turning to something much less pleasant than breakfast.

Wound noticed his distress right away. It even made him forget his concerns. Like that he was a terrible cook. Or that his offer was only made to create an easy exit. Because all the glamoured tom wanted was to jump into Gran's lap and spend the afternoon pleasuring each other. "What is it? Tell me, I'm sure I have something back in the apothecary for it."

"Uh... I think I died from starvation. Would that... you know," Gran spoke softly, fussing with the yarn in his lap. "Make me feel hungry forever?"

**Seven (Gran)**

Gran felt stupid asking the question. He was used to being hungry. He'd been told often that he was greedy, too chubby, and overate. But to feel this gnawing hunger forever... That sounded like actual hell.

"Never mind." He shook his head, taking back the question. "It's not important. If there's breakfast, I'll appreciate it. I've always appreciated food."

His ears drooped. Why had he said that? He was finally skinny after years and years of carrying around too much weight. Starving to death was possibly the best thing to ever happen to his body. He wondered if he looked like he had always hoped. Or if he was some kind of gruesome skeletal specter. What did happen after you died? Gran had no idea.

"Unless it's your eternal punishment, I don't believe so." The healer shook his head. "That wouldn't start until you met ol' Blackie, and this might be telling, but they aren't eternal for the most part."

"Ol' Blackie..." Gran felt a chill run down his spine.

The healer was talking about facing the Black Devil himself. That was not something Gran had considered. Though it made sense. All the religious stories said that was what happened to toms when they died, judgment by some sadistic tom god for all the sins of life. It sounded horrible to Gran, so he avoided religion during his living years.

"I won't be facing him before breakfast, will I?" Gran tried to keep his voice light, but there was no hiding the fear.

"I doubt it." The healer chuckled. "I'm just hoping my cooking isn't your true eternal punishment. I don't have a lot of skill in the kitchen despite being an excellent mixer of herbs. So I'm afraid the best I can do is medicinal sugar rice. And to be honest, ol' Blackie is off Topside, so you are sort of slipping under the radar at the moment. You are far from where the newly dead are supposed to go."

"That is weird." Gran put the sweater aside. "It is weird, isn't it?"

He shook his head, stopping the healer from answering him. He stood up, stretching his body and letting out an embarrassing yowl as his joints popped. "If you don't mind me puttering around the kitchen, I do know how to cook. Let's keep the medicinal herbs out of our meals."

"Well, I could do a little magick, I guess. Otherwise, all I have is milk, rice, and sugar. I shouldn't overdo it with magic unless you want a magically mangled meal. But I can summon a few eggs and things. Toms like eggs, right?"

The healer spun around nervously and almost ran into a wall as he walked toward the kitchen. It was almost as if the tom didn't know it was there. Like his home might have been renovated recently.

"Well, now that's a silly thing to say. Since I, myself, am a tom."

"Of course you are," Gran replied, wondering who the healer was trying to fool. He casually ran his paw over the purple-striped arm. "But you have been down here for a while. Maybe you forgot about some things. Let's see what we're working with, and we'll make do."

### Eight (Wound)

Gran could *cook,* Wound learned over several days of baked ham and muffins that were the size of his head. As good as the food was, Wound needed a break. He had yet to find a permanence spell for his cave, so he was using a great deal of demonic aura to keep it a cozy cottage for his guest.

But out here, he could stretch his limbs and bring home some fresh fish he didn't have to conjure for Gran to use. On one paw, this was very wise. Letting himself release the glamour he was using to disguise himself was the best course for his health.

And if that were why he was doing it, it would be fine. But it wasn't. He wanted to break the illusion to control an even greater one. Wound wanted Gran to look at him the way he did when he pretended to be a no-fur. He wanted to get lost in the mad passion they'd shared.

Sighing, he got to work. By noon he had two buckets of fish to bring home to Gran.

*Bring home*? How bizarrely domestic. How insanely wonderful.

He set the fish by the front door. No polar bear was going to steal it. Wound in his Demon form was the scariest thing in the tundra that made up this level of the Underworld.

He shifted to his tom form before entering and stopped in front of the mirror on the wall. He watched the glamour come over him. It would not last long and felt twice as hard to cast as last time.

Maybe this was a bad idea. What if he couldn't hold the no-fur form, and his limbs horrifically appeared during sex? That could be traumatizing for both of them. Not to mention what Gran might do when he saw the monster that had chased him on his first day in the Underworld suddenly sitting on his cock.

Wound stopped in his tracks. This had to be the last time, then. He would show up as Gran's beloved no-fur and get this out of his system. Gran deserved better than to be dicked around by a Demon.

So one last time, even if it was only their second time together. It wasn't right. It wasn't fair to either of them. But Wound's heart had never ached this much, and his hunger for another, if he'd ever felt it before, was lost in the memory of a former life Wound had not gone out of his way to find.

He focused with intent and got a hold of the no-fur glamour, feeling it settle over his skin.

Taking a deep breath, he called out to Gran and crawled into the cozy room with a fireplace, as was proper for a no-fur who had a keeper. "Gran? *Innehavre*? Are you here?"

"Hello, healer," Gran said with the same tone in his voice that he used with Wound in his tom glamour. He was knitting again, comfortably settled in front of the fireplace. "Did you enjoy your trip outside? It must be awfully cold."

Gran settled whatever he was making into his lap and turned to look at Wound. He frowned at the naked no-fur crawling across the floor. "Oh, yes. You must have been freezing if you were out in the snow like that. Come here and cuddle on my lap. Let me warm you up."

Wound had been concerned for a moment, but the glamour seemed to hold. "Grandeur," he whispered as he got to where Gran sat. He rested his head on Gran's knee before he began leaving light kisses along his thigh. "I need you."

The healer felt the home flicker around him. A reminder that the auric magick was working, but they didn't have long.

**Nine (Gran)**

"I think there's a draft in here," Gran said as he cupped his paw under the healer's chin.

He was trying to figure out why the healer had so many faces. Were they all real? Did he imagine them? Did it matter?

No, he finally decided as he looked down into the no-fur's sweet purple eyes. It didn't matter one bit. All that mattered was how he felt and did the healer feel the same. All that mattered was the word that kept echoing in his head. *Innehavre*. Was that even possible?

Some of the no-furs in his cousin's stable had talked about the sacred word a few times. One had desperately wanted Gran to be his *Innehavre*, his special soul mate. But Gran had never understood the idea of being connected to another soul. He was a gentle tom, and he loved that special no-fur as much as he could. But in the end, it wasn't enough. Another tom claimed him, and Gran hoped he was happy now.

But the draw to this healer was something different. It consumed him, driving Gran to think ridiculous things. He was losing his mind because the thought driving him the hardest was staying here and setting up a house with the healer.

"Come up here, healer," Gran said softly. "I have a gift for you before we lose ourselves to lust."

"Is that the name you have decided to give me, Grandeur?" There was something in the no-fur's eyes. It was only there a second. It looked like fear. "I will gladly accept it."

"No, it's a title. A way to call you something other than 'hey you' or one of the many slurs that exist." Gran sighed and stroked the no-fur's head. "Merely a word to fill the space until you tell me your name."

"Oh, I see." The no-fur leaned into his touch and gave him a sly grin. "So, what is this gift? Is it under this blanket in your lap? Can I peek?"

"You're being naughty," Gran grinned. At first, he had yet to catch on to what the healer was talking about. "That surprise isn't much of a surprise anymore, is it?"

"No, but what you might do with it could be." The no-fur nibbled on Gran's neck and nipped his ear before whispering. "Then what other treasure do you have for me? Show me so I can show you how much I appreciate it." He licked the inner side of Gran's ear in a slow spiral before settling in his lap.

Purring, Gran almost forgot about what he'd made for the healer. The little no-fur's mouth was very distracting. He finally managed to bring himself back into focus.

"It's this. While I was recovering, I found some yarn and needles... I find knitting very relaxing and thought you could use a sweater." Gran was feeling stupid while he explained his gift. He was curling his paws around the sweater and suddenly regretted mentioning it. He should have just let the healer distract him with sex.

### Ten (Wound)

"Looks more like a blanket." Wound was losing himself to how it felt to be with Gran like this. He didn't speak to him any differently than when he was in his tom form, but there was a way he looked at him when he was in the no-fur guise that spoke of an impossible future.

He tried to make the movement playful as he stole the gift and jumped off Gran's lap.

Wound didn't know what to feel. He forgot how to speak. As he unrolled the sweater, a huge unruly thing far too big for the no-fur body he wore, he counted just as many arms as his Demon form possessed. How could Gran have known to do that?

The shock made him lose his sweet no-fur shape, taking him to his smaller demon form. He felt a soft paw grip his shoulder.

Suddenly he knew what to say because he knew how much it would mean to Gran. He reached his paw up to cover the one offering silent comfort. In an instant, he knew this tom was his home and his future.

"Wound. My name is Wound."

# A Word from the Author – Dani Hermit

Hermit & Star are a pair of married writers who have spent the last 20+ years together, writing and laughing and generally being disgustingly cute. They specialize in dark Yaoi & MM romances, but occasionally dip their toes into sweeter tales. Curtis Star (he/they) is an art school survivor who has infused his love of horror and damaged characters into the stories. Dani Hermit (they/them) brought their love of filthy porn to the table and tempered it with a sweet touch that Curtis brings out in them.

Playlist

My Never - Blue October

The Real You - Three Days Grace

Find them and their books at https://hermitstarbooks.com

# Adventures in Demonsitting

## By AC Adams

"You summoned me, Lord?"

The slender demon, looking smaller than she really was compared to her master, bowed her head without averting her eyes.

Her network had failed her. For once, she had no idea what the immediate future held for her. If she had any friends, she would ask for sympathy, but she didn't, so she couldn't.

"I did. You are being recalled."

Her head shot up and she glared, a potentially fatal breach of protocol. A demon did not glare at a Prince of Hell.

"I—what? My Lord, did I displease you?"

"No. You are being reassigned."

Her lilac eyes flared in anger. "You can't! I've done what you ordered, but I need more time. They ferment grapes and make a drink which removes their inhibitions, leading to all sorts of evil actions, but there's no sin associated with it. It's not against any divine mandate they know of, only their own rules. They need religion before they can sin, and we haven't established that yet!"

"It is of no consequence for you any longer."

"Lord Beelzebub, I beg of you!"

Beelzebub 's voice softened. "It is decided. Not by me, Avareth."

Avareth glanced downward, towards the heart of Hell and their Master's demesnes.

"Precisely, Avareth. Sit, and I will explain."

This was a rare honor, and Avareth's anger cooled somewhat. No point in showing that, though, so she maintained the façade, dropping into the indicated seat with a thump.

"What do you know of the Thirteens?"

Avareth shook her head, concealing her curiosity. "Nothing, Lord."

"No reason for you to know. It is enough for you to know they exist, or existed. There is one remaining, and she is to be awakened to assist our efforts on Earth."

As explanations went, it told her absolutely nothing. Which was precisely what Beelzebub intended.

"What has this to do with me?"

"You are to be her companion. You will be there when she awakens, and you will stay with her."

"For how long?" The question was out before she thought through the rest of the statement and she mentally slapped herself. It showed weakness, and she hated to be seen as weak, even by a Prince who could eliminate her without a thought.

"Until I tell you otherwise. She needs to be guided, from the moment she is awakened until..."

He didn't complete the thought, which Avareth noted with interest. Then she picked up on the word "awakened." Demons were created as needed, not awakened, at least as far as she knew. Then the rest of his direction penetrated, and she burst from her seat. "I am not some sort of—of—minder!"

"You are what I tell you you are," growled the Prince. "You would not simply be a minder, Avareth."

"It sounds like it!"

"If you'll stop interrupting, I'll explain."

Avareth bit her tongue and nodded, settling down on the seat.

"Thank you." If Beelzebub's politeness was exaggerated, Avareth wasn't about to call him on it. He paused, contemplating his next words.

"All you need to know is Thirteens can be dangerous. They're more powerful than archdemons."

Avareth's jaw went slack. "And I'm supposed to watch her?"

"You are."

"She can smash me like a bug!"

"Not if she doesn't know she can."

Avareth's protest turned into a strangled, "What?"

"She doesn't know she's a Thirteen. She doesn't know her powers. Your job is to ensure she doesn't learn."

"How do I do that?"

Beelzebub shrugged. "That's up to you. Doesn't matter to Hell, as long as you don't fail."

"And if I do?"

His smile had no mirth in it at all. "You won't last long enough to regret your failure. She will be awakened shortly. Be there." The location popped into her mind.

Center of Hell. Lucifer's direct demesnes, and the most densely occupied part of his domain. The Princes maintained their lands well outside Lucifer's direct notice, the better to run their own schemes. Most of Hell's bureaucracy was clustered there, so she supposed it made sense that this resurrection center would be there.

It also meant that there weren't any portals from Beelzebub's palace. Portals worked both ways, and it would be too easy for a demonic assassin to slip in and out. Paranoia was a way of life in Hell.

It would take some time to cover the distance.

Beelzebub turned away, clearly dismissing her.

"One question, Lord?"

His attention returned to her.

"What is her name?"

"Kalili."

AVARETH STALKED ACROSS Hell. She was alone, as she preferred, and examined her new assignment.

It wasn't without benefits. Being selected for an assignment by one of Hell's Princes was an enormous honor. It gave her a name to drop when she was harassed by one of her fellow demons.

And she would be.

She wasn't well-liked. If she was honest, she was hated by a vast majority of the denizens of Hell. Those who owed her favors wanted her out of the way so their debts would be cleared. The unluckier ones, the ones whose unfortunate indiscretions were discovered by her investigations? They simply wanted her dead.

There were downsides, too.

The patronage of one of the Princes painted a target on her. The followers of the other Princes would happily dispatch her to curry favor with their patron.

And how was she going to deal with a Thirteen, whatever in Lilith's name that was?

Time for a detour.

THE LUCIFERI BIBLIOTHECA was centrally located as well, though set somewhat apart from the building Avareth now knew she needed. A minor detour and she'd had a much better idea what a Thirteen was and how to deal with it.

Unsurprisingly, the library was mostly deserted.

Demons weren't big on reading, even the texts provided by Hell for their instruction, and avoided the Luciferi.

Avareth found it relaxing.

Since she frequented it, she was greeted warmly.

"Avareth! It's been too long."

"Ariuk." She nodded at the taller demon, even sparing him a smile. He was always helpful and didn't ask stupid questions, two qualities she appreciated.

"I didn't expect to see you for a while."

Avareth answered the unspoken question. "I was reassigned. What can you tell me about Thirteens?"

"Thirteens?" He frowned, the black eyebrows nearly meeting above his narrow nose. "Doesn't sound familiar. Do you have any more information?"

"Not much. Terribly powerful demon."

The eyebrows separated. "Oh! An Original."

"A what?"

Ariuk was already off, so Avareth hurried to catch him.

"An original demon. Or angel, I suppose, though I don't have anything on them. They're practically legendary."

Now Avareth frowned. "There are angelic Thirteens?"

He waggled a hand. "No? I think the scroll we have will answer your questions better than I can."

They'd passed most of the spaces Avareth was familiar with and now headed down a set of stairs.

"I've never seen these," she said as they hurried past.

"No, most demons never come down here." He stopped at a stack of scrolls and began searching. "In fact, I think you're the first visitor here this year."

Avareth didn't doubt it. The crypt was dusty and close, and felt disused.

"Found it." Ariuk's voice held an unmistakable note of triumph as he lifted the scroll from the pile and extended it to her.

"Can I borrow it?"

That drew an unexpected bark of laughter. "No, but you can bring it up to a better location for reading."

It would have to do.

As they walked back, Ariuk asked, "Why the interest in a legend?"

Tell the truth, or feed him the lie? Avareth didn't hesitate.

"Curiosity. I overheard a pair of archdemons telling stories, but they seemed too precise to be fantasy. So I came to you." She ended with her most winning smile.

"Well, when you finish, you'll probably know more than they do."

*I'm counting on it.*

THE SPAWNING CHAMBER was quiet. Few demons were being created during this slack time in the Celestial War, so Avareth had no trouble finding her assignment.

She lay on a carnelian crystal slab, naked, her red hair spilling out in a plume around her. She was utterly motionless, not even breathing, and Avareth didn't know how to react. Dead bodies, she knew. She'd caused enough of them in her millennia on Earth, after all.

This one didn't seem dead, though the grayish skin wasn't helping.

She was waiting.

For what? Avareth didn't exactly know. Awakening, whatever that looked like.

After a few moments of waiting, Avareth pivoted, searching for anyone else to make sense of what she saw, but the chamber was empty, save for her and her silent companion.

"What do I do?" The words echoed, answering themselves without eliciting a response.

Avareth wandered around, searching for anything that made sense, but nothing came to light.

no effect Avareth could see. Kazraxas repeated the sequence twice more before Avareth's patience was exhausted.

"When will she wake up?"

"You stupid demon! You broke the ritual. Now I have to start over, and you'd better hope your clumsiness hasn't ruined her!"

"That's possible?"

Kazraxas ran her hands over her knobby skull. "It's likely. You said the Prince sent you?"

Avareth nodded.

"Then you'd better hope she's not broken."

THIS TIME, AVARETH remained silent until Kazraxas gestured for her to come over.

She hurried across and peered at the body on the slab. It wasn't breathing. That seemed wrong to Avareth.

"Damnation." Kazraxas laid a hand on the body's forehead, then pressed it to various places. When nothing appeared to meet her expectations, she returned to her bag and rummaged.

"What's wrong?" The possibility of failure chilled the blood in Avareth's veins.

"She's not awakening." Kazraxas continued searching.

Avareth groaned. "I thought you said this would work!"

"It would have if you hadn't screwed it up."

"You can't blame this on me!" Avareth said, a hint of panic in her voice.

"If I can't wake her? You bet I can. I won't end up in the Lake of Brimstone for your mistake. Found it!" She pulled a large, multi-faceted indigo crystal from the bag.

"What's that?"

"It's the life-bearer."

Avareth leaned forward, trying for a better look.

"Dammit, what do I do?"

"You can stop shouting, for a start."

Avareth spun to the voice. A tall female demon, one who towered over Avareth, emerged from a dark alcove. She was wearing a loose wrap and carrying a bag.

"Who are you?"

"Kazraxas."

"That tells me nothing."

"I answered the question. It's my turn. Who are you, and why are you here?"

Avareth was about to refuse before remembering her need for information.

"I am Avareth, sent here by Prince Beelzebub for the awakening of Kalili."

"Who?"

Avareth pointed to the redhead.

"Oh, her. She'll be awake soon."

Despite herself, Avareth was curious. "What do you have to do?"

Kazraxas stared down at her. "How much do you understand about the cessation of suspended animation?"

"Nothing." She hadn't even heard of it.

"Recovery of the soul and uniting with the body?"

"Nothing."

"Then be quiet, stay out of my way, and let me do my job." Kazraxas didn't sound upset, but there was no arguing with her. As she pulled crystals and powders and rocks from her bag, she continued. "Awakening a demon is almost never done, and I am the only one in Hell who has the knowledge to do it. The ritual is finicky and requires my full attention."

Avareth stepped back from the pedestal.

The next little while was confusing. Kazraxas waved her hands around, chanted, burned some terrible-smelling compounds, all with

"I've never heard of it."

Kazraxas placed the stone between the figure's breasts. "You wouldn't. It's difficult to find." She stepped back and closed her eyes. "I need to concentrate."

Avareth learned quickly and remained silent as Kazraxas chanted. This time, she paid attention to the words, their rhythm, and the gestures which accompanied them. Knowledge was power, something Avareth was familiar with, and power kept demons alive and out of the Lake. Knowing how to resurrect a demon?

Potentially priceless.

After Kazraxas ran through the routine a second time, Avareth gathered her courage. "What's wrong?"

"I don't know!" The words were a snarl. "And don't ask if I'm doing this right."

Avareth closed her mouth and thought of a different question. "Can you explain it to me? Maybe that will help. Or is there anything I can bring you?"

The resurrection specialist nearly barked an automatic refusal, then gave a grudging nod. "It can't hurt."

"Great. Tell me about the life-bearer." Kazraxas frowned at her, and Avareth spoke quickly. "It can bring someone to life?"

Intellectual snobbery warred with the desire to spread knowledge, and the latter won.

"No."

"But the name...?"

"Is wrong. It doesn't cause life."

"No?"

Kazraxas shook her head. "No. It restarts a life which is suspended, or awakens a demon who has been created." She waved a hand at the body. "Like this one."

Avareth pounced. "She's not a demon."

This earned her a glare from Kazraxas. "What do you mean? Of course she's a demon. What do you think she is, an angel?"

"No, but the Prince said she's a Thirteen." She watched Kazraxas for any hint of familiarity. She didn't expect a pained groan from the other demon.

"What?"

"The life-bringer and the curse I've been using works on demons." She plucked the stone from the body and returned to the bag.

"Isn't a Thirteen a demon?"

"No, they're—" She turned her attention from the bag to Avareth, intense eyes boring into her. "You don't know?"

Avareth thought quickly. "I need to make sure you know." Kazraxas looked like she was about to argue. Time to add a little pressure. "Prince Beelzebub wouldn't trust this to someone who knew nothing of Thirteens, but he needs to be certain of your ability. You're not impressing me so far."

That was enough. Distrust and backstabbing were survival traits in Hell. "A Thirteen is a being created to battle another Thirteen, neither good nor evil, not an angel, not a demon. Something other."

"Go on."

Kazraxas returned her attention to the bag, pulling bizarre items out and scattering them around. "Since this isn't a demon, I need to use a different crystal to provide a focus for the energies I summon. Ah!" She pulled another blue stone from the depths, but this was rounded, not faceted, and opaque, not clear. A six-pointed white star seemed to float just above the surface.

"Before you ask, this does the same thing as a life-bringer, but for a Thirteen. This is the only one in all of Hell." There was undeniable pride in her voice at being trusted with the unique object. She laid it on the body's forehead instead of above the heart.

"Why there?"

"Different curse," she explained. "Demons are created knowing their purpose and are given a basic knowledge of their abilities. Language, things like that. Understand?"

Avareth nodded. Languages weren't a problem for her.

"Thirteens know nothing. This stone imparts the collected knowledge of the cosmos to them. Otherwise, they couldn't fulfill their purpose."

Avareth frowned. If she was supposed to keep this Kalili ignorant, surely she couldn't allow Kazraxas to implant all that information in her skull. Could she?

Some of that thought showed on her face.

"What's the problem?"

What to tell Kazraxas? It went against the grain, but she'd have to tell the truth.

"My Lord wishes her to remain ignorant."

Kazraxas chuckled. "The knowledge will be there, but it won't be accessible without another curse, which I don't know."

Avareth's shoulders sagged in relief. "What will she know when she wakes?"

"No more than any demon."

"Perfect."

"Now shut up."

Kazraxas did a set of chants and gestures, similar to the earlier ones but distinctly different. When she stopped and stepped back, there was a smile on her face.

"Did it work?"

"It did. The stone is connected to the all, implanting the information."

Avareth approached the body, which still hadn't moved, or breathed.

"How long?"

"A while." Kazraxas packed the other items back into the bag.

"Do you need to do anything else?"

"No, the stone does the rest."

Kazraxas never felt the blade that entered her spine and emerged from her throat, which was a mercy. Ugly red cracks snaked out from the wounds, flooding the chamber with a ghastly light. They spread and multiplied, connecting and crossing, dividing the flesh into smaller and smaller sections. Finally, Kazraxas' body was entirely aglow, then it faded. When the light had gone, so had the body.

"Then you're no longer needed."

HOURS LATER, THE STAR continued to hover over the smooth blue stone, and the body remained still. Avareth reconsidered her decision to eliminate Kazraxas and muttered to herself.

"I may have been hasty." She rummaged through the contents of the bag. Most of it she couldn't identify, but she wasn't about to leave anything behind. Information was her best bargaining chip, and the items beneath her hands were probably priceless. Kazraxas certainly behaved that way.

"But who do I ask now? A problem for another day."

Avareth loaded everything back into the bag.

A change in the lighting drew her gaze back to the crystal pedestal. The star had brightened considerably before sinking back into the gem. Now it was fading and disappeared as Avareth watched.

"I wonder what happens next?"

As if in answer to her question, the body drew in a ragged breath.

Avareth jumped back in surprise before recovering her equilibrium. She tried to reassure herself.

"This is normal. It's what's supposed to happen. Right?"

Gathering her nerve, she approached the plinth. The figure drew in another breath, steadier, and Avareth leaned over. Color was spreading to her limbs, stripping away the gray pallor. Avareth reached for the stone and lifted it, tucking it into the bag.

The breathing evened out, slow and steady, and Avareth examined her for any other signs of life. She pressed a hand to one breast and felt the skin's warmth and the steady lub-dub of a heartbeat. It was nearly hypnotic, and Avareth let her awareness sink into the sensation.

"Hello?" A quiet contralto broke the spell. Avareth pulled her hand away as if suddenly frostbitten, whipping her head to face the source of the voice.

"Lucifer!"

The blue eyes, wide open and staring curiously, crinkled in confusion.

"I don't think that's my name."

Avareth caught her breath, then her brain caught up to her. She didn't think there could have been a mix-up; after all, how many Thirteens could there be? But it would be just her luck to have gotten the wrong one. Best to check. "What is your name?"

"Kalili. I think. At least, when you asked me, that's what came to me. I might be wrong." She shrugged against the carnelian.

"I'll call you Kalili." Avareth felt a measure of tension drop away. At least she wouldn't be killed for waking the wrong demon.

Kalili smiled, a wide, joyful expression that lit her face and surprised Avareth. Smiling wasn't something often seen in Hell, and the corners of her mouth involuntarily twitched in response.

*Stop it! It's a job, and if you screw it up, you are one dead demon!*

Kalili swung her legs over the side to dangle down and levered herself into a sitting position.

"Who are you?" The smile didn't leave her face.

"I'm Avareth."

"Avyreth?"

"Not quite. Avareth." She stressed the second syllable.

"Avyreth."

She groaned, but nodded. Close enough. "Come on."

Kalili dropped lightly to the ground and took a couple steps. Unexpectedly, she grasped Avareth's hand. Suddenly, Avareth's mind was filled with Kalili's thoughts. Confusion, anxiety, joy, eagerness, all jostling for position.

Demons were touch telepathic and could read the thoughts and emotions of anyone they came in direct contact with. New demons learned early to block their thoughts from casual transmission. Kalili was clueless, and the idea she'd need to be taught had completely slipped Avareth's mind.

Avareth jerked her hand away, and the smile disappeared, replaced by a look of dismay.

"Why did you do that?" Kalili's voice matched her face. Avareth stumbled over her response.

"I—I was surprised."

"I didn't do something wrong?" She sounded genuinely concerned.

"No. It's okay." Avareth raised her mental barriers before offering Kalili her hand. Kalili took it and the smile returned, full force. She wasn't about to allow this stranger access to her thoughts, no matter how innocent she seemed.

"What now?"

Avareth shouldered the bag. "First, we get you dressed. You'll attract too much attention looking like that."

"I like what you're wearing."

Avareth surprised herself by laughing. "It wouldn't fit you. You're taller and fuller than me." She felt Kalili's gaze on her.

"That matters?"

"Yes. Trust me."

"I do."

The instant response was unexpected. Trust, like genuine happiness, was rare in Hell. Kalili didn't have any barriers up, allowing Avareth to see into Kalili, and there was no deception there. Lying wasn't a requirement in Hell, but it helped.

She'd have to teach her. Otherwise, this Thirteen wouldn't last a week.

"LORD BEELZEBUB WILL see you now." The imp sounded both terrified and pompous, a challenging feat he pulled off with no visible effort. The quiver in his hands added to the effect. Avareth tapped Kalili's shoulder.

"Come on."

"Where are we going?"

For the third time, Avareth repressed a growl and said, "To learn your task."

"Oh."

She followed with no further repetition.

When they were before Beelzebub, Avareth averted her eyes in respect, then noticed Kalili was staring at the Prince.

"Drop your eyes," she hissed.

"What?"

"Do what I'm doing."

"Oh."

That seemed to be Kalili's pattern: a question, followed by a monosyllable. It was irritating, but predictable, and Avareth could deal with predictable.

"You brought her here. Why?" Beelzebub didn't sound irritated, which bade well for Avareth's continued existence.

"She's awake."

"I see that. I told you about your assignment, Avareth."

The slightest frown creased her brow. It wouldn't do to contradict or argue with a Prince, but she might get away with asking for clarification.

"Yes, Lord, you did. But you didn't tell me hers."

He glared at her. "I did."

Now she was stuck. All of her options sucked. Calling Beelzebub on his lie to his face would end with her dead, if she were fortunate. More likely, she'd be given to demons as a toy.

No, thank you.

She could call it a faulty memory. It was risky, but better than directly contradicting him. Still, if he was offended, she would be done.

Unfortunately, her preference, turning Kalili loose to find her own way, wasn't an option, dammit. She had her orders directly from Beelzebub and she got to play minder. Anything Kalili did to screw up her assignment would be held against Avareth. Lucky for her.

Disobedience was a terminal condition in Hell.

As a last option, she could try to discover Kalili's assignment through her own channels, but what if it was a trap? Avareth's information network was top-notch, but this was Hell. Plots didn't simply seem to lurk everywhere; they actually *were* everywhere, as all the denizens attempted to better their situation. Using her sources for Kalili's benefit might end up costing her more in the long run.

It was still the least shitty option, and the one which had the best probability of keeping her alive.

"My mistake, Lord. Of course you did."

Was that a gleam of respect in his eyes? Or, more likely, malice?

Time to leave.

"Come, Kalili."

Avareth bowed and backed away, pleased to see Kalili copy her actions without questioning.

*She can learn. Good.*

When they'd left his presence, Avareth cornered the imp.

"I need all your information on this one's assignment." She jerked a thumb at Kalili.

"On whose authority?"

"Lord Beelzebub needs her in place. Do you want to prevent it? He wouldn't be happy." She smiled inwardly at her clever non-answer.

As she hoped, invoking the Prince's name made the imp jump. In moments, she had everything the newly invented bureaucracy had produced regarding Kalili. She perused the files.

"Avyreth?" Kalili didn't sound like herself. Then again, what was she, usually, besides a burden?

Absently, still scanning, she said, "That's Avareth. Yes?"

"There's something wrong."

That got Avareth's attention. "What?"

"I don't know. It's like my middle is tight and grumbly."

"You're hungry." Avareth sighed. Demons didn't need food. Their *taaqat* supplied them with all they required. Human bodies still desired food, and it was easier to provide some than force the feelings aside. Kalili wouldn't know any of this, and Avareth didn't have the patience to teach her. Not yet.

"Hungry? What's that?"

And the questions began again.

SHE WAS GOING TO KILL her.

That was all there was to it.

How many questions could one person ask?

Wasn't she supposed to have basic knowledge?

If she did, she wasn't listening to any of it because she bombarded Avareth with question after question. Even finding her food hadn't slowed the onslaught.

And she insisted on calling her Avy.

"My name is Avareth," she growled yet again, after what had to be the fifteenth Avy.

The growl bounced off Kalili. She was utterly oblivious to the menace behind the reminder.

Or stupid. Avareth hadn't ruled that out.

"Avy, what's that?" Kalili pointed to something in the middle distance.

"That's an archdemon's palace."

"Do you live in one of those?"

"No. I'm not an archdemon."

"Will I?"

"No, you're not an archdemon either."

"Where will I live?"

"I don't know yet."

"Why not?"

"Do you ever shut up?"

"Sure." Blissful silence descended for all of ten seconds. "See?"

Avareth's hand caressed the handle of her blade.

*I can't kill her. That would annoy Beelzebub, and he'd send me back to Earth for good.* Much as she enjoyed being out of Hell, the prospect of an eternity on Earth nauseated her.

"Why's your hair that color?"

Avareth stroked her straight brown hair. It reached the middle of her back and helped with the illusion she was taller than she was.

"That's the color it is."

"But we can be whatever we want, right?"

Avareth nodded. On this interminable walk, she'd summarized the most common abilities of demons. One of those was bodily transformations and the cost that came with it.

"So you want your hair to be that color?"

Avareth started a response before considering the question and giving a more thoughtful answer. She twirled her hair around a finger as she spoke. "I'm not unhappy with it, and I like the length."

"I think you'd be pretty with different hair."

"I'm not pretty?" Avareth didn't think herself vain, but the casual way Kalili tossed out her comment cut to the quick.

"No, you're really cute!"

What?

Avareth had seen into Kalili's thoughts enough to know there wasn't an ulterior motive behind the compliment. Hell, there was doubt Kalili knew what a motive was. Everything she did or said was an in -the-moment reaction.

Avareth thought about her response. *Cute?* She'd heard it before, but coming from Kalili was different. Somehow. That genuineness that pervaded Kalili, which Avareth would have to burn out of her before it got her killed, was at the forefront of her behavior.

Before she composed an appropriate response, Kalili spoke again.

"But you'd look better with different hair." Kalili stopped, forcing Avareth to stop. "Avy, look at me."

Almost unwillingly, Avareth turned. She didn't like being reminded of their height difference.

Yes, she could change her body to be taller, stronger, and even have different hair. But she liked this body. It suited her. Other demons overlooked her, dismissed her, which allowed her freedom a larger presence wouldn't. She could sneak in and out of spaces without notice, strolling through as if she belonged. On the rare occasions she was questioned, her diminutive stature allowed her to play the meek and innocent card and escape.

Unexpectedly, Kalili put her hands on Avareth's cheeks and pressed her lips to Avareth's. Avareth's eyes went wide. This was completely out of the blue, but she didn't break the kiss.

There was nothing behind it except a desire to do it. No ulterior motive. No scheme, no plan. Just... Kalili wanted to kiss her, so she did.

When Kalili broke the kiss, Avareth almost drew her back in. Almost.

"I think you're pretty, but you could be beautiful. Your eyes are..."

Avareth waited. That was one thing she didn't change. Eye color was challenging, though she'd never been able to discover why. Temporary change was possible, but no matter her form, she always had the same pale lilac irises.

"Are what?"

"Gorgeous. You ought to let your hair match them."

Kalili dropped her hands and continued their walk. Avareth, stunned, lingered a moment before hustling to catch up. They walked in silence for a few moments before Avareth asked the question on her mind.

"You think so?"

"Uh-huh."

Gorgeous?

It had to be Kalili's newness talking.

Nobody ever called her gorgeous. Cute occasionally, and never by a fellow demon. The humans she interacted with during her sojourns on Earth were more interested in what she could teach them.

Despite her internal protests, the comment warmed her.

"Maybe." She grunted the word, denying the warmth, and continued walking.

A few paces further on, Kalili spoke again. "Are you going to do it?"

"Do what?"

"Change your hair."

Avareth pivoted, hands on hips, ready to snap at Kalili for persisting. The snarl died on her tongue when she saw Kalili's earnest face. There was still no deception behind her words. She was innocent, which struck Avareth with the force of Lilith's spells.

"You think I should?" Avareth permitted her cautious optimism into her words.

Kalili's plume of red hair waved with the vigor of her nodding. "Yes!"

"I'll think about it."

Kalili clapped her hands in glee. Avareth suppressed an unwilling grin. Something about the woman's enthusiasm was contagious.

Dangerous, too, if they spent much time in Hell.

Time to get her to Earth and her assignment, so Avareth could start hers.

Hmm. Could she use Kalili's assignment to return to her own?

"What do you know about wine?" she asked.

"What's wine?"

*That would be nothing.*

This time, Avareth was happy to explain.

THEY STOOD IN FRONT of a portal to Earth, one of hundreds scattered throughout the realm. With these, they could transit without relying on the whims of an archdemon. Or at least no more than they ever did.

"Tell me again?" Kalili was nervous, eyeing the swirling orange vortex with suspicion.

"I know where we're going. You hold my hand, and we step in here, and come out on Earth. It's easy. I've done it thousands of times."

The waves of unease rolled off Kalili, but Avareth could tell she was trying to control it and approved. "You're sure?"

"Positive." Avareth reached out her hand and brushed her fingertips against Kalili's palm. A trickle of energy spread up her arm as their *taaqat*s attempted to balance.

"What's that?" The nerves were back, and Kalili's hand separated from Avareth's fingers.

"It's your *taaqat*. Your soul energy. When we touch, our bodies want to balance it. You have more than me, so it's flowing from you to me. You can stop it." It was an effort of will, but not difficult, for a demon to stop the transfer.

"No. It feels good. I was surprised." This time, Kalili's fingers sought Avareth's hand, clasping it. The flow of *taaqat* resumed. "I'm ready."

Avareth already knew. Kalili's mind was open to Avareth, and she took full advantage.

Wonder. Joy. Confusion. And... love? The flavor was unfamiliar.

Impossible.

Demons didn't love.

They weren't capable of it. Not truly. Not without having an eye on a larger goal.

Love was weakness, allowing someone else to enter your mind and soul and heart. An attack from within was always more devastating, as Avareth had proven on many occasions.

A false flag, only valuable for the cover it provided.

But Kalili didn't know any of this.

Whatever she was feeling, it was...real.

Could it be possible? Avareth dove deeper.

No, not love. Not yet. But fondness and certainty and trust, all evoked by Avareth?

Astounding.

She gave herself a mental shake and withdrew to the periphery of Kalili's mind.

"Here we go."

Hands firmly entwined, they stepped into the portal, instantly emerging on the far side among scrubby pine trees on the side of a worn mountain. Bright sunlight streamed down through the scattered clouds, warming them.

"Wow." The awe Kalili felt at the change in their surroundings suffused their connection and colored Avareth's view. She'd been here many, many times before, but Kalili's emotional overlay added unexpected depth. The blue sky and green trees, which Avareth had long ignored, suddenly appeared striking and vibrant. Even the browns and grays of the ground were noteworthy.

Avareth tore her gaze from the landscape to search for the signs of the settlement she'd been working with. Ah, there were the traces of smoke from their fires.

"This way." She tugged on Kalili's hand, and the redhead followed.

They descended the mountainside, still holding hands. Avareth snuck peeks into Kalili's mind to get her perspective on the scenery, relishing the untainted visions. Finally, when Avareth reckoned they were just out of earshot of the humans, she dropped her hold on Kalili's fingers. Kalili turned in confusion.

"Why?" Her hurt and surprise came through clearly.

Avareth didn't have a better answer than an unwillingness to give any more information about herself away. Kalili wouldn't understand that; not yet, at least, and Avareth found herself reluctant to crush that innocence.

"It's only for now. They don't know you yet. To them, if we walked in holding hands, it would mean we belonged to each other."

Surprising herself yet again, Avareth told Kalili the truth, or at least a portion of it.

"We don't?"

Avareth's immediate "of course not" died on her lips. In an odd way, they did, didn't they? Kalili was certainly hers; her assignment, at a minimum.

"Let's start by introducing you before we do anything else?"

Kalili considered, then nodded. "Whatever you say, Avareth."

The sound of her proper name from Kalili's lips after so many corrections shocked Avareth, so much so that she said, "Call me Avy."

Kalili's smile was brilliant, echoed by Avy.

Maybe this assignment wouldn't be so bad.

# A Word from the Author – AC Adams

Yes, I'm back!
There are perks to being the publisher; one of them is, when my co-editors tell me I hafta put a second story in, well, I gotta!

Or maybe that's not a perk.

I'll have to figure that out.

So this story is the one I planned to have in here. After all, if you've read my books, you know Kalili and Avareth have a complicated past. It's alluded to a couple times, but I thought it would be fun to dive in, because they really start off as total opposites. Tell you a secret: I think Faith reminds Kalili of herself, way back when, and that's one reason they resonate so well. But who am I to say? It's her story, not mine.

Playlist? Not really, sorry. This was an offshoot of both Testing Faith and Keeping Faith, so both of those playlists have been bouncing around my head. I'm not gonna list all hundred songs!

Now for my thank yous. First, always, my wife, my biggest fan and cheerleader. I only drive her nuts on days ending in Y. Next, my co-publisher, mentor, editor, and friend, Adam Gaffen. He kicks my butt when I need it, and I'm a better author because of it. And I'd be remiss if I didn't mention my friend and co-author Nat Paga, who came on board as an editor for this book when Adam and I realized we'd bitten off more than we can chew. She's also a kickass writer! And finally, you. My readers. Knowing that I bring some happiness to you through my words makes the days teaching much, much shorter!

Since this is definitely a Kalili & Faith story, you need to go to my site! That would be https://kaliliandfaith.com

AC

# Death Do Us Meet

## By Rose Sinclair

### Act 1: First, Birth

The first time Layla saw her was in the bustling hallways of their middle school.

Time had brought them together, and time had separated them. Though in high school they had few classes together, Layla's glimpse of Maryam's familiar silhouette was a comforting backdrop amongst the noise of lockers slamming and the clanging of demanding school bells.

She was standing at the far end of the hall, her shoulder-length hair a waterfall of black silk, the frame of her shoulders an uneven slope under the collar of her school uniform.

Maryam's eyes were the same deep brown Layla remembered from many sleepovers when they had been inseparable friends. Friday nights where they shared secrets and stories, and promises that seemed like they'd last forever. The distance between them grew. Not from their own choices, but the hurdles of life that had once only been chutes and ladders on a board game.

As Maryam looked back from afar, she felt a wave of sadness wash over her. The passing of time doesn't cure love. By the time college came around, Maryam knew exactly what she wanted from life. She stepped onto the porch of her beloved's house, the cicadas singing in the trees above. Her heart was pounding as she knocked on the solid wood door, her palms slick with sweat.

When Layla's father opened the door, he greeted her kindly. Maryam left her shoes behind and stepped inside the familiar room. Its wooden ceiling beams and polished floors framed an heirloom tea set on the table that left a lingering aftertaste in the back of her throat from the mere sight. This place used to bring her such comfort. Now, it was filled with a strange uncertainty as she summoned the courage to ask Maryam's father for his daughter's hand in marriage.

Love was a sickness and a remedy, a virtue and a vice, from God, and utterly without. Even knowing the right thing to do could not shake the fear of what the response might be.

This offer of marriage had been quickly refused. The words of Layla's father still rang in her ears. "A poet is good for nothing. You cannot eat flowery words, or burn them when the winter grows cold."

Layla and Maryam had known each other for nearly their entire lives. They had grown up in the same small suburb, gone to the same school, and shared stories and secrets. Their friendship had been a source of strength and comfort for both of them. Maryam had thought this might have been enough to transcend class, status, and tradition.

No. Layla's father was adamant; she could not marry Maryam. He had been raised in a culture where same-sex marriage was not accepted, and his beliefs had never wavered. He had warned Layla that if she married someone of the same gender, she could be excommunicated, shunned, and excluded from the community. "And to add in such a frivolous field of study," her father said, with a shake of his head, and a tightening of his brow. "And one might as well pack a bindle now."

Layla knew that Maryam was special to her, and she wanted nothing more than to be with her. But she also knew that following her heart would mean defying her whole family, a path she had never before considered. The world wasn't about blindly securing your desires when so many couldn't even meet their needs.

After college, her father's words rang true. Layla was still only able to watch from afar. A heavy silence hung between them as Maryam's poetry books were now tucked away in flour-covered pockets of her apron.

Art doesn't pay. The best way for a woman to secure herself in society was to marry a rich man. Something Layla was running out of time to do.

The unspoken tension bloomed between the two women from the soil of unfulfilled promises that each of them had made to the other. Even from outside the glass-faced building, the scones in the window display made the air sweet with cinnamon and nutmeg. The bells over the door jingled as customers entered the bakery. The conversations inside were hushed as a secret as Layla nervously licked her lips desiring a taste. The wind nipped at her neck, the earth hard beneath her feet. Both urged her to take a step. But at this crossroad, which way?

At that moment, Layla realized the decision wasn't ever hers. When her father's permission was needed, love had never been her choice.

Maryam's eyes lifted from the cash register, meeting with Layla's for a brief moment. The fleeting glance seemed to linger for an eternity. A wave of emotion washed over them, a reminder of the childhood bond that had connected them since the first time they had set eyes upon each other.

At that moment, they both knew that no matter what happened, they would always remain connected. Dreaming of the fantasy that they could never have.

Her phone chimed an unhappy reminder of where she was meant to be. As she glanced down at the phone, her mother's name was a family banner full of duty and honor. It didn't even matter what the message said. She took a step down the sidewalk and away from the bakery.

Layla nervously adjusted her headscarf as she picked up the pace to make it to the restaurant on time. Her parents, along with three other people sat at a table under a canopy that shielded them from the afternoon sun.

Everyone stood as her father made the proper introduction. Voices lifted in pride over Ibnu, who worked in finance alongside his father. After pleasantries were exchanged they all sat at the table to eat. While breaking bread, Layla noticed the sly glances and subtle nods between her father and Ibnu's. Discussions of the future shifted from vague comments about the academic accomplishments of their respective children into open plans for how the marriage would be arranged.

Inbu seemed well-mannered and friendly. But his eyes flickered away and down to his plate whenever Layla tried to meet his gaze.

**Act 2: First, Life**

Layla felt a strange sense of déjà vu as she stepped into the store. This was the same shop she had been to with Maryam back when they were kids. She remembered the giddy excitement over discussions of what their dream wedding dress would be. The feeling of the expensive, high-quality fabric slipped through their young fingers as they ran through the racks of pristine white dresses.

As children, they quickly got kicked out of the store by a saleswoman who angrily shooed them out of the stop. Yet today, the saleswoman glanced up from her desk with a wide smile and greeted her like an honored guest she'd been patiently waiting to see.

Given this was an arranged marriage she suddenly didn't know if she should pick something traditional or the one she had always pictured. She had no idea if her soon-to-be husband would even like that.

The saleswoman must have sensed her hesitation because she cheerfully and quickly suggested different options. Layla was surprised to find that there were many different styles to choose from. How did arranging this whole thing somehow make things even more complicated?

Both mothers joined her a moment later, to help her choose ones to try on. As Layla slipped into the first dress, she felt a wave of emotion wash over her. She was about to embark on a new journey, one that she had never expected for herself. But, she was determined to make the best of it.

She thought of Maryam, and the dreams they had shared as children. She whispered a silent prayer that Maryam would find happiness, wherever her life might take her. Because her own life was going to be blessed and full of bounty and security that she came to value as an adult.

Layla stepped out of the dressing room and the trio of women gasped in delight. The fabric was delicate and shimmering, making her feel like a princess. Layla smiled as she looked at herself in the mirror. She knew that this dress was perfect. Even if it wasn't the one she had dreamed of wearing when she married Maryam, it was the one she was meant to wear. Layla smiled as she looked around the room. She was surrounded by love, and she was determined to make the most of it.

Later that week, Layla sat at the small table in Maryam's bakery, fidgeting with the napkin in her lap. She had been nervous about this taste test once she heard where her father had chosen. From the moment she arrived, she was practically shaking. So visibility that Maryam's mother offered to turn up the bakery's heating.

Layla sat across from her new fiancé, who reached out and took her hand to give it a reassuring squeeze. In the short time they had known each other he seemed sweet. They could become good friends, but love? Maybe that wasn't for marriage.

"It's okay, Layla," he said softly. "This bakery has wonderful cake. As soon as you warm up from the cold outside, I'm sure you'll start to enjoy your day."

But Layla couldn't help feeling a pang of guilt as she looked around the bakery. She wasn't sure if Maryam would be here working with her family today. It felt taboo to be here, as if moments away from tying the knot with someone else. A place that had once been filled with so much of the girl's childlike joy, was now being used to select a cake for a legal ceremony to someone else.

Just then, Maryam emerged from the kitchen, with a tray full of colorful cake slices. Surprise melted into a warm smile on her face. "Hello, Layla," she said, her voice friendly and professional. "It's nice to see you again."

"Good afternoon," Layla replied, trying to keep her voice steady. "Honored to have your family allow us this private tasting today."

"Of course," Maryam said, glancing at Inbu as her expression slipped into a neutral mask. "It's always a pleasure to work with a happy couple. I've prepared a selection of our most popular flavors for you to try."

Layla tried to focus on the task at hand as Maryam placed slice after slice of cake in the middle of the table for the couple, describing the flavors and ingredients of each one. But no matter how hard Layla tried, she couldn't shake the feeling of guilt and sadness that seemed to weigh down on her.

After they narrowed the choices down to two, Ibnu excused himself to go to the bathroom. An antagonizing moment later, Layla couldn't take it anymore. "Maryam, I would have told you––should have told you first... I'm so sorry," she blurted out. "I never meant to hurt you. I never meant for any of this to happen."

Maryam looked at Layla with kindness in her eyes. "I know that, Layla," she said. "I want you to have the best wedding and the best life possible. That's all that matters."

Tears sprang to Layla's eyes as she knew just how much Maryam cared for her. "There's no love in marriage," she mumbled to the unfinished cake slices.

"It is to make children," Maryam added to finish the thought. This was such a brutal take on such a romantic moment that Layla glanced up at someone who she had known to be so full of the creative spirit. "I've heard it from your mother plenty."

"And now, let's get back to business," Inbu said, unaware of what he had walked back out into. "Do you know which you desire for the big day?"

"I..."

"Layla," Maryam said softly, "which cake do you like?"

She pulled on a smile as she looked at the delicious array of cakes in front of her. Layla knew had to be ready to move on and start the next chapter of her life with Inbu by her side. Everyone reached the age where they had to put childhood toys and dreams away.

When it was time to pick up the wedding cake, Layla stood in front of the bakery, staring at the sign in disbelief. "Sorry we are closed ...my heart is broken, I'm too sad to make crepes </3." For all the blessings and hurdles of an arranged marriage, she was unsure what to make of this one.

She'd never seen the bakery closed like this. Maryam's family was large enough that there was usually someone who could run the family business for the day.

After seeing Maryam, so confident and firm, it was almost hard to believe that this had anything to do with her and Inbu's cake being ready for pickup. The woman had always turned everything into flowery-filled prose. Layla stared at the handwritten sign wondering if this had grown from that same soil. Maybe Maryam had been struggling more than she had let on in person.

Feeling a mix of guilt and concern, Layla reached for her phone and dialed Maryam's number. When it went straight to voicemail, she tried her mother's number which sat there untouched since their last childhood sleepover. It rang and rang, but there was no answer.

**Act 3: First, Death**

Maryam stood at the edge of the woods, staring at dense trees and tangled underbrush. It was a crazy idea that she'd only seen people joke about doing. But life was never a joke for Maryam. Nature was wild and giving. Why shouldn't she just forget all the ties that bound her to the world's horror and be free?

She started to walk through the woods, moving around what nature provided to start building a new home for herself. As the night grew dim, she heard a voice calling her name. "Maryam! Maryam! Allah, have you gone majnun? Where are you?"

She turned towards the sound of her mother's voice, as her father's call followed. "Maryam, please come back," he pleaded, "We miss you, we need you! The bakery isn't the same without you."

But Maryam couldn't bring herself to leave. She might have been able to find her way back, but she was too lost in the wilderness of her own emotions to have the will to do so.

Out of the shadows of the trees, a figure emerged. Maybe she had gone mad like her mother had asked God because standing there was herself as a child.

"We know beauty and pain," she told herself, "We sing poetry as medicine."

As her parents called out again their voices grew distant that Maryam had to turn to listen, the child spoke again. "Don't listen to them," she said with a playful laugh. "You don't need to go back to that life. You have me and you have poetry. Live in the wilderness and be sustained by the earth holding us up."

Maryam pressed her lips together, surveying the fort she had built for herself. It was a fantasy built for a child, but could it hold the life and death of an adult?

"Run away," her childhood self said. "Be like Layla and Majnun of old. Live for love and art alone. You do remember what we told Mother when she asked if we loved Layla?"

Maryam's eyes fell to the shadows on the ground. "I said, no. Love is a string that connects. Layla is me."

"And, I am Layla." When Maryam lifted her head once more it wasn't her younger self standing there anymore it was Layla. Layla, dressed in a hand-stitched kaftan that looked out of some historic past as her deep brown eyes signaled a rich future.

Maryam took a step forward as love offered out her hand. "Yes, Layla," she said, "I'll go with you. Follow you to where no one can take this away from us."

Layla and Maryam fled deeper into the wilderness, leaving the bakery and the pain of false promises behind. They danced, sang, and loved under each phase of the moon. Ran across streams that cleaned their feet and washed their footprints away as if never to be found again.

"Maryam, wait!" Layla called.

She turned away from a future mad with love and to the past where Layla was standing. Layla with a golden ring and shining stone on her finger. This was, and wasn't, Layla. Maryam blinked like a frozen deer that didn't know what to make of humans and their dangerous wild.

"Forgive me?" Layla asked.

"There's no love in the world that needs to be forgiven," Maryam said, "There's no love in the world that is wrong."

Layla smiled as if Maryam had just given her an exquisite gift. She looked at her engagement ring and shook her head at the shimmering promise it represented. "Love feels like a native language that I never learned to speak."

As Maryam held still as the mountains behind her, Layla pulled her bag forward to draw forth the notebook of poetry. She pulled open Maryam's book, turned to a page, and began to sing the words as bright and sharp as a bird. "O' friend, be my layla for I am majnun for you." A page turned like the day to night. "I don't have the right.

Only a wish under a twinkling of silvery white. With rose and woes, along with a song, we could instead, measure our treasure in the warmth of our bed."

Maryam paced during the poetry reading. Finding new shelter in the shade that a tree cast as if that life had already passed.

"I'll go with you," Layla said, no longer reading from words on the page. "You are my love. And I am yours." She gingerly put the notebook away, before tugging on her finger where the shining stone sat until it pulled free from her hand. "This vow? It was never made by me. A son of man can live without me, but I can't live without you. Marrying anyone besides you would be like dying before death."

Maryam laughed out loud. "You love me, Layla?"

She nodded and ventured closer to stand the closest they had in years. This felt more like home than anywhere else she'd been in far too long. "When we stopped talking, I didn't realize the depth of your love. If I had known, I wouldn't have been able to bury my own. When you wrote that you would fail an autopsy because there's nothing left inside? That humans need fantasy to make life bearable. And without it, there is no magic or hope. Living, but no life. We don't need to wait a lifetime. The poor can marry for love. We will be rich in our own way."

Maryam's eyes filled with tears as she looked at the woman before her, and lifted a hand to Layla's cheek, feeling a warmth and connection that she had never felt with anyone else. "What will that be like?"

Layla gazed into her eyes with a look of love and devotion. "It will be every fantasy we still enjoy that was first dreamed up together as kids."

As the sun rose above the horizon, Layla leaned up and pressed her lips gently against Maryam's. The world brightened as they shared their first-ever kiss. Tender and passionate. A brush of lips that sealed their commitment to each other.

They stood on the hill, gazing into each other's eyes, lost in the beauty of the moment with a love that would last beyond life and death itself.

# A Word from the Author – Rose Sinclair

**Why I Wrote This Story:**
W Given the prompt of spring origins and romantic firsts, I was trying to think of the oldest love story I could think of. The Greeks, and the English tales weren't doing it for me so I thought more about my own background and came across Layla and Majnun's story. Many have cited this Arabic story as an inspiration for Shakespeare's Romeo and Juliet. But unlike both of those tragedies, I wanted my third act in this collection to put hope and choice in our own futures as the central point.

**Acknowledgments:**
I wanted to thank the team of (AC) Adams and Adam (Gaffen). People talk a lot about doing things, but actually showing up for not only the work, but for each other is much more rare and important. I think community has the ability to keep people cruelly apart or bring them together and I'm happy that this book is an act of togetherness.

**Bio:**
Rose Sinclair is a queer author and former community leader who started with a blog in 2013. The biggest noisemaker they spearheaded was a protest in 2015 that made GLADD step up for the wider LGBTQIA+ community, and paved the way for future acceptance of those communities and on-screen TV representation.

Before becoming a full-time writer, they popularized several community terms and set up a decentralized support system with a "Dear Abby" style approach. They are the author of HELLO

WORLD, and have a steamy BIG BAD MAGIC series that is available now wherever books are sold or downloaded to kindles!

You can find more of Rose Sinclair's mythological retellings in The Cupid Fate, or visit https://RoseSinclair.com

**Playlist:**

Ha'oud (I Will Return) — Yo-Yo Ma

Kalam — Mashrou' Leila

# We Got the Beat

## By O.E. Tearmann

"Come on, Jen! It'll be amazing!"

Bunny made like her name and jumped three feet straight in the air. She grabbed her bae's hands and spun them around.

Jen laughed, sandy hair flying as their bae spun them. They shoved their hair out of their eyes when Bunny let go. She was so cute when she got excited like this. But still...

"Bunny... I dunno... all those *people*..."

Bunny bounced on the balls of her feet, the long brown ears that had given her the nickname stuck straight up and quivering. "Jen Jen Jen the people are *the point*!" Teeth bright in her dark face, she held out her tab.

"See? The Beat has kinetic tiles. When people dance there, the kinetic energy they generate powers, like, ten blocks of their neighborhood! Isn't that cool? Isn't that the very absolute best?" Hugging her tab to her chest, she spun in a circle. "And Nine Tails is playing! Oh, my god Jen! I've loved Nine Tails like forEVER! And the folks said we can go! I'm finally sixteen now, and you're seventeen, and the Meet says anybody sixteen plus is cool to go into Denver on their own, and the whole fam is doing a group trip, and my folks cleared me and once my folks say yeah you know your dad will, and the Beat's got an under eighteen night! Oh my god oh my god!"

She bounced straight up in the air, high enough to bump the ceiling panel with her hands. A little cascade of dust drifted down to salt her hair with white as she laughed. "And Lucky, she sings lead for the Nine Tails, she actually holds her *mic* with her *tail!* It's that long, and it's *prehensile!* Isn't that just the *best thing?* I mean, how often do we see Gammas like us showing off like that on stage?! Like, never!"

Jen glanced down, rubbing a hand up and down their arm. They sure didn't want to show off their eyes, or anything else that marked them as one of the genetic lines that the old corporate powers had screwed around with when they were trying to make people who didn't need so much food and water. Really, they didn't want to show off. Period.

"Isn't it going to be kinda noisy in there for you?" Their bae waved a hand.

"Psh! That's what ear plugs are for! Mo and Uncle Tafarah can print me a nice set like Papa has, yeah?"

"Oh," Jen said to their shoes. "Yeah. I guess so."

Bunny's ears shifted down from Bonkers Setting to Happy Setting, and she cocked her head. "Jen babe, what's up?" Stepping in, she rested her hands on Jen's shoulders.

Jen looked up, blinking to refocus their eyes on their bae's face. They did their best to smile. "Nothing, Bun. We're good. Sounds fun."

Bunny raised her eyebrows; her ears went in the other direction, sticking out on either side of her head like no-crossing bars on the rail line. "Jen, don't play. What's up?"

Jen could feel their insides tightening up. They didn't want to hurt their bae, but they needed Bunny out of their face. They needed space to think, bad.

Gently, they disentangled themselves. "Need some headspace, kay? I'll let you know in time to get tix. Sound good?"

"Yeah... sure..." Bunny agreed, but her ears sank. "I... guess I'm gonna go help Mama and Aunt Billie for a bit. See you later?"

"Yeah, later." Jen tried for a smile. Turning, they headed for their room. They had some studying for their next Community Career Accompaniment, and in their room they could *think*.

Crossing through the common area of the farm, they acknowledged a few waves from friends and fam. A guy bringing in stuff from Denver nearly ran them over, backpedaling with his boxes in his arms. "Oh jeez, sorry miss, uh, pal. Didn't see you there." He stared for a second, gave them a sickly smile, and rushed past.

Jen's gut dropped like a concrete block. Miss. City people were always seeing them as a girl. City people always stared at them in the way that made Jen want to climb into a hole. Like they were something *weird*. Something *dangerous*.

And Bunny wanted them to go with her and deal with *a club full of city people*.

Pulling the hood of their shirt up, they booked it down into the residential wing and into their own cozy family space. Climbing the stairs to the second floor, they flopped down on their bed and caught their breath.

Outside, shade tarps fluttered over the canopies of produce trees that protected the rest of the food forest that made up Four Aces Farm, stretching all the way to the edible agave species against the pylon walls two acres away. The wall of water-condensation pylons shimmered in gentle shades of cream under the sun, painted murals gleaming along the base. Beyond the wall, re-seed prairie rippled in the hot wind. If they turned their head to the side and squinted, Jen could just spot a herd of buffalo, placidly grazing under the gene-modded fur that kept them cool in temps that'd kill an Alpha human.

Most Alphas couldn't see as far as Jen could, especially if they turned their head to one side and looked out of the corner of their eye. But hey, that's what goat genes were good for: good panoramic eyesight, good glycogen storage. Weird looks.

Rolling onto their back, they watched pollination drones fly around the skylight like little pieces of stained glass. Slowly, they ran through a breathing exercise.

When their pulse was closer to normal, they got up and opened their closet, pulling out their study stuff. The mirror inside the door flashed in the sun. For a second, they studied themselves. A fluffy person, all rounded curves. Tan skin, sandy hair. Round face. Yellow eyes, the pupils horizontal rectangles like power ports. There were their stubby hands with their three fingers. And their boobs, of course. Too big. Too obvious. Too out there, making people assume stuff about them. Making people weigh them up and judge them. Like they didn't get enough of that already when they left home.

Damn it, why did they have to leave home and go to some stupid club? People *got* them at home. At home they had fam, and they had friends, and they were okay. Out there...

Jen sighed and closed the closet door. Yeah. *Out There*. They were going to have to figure out *Out There*. And soon.

"WELL, THAT WAS WEIRD," Bunny muttered to herself, watching her bae head off. She worried about Jen sometimes. Some stuff freaked them out, and she got that. But why would this do it? Tickets to an amazing show they could go to together? Ears twitching uncomfortably, Bunny stood and tried to think it through. She'd thought Jen would be over the moon right along with her. Instead they were, what? Sad? Scared? No, that didn't fit.

What was going *on* with Jen? They loved to crank the music and dance with the fam. Wouldn't that be so much better at a place built for it?

Finally, Bunny let out a breath, shrugged it off, and jogged down the hall. Jen would tell her what was up when they'd had some time and some headspace. She only hoped they got to it before the fam got together to buy their tickets and get their ride set up. Right now, Bunny had her shift in the kitchen. And crap, she was running late. Picking up the pace, she kicked off a corner and bounced off the opposite wall, giving her an extra boost of speed. People ducked to either, grinning as she passed.

A sharp voice barked out of the admin wing. "Bao Li Amanzi! *Walk* in the halls! Don't run, and *do not parkour*!"

Bunny dropped to the floor with a wince. "Sorry, Miss DeLiquisha!" She kept her feet on the floor the rest of the way to the kitchen.

Walking in, she ticked her name on her Common Ground app to register her shift, washed her hands, and grabbed the first big bucket she saw. "Hey Mama! Hey Auntie Billie!"

"Hey Bunny!" the smiling Black woman called, just visible over the mountain of eggplant she was chopping. Seeing the veggies, Bunny groaned. "Auntie! Eggplant *again*?"

"It's ripe in the gardens," Auntie Billie agreed. "And it's good for you. Full of micronutrients that'll help you grow."

"Crap. Helps her g-g-grow? D-don't give Bao Li none." The tiny Asian woman fiddling with the beast of a bulk processor on Aunt Billie's left muttered, pulling something out of the mech'n'tech bag by her side. "Too tall n-now!"

Bunny laughed, trotting over and giving her mama a hug and teasing right back. "Jealous, dragon mama?"

Her mama snorted, hair like a skein of black silk swinging as she turned to look up at Bunny with eyes set at the same angle as her own. The light caught along the golden scales covering her mama's arms, gleaming amber from wrist to shoulder. "Honest, rabbit d-d-daughter. Tall alr-ready. Tall as Papa, soon. See?" She stood on tiptoe to return Bunny's squeeze. "Now c-c-c-come help, kay? R-roaster's being an ass again."

"You overload it again?" Bunny teased.

"She did," Billie laughed.

"You hush," Mama retorted. "It was taking f-f-forever."

"And now it'll take longer because we gotta fix it," Bunny added. "You gotta learn to just chill, Mama."

Auntie Billie chuckled as she chopped. "Kid's telling it to you straight, Tweak. Listen up!"

Bunny's mother shot her A Look from bird-black eyes. "Next time Mo gives you c-crap, I'll r-remind you of that."

"Feel free!" Billie's knife made soft clickity-click noises on the chopping board.

Mama snorted and turned back to Bunny. "You want c-c-coffee and chocolate or not, Bao Li?"

"Okay, okay." Mama was one of about ten people in the entire world who always called her by her real name, grabbing her attention without even trying. "I'll go high, you go low. Sound good? It's unplugged, yeah?"

"Well, duh," Mama agreed, tying her silky hair up in a bun and putting on a hat, grumbling. "Should c-cut this again."

"No, you shouldn't," Auntie Billie admonished. "Short hair was for the bad old days."

"Eh." Mama shrugged. "Point. Kay. Problem's in the r-roasting b-box. Temp's n-not getting high en-en-enough to do the b-beans right. Bao Li, you check the v-v-venting."

"Kay." Bunny grabbed a couple tools out of the mech'n'tech bag. She pulled on a mask to protect against dust particles, flattened her ears down, and stuck her head into the roasting chamber. "Hey Mama? You need your focus?"

"Nah," Mama's high voice drifted up through the ductwork of the machine. "This's easy."

"You got bandwidth?"

"Sure. You got t-t-trouble?"

"Not really trouble. I'm just confused. Can I talk it out with you?"

"Course," Mama's voice chirped back.

Bunny drew a deep breath. "Kay, here goes. Nine Tails is playing and they're even gonna play an under eighteen night, and I was so into it, and me'n the fam are getting us tix for it on Friday, and I went to Jen and I squee'd about it, and I thought they'd psych about it, they love to dance, but they... Mama, they acted like I was asking them to eat my plate of eggplant along with theirs."

"I heard that!" Auntie Billie called. "You know it's good for you!"

Bunny rolled her eyes. Eggplant was *so* not the point.

"Mama, what do I do for Jen?"

Silence.

"Vents okay?" Her mother's voice asked.

"Mama!"

"Vents? Okay?"

Bunny sighed. "I got the covers off, and... eugh no, not okay, they're stuffed full of cacao husks and dust again."

"Fuck," Mama grumbled. There were a few clanks below, and then her mama's hand was on Bunny's shoulder. "Kay. That's our p-problem. Need b-better f-filters on these. Move. I got it."

Bunny got out of the way and stood, fidgeting as her mother worked. With Mama, you had to let her process on anything that wasn't a machine or a computer. But waiting was so *hard*.

"Still don't l-like you guys g-going to Denver on your own," the shorter woman offered after a couple of minutes. Bunny rolled her eyes.

"Mama, we've talked about this. The Corporate Powers went down *sixteen years ago*. The United Communities of America been in charge for forever now! Things are *good*. Denver isn't a *war zone* anymore. It's *nice!*"

"Lotsa things look nice that aren't," Mama pointed out. Bunny rolled her eyes, ears stuck out in a flat line of annoyance.

Mama didn't even spare her a glance. "Your dad's w-worried too."

"Yeah, but that's 'cause you two are both paranoid! Papa isn't worried! And he says you two are paranoid!"

A little growl of irritation came out of the roasting box. "Inyoni told you that?"

"Yeah, he did," Bunny crossed her arms. "So?"

"That guy." Mama pulled herself out of the roasting box. Looking up at Bunny and away again, she crossed her arms, tapping one foot as she thought.

"Jen's acting w-weird about g-going to a p-place with l-lotsa s-s-strangers, yeah?"

Bunny hadn't thought about it like that. "Um. Yeah." Slowly, she dropped her eyes. "Mama... I think I hurt Jen's feelings. But I don't know how I did it, and I feel awful. I don't want my bae hurting. I wanna make it better."

Tweak nodded, staring at something around Bunny's hip-level. She had lots of trouble with eye contact; if she wasn't looking at you, that meant she needed the bandwidth for thinking. Slowly, she nodded to herself. Hey eyes flicked up. "I got g-guesses, Bao Li. But you don't want me on this. Go check it with your dad and your Uncle A on r-rec hours, kay?"

Bunny nodded, swallowing back her feelings. "Kay."

Around fourteen-hundred, Bunny trotted through the common hall, looking for two men who could help her get this straight.

Nope, her dad and her uncle weren't down here.

She passed the holo screens on the walls explaining Four Aces Farm to newbies and visitors: there was all kinds of stuff about the work to build a self-sufficient farm free of corporate control way back when, the creation of the open-source, gene-modded crops thriving outside despite the heat, the fifteen other open-source farms that started on the same model to feed the Denver Metro, and the land-revitalizing work that spread across the West from those starting points. They still did a ton of the testing for modifications to native species here at Four Aces, double checking all the plants and some animals being resurrected and gene-modded with everything they needed to survive the climate the Corporate Years had created.

Bunny had read the signs a million and a half times, so she passed them without really looking. She'd been born on this farm, and she knew *all* about its story. She was one of Four Aces' gene mods herself; her mama and papa both had Gamma genetics, and some abnormalities that threw out could have been bad, so her dad had offered his DNA to smooth everything out and make sure she was born okay. She was pretty happy with how that'd worked; she got her mom's eyes, her papa's pretty ears and good dark skin, and she got her dad's good health and hair color. Her hair was curly as anything, more like Papa's, even so, she liked the red in it.

Of course, if she'd got her mama's eye for detail, her papa's common sense, and her dad's brains, she'd already *know* what was going on with Jen. No such luck.

When she didn't find Dad or Uncle A in the library or the movie room, she bit the bullet and headed for their place in the residential wing. Her dad opened the door, smiling down at her.

"Well hello there, Treasure!" He translated her name out of Cantonese into English the way he did when he was happy. "What can I do for you today?"

Bunny could feel her ears droop as she smiled. "Hey Dad. Mama sent me your way. I got a—feelings thing to talk about."

Her dad leaned on the doorframe, light glinting off the lenses of his glasses. "A feelings thing. Sounds dire." He put out a thin white hand, giving her shoulder a gentle squeeze. "Come on in. I'll start the kettle and we'll have a chat."

Ears weighed down with embarrassment, Bunny followed her dad into his living space; a cozy one, all done up in stuff him and Uncle A had thrifted around the country when they went to the big Regional and National Quadrant Council Meetings or the Mayors' Summit events. Some of the stuff was really ancient, like the analog books or the engraved brass kettle that Dad filled and put on its heating base.

"Kev?" A man's voice drifted down from upstairs. "Something up?"

"Bao Li's come over for tea, love!" Kevin poked his head out of the kitchen to call up. "Got time to join us?"

A couple minutes later, Uncle A wandered into the kitchen. Bunny gave him a smile. She'd called him Uncle A since she was tiny; Aidan wasn't a real easy name for her to say as a baby, and the name kind of got stuck after that.

"Hey Bunny." Her uncle gave her a smile as he chose a tea from the cabinet. She always had to explain to newbies that no, he wasn't blood family, but he was uncle the way fam was fam; he was there, and he loved her, and he helped things get better. And wasn't that what family was?

"Bao Li's got an emotional upset she'd like a hand with," Dad offered. Uncle Aidan turned to look at her a little closer, blue eyes thoughtful.

"Yeah? What's up, Bunny?"

Bunny felt her ears flatten themselves. God, this was so embarrassing. Now she had to explain it in detail. Was she being a whiner?

She looked up when a hand, pale as apple blossoms, covered hers, and met Dad's kind grey eyes. He gave her hand a squeeze.

"In your own time, treasured girl. No rush."

Bunny drew a deep breath. "Okay, so..."

NIGHT CAME LIKE A DAMP cloth to cool the daytime fever. Out between the orange trees, Jen closed their eyes and breathed.

Far off, the gray wolves that had been reintroduced when they were eight howled. There were probably wolves from the third generation in the pack now, growing up on the prairie right along with them.

"Nice to hear them, hunh?"

Jen looked over their shoulder at the sound of the voice and smiled. "Hey Uncle Aidan."

"Hey Jen." The older man took a seat beside them in the soft mulch. "How's it going?"

"Okay." Jen knew they didn't sound all that believable.

For a couple of minutes, they sat in silence together. Uncle Aidan was good at being quiet, and together, and there. Jen liked that.

Everybody talked eventually. And so did he.

"I hear you're feeling kind of squicked about going dancing."

Jen looked down. "I... yeah."

"Seems like one of your big things here at home," the sun-tanned man suggested. "You guys love to crank the music and dance."

Jen shrugged.

"But you're dancing with your fam then, not with a bunch of strangers. Yeah?"

Jen stole a look up at Uncle Aidan. He leaned against a tree trunk, eyes closed, blonde hair catching glints of light between leaves.

"Yeah." It was a whisper.

Uncle Aidan smiled, just a little. "I hear you. I used to be that way. Used to hate people looking at me. They saw things I wasn't, and it got to me. Sound familiar?"

"Yeah," Jen agreed. "I just..." They stopped, stuck. Nothing they could say fit.

"How about I ask some stuff, and you tell me if it's a yes or a no?" Uncle Aidan offered.

Jen nodded. "Sure."

"Is it a Gamma thing?" Uncle Aidan began quietly. "Is it the way people look at your traits?"

"I... sorta?" Jen managed lamely.

"Is it maybe a looks thing? Like, people don't want to see somebody fluffy dancing. Is that going through your head?"

Jen shook their head. "That's dumb."

"Yeah, it is." Uncle Aidan's agreement was quick. "So, is it a sensitivity thing? Is it too loud? Too weird having a bunch of people you don't know around you?"

Jen had to think about that one for a minute. "I don't think so. It's... I've done a lot of volunteer work in the cities, and it doesn't feel that way when we're working."

"Kay, good recognition. So, is it maybe a gender thing? Are people looking at you and seeing something you're not?"

Jen's heart clenched. "I..." Slowly, they nodded.

"What's giving you the most dysphoria?" Aidan asked quietly.

Jen waved at their chest. "These. People see boobs and... ugh."

Uncle Aidan gave a quiet little grunt. "Yeah. They do, don't they? Used to get to me too. I wore the tightest binders I could get my hands on back in the day, before Kevin got me some that actually fit." He opened his eyes, staring ahead for a second. After a moment, he continued, slow and thoughtful. "Actually. Jen, do you want to come to my place for a bit? I got an idea, and after we see if I'm right, we'll have peppermint ice. Sound good?"

"Sure." Jen was willing, if a little thrown. They weren't sure what Uncle Aidan was thinking, but he was good at coming up with stuff. That was why he was one of the few permanent members of the

Farm Council. Besides, he always helped them out with gender stuff. Standing, they followed along.

"Hey Kev?" Aidan called as he opened the door of his living space. "Where's the old boxes from the barracks?"

"Basement, storage room, against the far wall!" Uncle Kevin called back. "Please tell me you're actually going to clean them. It's been over a decade!"

"Working on it!" Aidan threw back up to the loft, taking Jen's hand. "C'mon Jen, let's go see if it's there."

"What?"

"Some old stuff we kept meaning to repurpose and never did," Uncle Aidan replied with a smile. "You're shorter than me, but I'm guessing my pre-transition chest and yours match up size-wise. Want to see what you look like in a binder? If I don't have them after all, we'll print you some."

Jen wasn't sure what they were feeling, not yet. Whatever it was, it was warm.

Down the stairs in the basement, Uncle Aidan flicked the bioluminescent bulbs to life. They stepped into the next room, and Jen froze. At their living space, the storage room had spare candles, some stuff that wasn't working, Dad's smellier work clothes and that week's recycling being saved up for processing. Here, there were six old military trunks like hunks of greeny-black concrete. In a weird way, they looked dangerous. They looked like pieces of the Corporate Conflicts. It made Jen feel... They didn't know what. Sure, they knew their dad and a lot of their older fam were soldiers back then, before the corporations had come down, but knowing it and looking at this was different.

Beside her, Uncle Aidan sighed. "Man. Kevin's right, I need to clean this stuff out... Okay, Jen, you take the one on the right, I'll take the one on the left. Look for uniform clothes. If you find one with dresses, move on. If it's got weapons in it, tell me and step back, okay?"

"Okay." Jen lifted the lid on the first box. "Looks like... old data tabs and analog maps?"

"Crap," Uncle Aidan sighed. "Kay, let me help you shove that one off the top..."

It took four boxes before Uncle Aidan stood up, exclaiming, "I knew we never passed them along!"

Standing, Jen cocked their head as they watched their uncle pull out three black things like t-shirts without sleeves. He held them up with a grin. "Binders with recessed zippers! Kevin got them for me way back when. I only wore them a couple of years before I got my surgery, so they're still in great shape. Here." He held them out. "It's okay, they're clean. They're yours if you want them. Take them upstairs and try them on. See if they fit?"

Heart in their mouth, Jen reached out and took the handful of cloth. "What if they don't?"

Uncle Aidan shrugged. "Then I help you get fitted and we get you ones that do. Go see?"

They nodded. Stepping upstairs, they slipped into the bathroom, locked the door, and pulled off their shirt. The binder felt funny going on, and it was a little tight, but when they zipped it up, it was like being wrapped in a hug. And when they put their shirt back on...

They stared at themselves in the mirror. Slowly, they smiled.

"Good fit?" Uncle Kevin asked when Jen sat down at the table. They nodded.

Uncle Aidan set a cup of peppermint ice down in front of them. "If you want, DeLiquisha can help you do your hair. How's that sound?"

Jen grinned.

"MO!" BUNNY CALLED DOWN into the open floor panel when Friday afternoon rolled around. "Hey! Mo!"

Cocking her ears, she heard nothing but the clink of tools. Rolling her eyes, Bunny shimmied down a little, hooked both feet into the rungs of the ladder, and let herself drop until she was hanging upside down inside the maintenance area. She drew a deep breath.

"Mir-iiiii-am!"

There was a thunk, a clang, and an "Ow!"

"Bunny! You made me snag my hijab!" Mo's complaint rose from somewhere down in the works. "Crap!"

"Hold still, I'll come get you unstuck!" Bunny called. Scrambling down into the climate-support works, she trotted over to her friend and carefully pulled her blue hijab loose from the fittings of a pipe. "What're you doing down here?"

"I *was* taking an impression of the socket for a broken gasket control to make sure Baba and me printed it right." Miriam grumbled while tucking her hijab right again. "Before I got *interrupted*."

Bunny gave her pal a shrug and an ear flop. "Yeah, sorry. How soon're you done? The fam and me wanna pick up tix for Nine Tails, we gotta decide where we want to sit! Remember, we put it on the fam schedule?"

"Oh, yeah!" Mo's dark eyes lit up. "Has the registration opened yet?"

"Not yet, but it will in a bit, and I want us in fast!" Bunny bounced on the balls of her feet to burn off all her hype. "Figured we could grab treats and do it together! It's gonna be so cool, all us Aces at Nine Tails!!"

"Okay, okay, don't start getting excited down here, Bunny!" Mo laughed. "You'll bounce and get stuck!"

Bunny's ears angled down as she crossed her arms. "Will not."

"Will, did last time," the fourteen-year-old shot back.

Bunny sighed, ears dropping. "Okay, fine, rub my nose in it."

"Forever, probably! C'mon, up the ladder. I got the impression; just need to drop it off in the fabrication room and we can go."

"Great!" Bunny grinned, ears bouncing back up. "C'mon!!"

They stuck their heads into the fabrication room, Mo giving her dad a quick hug and dropping the mold into his hand. "Seeya Baba, me'n the fam are going to land tix for Nine Tails."

"And leave me all alone fighting with the structural printing again." Tafarah laughed, giving Mo's shoulders a squeeze. "Good luck landing good seats! Hi, Bunny!"

"Hey Uncle Tafarah!" Bunny stayed outside the door. "What's for dinner?"

"Billie didn't tell me!" Her uncle called back across the workspace. "Guess we're both going to be surprised!"

"Man, I was hoping to find out if it was eggplant again so I could duck it if it was," Bunny sighed when she and Mo were out in the hall. "Why's she have to be into eggplant right now?"

"Because it's what's ripe in the planting beds." Mo's reply carried her 'you know better' tone. "And it's good for you; it's full of micronutrients."

"It's full of ugh!" Bunny groaned, ears drooping.

Her fam caught her eye with a wicked grin, sunlight kissing golden tones and sapphire glints out of her skin and her hijab. "It is, isn't it? Mom's begging Abigail not to plant it again."

She covered her mouth, leaning close. Bunny perked an ear out towards her.

"Truth is, Mom hates cooking it!!" Mo whispered.

"Whaaaat?!" Bunny squealed. Mo tried to shut her up the rest of the way down the hall.

In the common area, the fam had got together: twenty-some teens anywhere from thirteen to eighteen, all chattering and comparing tabs. In theory, Max, Thea and Oxeye were the organizers and the reason the younger kids could go along, but the fam was about as hierarchy-based as an amoeba.

"What's the word?" Bunny asked, hopping into the middle of the gathering with ears up like flags. Dove and Hawk grinned at her, identical faces bright.

"Check it! We can hop the Outer Loop train at fourteen-hundred, get there by sixteen, have dinner and some fun downtown, and then hit the floor at eighteen!" Hawk crowed.

"And we can take oh-hundred, two hundred or three hundred train back!" Dove added.

"Cool! Are there enough seats for everybody?"

"Looks like it!" Norah checked the train schedules she'd taken responsibility for. "There's what, twenty-two, twenty-three... Wait, where's Jen? They're coming, right?"

"Here! I'm here!" Jen came trotting down the hall, puffing. "Sorry I'm late."

"No big." Oxeye gave her with an easy wave. "Good to see you. Okay everybody, sign into the Common Ground, let's get tix!"

Bunny pulled up her app, but her eyes were on Jen as they dropped beside her. They were sitting with their shoulders thrown back, and, wow; they did something to make their chest look way smaller. It was amazing on them. They'd even done something with their hair.

Jen caught her eye and gave her a little smile. "What do you think?"

"It's a great look!" Bunny leaned over to give her bae a big hug and a kiss. Jen buried their face in Bunny's shoulder, squeezing back. "Thanks."

Oxeye brought everyone's attention back. "Guys! Focus, tix! We need to decide where we wanna be!"

"IS EVERYBODY READY to dance?"

Lights strobed out across the stage. Front and center, Lucky of the Nine Tails held her mic high in her prehensile tail, her hair a wonderful rainbow storm around her head.

Squeezing Bunny's hand, Jen yelled right along with their fam, cheering as the band launched into their signature song. As the guitar sang out, Bunny bounced and twirled around Jen, stealing pecks on the cheek that made them laugh. Hawk and Dove danced back to back, and Oxeye and Thea pulled each other close and shimmied. Around them, all types of families and groups danced too, a whole community on the move. The music swept them all into a good place, and they went gladly.

Jen moved with their bae, and their fam, and the world was perfect. Closing their eyes, they sang along with Nine Tails.

*We are Here!*
*This is Now!*
*We are what it's about!*
*We are future,*
*We are past,*
*We decide where it's at!*
*We are Here!*
*This is Now!*
*And while we're here let's dance!*

# A Word from the Author – O.E. Tearmann

B ringing their own experiences as a marginalized author to the page with flawed and genuine characters, O.E. Tearmann's work has been described as "Firefly for the dystopian genre." Publisher's Weekly called it "a lovely paean to the healing power of respectful personal connections among comrades, friends, and lovers."

Tearmann lives in Colorado with two cats, their partner, and the belief that individuals can make humanity better through small actions. They are a member of the Science Fiction Writers of America, the Rocky Mountain Fiction Writers, and the Queer Scifi group. In their spare time, they teach workshops on writing GLTBQ characters, plant gardens to encourage sustainable agricultural practices, and play too many video games.

Get in touch with them here:

WEBSITE https://www.oetearmann.com

FACEBOOK https://www.facebook.com/wildcards1407

TUMBLR https://www.tumblr.com/blog/wildcards1407

MAILING LIST http://eepurl.com/d!4Oqb

AMPHIBIAN PRESS https://amphibianpress.online/index.html

# Shift Together

## By Poppy Minnix

### CHAPTER ONE—MEETING RETRIBUTION

The shifter has followed me for two days, yet I can't figure out what type he is—Valkyries don't have super-smelling abilities like some beings and he's not my goal—but he's as quiet as a panther, even on a forest floor of autumn leaves. He's not pouncing, showing that he's either intelligent, curious, or going to be a problem.

I veer Freya west through a wide path of ash trees, continuing to follow the tingle in my chest that tells me war is building. She feels it too. Blessed with the essence of our goddess, my mare and I are one on this earth; chosen for one purpose, bound by the gods. She is my sister as much as my other blessed Valkyrie sisters.

My quiet stalker goes silent. Freya pauses her steps as well and I close my eyes, hand on my blade. An escaped dark tendril from my braids tickles my chin and I blow it away from my lips. Freya stays still as an ancient stone.

Call it second-sight, sixth-sense, or witchcraft from the original Valkyrie that thrums the warning through my blood. I feel his movement above me before he drops and I unleash my sword, sliding from Freya's saddle. To my surprise, my attacker blocks my blade with twelve-inch claws sprouting from three of his tan, human-formed fingers. I stare at their creamy color and dull edges. It's distracting enough for him to get in a swipe across my armor with the black claws on his other hand. Those are sharp enough to engrave the metal. My enemy is vicious, but not smart. He should have gone for my exposed neck while I was distracted.

Dropping the tip of my sword out of his grip, I spin backwards and get into a defensive stance. Freya moves behind me, ready for me to mount, but this standoff is intriguing, so I stay grounded. The shifter is only in jeans, and is a mass of muscle. Chestnut hair flops across his denim-blue eyes and a scar dents his sharp, thick lips. For the quickest moment, I have the oddest need to trace it and see what it feels like. Besides the oddity of mismatched claws, he looks like an attractive human. I stand straighter. "What are you and what do you want?"

He gives a sarcastic laugh. "A shifter who wants to live in peace." The slight jovial intent of his expression turns to furrowed-brow determination. "But it's too late. Valkyries don't allow that, do they?"

He knows what I am? It's not like my kind speaks of it, or parades into towns as a group like some warriors do on the holidays to visit their families. There are no holidays for the Valkyrie. Or family. After we're taken from our blood parents, we breathe, train, and learn our role in the universe alongside our horses. We're the elite soldiers who carry the final blow to those who would alter the world with their doom. We rely on our mounts and other Valkyries, though after leaving training at the righteous age of seventeen, we only see other Valkyries at major war events. I haven't seen a sister in the flesh in two years. So why does this odd and handsome shifter know what I am?

I back up with a shuffle, Freya moving with me, as he steps forward. There we stand, staring at each other, facing off. A pattern of shimmering scales slides over his neck from under his jaw.

I shake my head. "Tell me what you are?"

He snarls, but his eyebrows furrow as if worried. "I am retribution." He springs forward.

Twirling from his whip-sharp swipe, I back away again. "Retribution for what?"

"Like you don't know." His fangs grow longer and whatever hesitation he harbored disappears with a menacing growl.

"I really—" I sidestep and thwack his backside with the flat of my blade. "—do not know—" I dodge another vicious slash through the air. "—what you're—" I leap back and gain another four scratches over my armor. "—talking about. You're fast."

"So are you. Faster than others."

My heart sprints at the options of how he would know one or more of my sisters. "What others?"

A horn sounds in the distance and we both say, "hunters," in sync. There will be too many to defend by myself.

I hold my sword out, no longer playing. "Are they with you?"

"No." He backs from me, head pivoting between the distant calls and me. He lifts his upper lip. "Leave this area and never return."

I back toward Freya, not taking my eyes from him. "If you know I'm Valkyrie, then you should understand that's not an option."

"This is your only warning."

I glare. "Then I'm thoroughly warned." Not that it means anything.

The sound of footsteps crunching through leaves has me leaping into Freya's saddle. I look back, finding denim blue staring right back at me. The stranger inhales and shifts into an owl with impossible speed.

## CHAPTER TWO—APPLES AND ANGER

IT'S TWO MONTHS BEFORE I feel the eyes of my quiet stalker on my back again. It makes me flinch. Freya reads my body well and clops to a halt, turning her head to nip at my boot impatiently. I give the slightest squeeze of my heels to send her forward again. We're not in the section of woods where I met him, though it was difficult to stay away. He's sparked my curiosity, and it's not my job to be curious. The temple trainers would be disappointed in me.

My curiosity was sensible, though. The shifter had different claws on different hands. At the same time. No being we know of can do that, so I should learn more about him, shouldn't I? Maybe that's where my endless curiosity about him is coming from—wanting to study his species.

His energy approaches and the urge to dismount and run to him is strong, but the last time we met, he tried to dice me. I'm not sure how to broach a conversation after that brand of meeting, so Freya and I walk. Her ears turn back, head raised, ready to spin and stomp at my command.

"I warned you, Valkyrie."

"You did." I remain on my path, though my senses are open. He's merely following.

"Why this forest?"

I shrug a shoulder, making my armor creak. "Because it calls to me."

"Explain."

"It. Calls. To. Me—to us." I turn in my saddle. "It is our duty as Valkyries to follow the call. Why are you here?"

He's even more attractive than the last time I saw him. His light camel-colored jacket and jeans fit perfectly. Big brown boots are untied, as if he was too nonchalant to worry about tripping over laces. Or maybe he's ready to shift. His scruff is days old, and he looks exhausted. He steps over a log. "Because it's my home and I need to protect it."

I wave a hand toward him. "You're doing a splendid job with your claws." I want to ask. I want to ask so badly. *What are you? Show me what else you can do. Can I come closer without you attacking me?* But I don't. Because this isn't a war and he's not a soldier for me to judge. I may be part of the mystical world, but I am not allowed in it. He does not pertain to me. So I turn forward again. "Enjoy the lovely afternoon, shifter."

He continues to follow me. "How does it call to you?"

"Mystical intervention from the gods." Shrugging a shoulder, I move again but sit side-saddle in case I need to drop. Freya nickers at me, but continues forward at a slow walk. "How can you shift in parts? Different parts?" I shouldn't have asked that. I do not care.

The way he licks his lip scar should be outlawed. It makes the world hone into that one small, slow flick of his tongue. He looks past me. "You may want to—"

A thwack to the back of my head makes me yip and duck from the invading branches. I rub the sore spot and glare at Freya, who keeps her pace, one ear turned back. She doesn't enjoy being followed and apparently would like me to remember that.

"So..." I drop from the saddle and roll my hand through the air. Freya continues on to a patch of grass tucked among a grove of short elms. Clearly, she's not as concerned with the shifter as I am.

He takes another step closer, moving a shadow over me, blocking the afternoon light as a mountain would swallow the sunset. "I'm part god."

It's impossible to keep the shock off my face. I'm the sword of the gods, the dealer of justice, yet I've never met one. "Which one?"

He huffs a laugh and looks towards Freya. "Why would I tell you that?"

"Why would you tell me you're part god?"

For the first time, there's a crack in his threatening demeanor. He scratches the back of his neck, appearing smaller than the mountain he is. "I don't know. Can you tell me why you're here now?"

I tap my chest. "Because I feel the call. There is a war and the gods have spoken. They need justice served." The call keeps slipping away, though I won't tell him that. The lines are eluding me. When I reach a call point, there's nothing but blood where a fight took place. Even now, my soul quiets and once again I am lost.

The stranger runs a hand down his face and shakes his head. "That's not an excuse for what you do." He flexes his fingers and claws come out once more.

My fingers automatically encircle my sword's hilt. "You don't like justice served? The worst of mankind and immortals taken from the earth? That's not an honorable enough reason beyond the call that comes directly from the gods?"

"There was nothing bad about my clan. Nothing." He yells the last word with so much raw rage an ache forms behind my eyes. I don't have time to question what he means, or why I'm feeling an inner pain for him, because he lunges. My sword is out in a quarter second and I block his claws with the flat of the blade, confused again why he's attacking.

He kicks out and connects with my midsection of armor. I soar, hitting the ground and rolling back up. Freya whinnies loud and close.

"Stay back, Freya." She would stomp him, but he could impale her on the way down.

He's nearly on top of me and I block again, punching his jaw with my other hand before he remembers the claws he has yet to use. His head whips back and I rush past him to the cover of the trees. I leap for a low branch to swing to Freya, who turns to me, backside dancing about. The shifter grips my ankle, jerking me to the ground. I smash my hilt into his collarbone as I fall and knee him in the side, but he pins me to the ground with his whole, big body.

Panic bubbles up as the air refuses to return to my lungs. My plates of armor are excellent for preventing stab wounds, but not crushing death. I crash the hilt against his shoulder and he grunts. He must weigh as much as a bear. Claws touch my neck and I go still, breathing what tiny amounts of air I can.

Freya whinnies again, but I hold my hand up, fingers wide, to tell her it's okay. It's not, but I'm her guide as much as she is mine, and we're not to take him.

His denim eyes are wet. "Why aren't you trying to kill me?" he growls through gritted teeth.

"Why... a-are... you—" I inhale hard when he shifts enough to let me breath. "—trying to kill me?" And why did he stop? He has me. A quick flick of his fingers and I'm done.

"Goddammit, answer me." His breath is apples and anger.

I give him the truth. "You don't deserve to die." There is no darkness surrounding him. No chill of danger, besides the claws tickling my jugular. I have no urgency to end this being and relax under him. "Do as you will." I release the hilt of my sword and tilt up my chin. This isn't the worst way to go, staring at the beautiful face of a worthwhile opponent.

The lines around his tired eyes tighten, and he swallows. He heaves himself up and pivots, slashing the closest tree. He kicks it as well and a popping crack shatters the stillness of the forest. His enraged bellow makes a murder of watchful crows take to the air and disappear over the canopy of red, orange, and brown leaves.

I breathe deep and sit up, sheathing my sword. Freya's breath tickles my neck and I reach back to rub her fuzzy muzzle. From the ground, I watch his rage unfurl. It's exuberant how much this being feels. Emotion was trained out of me, or capped. Bottled up and left in a far corner, undisturbed. It has to be that way. There's no place for hesitation if an enemy needs ending. Feelings would interfere. Maybe that's why this stranger makes me so curious. He sparks something inside me that the world isn't privy to. It's unnerving, this ball in my chest that cracks as he drops to his knees. His anguished sob unseats the water in my eyes and I swipe at my cheeks. The moisture mixes with the dirt on my fingertips.

The forest grows dark and quiet after he pummels and fells two trees. I should be far from here by now, instead of staying. I've seen emotion before, tears before my sword falls, but apologies and pleas mean nothing when that person has disrupted the balance. They took too much. Maybe I'm the same way. I'm an executioner, but what do I give back? Taking a judged life does not undo the past, only prevents them from harming the future.

An itch strikes my soul, and my time in this quiet forest with this beautiful shifter is done. I rise and escape on silent feet with Freya following, leaving him to his fascinating cornucopia of emotions.

## CHAPTER THREE—UNWORTHY

I THINK ABOUT THE STRANGER often during the next months as we work our way north, then back again. My only work fodder is two minor altercations, and one ending blow. It always seems that we're a mile behind where we should be and then my mind works too hard, running over every interaction between the shifter and I. Something has changed in me.

I see colors for more than coverage and I smile at squabbling birds, wondering if their arguments are an in-depth lovers' quarrel or merely a shallow fight over a seed. I wonder what the shifter is doing since he's no longer stalking me, or not outwardly like he was before. There's still a familiar energy lapping at the outskirts of my path, like calm waves against a sandy shore.

Freya doesn't seem bothered by his presence, or maybe she's not honed in on him like I am. It's yet another thing that's different about me. It's as if half my mind is tucked away in the trees, staring southward and waiting for him to catch up.

What caused his pain and why do I feel connected to his agony? I go over our conversation relentlessly, trying to piece together a picture, because he thinks I am part of whatever happened to his clan, but nothing lands. I don't have all the information.

My senses spark a half a second before an arrow wizzes by my ear. It would have struck my forehead had Freya not shifted. I pull my sword, tilting my head to listen. Four—no, five—surround us, hidden among the trees. A tingle heeds a stark warning. *Take them all, for they're not worthy.* The tingle grows into a hot ember. *War is coming if they remain.* The gods' call is loud as a scream next to my ear. My breath quickens and Freya stamps a hoof. How did I not know of this sooner? Did they make up their divine minds just now? I pull a dagger as well. It's not my job to judge the gods. It's to carry out their will.

A body in front of me shifts, as does another to my left.

I throw my dagger as two arrows pass by me, one above, and one pinging off my blade as I block. There's a yelp and the closest attacker falls, my dagger lodged in his chest. The throat would have been faster, but I had a bigger chance of missing.

The forest erupts in chaos as another arrow flies and three bodies sprint toward us. *Hunters.* Their leather with the green stamp of their guild gives them away. I'm marked as Valkyrie as well, but no one but my sisters and trainers have seen the ink under my armor.

I pull a second dagger from my thigh holster and surge Freya toward the quickest huntress, but an arrow makes me halt as it passes by my nose, embedding itself in the crest of Freya's neck. She gives a whinny of rage and rears to avoid the swipe of the huntress's spear while I slide from her saddle. I pivot to grab a handful of raven braids, throwing the huntress into one of her incoming partners, a tall man with a mace. He needs to be avoided at all costs. Crushed armor is a painful death.

My blade slides brutally along the thigh of the other male and he cries out, falling to the ground and holding the gushing wound. An arrow strikes my shoulder, whipping me backward with its power, denting my small shoulder pauldron, but the next finds the weak point and I hiss as the arrow pierces under my collarbone. It's not deep, so I yank it out with a grunt.

A roar silences the forest and familiar energy washes over me. I switch my sword to my uninjured arm and swipe at the huntress. A blur of brown fur and spikes crumples the mace-bearer, who only has a second to scream before a ghastly crunch turns his voice to whimpering gurgles. The relief in my chest at his death fills the places the tension of the call lived, though there is still much more work to be done.

The huntress's wide eyes belie her calm, and she frantically swipes her blade toward my throat. I dart from her, then block. Tings sound as our blades collide again and again. How many innocents has she taken before today? She tires, but I don't. I end her with three quick slices to her major arteries.

My shifter bears down on the archer, but the other hunter—my dagger still in his chest—rises, pale and shaking. Freya barrels toward him.

"Liv," a familiar voice calls behind me, stopping my sprint.

I turn as Gunhild runs toward me, looking wild with her cherry-wood colored hair flowing. She's one of the eldest of my sisters at twenty-nine, deadly accurate and more determined than a wolverine. Relief pours through me. The battle will be quick now, except she's missing her horse. "Where's Tyr?"

Another screaming warning call sounds from my mind, but it's too late. Gunhild rams her dagger into my side, right between the hairline separation in my armor. "Hello, sister. Lovely to see you again." She kisses my cheek as pain spikes panic into my blood.

"Why?" I ask, as unfamiliar tightness enters my chest, making it hard to breathe.

She frowns down at me with crystalline blue eyes. "You've been judged unworthy. That's what we do, isn't it? Remove the unworthy."

There's a cutting tone to her words, as if the words themselves weren't sharp enough.

*No.* I drop to my knees as she jerks the dagger from me. I did everything I was supposed to. I've always done everything they trained me to do to the exact instruction. It makes no sense. "If the ache to end the judged remains in my soul, then where are the signals coming from, if not the gods?" My vision wavers, bringing my attention to the hot liquid spurting from my side.

"Probably demons." She raises the bloodied dagger to make her ending blow when my shifter arrives, clamping fangs down on her forearm and flinging her behind him. She cries out but rolls to her feet as the bear-porcupine follows.

Gunhild runs. That can't be right. Valkyries never run away when there's a mark. The judgment remains thick in my blood and I should follow, but can only watch as my shifter gives chase to a streak of retreating cherry-wood locks.

I gasp at the coldness settling into my skin and the numbness in my hands. Freya's fuzzy nose nudges at the hand covering my wound as I fall to the crunchy-leaved forest floor. Are the unworthy gone, or will they be with my last breath?

## CHAPTER FOUR—FOLLOWING STARS

MORE STABBING PAIN assaults my side, dragging me from the chilled dark. I go to push away whatever is causing the sharp discomfort and yell, but can only twitch and moan. My eyelids are too heavy to lift.

"Shh," a deep voice coos. "You're safe and we gave you something for the pain. I'm stitching you up."

There's a feminine huff. "Why you brought one of them here is beyond me. And gave her good meds. Should have left her in the forest for the crows to snack on." The voice goes soupy and quiet.

When I grip consciousness again, it's deep singing that pulls me to the surface. Something about the stars that look upon us and how we follow them to our fate. It's pretty and makes me need to see where it's coming from. Opening my eyes takes monumental effort, but I succeed, finding myself in a small room with dark wood walls and cream-colored curtains. Big bare feet are propped on the corner of the bed I'm on and the singing trails off.

"Good morning." My shifter lounges, fingers laddered together and resting across his stomach. He looks more comfortable than I've ever been.

I attempt to sit up, but the slightest movement sends a jolt of pain to my side and all the memories flood back. "Gunhild?" My voice is a weak rasp that sends heat to my cold cheeks.

"Was that the other Valkyrie?"

I nod, though it takes more effort than it should.

"She's gone. I don't know where."

"You did not catch her?"

He shakes his head.

Then why didn't she circle back and attack? If I'm judged, she won't stop until I'm gone. The others will join in. *I* will become a war. I force myself up to my elbows, biting back a cry from the sharp stab of every strand of injured muscle.

"Stop." My shifter sits up and puts a hand on my blanket covered leg. "Lay back down."

"You're not safe if she comes to take me. Where's Freya?"

"Your mare is fine. A dozen children are fighting over who takes care of her every need." He tilts his head. "What do you mean by take you?"

"She said I was deemed unworthy by the gods and needed to be—." My throat tightens and I cannot finish saying the words. "If that's true—" I hiccup a breath. "She won't stop. Others will come for me until the job is done."

"They won't." He rises from the chair and sits on the bed, making my hip slide against his. "Breathe, darling. What she said isn't true. There is nothing unworthy about you." He brushes my cheek with his thumb. "Besides, the others involved in murdering my clan members said nearly the same thing to my people."

"Will you tell me what happened?" I grip his fingers. "This is all confusing."

His lips firm, and he stares at the wall behind me, though he traps my fingers, lowering our hands to the soft blanket below. "Three Valkyries came through the forest half a year ago. Our clan protectors followed, unsure of why three armored women were searching our lands. When they approached, the women attacked." His grip tightens before he strokes my knuckles with his thumb. "They left the protectors barely alive, and tracked them back to our village. Then it was a bloodbath. My people killed one. The other two fled after taking two dozen."

There are too many questions, too much that makes little sense. "The only reason Valkyrie would attack is if there is war and the gods deem it so."

"Then those women were not Valkyrie. No god would punish innocent beings like those women did."

"That's why you followed me and attacked."

He nods, eyes angling to something like shame. "But you didn't fight back. Not really."

Our brief conversations and his expressions of pain make more sense now. He had an inner struggle between vengeance and righteousness. I think I would have had a hard time harming him if the gods deemed it necessary. Am I a ruined Valkyrie? Maybe that's why my sister came for me, though that's not adding up. She would have said more—declared my misdeeds before an attack. "I do not know why Gunhild would act as the very thing we were created to keep in check. What did the others look like?"

"I've heard one had blue eyes but lighter blond hair. She was the one our warriors stopped. My people call Gunhild the red demon and the other probably looked closer to you." His eyes take a slow meander over my features. "Green eyes, but not as bright. Brown hair, but not as shiny." The corner of his lips quirk.

"Sounds like Seda and Wen. Seda was like a sister to Gunhild, but Wen is one of the youngest of our kind. They didn't bring their horses into the battle?"

He shakes his head.

"I don't understand what they're doing."

"They meant to start a war," a firm voice says from the doorway, making me reach for the sword that isn't there. The woman is young, with tan skin and denim blue eyes that match my shifter's. Those eyes glare at him now, then sink to our entwined fingers. "That's what they spoke about as they were slashing down families. You're taking one as your mate, brother? Just when I thought you couldn't make any more poor decisions."

He growls at her before turning back to me. "This is my sister, Jubilee."

"Mate?" The word falls from my lips before I can think. I've heard the term, used about shifters. *United*. Together, potentially for the life of the two. It's not common for Valkyrie to pair with another, but it's not impossible either.

My shifter licks his scar again. "Not something to worry about. You need to heal."

Then it's not what his sister meant, which is for the better. There are too many things to work through that need my focus. I glance at our still connected fingers, which are warm and seem to pump energy through me. He lets go to stand. "I'll get you something to eat."

"Probably the good food," Jubilee murmurs, disappearing around the corner.

"I'm sorry for your loss and what pain my sisters have caused. If what you say is true, they are no longer following the ways of Valkyrie."

He leans against the door frame, hands in his pockets. "I realized that after meeting you." His gaze trails from my eyes down, as if he's viewing what's under the sheet. "You're smaller than I imagined."

I assess and realize I'm in a shirt, possibly his. "My armor?"

"In the other room. I had to clean it." The corner of his lips quirk. "It makes you look more... substantial than you are."

"Is that a disappointment?" Again with questions I shouldn't care about.

"I don't think disappointment in you is possible. But your inner fire buffs you up." Before I can question him further, he turns.

"What's your name?" I blurt.

His blue eyes hold mine and I'm transfixed, pinned, yet never want to be released. "Rekker."

"Rekker," I echo. "I'm Liv."

"I heard what she called you. Before—" His jaw clenches tight and his nostrils flare. "Rest now... Liv."

## CHAPTER FIVE—SOUL EXPANSION

"YOU CAN FIGHT WITH a blade, too?" I ask, slashing out again.

Our swords clash as he parries. "When I need to. You're still stiff."

I narrow my eyes. It's been five days. Plenty of time to heal. "I'm not warm yet." Another clash, a slide of metal. I spin and bear down on him.

Rekker grips my wrist and pulls me close. "I've seen you fight cold, darling. You're still in pain."

Against his warm body, staring up at the perfect angles of his face, I've forgotten what pain is. I've forgotten everything. The sword falls from my fingers, clanking against the rocky ground. This practice—this test of my healing—fades away as he releases my wrist and his coasting fingers slide over my neck, his thumb dragging over my jaw to tilt my head. "Liv," he whispers, closer still and with an intention that spears my heart.

At the first brush of his heated lips, my breath leaves in a sigh and my eyes close. Another sword clank and his other hand threads fingers through my hair. Whatever I thought a kiss would be, it wasn't this. It's consuming; a perfect exchange of breath and scent. I revel in it, opening to him with a moan that he steals with his tongue. My skin tingles and my stomach tightens in a way I enjoy. How could something so seemingly benign make the earth feel like it rotates for us alone?

I touch his chest and the quick beats of his heart tickle my palm. He pulls back to look down at me, eyes half-lidded like he's drunk, or half-asleep. I'm sure I'm wrapped in a dream as well.

His nose brushes mine. "Do you feel this between us?"

"The lightning under my skin?"

"Yes." His smile is ageless with peace. "The expansion of our souls?"

I nod and eye his lip scar. "Again."

He doesn't keep me waiting.

"By Bres's undergarments, can you two just—" Jubilee makes a crude sound of expulsion as Rekker and I jump apart. "Gross."

My cheeks go so warm, I touch one to feel the heat. Jubilee and I have grown closer over the last few days. She'd been cold towards me until I commented on the beauty of a rug in their kitchen, and found she was a talented weaver. Once I confessed I'd like to learn how to work a loom, Rekker had to physically pick me up and carry me away for dinner, hours into an impromptu tutorial.

"Leave, Jubi." Rekker moves closer, hooking a finger at the neck of my armor and pulling me closer. His grin is now mischief and flame.

"There's a problem." She crossed her arms, holding her stance. "A Valkyrie is approaching."

I stiffen and Rekker growls.

"One?" I ask.

"Yes."

"It has to be Gunhild. If it were the others, they'd come in at least a pair." I aim to pick up my sword—

Rekker pulls me closer. "Stay here."

"Like the devil, I will. I'm the one who knows her best. I trained with her and understand her mind... or thought I did. She's here for me."

"And she won't have you. You're injured, Liv. *She* injured you."

I narrow my eyes. "I only need to speak with her and find out what's going on. The call of judgement has faded." Maybe it was a mistake.

His jaw tightens, and he shakes his head. "She will cut you down, and I will not allow it." His voice grows dark and rusty.

"I won't allow it either, but it's my fight and I won't let anyone here to be injured. Not after what you all went through." I head toward Jubilee. She looks worried. I slide my sword into its holster. "Please show me to her."

Jubilee stares past me and frowns, no doubt trying to lure me in with sympathy or make me turn back to Rekker, but I can't. Won't. There are people in danger. Rekker and Jubilee could be hurt.

Rekker curses behind me and sidles up to me with heavy bootsteps. "Let's go. When they attacked before, they came from the East."

Jubilee shrugs. "She's coming from the Northern point between the falls."

"That is not a war move. She would be trapped in the canyon if we ambushed her."

I furrow my brows. "Valkyrie do not care for ambushes and will avoid areas of closure. It's easy to realize who the gods wish us to end. However, unarming the others without injury is stressful in tight spaces. Gunhild wants me to know she's coming." I whistle and push a request from my mind towards Freya. *Find Tyr.* Gunhild's horse may ease some sense into my sister's mind.

Jubilee blows out a long breath and veers right. "I'm getting my sword. The others are preparing for an invasion." She pauses and looks at us. "Be careful."

Those words have never been directed at me before. No one has ever cared enough to do so. I nod and swallow at the odd tightness in my throat before continuing north.

It's a quick path before the call of the gods hits like a mace and I stumble.

Rekker snags and steadies me. "What's wrong?"

I tap the armor over my chest. "Call of the gods. They can't ask me to do this."

Rekker's eyebrows scrunch. "Your sister?"

The slightest bob of my head feels like the longest conversation. "But to kill another Valkyrie... they're all I have."

"No, they're not. And you won't have to kill her. I will." He turns, but I hold tight to him.

"We're made to be the gods' executioners. She will kill you."

He raises an eyebrow. "I had you at your end, darling."

"I wasn't trying to kill you, Rekker. If I was, I would have, though you're the toughest opponent I've ever come across. But we're Valkyrie. I'm not sure how you stopped Seda."

"It was a hundred to three. That's how. But I wasn't there."

"Why not?" I tilt my head.

His expression goes distant, and he swallows. "Because we lost our mother and with her, any knowledge of who my father was. I lost myself for a long while after that, left the clan and wandered. Jubi called me in the middle of the attack to say goodbye and she loved me. I morphed, flew back, and arrived in time for the aftermath. If I had been here, things would have been different. I've been hunting Valkyrie since." He thumbs my chin. "Until I found you."

I lean into him. "Please let me protect you and this clan."

He brushes his lips over mine. "Only if we protect you in turn."

I'm not sure what to say, so I kiss him, needing to test how good that gesture was between us once again. It's somehow better, but there's no time, so I breathe him in and head toward our fate.

## CHAPTER SIX—THE HARDEST DUTY

GUNHILD IS WAITING for us by the edge of a crystalline pool, fed by a trailing series of short waterfalls. She holds the arm Rekker bit close to her body. With Rekker's bristling energy beside me, I halt twenty feet away and take in her appearance. Her cherry-wood hair is down and messy, and there's a new, wicked scar across her cheek. Her eyes are as lifeless as one of the scattered river rocks below her muddy boots.

"What happened to you, sister?" I ask. Bedraggled is the kindest word I can think of to describe her. Dirty and demonic is a better fit.

Gunhild barks a crazed laugh before her lips firm into a scowl. "That's what you ask me? You wouldn't prefer to send your—" She points to Rekker with the tip of her bloodied sword. "—thing to attack me."

"He's not a thing," I growl. "And it's not his duty to attack you. It's mine."

"No. He's a shifter." She spits the word. "Filth of the—"

"Stop." I raise my sword. She will not speak of him like that. "Why did you attack me?"

She gives a faint grin. "You wouldn't have left me alone, sister. You know that. And I have work to do. So much work."

Realization hits. "You knew you were one of the judged."

"Of course I did. And I find you with this kind?" Her upper lip raises in a sneer. "Disgusting."

"Enough."

Rekker's arm brushes mine, his eyes fixed on Gunhild. "Why do you take such an issue with my kin?"

Approaching quick clip-clops interrupts our conversation, but I don't take my eyes from Gunhild, and I'm glad for it, because I catch a sharp pain I wouldn't have imagined ever seeing on her face. I glance back at Freya, who the shifters have dressed for war. They follow in leathers, all holding weapons, even the small ones who shouldn't have to know this aspect of the world yet, if ever. My sisters caused their fear and their defense.

I wish for another day and no audience. I wish for our goddess's altar and a smoking pot of herbs as I ask for guidance—more conversation than a powerful message of judgment—a demand for Gunhild's blood. She's my sister. A Valkyrie. This isn't the same as the doom-bringers we annihilate.

"Tyr is gone?" I ask with a shake in my voice.

Gunhild's jaw works and she straightens. "Yes. A pack of cat shifters ambushed us, took him down as he drank from a pond." Her eyes dart to Rekker and narrow. "That's my issue with your kin."

The air leaves my lungs in a harsh whoosh. "Oh, Gunhild." I don't want to imagine her pain. Months ago, I'm not sure I would have considered what it would be like. But Rekker opened something in me, and a loss like that is a heavy burden to take on.

"Which clan?" Rekker asks. "We could have helped you. If what you say is true, it's against the code of shifters."

"*Code.*" She snorts. "I don't seek help from anything, nor am I allowed vengeance. The gods told me to back down." She gives a small smile. "But I didn't." Her smile draws back into her chilling sneer. "And I don't plan to."

I angle my sword and, along with Rekker, step between her and the clan. This is my stand. "Seda was killed in a battle you started. Where's Wen?"

That makes her forward motion pause. "Wen is dead. She couldn't stomach our cause and when Seda was taken—"

"Died when she attacked an innocent clan," Rekker growls. "She wasn't taken."

Freya snorts and paws at the ground behind me. She's prepared for what we may have to do; waiting for the word of which path we will take with this... enemy. My chest clenches. This is happening.

"Innocence is an opinion." Gunhild opens her arms wide. "The gods decide on a whim who to take and who not to. Now, I decide who pays and who doesn't."

I glance to Rekker, who looks like he feels this impending fight the way I do. There will be no gentle end to Gunhild. "Stay back," I whisper.

"Until I'm needed," he returns and eyes my lips, which tingle under his gaze.

Gunhild points her sword at me. "Join me, sister."

"You know I can't, nor would I." The fire in my blood is hotter than I've ever felt. "Back down. Rest and return with me to the training temple."

"That's what Wen said before she tried to find you. And *returning*? You understand that's not something I can do. We're at an impasse." She twirls her sword with her uninjured arm as she eyes the crowd. The golden embellishments on the hilt glint in the midday sun despite the dried blood. She charges and so do I.

The tips of our swords clash as we whip apart at the last minute, expecting the other to remain on the path. She crouches to slash and I parry, though the movement spikes pain through my wound. I leap and strike high. She cries out at my shoulder stick.

I continue backing her toward the water with quick guiding slices. "You can't fight like you need to with that injury."

She forward-rolls, kicking me in the armor over my wound, making me cry out as I crash to the ground. She leaps on me, raising her sword. "You can't ei—"

I grab a handful of her unbound hair and jerk her sideways.

She elbows my cheek as we roll.

"Submit!" I punch her with the fist clasped around my hilt. Maybe our training words will sink in. Help her remember who she is.

"Never." Her knee comes in sharp against that same spot and I can't get enough air. Then she's off me and running.

I stand and look at Rekker. He nods, shucking clothing to shift into a huge eagle, jumping to the air, sending a wave a wind against me from his massive wingspan.

Freya gallops by, lowering her head. I grip her rein and stirrup, and leap. She gives a sidestepping buck to launch me into the saddle. Then we really move. Valkyrie are fast, but our horses are like riding a hurricane. Gunhild uses the rocky canyon to her advantage and is climbing to stay away from me and Freya. Even with an injury, she's moving fast, the way someone who's studied the land moves.

Freya and I slow as I seek the best advantage for attack. There isn't one.

Rekker dives, claws out. She swings at him with the sword she refuses to release and falls. The pulse of the gods burns like fury. They're so angry. But I close my eyes at her scream and jerk when her body hits the rocky ground. Freya takes slow steps as she approaches the fallen Valkyrie. Shifters arrive, surrounding us, the ones on thick bear's legs first, then human form after. My eyes burn as I slide from the saddle.

Gunhild struggles to get up, but her leg is broken, and she coughs blood.

My fingers shake around my sword. "I'm sorry for your loss, sister. You shouldn't have had to carry that burden alone."

She screeches and swings at me, but her sword clinks against another. Jubilee stomps on the flat of Gunhild's blade, pinning it to the ground, but looks at me. "Go."

I shake my head, unseating a stream of hot tears. "It's my duty."

Her lips part as she looks behind me and nods. She takes a breath. "You're clan, Liv. Let us shoulder this for you."

Rekker's energy engulfs me one second before his arms do. He pulls me against him as clan members fill in the space between me and my sister.

I hesitate, but he turns me, taking my sword and lifting me against him. I grip his bare shoulders, my breaths coming in harsh pants. He strides from the group and I glance behind him, but Freya follows, blocking my view.

"Look at me, darling." His denim blue eyes are steady and hold me fast, but they don't stop the grunt of Gunhild's pain. When the gods' will flutters from my veins, I sob and press my face into the crook of his neck, letting him carry me to wherever he will.

## EPILOGUE

I PACE THE SMALL BEDROOM, rubbing my hands over the thin fabric of my dress. My pulse is wild, my hair is down, and I only want to see one person.

"You ready?" Jubilee isn't that person, but her smiling face is a relief. I make a choked squeaking sound that makes her laugh. "I'm going to take that as a 'ready enough.'" She steps in to fluff the curls she put in my hair, then takes my hand and leads me to the back of the house. Past the back deck is a sea of shifters, horses with flowers in their hair, and four of my Valkyrie sisters. And in the middle, my person—my shifter.

My soul expands at Rekker in his clan's formal garments. The rust-red embroidered tunic brushes his knees and I want to muss the perfection of his sleek hair.

Jubilee squeezes my hand, and we step out together. The path is long as I make my way to Rekker, eyes locked on his. His smile is the greatest joy of my life. When I impatiently speed up, Jubilee laughs and lets me go. I crash into Rekker's arms.

"Better together, right?" he asks against my ear.

I nod, overwhelmed with the soul expansion he described. He says it will only get stronger after today, though I'm not sure how.

Our groups, our people, watch us with smiles and hands over their hearts. Then I get a call from the gods; a different one than I've ever received.

I press a hand to Rekker's chest. "The gods approve of this union." The blessing takes my breath away.

He gives a sharp inhale, then smiles in disbelief as the call reaches through our touch. "Darling, we're going to do much good together."

END

# A Word from the Author – Poppy Minnix

**B**io: Poppy Minnix is an east coast romance author who loves to take readers for an emotional rollercoaster ride while her characters find love. She shares her life with a husband who's far more romantic than herself, two rambunctious kiddos, and many fur family members. An author was not what she expected to become, but when she needed a creative outlet that would pass under the radar of her tiny kids, she turned to writing scenes out on a tablet. In the hours when normal people sleep, she quickly became completely obsessed with her mythical new friends and building the worlds they live in. Her first writings were garbage fires, but are on the slate to be rewritten, so follow her on all the social things to discover her books and on-the-way works.

**Playlist:** Carry You – Ruelle ft. Fleurie, Stone – James Young, Where the Shadow Ends – Banners

**Why I wrote this story:** - I love fantasy worlds with non-human people getting sideswiped by unexpected love, so this short story was a joy to play with. Mythology is something I often incorporate into my writing, and once I started learning who Liv was, a Valkyrie background fit her so well. And Rekker! Who doesn't love a good paranormal hybrid? A blend between a shifter and deity lets him shift into any creature he wants—a concept I pulled from a series I'm working on, so you will see Rekker's alternate universe brother in my future work.

Find her stories at https://linktr.ee/PoppyMinnix

# Fate and Tea Leaves

## By Sienna Swift

### Dark Oolong

The bookstore was busy for the early hour. Normally the humans of the area were in their cars now, sitting in standstill traffic. Today, though, at least fifteen were milling around my shop at eight AM on a weekday.

I suspected that one of Hex's new marketing schemes was at work. My guess was confirmed when one of the fifteen approached with a book and a small piece of paper. Her hand was steady as she thrust it toward me.

**Tea Leaves Bookshop Sale! Buy a book, get a reading 20% off!**

I almost rolled my eyes. Hex could have asked me before offering my services at a discount. It wasn't like it took much effort, but that wasn't the point. It was the principle of the thing.

I pasted on my customer service smile and gestured at the menu behind me. The local woman who had painted it was crazy talented. Hex was sure that she must have fae heritage, but I was skeptical. Humans could be skilled, too.

"What kind of tea would you like?"

The woman responded, "Earl Grey," with all the confidence of a person who was completely wrong.

"Coming right up." I scooped the tea leaves into a green mug and added the water, muttering as I stirred it. The muttering was completely unnecessary, but Hex said it added authenticity to the reading.

I rang the woman up as the tea steeped, then handed it to her with instructions to drink down to the dregs before returning to the counter. As she walked towards the small cafe area, I turned to the next customer.

The scent hit me first, a blend of cooked bread and something sweet. My stomach clenched unfamiliarly, and I scanned the source of the smell with curiosity. The man was tall, taller than me in my glamoured form, and probably about my true height. He was an objectively attractive human, but that didn't normally mean much to my kind.

His ebony hair was nearly as dark as mine, although in the form I had taken today, my locks were blond and bouncy. I imagined I looked a bit like a human cheerleader. Hex would make fun of me when she came in later. She preferred to look older and intimidating, but I enjoyed being underestimated by the humans.

The man in front of me didn't look like he was underestimating me, though. His gray eyes were appraising as he placed the book in his hands on the counter. A glance at the cover revealed an obscure cookbook. We stocked two copies, the same two we'd ordered when the book was published. I made a note to place an order. I liked to have duplicates when possible.

"That will be $13.05, and would you like a discounted tea reading?"

Even though I had been bemoaning the sale, I was slightly grateful to Hex for the opportunity to learn more about this enticing stranger.

"No, thank you." He was polite, but there was an edge to his voice.

I looked at him from under my eyelashes, taking advantage of my cute form. "I insist."

He hesitated, but seemed to take in the way I was holding onto the book and read my intention easily. Relenting, he chose a dark oolong tea that I prepared happily. I muttered the nonsense as I stirred, but before I could give the instructions, the man consumed half of it. I wasn't sure the tea had time to steep.

If I wasn't so intrigued by his scent and my response to it, I would have been put out. The chocolatey smoothness of a dark oolong should be savored.

Stepping to the side, the man sipped the rest while I helped a far less interesting customer. He waited patiently as I served the tall woman her boring tea and sent her on her way.

"So what do my tea leaves say?" he asked, still too reserved for my liking.

I swirled the dregs and flipped the cup onto a waiting saucer. A human purist would leave them there, but I preferred speed over human authenticity, so I rotated and flipped it back over immediately.

The formation of the leaves was beautiful and nearly took my breath away. I stared into the cup for a moment too long, lost in the patterns, when the man cleared his throat.

"I see you are looking for direction. You wouldn't ever have found it, but you recently made a choice that will change everything."

The man failed to disguise his dismissal of my skills, and I felt my eyes heat and glow the tiniest bit at the rudeness. I wasn't normally thrown by something so small, but apparently Hex's antics had put me in a mood.

"Fine," I said, exasperated. "You work at a bakery. You feel lost, but you know what you have to do. In fact, you've always known you need to open one of your own, but until this recent decision, your path would never have led to a happy ending. Lucky you, though."

I added, almost as an afterthought, "You've recently met your soulmate."

His eyes widened almost imperceptibly before he blinked, hiding his emotions more effectively. He nodded and mumbled his thanks.

"When you come back, ask for Jinx," I said, smiling widely. I knew my glamour would hide my sharp teeth, but the man's uneasy reaction had me rethinking its power. He moved a little too quickly out of my shop, but his leaves told me he would return.

Mrs. Earl Grey came back, and I recited detailed drivel to her about her dreadfully monotonous life. Her eyes lit up, and she thanked me profusely, but my mind was still with the gray-eyed man. His credit card had given me his name, but I was more intrigued by his leaves, still in the cup in front of me.

"Who are you, Harmon Banks," I muttered to myself, "and why can't I see more of your future?"

## Darjeeling

THE REST OF MY DAY was uneventful, if fairly busy. Hex teased me about my bouncy curls and I pestered her about not having sales without telling me first. We bickered between customers until the shop closed and then went to our apartment upstairs and harmoniously made dinner. We stayed glamoured out of habit, Hex in her usual stern older woman form.

It was my turn to choose, and I decided on Indian food. The delicacies in Faeryland were all sweet and rich beyond a human's imagination, so when Hex and I first came to the human world and tasted spicy, bitter, and savory foods, we were utterly hooked.

The coconut curry we made was medium to mild by human standards, but it had Hex pouring us both large glasses of milk beside our Darjeeling tea. We laughed in delight as tears filled our eyes and our mouths burned. How lovely to experience all the human form offered.

I wanted to ask Hex about her day, what she had done before she arrived at the shop after noon, but I knew she wouldn't tell me. I smiled at her across the table and ignored how sadness pooled in her eyes even as we joked and smiled and ate our food.

"I met a human today," I said as we cleared the table.

"I'm sure you met many. I imagine you'll meet a few tomorrow, too."

I glared at her, but given I was still glamoured as a short blond woman with ringlets, I couldn't imagine it was effective.

"This one was unusual. I smelled him immediately when he walked in the door and—" I couldn't describe the way my stomach had clenched and pulled, so instead I added, "—I could barely see his future."

This got her attention, and she looked up from loading the dishwasher. "Even when you had his tea leaves?"

I nodded, and her eyebrows drew together. She didn't pause for long, though, before she continued cleaning.

"I guess it was a fluke. Or maybe he's protected by another of the fae?"

I shook my head. "I would have noticed."

Hex waved her hand at me. "I'm sure it was nothing."

I would have believed her, but I had scooped her empty cup of Darjeeling tea off the table. Three swirls, invert, three turns, and look. Hex knew what was going on and didn't want to tell me.

## Masala Chai

AS I WRAPPED MY GLAMOUR around myself the next day, I was thinking about Harmon. I didn't realize it until I looked in the mirror and saw a tall girl with long black hair staring back at me.

Shrugging, I added a nose ring, some dark makeup, and a slightly provocative outfit. Why not go all out?

Hex was still eating breakfast when I walked out the door, and I heard her calling after me about the "image" of our shop, but I shrugged her off. I would get my kicks wherever I could find them, thank you very much.

Fewer humans came in with coupons today, and those who did seemed intimidated enough by my blank stare that almost none of them actually asked for the reading. Hex would probably pitch a fit, but it wasn't like we actually needed the human money. There were more intricate motives at play for the shop, nothing as dull as pieces of metal and paper.

I was drawn from my thoughts by the same pull from the day before. I looked up, expecting to see Harmon, and struggled to hide my expression. The man in front of me was Harmon's height, had the same hair and eyes, but something was off about him.

Unlike many of my kind, I was pretty good at reading humans. I assumed it was from spending so much time around them. Because of this, I would never, ever admit to anyone that I took until he opened his mouth to realize that this man must be Harmon's twin.

"Hello." His tone was almost musical, his scent some sort of human concoction, sandalwood and maybe lemon? "I'm here for a reading of my tea leaves, please."

If I hadn't realized the man was not Harmon before, this would have been the giveaway. He eyed me curiously, but with none of the suspicion of his brother. I kept up my bored expression, testing his resolve.

"Teas are there." I gestured to the sign behind me.

"Of course." He glanced at the menu before declaring, "I'd like your masala chai, and your number, please."

This cracked my mask. I raised my eyebrows, even as my stomach did a little dance. I picked beautiful glamours, so of course humans had asked for my number before. But I had never wanted to give it to them.

I turned without responding and made his tea, murmuring as I went, taking a little longer than usual. I wanted to wait him out, test him, although test him for what I couldn't say.

"My name is Reave."

I finally turned and handed him his tea. "You can call me Jinx." I smiled at him.

Just as Harmon did, he glanced at my teeth, although there can't have been any sign of their unnatural sharpness through the glamour. Unlike his twin, Reave smiled back.

When he smelled his tea deeply, closing his eyes and savoring it before walking to the cafe area, my smile grew wider. That's how people *should* drink tea. None of this gulping it down nonsense. It should be appreciated, deeply and without regard for the opinions of others. Drinking tea should feel filling and holy.

Hex would make fun of me if she heard me saying that.

Try as I might, I couldn't stop peeking towards the cafe where Reave sat, and every time I looked, he was looking back at me. If this were my true form, I would be blushing, but as it was, I could feel an invisible heat on my cheeks.

I helped two more customers, one who bought a book, and one who requested a reading. He chose English Breakfast tea, and I wanted to glare at him. We had literally forty-three teas on the menu. English Breakfast should *not* be his first choice. But I held my tongue and directed him toward the cafe.

I pretended not to hear Reave approach me, though with my powerful senses I knew the minute he stood up.

"Hello, Jinx."

Seriously, what was going on with his voice? I felt I needed to look more carefully at him. Perhaps he was also a fae? He handed his teacup over, and I let my fingers brush his. Nope, definitely human. I did my tea leaf ritual and stared at the leaves, a little surprised.

These patterns were almost... worrying. Something deep inside my bones ached with concern at the whorls, even though what they said wasn't outside the ordinary.

"You came in on a whim today. You believe in fate, but have never been drawn to this shop before. Two days ago, something happened and made you rethink something meaningful, and you are now trying to figure out the right path to take." I glanced up at him.

He was not as shocked as most customers were with such an on-the-nose reading. Instead he looked expectant, like the answer to his question was about to be delivered on my tongue.

I was about to disappoint him.

"There is no correct path, not the way you're thinking of it. And unless something changes, you aren't going to choose at all. Which is, in itself, a choice."

Reave's face froze at the beginning of my explanation, but slowly morphed into disinterested stone as I went on. The man staring back at me when I finished was not the same one who walked into the shop. He gave me the barest hint of a smile before turning and walking out the door.

The smell of sandalwood and lemon lingered in my nose for the rest of the day.

## Vanilla Rooibos

I DIDN'T TELL HEX ABOUT Reave. She was gone for most of the day again, and despite it being several centuries since we were children, I could still be petty when I wanted to. I knew she was keeping things from me, and two could play at that game.

I found myself secluded in my room for the evening and putting on my glamour in a hurry this morning before rushing down the stairs, avoiding Hex's eye.

"What about the vanilla rooibos? Is that any good?"

The smiling blond man across the counter just pronounced rooibos like he was saying "row-a-bus," with so much confidence that I almost felt bad correcting him. Almost.

"That rooibos is a nice light blend, very little bitterness." I emphasized the first syllable of the tea, so it sounded like "ROY-bos," but the man barely looked chagrined.

"That sounds perfect."

I had been so focused on his faux pas, I hadn't realized my stomach was churning again. I nearly groaned. This was becoming an issue. If every attractive man who walked into my shop had me feeling this out of sorts, I would need to close up and see a healer. Something was clearly unaligned.

I made the tea automatically and the blond man leaned against the counter as he sipped it.

"Is that your natural color?" He eyed the mess of curls piled above my head in a bun. I was a ginger today, complete with the classic willowy figure and freckles. I also made my eyes green because they matched the rest of it so well.

"It grows out of my head like this." I could not lie and say yes, but not wanting the questions that came with the blunt truth.

"I hope you've heard this your entire life, but you're gorgeous, and I'd like to go out with you sometime."

I scoffed, even as heat once again warmed my cheeks beneath the glamour. What the hell was going on? "You don't even know my name. Anyway, we'll see what the leaves say first."

At that, he began sipping a little faster, which silently irked me. Rooiboses were so smooth and sweet, I hoped he was savoring it.

"I'm Lincoln, but you can call me Link."

"Then you can call me Jinx." I ignored the way his head tilted in confusion. It wasn't a common name, but I usually only got this response from older humans.

When I flipped the cup over to read his leaves, I was nearly blinded. I glanced up almost immediately.

"Why did you come in today?" I asked, forgetting myself.

"Aren't you supposed to tell me?"

I examined his face before saying anything else. It didn't seem like he was hiding anything.

"You don't want to know what I see in the leaves, not because you don't believe in readings, but because you do, and you'd like for your life to happen without outside influence." He nodded happily.

"Anything else in there?"

I wanted to be sharp with him, but a particular bunch of leaves caught my attention and I nearly dropped the cup. I didn't look up as I asked in what I hoped was a casual voice, "How do you know Harmon?"

"We got into business together. I came in to meet the woman who got us started, but apparently 'Jinx' isn't her name so much as a title worn by the leaf readers. Am I right?"

When he smiled, it was magnetic. His gaze was nearly worshipful, and I wanted to climb out of my glamour and feel it on my skin.

I shook off the unusual feelings and thought quickly. "Yes, sorry, I can't give you my real name." Not a lie, and not even that manipulative of a truth either.

"That's a shame. So when I take you out for dinner tomorrow night, I'll have to call you Jinx?"

"Yes." I answered before the entire question processed in my head. "I mean—"

"I'll pick you up at seven. That's a half hour after the shop closes, right?" He glanced behind him as though he could read the posted hours from the wrong side of the door.

"Yes," I said again, and he was gone before I could say another word, shooting me one last grin.

I was unnerved. Never before had I been so clumsy with my word choice, or so careless with my promises. Now I would *have* to tell Hex about Reave and Link. Maybe she would be more forthcoming on the second and third occurrence of the bizarre pull.

## Ginger

WHEN HEX GOT UP TO make me ginger tea after my description of the pull in my gut, I wanted to laugh.

"I don't have a stomachache." I patiently waited for her to finish making the drink before sipping it gratefully.

"Well, it certainly sounds like stomach issues." I heard a slight strain in her voice.

I reached across our tiny kitchen table to grab her hand. The bark that made up my fingertips gently gripped her satin smooth skin. She had shed her glamour when I asked, wanting to look my best friend in her eyes while I told her the story.

Hex's lineage was convoluted and mixed, but I thought her dainty form was gorgeous. It was a shame she had to hide her gorgeous blue wings that matched her brilliant eyes and skin. Seeing her small, delicate hand in my large and rough one gave me a familiar twinge, but when she squeezed it, I refocused on the moment.

"I know you, Hex. What is going on?"

"They're your mates," Hex said, shocking me.

Mates were rare and took centuries to meet. Admittedly, I was no young fae anymore, but meeting all three in three days was unusual. And they were *human*!

At my face, Hex smiled sadly.

"It's apparently more common to have a human mate than the Folk at home would have us believe."

"How do you know that?" My voice was curious and casual, but my mind was in turmoil. Mates meant forever.

"Do you remember the witch we met about a decade ago? I visited her and I—" Hex stopped speaking abruptly and pulled her hand back.

Despair was written in every curve of her small body.

"Is she your mate?" I asked gently, trying not to be hurt she had never told me. "What happened?"

"It's not important." Hex's denial was pointless because it clearly was. "She's aging like a human, and I'm aging like fae."

I let her sit in silence, trying to be respectful, but I was brimming with questions about human mates I desperately wanted to ask. I also felt something deep and ugly that felt a lot like hurt. Hex was practically my sister, but I had to acknowledge maybe some things were private, even from those you cared about the most. Although now that I apparently had human mates as well, maybe we could find a solution together.

"I'm not ready to talk about it," Hex said finally, and left the kitchen, closing her bedroom door behind her.

## Jasmine

PUTTING ON MY GLAMOUR the next morning, I felt more subdued than usual. I spent the entire night obsessing over what I knew of my mates.

Harmon. A skeptic looking to open his own bakery who maybe wasn't as much of a non-believer as I originally thought.

Reave. Friendly, right until I told him something he didn't want to hear.

Link. Forward and bold, a firm believer who wanted to let fate happen to him.

It bothered me a bit that I could only seem to read their past. Sure, I got glimpses of their futures, but only as much as a human psychic could glean from their leaves. It made me nervous, which wasn't a feeling I particularly enjoyed.

I ended up walking into the shop as an average-looking woman, unremarkable in almost every way. It had been a subconscious choice, but the message it sent me was clear: I wasn't interested in being seen until I figured everything out.

It wasn't until halfway through the day that I realized my date with Link was tonight, and he was expecting a ginger. I sighed and made myself a cup of Jasmine tea to soothe my anxious energy. As a centuries-old creature, I was used to feeling centered, comfortable in my mind. This was not a welcome change.

I cast a quick charm, unnoticed by the patrons of my shop, allowing others to see me as they expected to, at least for today. That should take care of Link. He would expect to see the woman from yesterday, and so he would.

A mother and her young daughter came in for a reading, and it was like the floodgates opened. After the third primary school-aged child entered the shop, my suspicions were confirmed.

"What a lovely shop," one mother said to me loudly, her mouth open wide as though to project the words directly into my brain. "We saw the ad in the school newsletter and my son was just dying to get his tea leaves read!"

The boy looked incredibly bored and disinterested as she shoved him forward, and I helped him pick out a heavily caffeinated tea that I was sure would have him bouncing off the walls of their home in no time.

If Hex pulled one more marketing scheme without warning me, I would have strong words with her about whose shop this was.

Some of the children had fascinating futures, and it was fun practice interpreting for young humans instead of the older ones. Even the bored little boy brightened up when I whispered that his plan to fake being sick before his next spelling test would be successful.

As the store emptied a bit, I finished my mug of tea. Out of habit, I flipped it over and turned it. The leaves spelled out the same message they always had.

Most fae couldn't use their gifts on themselves. I knew it drove Hex crazy that my gift was an exception, but I had humans to thank. Reading tea leaves was an effective way for them to channel energy. When Hex and I had arrived in the human realm decades ago, I had recognized the power of the act immediately. It was pure luck that my gift of perception worked in tandem with their rituals. It was thanks to humans that I could read my future perfectly in the aromatic leaves in my cup.

I would never return home.

The bell above the door rang out, and I looked up to see Link smiling at me. A glance at the clock above a nearby bookshelf revealed it was later in the day than I thought. With only half an hour before closing, I strode from behind the counter and past Link, flipping the open sign to closed.

"You sure your boss won't get mad at you for closing early?" Link was playful, with a slight edge of seriousness. "I'm happy to stick around and look at your cookbooks if you need to stay longer."

I looked pointedly at the empty cafe and lack of humans wandering in the stacks before returning my gaze to Link. "I think the shop will survive. Plus, my coworker can finish closing up." It wasn't totally a lie. I was sure Hex would come by later and insist on cleaning everything.

Link nodded, like that settled it, and offered me his hand. I stared down at it for a split second before recovering and taking it with my own.

"So, Jinx," Link said, my name sounding like an inside joke. "How was your day?"

"I read the leaves of a bunch of children, mostly."

"Anything interesting in their futures?" Link asked, his face sincere. I examined it, not entirely sure what I was looking for.

"Yes actually. One little girl's parents are about to win the lottery, and another one is about to meet her soulmate."

Link's eyes widened. "Aren't they a little young?"

I shrugged. "Hu—" I stumbled over the word, "—people meet their soulmates all the time. It's one of the easiest things to see in the tea leaves." I didn't mention it was the main thing I could tell without ever looking at someone's leaves.

Link slowly smiled and looked me up and down. I waited for the inevitable question, but it never came. Instead, he pulled me out the book shop door and into the brisk spring evening.

The street was one of the quieter ones in our small city, and some of the nearby stores had put out planters with early blooming flowers. The daffodils made me nostalgic for the yellow herlups and drandons that my mother grew in our garden when I was young, species of flowers that didn't exist in the human realm.

"What's the deal with the shop next door?" Link's question shook me from my thoughts.

"Oh, it's owned by the same people we lease our shop from. The owners are looking for new renters since the last ones moved."

Hex and I technically owned the entire block, but Link thought I was an employee. The half-truths were adding up, though. If Link really was my soulmate, I'd have to tell him I was fae, eventually. I just didn't know how, or when, the right time would be.

Link's eyes lit up. "It would be the perfect location for the bakery!" He surveyed the storefront carefully. "Harmon and I are starting a business. You might have seen it in my tea leaves. We've been going back and forth on where we want to base it. This would be great!"

Link's enthusiasm was contagious, and it made me feel youthful in a way I hadn't felt in decades. I couldn't help my smile as I pretended to inspect the building beside him, still grasping his hand. "I'll put in a good word for you."

## Peppermint

LINK LED ME DOWN THE street to the little diner on the corner. I knew the sweet couple who ran it and was happy when Link told me he and his friends ate there often.

The host took us to a booth by the window, where we had an excellent view of the slowly setting sun. Once we were seated, Link placed his hand on the table, palm up, and looked at me expectantly.

"I can't hold your hand for the whole date," I said, but a blush was once again heating my cheeks beneath my spelled appearance.

"Sure you can. We'll just both do everything with one hand." He grabbed his menu and held it comically with the hand not on the table, as if to demonstrate.

I tried unsuccessfully to stop the giggle that escaped from my lips. What was it about him that made me act like a human teenager? Did human mates always make fae behave differently?

I gave in, giving him my hand while I picked up my menu.

A bright faced server came by and asked us for our drink orders, smiling at our joined hands.

"I'll have your peppermint tea, please."

"Coffee for me."

I raised an eyebrow.

"I still have a lot of work to get done tonight after this," he explained with a slight shrug of his shoulders. "I'm practically nocturnal, anyway."

Interesting. I found myself filing away bits of information about Link, hoarding each nugget of knowledge like if I didn't, I might lose it forever.

"How did you get a start reading tea leaves?" Link's eyes were clear and curious.

I opened my mouth to answer when a powerful pull in my stomach turned towards the entrance of the diner. Harmon and Reave stood side by side, staring at Link and me with near identical confusion.

They walked over to us, and Link made a sound like a quiet groan. When I glanced back at him, his smile was tight but firmly affixed to his face.

"Looks like my friends might join us. Or I could tell them to go away?" He said the last part with hopeful inflection.

This was about to get very complicated, very quickly. A rapid assessment of the magic surrounding me reassured me that my facade was in place, but I was about to face the consequences of my actions. By only charming my appearance and not changing my glamour before my date with Link, I set myself up for the type of ridiculous mix-up only young fae fell into.

Because while Link was seeing me as a willowy ginger, Harmon saw the blond cheerleader, and Reave saw the raven haired emo woman.

"Here are your drinks. Do you know what you want from the menu?"

Fuck. Even peppermint tea wasn't going to fix this.

## Ginkgo Biloba

"I, UM, NEED MORE TIME," I responded distractedly, and the server left to check on his other tables.

"Jinx! How do you know Link?" Reave asked, and part of me was relieved that his cold exterior from the other day had thawed.

Harmon turned to his twin, a slight frown on his face. "How do *you* know Jinx?"

Reave waved him off. "I met her when I went into the shop the other day."

"You didn't mention it." A small divot formed between Harmon's eyebrows.

"Harmon, this isn't the same Jinx you met," Link said, clearly very confused. "You said she was short and blond. This isn't her."

Oh shit. Shit fuck. Sometimes human swears weren't vulgar enough.

The wrinkle in Harmon's brow was more pronounced. As he opened his mouth, probably to argue about my hair color, I cut him off.

"Listen, I can explain all this, but I can't do it here. Can we please go back to the tea shop?" I stood and pulled my hand out of Link's, reaching into my pocket to drop some money on the table for the server, hoping my plea would reach them all.

Link looked down at his hand, and then at the money like it offended him.

"Not sure what there is to explain." He wore a bemused expression. "But sure."

I rushed out of the diner, hearing the men follow me at a slightly more reasonable pace. I led them down the dimming street, pretending I couldn't hear them muttering behind me.

"Her hair *is* blond, Link. What the fuck?"

"It's so fucking ginger it's nearly blinding. It's not even *strawberry* blond."

When I glanced back, Reave was looking at me closely, not engaging in the bickering between his brother and their friend.

My stomach felt like it was doing backflips, and I spun forward again. The walk down the block felt like it stretched forever. In reality, I was unlocking the shop doors and ushering all three men inside in less than a minute, flicking on lights as I hurried behind the counter.

"What are you doing?" Link's voice was more even than I'd expect.

"I'm making us tea." I sent some magic towards my personal electric kettle to speed the process. As I measured out ginkgo biloba tea into four mugs, I carefully avoided eye contact with the three men staring silently at me. When the kettle beeped, I poured the water and distributed the mugs, still keeping my eyes on my hands. I was going to mess this up. I had found my three mates, and I was going to mess it up because of a stupid mistake.

"Hey." Reave's voice was soft.

I pulled my eyes up to his.

"What's really going on, Jinx?"

"Drink the tea," I said instead of answering.

Reave held my gaze as he blew on his mug and sipped, his eyes widening as the magic-infused tea hit his tongue.

"Holy shit, Jinx."

Seeing Reave's reaction, Link immediately took a gulp of tea, gasping as he burnt his tongue. He stared at me with an astonished reaction that morphed into his natural and playful grin.

"Holy shit is right."

I turned to Harmon, who was looking at his brother and friend with suspicion.

"What's in the tea?" he demanded, but Link shook his head, still grinning.

Reave rolled his eyes. "Just drink it."

I held my breath, and Harmon examined the mug before taking a small sip. His Adam's apple bobbed as he swallowed, and the only sign the magic had any effect was the slight tensing of his shoulders.

Knowledge sharing had been my father's gift, but with a tea that held memories as well as ginkgo biloba did, I could replicate a weak shadow of what he could do. My three mates now knew with complete certainty that I was not human, and what they saw of me was a disguise. I tried to infuse it with emotions as well, like how lying to them had felt like a dull ache behind my eyes, and I didn't want to hurt any of them, but Harmon's suspicious gaze made me question whether I had done it right.

Link spoke first. "This is so cool. Do you have extra heads? Or wings?"

Reave coughed out a laugh, and I smiled.

"No, but I know some fae who do."

Reave looked like he was trying to hide his amusement, and Link was absolutely beaming.

"Can we see what you really look like?"

"I, um." I looked to Harmon, almost for reassurance. This was not a standard way to react to the news that the woman you went on a date with wasn't human. His stiff posture confirmed it.

Reave stood beside him, quietly sipping his tea, observing the clusterfuck in front of me. When I looked back at Link, the man looked excited and hopeful.

"I don't want you to be afraid of me." I tried to inject some of my usual confidence into my voice, a hard feat when admitting insecurity.

"Why? Are you scary?" Link's question was fair, but it was Reave's that had my heart racing.

"Why do you care what we think?"

"I'm fae." I stared at my mug. "And in our cultures, we believe in soulmates." I looked up at the three of them, waiting for them to make the connection.

"Wait, you think one of us is your soulmate?" Link asked the question. Harmon's head snapped towards him before the dark-haired man turned on his heel and walked out of the shop.

Link looked apologetically at me. "I'll talk to him." He followed Harmon out.

I turned to Reave, who was still sipping his tea. I didn't know what made me want to keep spilling truths, but I said, "I think all three of you are my soulmates."

Reave's eyebrows rose slightly, but otherwise, he looked thoughtful. When he finally spoke, his voice was soft, as though he was talking to himself, not to me.

"My grandmother used to tell us about the fae. I loved them, and when we stayed at her house, I would leave a saucer of milk out on the doorstep." He glanced in the door's direction. "Harmon was never as convinced. He thought they were stories." A wry smile danced on his lips, sad amusement twinkling in his eyes.

I let the silence hang between us for a moment. I still felt unprepared for the conversation we were having and sipped my tea, trying to center myself.

"I'm more familiar with human culture than some of my kind, but I still feel a bit... uncertain about how to best handle this situation."

Reave looked softly at me, my confession unlocking something in his expression.

"Harmon needs some time. Link is clearly more interested in finding out more about fae than running in the other direction."

"And you?" I steeled myself for his response. I didn't expect his hand to reach out to cup my face. I instinctively leaned into it, barely noticing his other hand placing his cup upside down on the saucer.

"Read my leaves," he said, a playful hint in his tone.

Breaking his gaze, I turned the cup and then examined the leaves. They didn't fill me with the same deep-seated worry as the last time I had done a reading for him, and this time their patterns spoke only of the present.

I looked back up at him with the start of a smile.

"You're in?"

"Yeah." Reave leaned close enough I could feel his breath against my lips. "I'm in."

I closed the small gap to meet him in a gentle kiss. It was like being kissed for the first time. Fire burned in my chest, spreading outward across my skin. His lips were intoxicating against mine, and it wasn't until his hand moved to the back of my neck that I realized my glamour had burned away.

My eyes shot open and I pulled away, but my mind was too scattered to wrap myself in more magic. Instead of horror, Reave's eyes held curiosity as he scanned my face.

"It's like a crown." His eyes rested on the place where the pale skin of my forehead gradually morphed into bark prongs before they returned to hold my gaze. I guessed they did kind of look like a crown.

"You have beautiful eyes." He made no mention of their cat-like pupils or nearly glowing green hue.

Relief rushed over me, even as a hint of confusion shimmered at the back of my mind. I didn't know why Reave wasn't afraid of me, but I was endlessly grateful. He leaned forward again, and I happily met him halfway, our second kiss deeper than the last. No magic barrier separated us.

I was breathless when we finally broke apart, and Reave's satisfied grin lit up my vision.

"Let's go find the others." He took my bark-covered hand in his.

## Cinnamon

DESPITE REAVE'S OBJECTIONS, I wrapped myself in a glamour before we left the shop. It was getting dark, but we didn't need people seeing a six foot tall tree woman walking down the quiet street. Without letting myself think too hard about why, I made myself appear as the preppy blond woman Harmon had first met.

Reave smiled and took my hand, leading me down a side street and across another road.

"Where are we going?" I asked.

"The bakery Harmon works at. It's where he goes when he needs to think."

Harmon's tea leaves from the first day had told me he chafed at his job, so it wouldn't have been the first place I would've looked, but Reave knew him better than I did.

When we arrived, Reave pulled me past the dark storefront and to a side door in the alley that took us into a well-lit hallway. A wall of scents hit me as I walked in: breads and cakes, cinnamon and vanilla. Reave smiled at me and led me through another door.

The industrial kitchen was impressive, but my eyes went straight to the two figures at a counter in the corner. Harmon was kneading a mass of dough, and Link stood beside him, gesticulating with his hands as he talked.

"You're being so fucking stubborn, Harmon! This is cool and exciting and you're acting like it's a bad thing."

Harmon didn't respond, and his fists continued to work the dough. Link sighed and turned toward us. His eyes lit up when he saw Reave and me standing in the doorway. Even better, when his gaze moved to our joined hands, he smiled.

"You *are* Jinx, right?" he asked. When I nodded, he added, "Just checking."

Reave dropped my hand and walked across the room to clap Link on the back.

"Let's give them a moment." He shot down Link's brief protests with a meaningful look.

As the door shut behind them, I took a tentative step towards Harmon, and his hands faltered. He glanced up at me, an unreadable expression on his face. Instead of continuing toward him, I followed my nose to a cabinet and found some ground cinnamon. I made it all the way to a rack of cooking pots before Harmon spoke up.

"What are you doing?" His voice was more curious than angry, although there was a gruff quality to it.

"I'm making us tea," I said, grabbing a pot and filling it with water.

"We just had tea," Harmon said, still kneading the dough.

"I know. Don't worry, I won't read your cup." I stared at the water long enough for it to heat, but stopped before it boiled. Scalding tea wasn't helpful to anyone. I added the cinnamon and covered the pot.

"Is it really tea if it's made with cinnamon?" Harmon seemed to surprise himself with the question and hurriedly rearranged his face into its previous expression.

"Cinnamon is a bark. It's close enough to a tea leaf to me." I nodded at the dough. "You're going to overwork that bread."

Harmon looked down at the dough, stopped kneading it, and sighed quietly. I leaned against the counter, waiting for him to speak.

It took a moment, but he finally said, "Can you stop looking like that, please?"

"Do you... do you want me to look like someone else?"

Harmon stared straight at me. "No, I want you to look like you."

With a breath out, I dropped my glamour. I knew, to his eyes, I rippled for a moment. Then my true form stood where a short blond woman had been standing before.

To my immense surprise, Harmon's mouth briefly twitched up. His eyes rose to my forehead the same way his brother's had. I gave him a tentative smile.

"Can you tell me what part bothers you?" I asked bluntly.

"I don't like people who lie. Please don't do that again."

I paused for a moment before I answered. "Alright. You should know my name isn't Jinx."

"What is it?"

"Fae don't give out our true names. It gives others power over us. We only tell those we really trust."

Harmon pondered this for a moment and then nodded. "Other than that. No more lying."

"Okay."

Harmon grabbed a loaf pan from under the counter and greased it with some olive oil before placing the smooth dough in the pan. He washed his hands in the sink behind him and then looked at the pot of cinnamon tea.

"I'll grab some cups." He disappeared behind a door, reappearing a moment later.

He handed me two paper coffee cups, and I poured the tea into them. I sipped mine and my eyes slipped closed. It was the perfect temperature. I opened them to assess Harmon's reaction and was rewarded with a confused frown.

"It tastes like cinnamon," he said.

"And isn't it delicious?"

He considered this for a moment. "Yeah, I guess it is."

We sipped our tea in silence before I noticed Harmon steeling himself to ask a question.

I waited patiently until he asked. "Which one of us do you think is your soulmate?"

I blinked. "All three of you. Most fae are polyamorous."

Harmon's cheeks darkened a bit, and his brow furrowed.

"Can you forgive me for reacting like I did?" he asked.

"What? Of course I can," I said, shocked. "I'm not human. You reacted exactly like I assume most humans would."

"Let's go see where Reave and Link went off to."

"You're okay with it, then?" I braced myself for his answer.

"You being fae, or you being my soulmate, or you also being the soulmate of my brother and best friend?"

"All of that."

"I think so." He gave me a genuine smile for the first time. "Let's talk to Link and Reave before we get ahead of ourselves."

I thought that was it, and turned towards the door. As Harmon brushed past me, he grabbed my waist, pulling me against him and brushing his lips against mine.

He pulled back quickly and my lips tried to follow him.

"Couldn't help myself." His eyes twinkled as he continued out the door.

## Chamomile

I RE-WRAPPED MY GLAMOUR. The strain of doing so much magic today, combined with the buzzing in my veins from the kiss, distracted me slightly. As soon as we exited the kitchen and made our way out to the street, Link greeted me loudly.

"Jinx! We're soulmates?"

I widened my eyes at Reave, who shrugged.

"He kept asking."

Link was leaning against the front of the bakery, but pushed off of it and strode towards me. He stared intently at my fingers and then at my forehead. I had the feeling he believed if he looked hard enough he'd be able to see through my magic.

"Reave said you're some sort of tree lady. Can I see?"

"I did *not*," Reave said, but he was smiling.

"Do you guys want to head back to the shop? The children's book section has bean bag chairs." The men nodded their approval.

Link held one hand, and Harmon grabbed the other, while Reave led us back up the street. The night was truly upon us now, and a light breeze wove its way through my hair. Link was uncharacteristically quiet, seemingly also feeling the magic of the night.

When I unlocked the shop door, the spell was broken and questions spilled out of his mouth.

"Are you actually from another universe? Does that make you an alien? And how does having three soulmates work?"

"Slow down." I laughed at his barrage. "I'll answer all your questions. Let's just go get comfortable."

In the children's book corner, Reave and Harmon piled all the bean bag chairs together to make one big seat. Link sat first and pulled me down on top of him. I let out a squeak, and Reave laughed. The twins sat on either side of us, and I leaned back against Link.

"So you're all okay with this? That all three of you are my soulmates?"

Reave nodded, Link sounded an enthusiastic "yes" in my ear, and Harmon smiled.

Harmon took the lead. "Now that that's settled, start looking like yourself again before Link loses his mind.

I peeled my magic away, and Link grabbed one of my hands, holding it close to his face.

"Wow, it really is bark. That's so cool."

I turned my head towards where his chin was brushing my shoulder, and he met me with a soft kiss. My heart pounded at the gentle caress, and I smiled against his mouth.

"Perfect." He stared into my eyes.

I felt Reave pressed against us on the left and Harmon on the right. I felt more complete than I ever had, and leaned my head back, looking up at the constellations painted on the ceiling above us.

"Perfect," I agreed.

# A Word from the Author – Sienna Swift

Sienna lives in Boston and spends her nights typing up the kind of stories she likes to read. An avid reader since childhood, Sienna has always enjoyed romance books that take her away from everyday life and into a world where happily ever afters are a given. Writing paranormal and fantasy romances are her favorites, and there is a special place in her heart for any story with positive LGBTQ+ representation.

This story is for Mya, the barista who made me the best vanilla latte of my life while I was writing the ending for this piece. I'm going back to the coffee shop to give you a copy. It's also for Morgan and Mackenzie, who read as I wrote and pestered me for updates. I love you guys. Finally, it's for Charlotte, who introduced me to the wonders of tea. My life wouldn't be the same without you.

Playlist: Almost by Hozier Old Pine by Ben Howard Bloom by the Paper Kites Hello My Old Heart by the Oh Hellos

Find all her stories at https://linktr.ee/siennaswift

# Afterword – from the Publishers

## (Adam & AC)

Adam:

Thank you for reading our second anthology.

When AC approached me last spring and said, "Hey, Adam, I want to do an anthology!" I was all for it.

"Great!"

"I don't know how to do it, though."

"Oh. Well, neither do I." Not the way she wanted. I'd published a collection of my own stories, but I didn't have to do royalty splits.

"That's okay," she said. "You'll help."

"...what?"

"And I need you to edit it."

"...what?"

In the end, AC got what she wanted, and we put out "Spice & Steam" in November 2022.

At which point, AC started recruiting for this anthology.

Most of the authors from S&S came back, and we recruited some additional authors. The result? You have in your hands.

We also recruited another editor. Nat Paga, a close friend of AC's and a talented author in her own right, agreed to help. She's been a tremendous asset and valuable addition, as well as a pleasure to work with as a co-editor and author.

Speaking of authors, the cover was designed by our own Lila Gwynn. Who knew?

I'd like to express our appreciation to all the talented authors who submitted stories for this anthology. You put out an impressive collection, hitting our theme of romantic origins with a broad variety of styles and genres, and we're in awe of your talent.

My wife deserves another mention. It can't be easy, being married to an author/editor/publisher, but you never pressure me to do anything but what I love. This is a gift beyond price.

I hope you've enjoyed these stories, and we're not done yet. But I'll let AC tell you about that.

Adam Gaffen, Trinidad, CO

AC:

OR NOT!

No way, not gonna spoil things for the next anthology except to say there is gonna be one and I wanna have a kickass lineup!

It wasn't quite like Adam said, but close enough. I *did* want to put an anthology, and *did* ask him to help. I don't think I *told* him he was going to be editing it.

Maybe I did.

In any case, it was a natural evolution of our ongoing partnership. I write, he writes, he edits, I edit, we publish. Now that we've done two of them—and I did all the formatting for this one, so thank you very much for all your kind words!—it's getting easier. I think.

The first anthology made me sweat, reading through the stories, because that's totes what they were supposed to do. This one? This was a joy to read and edit the stories, with such hope and love in every single one of them! That's all because of the wonderful, talented, creative writers who contributed to the anthology.

Nat and Adam, I wouldn't want to edit a book with anyone else! You have a great ear for language and can fix things in a passage which makes a vast difference in how it reads. I hope our partnership—and friendship—continues for many, many years to come!

Leila and Pixel, I love you both. Pixel, you're a stinker and always try to sleep on my keyboard, but I guess that's your job? And Leila, you are the perfect woman for me and I'm thrilled I get to be your wife.

Imma so happy to be doing this! No, it's not what I do for a living, but it's what gives me joy. That you—yes, *you*—come along with me on these fanciful rides makes my pleasure skyrocket. Thank you!

AC Adams, Boston, MA